31472400382135

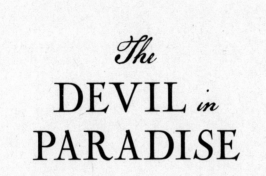

*The* DEVIL *in* PARADISE

# The
# DEVIL *in* PARADISE

— • ❖ • —

## Captain Putnam in Hawaii

## JAMES L. HALEY

G. P. PUTNAM'S SONS
NEW YORK

**PUTNAM**
— EST. 1838 —

G. P. PUTNAM'S SONS
*Publishers Since 1838*
An imprint of Penguin Random House LLC
penguinrandomhouse.com

Library of Congress Cataloging-in-Publication Data

Names: Haley, James L., author.
Title: The devil in paradise: Captain Putnam in Hawaii / James L. Haley.
Description: New York: G. P. Putnam's Sons, 2019.
Identifiers: LCCN 2019011055 | ISBN 9780399171123 (hardcover) |
ISBN 9780698164086 (epub)
Subjects: | GSAFD: Sea stories. | Adventure fiction. | War stories.
Classification: LCC PS3608.A54638 D48 2019 | DDC 813/.6—dc23
LC record available at https://lccn.loc.gov/2019011055

Printed in Canada
1  3  5  7  9  10  8  6  4  2

Book design by Tiffany Estreicher

*In Loving Memory*

*Thomas Craig Eiland*

*1951–2018*

[Kaahumanu], with all her haughtiness and selfishness, possessed, perhaps, as true a regard for the safety of the state, as her late husband or his high chiefs . . .

—HIRAM BINGHAM,

*A Residence of Twenty-One Years in the Sandwich Islands*

# CONTENTS

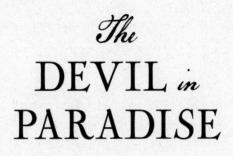

# The
# DEVIL in
# PARADISE

## { 1 }

## *The* Rappahannock, *Twenty-six*

Bliven's eyes snapped open at the first rap on his cabin door, the first of three—always three—and he knew it was his steward. "Enter!" His voice was hoarse, and he coughed out a small clot of phlegm into the handkerchief that stayed by his pillow. He had slept soundly, the sea swell directly astern of them, powerful, gentle, rhythmic, and as he had fallen asleep it seemed to propel him forward into his dreams.

"Good morning, Captain."

"Good morning, Mr. Ross." His steward was a short man, of gracile build, with very wavy ash-blond hair, slightly dish-faced but not unpleasantly so, and with hazel eyes beneath woolly brows so heavy that they seemed always knit in worry. He bore a wooden tray with water, coffee, and a covered plate.

Bliven rubbed his eyes, rose stiffly from his berth, and entered his sea cabin. "I am eating alone this morning?"

"Sir"—Ross scooted aside a chart of the southern coast of Cuba that lay on the great mahogany table and prepared to lay breakfast—"the lookout sighted a sail just a moment ago. The officers are already on deck."

"Where away?"

"They make her three miles, sir, northwest."

Bliven paused to enjoy the morning sun streaming in the stern windows. "Toward the reef."

"It would seem so, sir."

"M-hm." If it was a pirate or a slaver, he was doing just what he needed to: trying to draw them into shallow water. Well, as dearly as Bliven would have loved to take a slaver out of the trade, he would not be drawn in. Even after more than a decade it made his gorge rise to think of how Bainbridge lost the gallant *Philadelphia* at Tripoli, racing into shoal waters where he had no business going.

Ross set his breakfast down next to the still-open logbook in which Bliven had been writing the night before. Even before his first sip of coffee he took up the pen, flipped open the inkwell, and dipped the nib. He paused to wake up a bit more, for if there was one thing that had come to irritate him, it was an inconsistent hand in the captain's record of the ship's operation.

*October 20, 1817. At dawn, sail sighted three miles northwest, toward the reef. Suspicion of illicit activity, will give chase and investigate, but not enter Spanish territorial waters.*

Bliven cleared the pen with a tidy rubric and set it in its stand. "How is the wind?"

"Easterly, sir. We have our will of him."

"Maybe." Yes, they held the weather gage, if they chose to use it. Bliven rose and walked stiffly across his great cabin and closed himself into the privy. In the old design of ships he would have had to exit onto a narrow quarter gallery to access it, and as in the old design the close stool itself emptied over the open water, but for this new generation of ships the architects had reworked the whole design of a captain's accommodation. Now it was divided by partitions into a six-compartment suite, with separate areas for working, sleeping, hosting guests, all surrounding the great sea cabin with its fine mahogany furniture—heavy, polished, elegant, but no longer fashionable and no doubt appropriated from some earlier vessel now stricken from the list—for dining and entertaining. Along the after bulkhead of his study, which lay to starboard and was matched by a guest berth to port, reposed the ten-foot assemblies of twenty-four-pounders on their carriages, their gunports closed against the weather. They served as reminders that in a battle even the captain's suite fought, and one feature of the new architecture was that its partitions were collapsible. In beating to quarters, the partitions were lowered and the captain's furnishings were stowed below in the wardroom, shared by the other officers at the stern of the berth deck. Thus the working frenzy of the gun deck in battle extended the whole length of the ship, from stern windows forward to the sick bay in the bow. Then, after the fight, even if the ship was ravaged by raking fire through the large, sunny windows, the partitions could be raised again and the furniture brought back up, and the captain and his guests could still dine in elegance and privacy.

In the privy, on a shelf bolted to the bulkhead, Bliven saw a new stack of small cut squares of lamb's wool, and wondered when Ross could have replenished them, for he did not remember them from the night before. He crossed again to his berth, where hot water steamed in its basin next to his razor and towel, and Ross had laid out his uniform, complete except for the body within it, then regarded again the breakfast laid out on the vast slab of a mahogany table with its silver accouterments. For a Connecticut farmer raised to do for himself,

Bliven decided that the perquisites of command were not to be disdained.

He did not sit again but ate—eggs, a fresh pork chop, and toasted bread with jam—as he dressed. Their stores were fresh and plenty, for they had made a port call at Santiago de Cuba to spend money and try to assure them of America's friendship in the face of General Jackson's incursions into Spanish Florida chasing Seminole Indians, and their unending boundary disputes. That required diplomacy: Spain's crumbling empire could no longer afford to contest for Florida, which the United States wanted, but it was also desirable to preserve Spanish pride and good relations. Bliven had always been curious to see Santiago's looming Castillo de San Pedro de la Roca, to see for himself what kind of harbor fortification could take more than sixty years to build, and he got an eyeful, for they had anchored in its very shadow. The oldest parts dated back two centuries, separated from the mainland by a yawning moat, and supplied by sea, its storehouse cut into the living rock of the cliffs. The fortress's rising, receding terraces were lined with batteries of heavy guns, not unlike the decks of a ship of the line. Bliven had saluted the fort as he came gliding in under topgallants; the answering guns shook the *Rappahannock's* timbers, and he realized there was a reason that Spain, whatever her fallen state now, once ruled the western hemisphere.

After Santiago they rounded Cabo Cruz, on the lookout partly for slave runners—a task to which they were bound, since the African slave trade was outlawed in 1808—but still more alert for pirates, who now infested the Caribbean in more, and more devious, ways than in years past. The ongoing liberation of South America from Spain created new nations, who needed some semblance of navies and who even, as the United States had once done, turned to the contracting of privateers to establish a presence at sea. Many of those privateers, they now knew, were merely former pirates plying their old trade under the protection of new national flags. Since the close of the Second Barbary War, more than a thousand merchantmen had disappeared in the Caribbean, and, while maintaining some presence in the Mediterranean, much of the U.S. naval strength was now turned to the Caribbean to pacify that historically lawless sea. The very capable Hazard Perry had been dispatched to newly independent Venezuela—again, officially to demonstrate American friendship, but when out of sight of land to put pirates out of commission when they could not prove their bona fides. Bliven's task, in the northern Caribbean, was to intercept buccaneers whom Perry flushed from the coast of South America.

It was impossible not to think of President Washington's often-published farewell warning, that the United States should avoid entangling herself in foreign alliances, and smile. In the mere three years since the British had burned Washington in the attempt to reestablish her North American empire, the United States had become irretrievably enmeshed in world affairs. And this was no bad thing, from the standpoint of trade, by which America was profiting most handsome, nor from the standpoint of those many who viewed their homespun democracy as a light to the world, who believed in it so ardently as to see it as the desired hope of mankind. There was even the latest talk in the Navy of showing the Stars and Stripes again in the Pacific, that giant quadrant of the globe with exotic and potentially vast trade in which the United States had only dabbled in the most exploratory way.

To all this was required a Navy commensurate with the responsibility, and it was a thrill, a daily thrill every morning when Ross rapped on his cabin door, to be a part of. Ross was pouring coffee, elevating the silver pot as he did so as to aerate the brew as it swirled into the cup. "Sugar yet, Captain?" He grinned with a faint slyness.

"Thank you, no, Mr. Ross, I have not acquired a taste for sweet coffee in the past twelve hours." He knew Ross was joking, a venturesome familiarity for a steward with his captain, but Bliven had never attained the full stiffness of his rank, and he allowed something like friendship between himself and those whose duties touched him most closely. At Santiago de Cuba they had bought thirty barrels of sugar to leave some silver in their wake, with little use for it but to serve the crew the sweetest plum duff in the history of the Navy.

After Santiago they had put in at Cienfuegos, four hundred miles by sail west of there, a settlement less than a year old, to check on how their Louisiana colonists were faring. Here, too, there was a double purpose to the call, most assuredly to show their home country's amicable interest in developing this fertile and potentially rich portion of the island, but also to satisfy themselves that, being Louisianans about to engage in large-scale agriculture, they were not crossing that filmy boundary between utilizing slaves on their plantations and profiting from any transshipment of slaves to the U.S. mainland.

Bliven sawed easily through the tender chop of pork, to which he added a yellow fluff of egg, and slurped a sip of the hot brew. Every time he drank coffee he thought of Sam Bandy, who still made the Putnam family a present every Christmas of a sack of the finest Martinique beans. And they reciprocated with a jug of the first and finest draw of maple syrup, and always a barrel of their Putnam Farm cider. He and Sam did not correspond as frequently as they had during Sam's recuperation after the War of 1812. And directly after hard service in that conflict Bliven had been sent under Decatur on the *Guerriere* back to the Mediterranean for the Second Barbary War. That was a cruise he actually enjoyed, for he had come to like Decatur, and he especially took pleasure in reducing and capturing the cursed *Meshuda*, which had slipped from their grasp in the first Mediterranean conflict. That was more bracing duty than trying to explain to people since then that this *Guerriere* was a new American frigate, not a resurrection of the British ship destroyed by the *Constitution* in 1812. The U.S. Navy had, on occasion, adopted the English penchant for naming new ships after defeated enemy vessels. The custom tasted of British arrogance and, he believed, had no place in the fleet of a democracy, but his consultation was not sought in the matter.

Home again, he'd barely had time to turn around before being sent to the Caribbean to help quell piracy and the slave trade. Clarity and his parents had all let Bliven know their despair at losing him back to sea so soon after coming safe home, to the point that they could barely share in his triumph at being once more elevated to his own command, and in the rank of captain, at last.

"Shoes, sir," said Ross as he plopped them onto the Brussels rug that Bliven had spread in his compartment. Bliven stared at them with disgust and then slipped them on. Boots were harder to get on and off, and were lost if one were wounded and they had to be cut away, but that was a small price to pay to avoid fighting a battle feeling like one was kitted out for a dancing lesson. Ross helped him into his blue cutaway coat, and pulled lightly at the gold lace around the cuffs and collar. "Three-eighths of an inch, Captain, not a tittle less."

"Oh, for heaven's sake." The Navy had found the most astonishing regulations to insist upon other than defense. Ross handed him his sword, which he buckled on, and bicorne. With the hat tucked in the crook of his arm, he regarded himself in the full standing mirror, satisfied. He took several more rapid bites of breakfast, drained the coffee, and said mostly to himself, "All right."

He started to leave but heard Ross's voice behind him, "Your glass, Captain." He turned and Ross had it almost into his hand.

"Oh, yes, thank you." Outside his cabin he strode quickly forward down the gun deck, surveying its double file of twenty-fours and finding all in order as he reached the ladder. Below on the berth deck he could hear the crewmen greedily downing their breakfast as he ascended the ladder to the weather deck.

His new sloop of war, *Rappahannock*, twenty-six, fresh from the yard, represented something of a change in policy for the government. With the end of every conflict, after the Navy had more than proved its worth, the Congress would pare it down to save money, lay up ships in ordinary, and furlough officers to half pay. The country would retreat into its shell like a hermit crab, hoping the world that it refused to see by covering its eyes would therefore not exist. Bliven admitted the expense of maintaining ships at sea, but the United States would never assume a place of respect in the family of nations until they deployed the means to defend that vast merchant fleet on which the American economy depended more than ever.

The end of the Second Barbary War, however, presented such a new set of circumstances that for once the nation took a different tack. James Monroe, secretary of state under Madison in the last war, was now president. He was a diplomat, he had been abroad, he understood the still-colonial attitude of the Old World toward the New, and he wanted to make it clear that this was no longer acceptable. On land the War of 1812—the Second War for Independence—had gained them no new territory. As Bliven's father had foreseen, the invasions of the Canadas had been a collective disaster, but conquest had never been the primary goal. At sea American victories, and America's willingness to pay the price for those victories as with the loss of the

*President* and the *Chesapeake*, won America freedom from impressment, which indeed had been their primary reason for going to war.

And now the United States owned Louisiana, which enlarged her superficies to some one and a half *million* square miles, and that dwarfed every country in Europe save Russia, which was equally empty. There was iron in the Northwest Territories, and well-proven lead mines in western Virginia and Missouri. America wanted only development, and the determination to pursue it, to become the dominant power on the planet. That, and Monroe's determination that Europe must no longer look to the western hemisphere for more colonial tributaries, required a navy—a navy ever increasing, ever more present around the globe. For once, the Congress lived up to its responsibilities, and in 1816 approved ten million dollars—an almost inconceivable sum—to begin building an impressive dozen new heavy frigates and nine capital ships of the line, two-decker seventy-fours that were not just the equal of their British and French and Spanish counterparts but designed to be tough and resilient, an advance over European design just as the *Constitution* and her sisters had outclassed their supposed equals in foreign service. And the standard armament was increased from batteries of twenty-four-pounders to thirty-twos. The *Ohio* had been abuilding in Brooklyn for two years and would be ready for launch next year, as was the *Delaware* under construction in Norfolk. Trumping them was the mighty *North Carolina*, laid down in Philadelphia, announced as a seventy-four but actually pierced with more than a hundred gun ports, with the lower deck at least to mount shattering forty-two-pounders.

Bliven's own command, the *Rappahannock*, was but a small part of this muscular expansion. With twenty-six guns she might have been classed as a light frigate, but the Navy still found it a useful policy to underrate their strength rather than boast. Just as the English once engaged American frigates, wrongly supposing them to be equals, it might again prove useful for some future foreign adversary to bite off more than it could chew.

Emerging onto the weather deck, Bliven felt the wind's push from astern, not yet warm with the sun, and snugged his bicorne down onto his head. *Rappahannock* was a sloop of war, yet she almost equaled the old *Constitution* in size and displacement: one hundred thirty feet long, plus seventy for the bowsprit, thirteen hundred tons, drawing twenty feet of water, a deep draught for its size. Bliven sucked in a lungful of fresh morning sea air.

The sky was clear, and in scanning the distance he could see, far out, the lumpy white mounds of thunderclouds just rising above the horizon. He disliked the Caribbean, for it was a fickle sea. For nearly half the year, from May until September, a day that began with the most blessed gentle breeze and sun could end in a howling, deadly gale out of nowhere. Now, in October, they should be safe enough, but tempests this late were not unknown.

Bliven glanced up and saw they were running under easy sail. That was another innovation in his new ship of which he heartily approved. His topsails spread nearly double the square footage of his courses, making for better headway in a fight, when the courses were reefed. The practice was a near necessity in a frigate, with their battery of guns on the spar deck whose flames might catch on the mainsails. Sloops lacked this additional armament, although Bliven exercised his captain's prerogative to mount one chaser each on bow and stern, and six carronades, three on each beam. He well remembered Preble's preference for long guns on the weather deck to help disable an enemy at a distance, but life and longer service had inured him to the gore and suffering wrought by carronades when the gain—thanks to a distant spray of grape to spill the wind through enemy sails and a close spray of grape to clear living men from her deck—might be a more seaworthy prize won with less gore and suffering among his own men.

He was seen first by his first officer, who approached and saluted, which Bliven returned. "Good morning, Captain."

"Good morning, Mr. Miller." They had become good friends, but they were careful to address each other formally when about their duties. "What do we have?" Miller was of medium height and solidly built, his hair very straight and rich brown, willful that it would fall straight forward over his brow as it chose, and Miller did not resist. He was fair complected, with light brows and a large and almost Roman nose over delicately turned lips like a portrait of Byron. Bliven found Miller's eyes to be his key and strange feature. They were clear and impassive, betraying no emotion no matter what he might be feeling. They were predominantly hazel but contained flecks of pure brown and pure green, as though his components as they came together could not resolve among themselves what visage to present to the world. But what drew Bliven to him was Miller's education: a love of history and literature and a curiosity of geography such as he had not encountered elsewhere in the Navy, or anywhere else save among the collegiate scholars and seminarians at home. Miller was a Philadelphian but not a Quaker, which gave him a moderate demeanor yet with a willingness to fight when called upon. He was a decade younger than Bliven and a man who must rise in the Navy, and Bliven was determined to help him, although it would grieve him to his core to lose Miller to his own command.

"Lookout sighted a sail to the northwest and we sent down for you straightaway," said Miller. "I am guessing not a large vessel or we would have seen him sooner."

They were walking toward the starboard rail and Bliven raised his glass to his eye. "Has he altered his course?"

"Yes, sir. Since we sighted him he has changed from a westerly heading to northwest."

"M-hm. First indication that he is up to no good. Have the helm come northwest to follow him. The bosun will want to haul closer when we do."

Miller relayed the orders. They were too far out to know by land, but both knew from the charts that a course northwest would lead them into the long, narrowing funnel of deep water that ended at the Bay of Pigs. "Well, he must have seen us. Break out our colors, Mr. Miller, and we will see how he responds."

"Very good, sir."

"Excuse me, Captain." A small voice approached from the waist, and Bliven turned to see a black-haired midshipman of fourteen saluting as he approached.

"Mr. Harrison, good morning." Bliven returned his salute.

"Beg pardon, sir, the ship's carpenter asks to make report to you."

"Very well." That was concerning, for carpenters didn't make morning report. "Send him over."

In a moment a grizzled man, extraordinarily tall with tousled gray hair and deep-set, almost gaunt gray eyes approached, saluting, but clumsily, as old carpenters were wont to do. "Good morning, Captain."

"Good morning, Fleming. How are things?"

"Captain, we found fourteen inches of water in the bilges this morning."

"What! From where?"

The carpenter shrugged. "Well, she's a new vessel. If one of her ribs was not cured properly, it might have warped and pulled a seam loose in the copper plates. Or some such matter."

"Fourteen inches? Since when?"

"Last evening, sir. Certainly not normal, but not grave."

*"Grave"*? thought Bliven. To his mind any leak at sea was grave. Leaks did not spontaneously repair themselves; they could only get worse. "Well, pump it out at once, and station a couple of men down there to see if they can discover where it is coming from."

"Very good, sir." Fleming saluted again and started to leave.

"And keep me informed."

"Yes, sir."

Bliven heard the soft snaps of their ensign as it unfurled from the spanker boom even as Miller rejoined him, raising his glass and studying. "Ha! That did not take long."

The ship they were spying loosed a flag of three stripes, yellow above blue above red, with a row of blue stars on the yellow stripe. "Venezuelan," said Bliven evenly. "We might have guessed."

"Venezuelan, so he says."

"Yes. If he is truly Venezuelan, what is he doing so far from home? Come to full sail, Mr. Miller, we will just go have a look."

"Aye, sir." He barked the command for full sail to the bosun but then cocked his head, listening. "What is that?"

Faintly they heard the splash of water spilling from the scuppers on the gun deck. "The pumps, Mr. Miller. We took on just over a foot of water overnight."

"Oh, my good God damn!"

"Yes. I'm going down and have a look now. I will be back directly."

"Yes. Yes, sir . . ." Miller's voice trailed away, and it was plain he was as concerned as Bliven was.

On the gun deck Bliven heard the click-clack of the elm tree pumps and saw teams of sailors getting some unexpected morning exercise pushing and pulling the plungers as the bilgewater splattered out of the brass bulbs at their feet and flowed across the deck to the scuppers.

He descended to the berth deck, for *Rappahannock* was a bit of a hybrid vessel, armed as a sloop with all her guns on one deck, but decked rather as a frigate with a separate deck for the crew's housing. What she lacked was a distinct orlop deck, but there was plenty of height for one, given her deep hold, and if he remained long in command he would see if he could not remedy that. The hold was partially decked, which allowed for a carpenter's room and sail room forward, and magazine and bread rooms aft, with the forward and aft compartments connected by a wooden catwalk that allowed an unobstructed view down to the ship's ribs as they curved inward to meet at the keel. The whole configuration gave *Rappahannock* both a deep draught and a high freeboard, making her not the sleekest sailer, but the value of this arrangement was yet to be proven or disproven.

Bliven descended from gun deck to berth deck to hold, where he saw the carpenter observing the water level as it slowly lowered, and a clot of the crew, shirtless and sweaty, standing gingerly on the kentledge in water past their ankles. "How is it, Fleming?"

"It is a damned inconvenience, Captain. Once we get the water level down, we shall have to move away sections of the ballast by turns to try and discover the leak."

"Were any of the stores affected?" The architects planned to install metal tanks for drinking water in some of the newer ships, but *Rappahannock* still stowed ranks of wooden casks, and food stores above them.

"No, sir. The water never reached the hold's decking."

"Can the pumps handle the job?"

"Most certainly, Captain. It is a nuisance, but Davy Jones will have to get along without us for now."

"Well, good. Keep it that way. Report to me when you know something." Bliven cast his gaze higher up the curve of the hull. A sloop of war was more lightly built than America's famous frigates, and lacked the diagonal riders that gave those ships their legendary toughness.

For the sloops, however, the builders had crafted an ingenious compromise: the knees that supported the berth deck were affixed to the hull at a similar diagonal, shaped by saw and adze to match the angle to the curvature of the hull, and reaching down several feet to provide a similar bracing. Their proof must come in a battle, but until then the ingenuity of their concept gave him a swell of pride every time he saw them.

Back on the quarterdeck Bliven found Miller peering steadily through his glass at the strange vessel, now about two miles distant. "Captain, we may not yet know the name of the ship, but for the present we may call her the *Atalanta*."

Bliven raised his telescope and nearly lost the suspected pirate ship in its magnified circle as he began laughing, for he beheld a small dinghy laden to the gunwales with hapless-looking, half-naked Africans. "Yes, I see. He has tossed aside a golden apple to distract us. Ha!" He lowered the glass, thinking for a moment. "Except, you realize, if he is the one casting the apples, that would make *us* Atalanta, would it not?"

Miller chuckled. "Oh, hell, you are correct. I misremembered . . . I should know better than to mention such things to you."

"And if we are Atalanta, that would make him . . . What was that fellow's name?"

"Hang him, I don't know. Something with an *H*? Greek; they all sound alike."

Bliven raised his glass again. "Hippomenes, Mr. Miller. His name was Hippomenes."

"Oh, you show-off. Of what possible use in the world is your mastery of silly Greek myths?"

Bliven stared at him, amused. "Well"—he gestured ahead of them—"he seems to know the story of Atalanta well enough, doesn't he? And he is using it, and it will save him. History, Mr. Miller! I tell you, men who know history have more weapons with which to deal with the world."

"Yes, well, Captain Hippomenes is laying on more sail, and we should do the same if we wish to catch him."

"True enough. How far away do you estimate the coast?"

"Without looking at the chart, sir, I would guess twenty miles, perhaps fifteen."

"M-hm. We could not catch him in any case before he reaches territorial waters, but we can make his heart race a little bit. Have the bosun come to all sail, set the stuns'ls. Beat to quarters when the watch have finished their breakfasts, but ready the starboard guns only, maximum elevation. And there is no need to break down my cabin; we will not need those guns."

Miller stepped back and saluted. "Very good, sir. Mr. Yeakel!" he called out to the bosun. "Make all sail, if you please! Set your stuns'ls!"

Within the moment men were aloft, gripping the rigging with their almost prehensile toes, lashing fast stuns'l yards and lowering canvas far outboard the hull as *Rappahannock* spread her wings like a giant raptor to ride the wind. Her royal yards when hoisted rode nearly two hundred feet above the waves, and their increase in speed was palpable.

Miller returned. "The sergeant of marines has his eye on the watch. He will beat to quarters when they are done eating."

"Good," said Bliven, gesturing out to their quarry. "At least he has given himself away. If he were as Venezuelan as his flag, he would not cast pathetic innocents adrift. I wish we had room to catch him before we cross into Spanish waters. She's a fine fat brig and would make a nice prize."

Miller nodded. "Yes, and we might see Mr. Hippomenes brought to justice." He raised his glass. "Look there in the dinghy. Old men, women, children. They would never fetch a decent price in a slave market. Why even bring them along?"

"As bait for us, Mr. Miller. They know we have a conscience about life, where they do not. Oh, shit!" Bliven's face went slack. "We must be getting into the channel, and our chart cannot be all that reliable. Send a midshipman down to the carpenter; he's in the hold. Have him send up his mate and start taking soundings. I'm not going into less than eight or ten fathoms."

A quarter of an hour later they jumped at the sudden drum tattoo at the head of the ladder, and the crew leapt to life at beating to quarters; loose gear was stowed; mattresses rolled up and stuffed in the netting; the bosun and his mate ready at the rigging with marline-spikes, even though it was apparent there would be no contested action; and guns rolled in and limbered—in this case just the starboard main battery of twenty-fours.

Within ten minutes they had a reading that there was no bottom, and they bore down on the renegade brig. Rapidly they overtook the drifting dinghy laden with slaves, and Miller shouted down to them that they would return for them. Three miles farther on, the carpenter's mate called out a sounding of thirty fathoms.

Bliven turned to Miller. "Who has the starboard battery? Is it Rippel?"

"Yes, sir."

That was their second lieutenant, only twenty-two, a Kentuckian and therefore somewhat raw in manners, but hale and informal in that frontier way, tall, with finely drawn, almost beautiful, features, brown hair that bleached blond in the sun, and small brown eyes as quick and comprehending as a bird's. He was attentive to duty, to the point of worrying almost too much whether he was doing something properly. He needed reassurance, but his continual fretting would either turn him into one of the finest officers in the service, or else must abrade him into ruin. He was new at working twenty-fours, and Bliven felt a certain tolerant, paternal fondness for him, for like Bliven he had learned gunnery with twelve-pounders on a schooner. "Tell Mr. Rippel that as we overtake him we will begin a turn to port. He will fire on that brig as his guns bear, one rolling broadside only. He will not reload but secure the guns immediately thereafter."

"Aye, sir." Miller clattered down to the gun deck and returned in a moment. "Mr. Rippel's compliments, and he begs to say, if you get him within range, he will hit the bastard."

"Oh!" barked Bliven. "The confidence of youth, I remember it well."

Several moments elapsed. "You're thinking about it, aren't you?" ventured Miller.

"About what, Mr. Miller?"

"About going in after him."

"I am. I want to. But our orders do not embrace violating Spanish waters." He strolled over to their great double wheel, standing as high as a tall man. "Helm."

It was their third lieutenant who responded. "Sir?"

"Stand by to ease your helm to port—slowly, if you please." Whenever he gave this order he laughed, for he remembered Sam Bandy at Messina, leaving whoever was at the helm to wonder what was so funny. "Bosun!"

Evans Yeakel knew to station himself nearby. "Sir?" He was rather shorter than average height but powerfully chested, his short, straight blond hair perpetually hidden beneath his bosun's hard hat so that he could be easily found in the confusion of the deck.

"After we chase him off we will come about. We must go back for those people and bring them aboard."

"Yes, sir."

With closing distance their quarry grew larger quicker. "Begin your turn." Gradually they felt the bow point more to the west, and Yeakel's men eased the yards as the wind came more astern of them. Even though they were expecting it, all jumped with the concussion of the forwardmost twenty-four-pounder's deep boom, and they saw the stream of fire jet outward for fifty feet before it faded into a ball of smoke that hung suspended. Five seconds later there erupted a second huge boom and sheet of flame, then a third, and they knew that Rippel was leaping from gun to gun, sighting each before pulling the lanyard, as he was trained to properly do. They counted out twelve shots—the starboard broadside less the after gun in the captain's cabin, which was not rolled out—before the silence descended again. Through their glasses they saw all the balls fall a quarter mile astern of the scampering brig, but truly on a line that would have struck him had they been closer. Then they saw a small flash from the brig, and seconds later heard a snotty little bang, a small gun, probably a six-pounder of the kind commonly mounted on pirate privateers. It was a mocking little gesture of defiance, a taunt.

"You lucky little hellion," growled Bliven. "I will hang you if I ever get my hands on you, and no mistake."

"I will help you," said Miller. "He is probably wondering why we don't close and finish him off."

"Oh, I think he knows he's just reached safety. See?" Just visible on the northwest horizon lay the thin green line of the Cuban coast. "Dog's son. Come about; let us pick up those castaways."

"Twenty fathoms, Captain!" called out the carpenter's mate.

"Very well, thank you." They shortened sail and tacked back toward the bobbing dinghy, its ragged black passengers waving, not in greeting, but helplessly. "Mr. Yeakel?"

"Sir?"

"They have no oars and cannot come to us. You must lower the cutter and tow them over."

Yeakel considered it. "Well, that will be easier than trying to maneuver this big girl right next to them, for certain. Poor blighters."

Bliven and Miller followed Yeakel's skillful operation from the quarterdeck, mindful of how indispensable a decisive, experienced bosun was to a ship's operation, although he was rated only as a warrant officer.

None of the slaves was so broken-down as to need hoisting up to the deck; all were able to mount, albeit uncertainly, the ship's boarding ladder. It was Yeakel, standing somewhat apart from them, who led and beckoned them aft, and they followed.

Bliven saw the clot of slaves approach him. "God in heaven!" He pulled a handkerchief from his pocket and covered his nose. "Oh, God in heaven!" He had spent much of his life at sea and was accustomed to the odor of sailors, but this was a shock to his senses, an almost visible veil of stink that wrapped itself around him like wet muslin. "Do any of you speak English?"

They stared at him, mute.

"*¿Habla español?*" he tried again. Again no one spoke up, but one black man, on the far side of middle age but still powerful looking, seemed to mark what he was attempting. "*Parlez-vous français?*" he tried once more.

The man he had noticed stepped forward. "*Un peu,*" he said. He was barrel-chested, with yellow eyes and a very flat nose. Bliven surmised that they must have been taken from the Guinea coast or Senegal.

"*Très bien.*" This was lovely. He had just found a man who knew some French, and Bliven had just spoken about the only five words he knew. Clarity had teased him that she could make herself useful on board a ship, and at this moment he would have given a month's pay to have her on deck, for her French was faultless. "Mr. Miller?"

"Captain?" Instinctively he had also placed a cloth over his nose.

"Who on this ship speaks French?"

Miller thought on it. "Our surgeon studied in Paris, did he not?"

"Yes. Yes, he did. Send for Dr. Berend; have him take charge of these people. Get two casks of water forward to the heads, get them washed, men and boys on one side, women and girls on the other. Tell the purser to find them something to wear. Get pallets ready in the cable tier, and have the steward make them something to eat. Have Dr. Berend learn what he can about them and come make report to me."

Miller was paying the strictest attention. "Beg pardon, sir, but this is a pork day. Many Africans would rather die than eat pork."

"Oh, hell, you're right." He gave Miller a cold stare. "One would think that when people are starving, they would be less particular about their diet."

Miller nodded. "Well, perhaps when the next world is all you've got, you're not so keen to risk losing it."

"Simple people, persuaded to nonsense." He checked himself before he said more, aware that his disgust with slavery was spilling over into hate for the reality that in this early nineteenth century there could still be a continent full of tribes who were prey to it.

"Suffering people, Captain Putnam, who have been stripped of everything they know."

Bliven slumped from his wonted on-deck erectness and sighed. "You're right, of course. Is there pork in the steep tub yet?"

"I don't know as a certainty, but I don't believe so."

"Well, regulations are overridden for today. We shall have rice and cheese, then, and peas. I am going below to check the hold, then I will be in my cabin. Send Dr. Berend to me after he's got them settled."

Again he looked aloft. "Easy sail, Mr. Miller. Come sou'-sou'east. Have the lookouts keep their eyes peeled for any reefs."

"Aye, sir. Excuse me, did you order a course of south-southeast?"

Bliven glanced at their pennant aloft. "Oh, yes I see." With a strong east wind she might not take a south-southeast course. "Well, have the bosun haul as close as she'll take, but then come sou'-sou'east if the wind allows. My intention is to not turn west until we get clear of the Isle of Pines. South of there we will have deep water and a clear shot through the Yucatán Channel. I am not going to waste time poking and sounding through this labyrinth of cays and rocks."

"I understand," said Miller. "I just thought that, since we sprung a leak, we might want not to venture too far from land."

"And I thought, since we sprung a leak, we might not wish to run aground. Course sou'-sou'east when you can, Mr. Miller." Bliven did not need to say again that he never trusted the Navy's charts in foreign waters.

"Very good, sir."

How very glad he was to have a Pennsylvanian for his first lieutenant and not a Southerner who would arch his brow over treating the Africans like human beings, and an officer and friend who could function as an added compartment of his own mind.

Back in his cabin—where Ross, amazing Ross, had foreseen his coming and had fresh coffee on his desk—he thought on it, and Bliven found himself grateful to be homeported in Boston. With a leaking ship he should put in at Mobile or Savannah and heave her down, but he knew what that would mean for his miserable Africans. No, if he could take her back to Boston, he would do so, and give these people some fair chance at a life.

For the first time in a long time he thought of Jonah, the slave chamberlain of the dey of Algiers. Once safe in Boston, Jonah had not disappeared into but immersed himself in the colored population there, applying himself to it. He had shed his Mohammedanism and become a Congregationalist—how fortunate, Bliven thought, to be so adaptable—albeit a Unitarian, the news of which had nearly given Reverend Beecher a fit of apoplexy. Jonah took the Putnam surname for himself, which gave Bliven a warm and rather honored feeling, and he had become a teacher: basic education to his own people, but also tapped to teach Arabic at Harvard College, which gave that school a significant boasting point and kept Jonah living in some comfort, for a black man. And Harvard, as all knew, had gone over bags and baggage to the Unitarians, which might explain Jonah's new profession of faith. They were not correspondents, but if he had died, Bliven would surely have learned of it. He determined, once they put in at Boston, to inquire after him. Perhaps Jonah could do something to help settle this clot of wretches he had taken on.

# Miss Clear Day

Litchfield lay white, quiet, and snug beneath a deep February snow, its cedar rooftops steep enough to shed new-falling powder, its main street frozen even where the snow had been knocked aside, and gray smoke curled from bluish fieldstone chimneys.

The knock came not at the Putnams' front hall door but at the keeping room door, at once muted but insistent, as though by an urgent, gloved hand. Dorothea Putnam was sitting at the great old pine table, as erect and prim as a pilgrim, reading in her dress black beneath a white cap, as Clarity stirred a pot of beef stew, almost ready to take in to Mr. Putnam, who lay in bed awake and waiting.

Clarity crossed the room and spied through the curtains for a tiny second before swinging the door open wide. "Harriet! What on earth are you doing out? Come in and be warm!"

"Thank you, Mrs. P."

"Give me your cape. Come, warm yourself by the fire."

Harriet Beecher strode less than ladylike to the fieldstone fireplace, handing off her cape and peeling away her gloves, and rubbed her hands before it. She was now thirteen, in the first bloom of slowly revealing maturity. As she had grown, it became all too apparent that, as those closest to her had foreseen, she had inherited the melting-wax features of her father, his mouth that turned distinctly down at the corners, and the eyes that seemed to have begun sliding down the side of her face. She knew very well now that she was not pretty, nor ever would be, a hard revelation for a girl of precocious intelligence but a fate that she accepted with the stoicism of her father's faith, and not surrendering the remaining prospect that by training herself to be a woman of warm sympathies, content to be a doer of good works, she might one day merit the love of some worthy man, albeit not a young or handsome one.

"How do things go on with you and the Misses Pierce?" asked Clarity.

Harriet curtsied at the pleasantry. *"Tout bien, merci."*

It was strange to think of the aging Pierce sisters, Sarah and Mary, and their married sister Susan and her husband, who also taught there, still managing their school after more than a quarter of a century. But as their fame grew and its name was formalized into the Litchfield Female Academy, the family had become pillars of New England education and likely could not have retired even had they desired it. Indeed, the institution had only become more exclusive—and expensive. "And how is your father getting on there?"

After the death of Roxana, the education of the Beechers' three daughters had become a serious consideration. Their five boys could make their way through school, but Reverend Beecher's income had never matched his social and ecclesiastical prominence, and the proper upbringing of his girls required the laying of a strategy. Beecher had attained fame as the most passionate and articulate conservator of the

Congregationalist faith, holding fast against the more liberal thinking and even Unitarianism that had engulfed Boston. It was a celebrity, however, that came with only a parson's modest living, which
had constantly to be supplemented with honoraria for guest preaching and a stream of tract and pamphlet publications. Beecher had
therefore reached an arrangement with the Pierce sisters to teach
religion classes at the Female Academy in exchange for the tuition for
his daughters that he could never have afforded. "In truth, Mrs. P., he
was overburdened before, and now I fear he has taken on too much
altogether."

"And how is young Charlie?" asked Clarity. "Will you have a cup
of tea?"

Roxana Beecher had finally given out after the birth of their ninth
child, who was now almost three. "Charlie is rather spoilt, I fear.
Since dear Mama passed away, Papa seems to hold him most precious
of all of us." Harriet's visage changed dramatically. "Oh, Mrs. P., forgive me, I must come straighter to the point. I have news of a most
distressing nature."

"Oh?"

"Perhaps you should sit down."

Clarity observed her earnestness. "Yes, perhaps I should." She sat
and indicated the chair next to her. "Please."

"Oh, Mrs. P." Harriet sat on the forward edge of the chair. "Papa
has just returned from Cornwall. Your friend, Henry Obookiah, that
first convert from the Sandwich Islands, has taken ill. I fear he has
taken most dangerously ill, and he has asked for you."

"Oh, no!" Clarity's hands raised to her chin, fingertips together
as if in prayer, but she was not praying. Winter and its close quarters
had brought an onset of disease in Litchfield and the surrounding

towns, and for two months none knew who might be the next taken.
"Oh, no."

"Papa is getting the sleigh ready and will come down for you as
soon as he finishes a letter. He says if you can come to please make
haste, but if you cannot come, he will take your message."

Dorothea had laid her book aside and was listening intently. "Is it
typhus, Harriet? Do they know?"

"They fear so. It appears to be the same sickness as the others."

Clarity looked at her sternly. "How do you mean, 'others'? Others
generally, or others at the mission school?"

Harriet hung her head. "Six new students arrived a fortnight ago.
One of them—I believe Papa said he is from China—became ill right
away, and then another. They are all that I know of."

*The mission school,* thought Clarity. For seven years Henry Obookiah had given the church leaders no peace in hectoring them on the
point of sending missionaries to his Sandwich Islands home. Beecher,
Mills, and both Timothy and young Henry Edwin Dwight had remonstrated with him that this was an undertaking quite beyond their
means, but Obookiah had proved implacable, holding up to them the
Great Commission of Christ, gaining his own sympathizers among
the Connecticut churches—even gathered about himself further refugees who had made their way to New England from their violent and
benighted country. There was Hopu, who had escaped Hawaii on
board the *Triumph* with Obookiah, and Honoree, and Tamoree, who
was a prince of one of the islands whose royal father had sent him
abroad to gather knowledge of the larger world to bring home to
his people, and now half a dozen others. Two years previously, great
was Obookiah's victory when the church established the Board for
Foreign Missions and opened a school overseen from the church in

Cornwall. There they crafted a course of study to train those who felt the missionary call in not just biblical precepts and practices but in the evangelical arts, the persuasion of the heathen to the light. This past term they had increased the number of students to twenty, accepting the additional number from other Pacific islands, including, Clarity had heard, one from Feejee—which could prove a mighty challenge indeed to a missionary effort, for there was a reason that Western sailors knew them as the Cannibal Isles.

Dorothea rose stiffly and poured tea from the still-hot pot, handed the cup to Harriet, and patted her shoulder. "Warm yourself, child. Clarity, daughter, such an errand, if you undertake it, would show great compassion but it would not be without risk, as you must realize." She studied Clarity's face, still delicately featured as porcelain but now in the maturity of her thirty-one years, and she read there Clarity's full understanding of the gravity of visiting not just a house touched by disease but one in which a dozen languages were spoken by people—not white people—of uncertain history and habits.

Clarity found herself staring into the fire, as though it had suddenly become a metaphor of a trial she must undergo, a trial not dreamt of ten minutes previous. She shook her head. "Well, I must go. We preached our religion to Henry, and he believed us. He believed it all; better than we ourselves, he gave himself up to it, body and soul. If we—if I—abandon him now, we shall show ourselves to be not just cowards but frauds." She shrugged lightly. "There are some points on which I may be a coward, but I will not be a fraud."

Having given Harriet her tea, Dorothea crossed to the fireplace. "I thought no less, my dear." She swung the cast-iron hook from which the pot of stew was suspended away from the fire, and with two pot holders hefted it onto the hard maple butchering block. "You make haste to get ready; I will take care of my husband."

Clarity squeezed Harriet's hand before heading into her small suite behind the keeping room. "I will be only a moment." When she returned, she wore heavier shoes, and gloves, and Bliven's great cloak, which she fastened about her throat.

"Let me just take a brief leave of my father-in-law." She crossed the hall into the parlor and, finding the door to the bedroom open, knocked lightly on the jamb. "Father Putnam?"

"Come in, daughter, come in." He had arranged his pillows unaided and was sitting up in bed.

"Your lunch is almost ready."

"Yes?"

She sat on the edge of the bed and took his hand. "I am called away to Cornwall. I will be back tonight."

"Yes, I know."

"You know?"

"I know all. I am not so deaf, daughter, that I cannot eavesdrop." He wagged his finger. "If I strain hard enough, and perhaps creep over to the door."

They laughed together. "You are feeling better?" They heard the door open and knew that Beecher had arrived.

"Yes, daughter. Yes, yes." They understood that his answer was relative, for he was always in some pain. "Now, you hasten on and visit your sick friend lest you arrive too late." Her countenance fell. "Oh, damn me, I am sorry. I hope that he may recover."

"Some do recover," she reflected, "but apparently he is gravely ill."

He took her hand in both of his own. "God's will be done, but I hope he may yet be well again."

In the keeping room she found Beecher and Harriet flanking the door, and Dorothea saw them out. "God bless you, my daughter." Dorothea kissed her cheek and tightened the cloak about her neck.

"Do as you feel God directs you," she whispered, "only, I beg you, do not mingle with the foreign students, do not go into their common area. Keep yourself covered in your cloak and leave it outside when you return. I shall make up a fire and boil it tomorrow."

Clarity kissed her cheek in return. "It will surely be after dark when we return, perhaps late."

Beecher helped her up into the sleigh, and Harriet after her, then sat on the opposite and facing seat; he tapped his driver on the back. "Off we go now."

They paused at the Beecher house to deposit Harriet and continued on at a trot, in gloom and silence for over a mile. "I want to thank you for coming, Mrs. Putnam," said the minister at last. "Henry has long regarded you as a special friend."

"You fear it is typhus."

"Yes."

"Some do recover."

"Yes, but Henry is very sick."

"Poor Harriet," she said. "Her disposition is so naturally sunny, it nearly destroyed her to have to tell me why she had come."

"She is a great joy to us. And she appreciates your tutelage in her composition. Just keeping her in paper and ink has become a considerable household expense."

Clarity felt a swell of satisfaction. "She could be a great writer someday. Do tell me," said Clarity above the clip-clop of hooves on the frozen road, "when you call out 'Harriet!' who answers?"

Beecher's face cracked into a smile. "They both do, in fact, sometimes." After a proper year of mourning Roxana—his parishioners were too sympathetic to count on their calendars that it actually had been less than a year—he married Harriet Porter, who was now already great with child—her first, though his tenth.

Clarity had remained silent on those occasions when Bliven brought up the incongruity of such a religious man having such an appetite as to have fathered ten children by his fortieth year. She was willing to accept that Beecher was such a furnace of energy that his preaching, writing, and church building were simply not sufficient outlets, and that he was impelled to leave a legacy also of children, and more children.

As the sleigh passed up North Road beyond the limits of the town, they remained in their facing seats, each under a thick lap blanket. "You know," said Beecher, "the other day I was perusing a book of architecture. I know your husband has a great interest in the subject."

"Indeed, he does."

"I read that the Greeks, apart from their three famous orders of columns—"

Clarity sensed that he was about to wax didactic, and perhaps name them, and determined to move him along. "Yes, I am familiar with them."

"Well, apart from those, they had another kind of column, one that was carved in the shape of a woman, that sometimes a rank of these columns bore the weight of the portico. There was a special name for them: they were called caryatids. So we see that, in a very real sense, sometimes it was women who supported the temple. It put me in mind of you, and your mother, and how grateful we all are for your support, especially of the mission school. I know it has been difficult since God called your father to his heavenly rest."

*My God*, she thought. *He is good. He has honed his fund-raising skill to the sharpness of a Toledo blade.* "Thank you, Reverend. It is our privilege to be able to help, and it is kind of you to acknowledge us." *So help me, if he mentions money at a time like this, I will throw him right off his seat into the snow.*

"You must know that you and she have given Obookiah and the others the realistic chance to return to their home countries and preach the light of the gospel to their people in their own languages. I cannot believe that God would call him home when he is"—his voice broke—"so, so close to obtaining his object!"

In her heart Clarity forgave him, and indicted herself. "To believe that, Reverend, one must believe that it is God who sends disease among us. The Bible itself tells us that there is evil in the world. Therefore I do not believe that God sends disease, but that it is God who will ransom his poor soul if these are indeed his ultimate hours."

"It is a rare gift," he said after a full minute of silence, "to be able to comfort the minister. I shall hold to that, and thank you for it."

After more than a mile of silence she relented and asked, "How are the affairs of the mission school this term?" She knew she had opened the door to voice their needs, but he had earned the privilege by forgoing it before.

"Quite good, actually," he answered. "Surprisingly solvent just now. I believe it was a wise step to begin admitting Indian candidates from the West. It seems that a number of our parishioners believe that our first duty is to effect the conversion of the natives on our own frontier before turning our attention to farther shores, and the admission of our Cherokee and Choctaw pupils has had a good effect on the giving."

Outside Cornwall they turned into the drive of the school's eighty-acre estate, given over mostly to farming and to teaching that skill to the foreign students, and there was also a compound of buildings the size of a small village with its outbuildings. They skirted by the school itself, which was in the Dutch style, having a gambrel roof, with a chimney at one end and a belfry at the other, and two small slant dormer windows between them. Clarity's thin lips twitched into a smile.

It was a unique school, but the architect must have felt that every school must have its bell.

Separated unto itself was the great manse, high and white and Federal in its architecture, of the principal's house where lived Edwin Dwight, Obookiah's special friend and benefactor, who had been entrusted as the school's first chief administrator. She expected the sleigh to stop there, and expressed her surprise as they went on. "Is Henry not being cared for in Mr. Dwight's house?"

"No. A number of people are keeping watch over him, and with so many coming and going it was more sensible to put him in the steward's house."

The sleigh stopped and they descended at another great house, two full stories of black-shuttered windows in white clapboard, and atop that a steep roof with eave windows flanking mighty chimneys. Clarity scarce had time to wonder why school employees needed to live in such state before the housekeeper appeared and conducted them inside. She peeled Beecher's coat from his shoulders and made to help Clarity out of her cloak.

"No, thank you." She grasped it more tightly about her shoulders. "I still feel quite chilly. I believe I will keep it on for the moment."

"Yes, ma'am." The housekeeper gestured up the stairs. "Mr. Obookiah is in the west bedroom."

They mounted the flight of steps, steep and narrow, and found the door open.

"Oh, Miss Clear Day, you have come! Oh!"

Clarity approached the bed, appalled at how much weight he had lost, his eyes white and deep in the sunken black skin around them. The speaking and the sounds of footsteps on the plank floor awakened a middle-aged woman who had been dozing in a Windsor chair by the window. As soon as she moved she grabbed at her neck, which had taken a crick as she slept.

"Oh, Mrs. Mills," said Clarity. "Please, do go down and stretch and rest. We will watch over Henry for a while." They held hands for a second before she left, and heard her descending the stairs.

"How are you feeling, Henry?"

Obookiah caught sight of Beecher hanging back by the door. "Oh, Mrs. Putnam, I fear that I will not live to see my home again, my beloved *Hawaii nei.*"

"We cannot know that. If you rest and eat, you may grow strong again." She saw the sheet beneath his back soaked from sweat, as was the pillowcase. "Reverend, come help me." She removed a thick towel from a quilt spreader at the foot of the bed and shook it out to its full size. "Don't stand there; come help me."

She looked in the drawer of a nearby lowboy and found a dry shirt. "Can you sit up?" She and Beecher pulled the wet shirt from his back.

"Oh, Mrs. Putnam, it is not fitting that you should see me thus!"

"Hush, Henry. This is no time to be squeamish." She spread the dry towel behind him and turned the pillow to the dry side up, and they pulled the dry shirt down his back. Gently they laid him back down, and Clarity washed his face with the cloth from a basin of water.

"That is so very comfortable. I am sorry to be such trouble."

Clarity did not sit on the bed or remove her gloves, but she held his hand and they looked deep, eyes into eyes. "Dear Henry," she said.

His tears welled up but he held them in check. "I wish . . . for someone . . . to see my family—my grandmother, if she lives—to say that I remember her, and I love her. And my uncle, priest to the storm god . . . Tell him that I thank him for raising me, that I love him, and that I hope, I hope he can find peace in true religion, as I have. Who can tell them these things?"

*Who indeed?* thought Clarity. They heard a commotion downstairs, and realized that their arrival had been noticed, and now the younger Dwight, and the other Hawaiians, Hopu, Honoree, and Tamoree, were coming up the stairs.

"See?" Henry pointed weakly to the desk nearby. "I have not been idle." She looked at the desk, with papers and an inkwell and quills. Henry released her. "Go and see, please."

Atop a short stack of paper she saw a title page, written in a large, simple hand, that read: *Ka Baibala Hemolele.* She lifted the covering sheet gently and saw the text on the second page, in single lines, numbered by verse with a blank line between the verses, the script clear but rote and childlike. *1. I kinohi hana ke Akua i ka lani a me ka honua.* She recognized some of the words that he had playfully taught her over the years: "beginning," "God," "created," "heaven," "earth."

She looked, stricken, back at the bed and saw Obookiah studying her. "It is correct," he said weakly. "I am certain, I have not made mistake."

"Oh, Henry!"

"Is not easy. My language has never had writing. I must be guided by the sounds. And I have only begun. I do not know why the Lord should take me before I finish, but He know best." He sank into his pillow, exhausted by speech. "Surely He know best."

She returned to the bed and took his hand. "Yes, Henry, surely He knows best."

"Oh!" he cried suddenly. "Oh, Mrs. Putnam, can you go? Can you go, with missionaries to my home? Who can better give my love to my family?"

"Henry—"

"Oh!" Obookiah cast his gaze to see Beecher still standing at the end of the room, but he was past caring who could hear. "The preachers, they are men of God, but they lack . . . human understanding. My people will understand you better than them."

"Thank you for that, Henry," she nearly whispered.

The others came into the room, and Obookiah brightened without raising his head again. "And now, I want my friends to speak to me in my own language one more time."

Beecher held the door open for Clarity and closed it behind them, and they walked down the short hall to the stairs. "Perhaps," he said, "you ought to have told him that it would be quite impossible for you to grant his request."

"And vex him during what may be his final breaths? Perhaps, Reverend, you should have taken his words about you to heart."

LITCHFIELD, CONNECTICUT
20TH FEBRUARY, 1818

*My dearest husband,*

*Oh, my captain, where are you? What ocean are you sailing upon, when I have such need of your society, your comfort, of your great strong arms?*

*Yes, there has been a tragedy, but not touching you directly, for your parents and my mother all enjoy tolerable health in this frost unseasonable even for New England in mid-winter. Our foreign friend, Mr. Obookiah of the Sandwich Islands, took sick and went to his heavenly reward a few days since, and I have just returned home from the service held for him. He was resident in New Haven, or*

*Andover, or Cornwall for nine years, since he was but a youth. He became highly educated, and when he sent for me, I saw in his room the pages he had written to translate the Bible into his language.*

*Over the years we passed many pleasant hours together, I telling him about America, and he telling me about his country, his language, the flowers and birds, but also the volcanoes that throw fire a thousand feet into the air, and telling me with grief of their heathen priests and hideous idols. He said there were many things about their society that were not fit to relate to a lady, which I doubt not but, as you know me, made me only the more curious about them.*

*I knew nothing of his illness until our dear Harriet came to fetch me about ten days after the great snowfall, and Rev. Beecher came for me in their sleigh, and drove us to Cornwall, where Henry lay in his room. I tended him for a couple of hours, to relieve Mrs. Mills who was quite exhausted, and he was by turns delirious and in perfect possession of his senses. He spoke affectionate farewells to all present, including to his countrymen in their own language. We departed when he said he felt he should sleep a little, and the last he said to me was, "Aloha oe," which he told me many times is their universal hello and good-bye, but deeper in feeling, it means, my love be with you. Downstairs we took tea, and after a time Hopu went up to check on him. He returned in shock and tears and said, "He has gone."*

*At the last, when we rushed back to the room where he lay—you will think I am carried away in this by my emotion, but I declare to you I am not—he lay dead, but he was smiling, he was smiling as surely as you shall smile, when next we meet. Doubtless it was because of the prank he played on Death, who came for his body but could not take his soul.*

*Reverend Beecher was much affected by this turn of events. Downstairs, he and Mr. Mills and Mr. Dwight the Younger all confessed to one another that each had tried to talk him down from his mighty zeal to return to Hawaii and preach to his people. They had many times adjured him to realize the danger of such a mission, that he might very truly be taken and killed by the priests of the wooden idols, but he met them at every turn. He held up their own Bible to them. He said he was ready. Does not the Bible say, he who loses his life for My sake shall find it? And do you know, dearest? When these high church men realized that each had opposed him and been bested, the great dark pall cast over them was more than grief, it was shame, and when the room was at its most silent, it was because they were ashamed of themselves.*

*Rev. Beecher preached the funeral, and it was quite unlike his wonted orations. You would not, as you have many times threatened to do, have wrapped yourself in your cloak against the gusts of his "much saying." He was still deeply moved, and vowed that while the world might see Mr. Obookiah's death as the end of a wasted education, or a sign of the Almighty's disfavor to the mission venture, they instead took increased devotion from the example of his simplicity of faith and steadfastness of purpose. There will be missionaries of this school who take ship for the Sandwich Islands, one day near or far—not just Americans knowledgeable of the Bible but also doctors and teachers and those skilled in agriculture and manufacture, and also Hopu and Prince Tamoree, and other natives who can give great assistance in the language and smooth their way. The question really is one of money, and how to raise it.*

*And this brings me also, and briefly, to another point on which I wish you were here to consult with me. I received a letter from my father's financial advisor in Boston, urging me to liquidate anything that my mother and I hold in mortgages, either as creditor or debtor. He says there is talk of credit having become overextended, and that*

an uncertain time is approaching. At his alarm I am dubious—yet he
is in some position to know whether the mighty banking houses of
Europe are becoming worried over the moneys they have poured into
America. The great Bank of the United States, which has acted as
their principal agent here, and which has grown so powerful on the
investments of the people, surely would not let speculations run so
rampant as to create what some are calling a bubble.

I do not know what exact steps I shall take, but without acting
rashly I believe I should do something to "lighten ship," as you
would say.

Oh, my darling, I know not where to send this, therefore I will
entrust it to the Navy Yard in Boston. Perhaps if you are on your way
home you will read it there, or they will know where to send it. Your
parents send their love, and I pray that your father may live to greet
you again. This I tell you as a certainty, if his body were as strong as
his spirit, he would outlive us all.

Farewell my dearest love,
Clarity Putnam

BLIVEN PUTNAM, CAPT. USN
*WARSHIP RAPPAHANNOCK*

# ❦{ 3 }❧

## *Conspirators*

Alone in his study on the *Rappahannock*, closeted with his coffee and his chart of the Cuban coast, Bliven studied out what he should do next. Cuba, though it was a mountainous island, at its western extremity sank almost imperceptibly into the sea with miles of mangrove swamps, vast sandbars and tidal flats; and miles out at sea, just when one thought there must be a passable depth, there rose up reefs that were a graveyard for Spanish galleons.

If Fleming reported the leak to be serious, he must put in at Mobile, six hundred miles north northwest of the Yucatán passage, which he did not want to do. If Fleming could find the leak and isolate it, keep it controlled, that would buy some time to act further against the piracy he was sent to suppress. Indeed, the game of piracy changed in nature when passing from the Caribbean into the Gulf of Mexico. The Caribbean was beset by the spiritual heirs of buccaneers who had plundered the Spanish Main in centuries past, only now they masqueraded as privateers for newly independent countries of South America. Piracy in the Gulf brought to mind, realistically, only one name: Jean Lafitte. That smooth-talking, oily, ingratiating, murdering Frenchman who had turned piracy into something like a business, as sophisticated in its way as a Boston brokerage.

For years, Lafitte had operated a thriving pirate's nest on an island deep in the recesses of Barataria Bay, which lay to the south of that long tongue of the Mississippi River delta, his lair approachable only through a maze of narrow channels among miles of reedy marshes. Lafitte had a brother, Pierre, older by ten years, who was the bolder seaman, unafraid to claim his station as a pirate of the high seas, capturing merchantmen, killing crews, and stealing their cargoes. The booty was taken to Barataria, and from there the stolen goods were poled on pirogues through the marshes to New Orleans and sold at pure profit, for the consumer there asked no more than did consumers anywhere what was the source of this bargain merchandise. The Lafitte brothers' inroads into Gulf commerce were such that shipowners and insurance companies applied pressure to the government. In 1814 the United States Navy flushed Jean Lafitte out of Barataria Bay and turned him into a wanted man—only for him to turn up in New Orleans the next year, winning a pardon for himself and his brigands by aiding Andrew Jackson in the defense of that city, and in Jackson's crushing defeat of the British army that opposed him.

Since then, Jean Lafitte had transferred his allegiance to the king of Spain, who had been fighting an insurgency in Mexico since 1810, which occasionally spilled over into Mexico's eastern province of Texas. Lafitte agreed to spy on the inhabitants of Texas and report or eliminate revolutionaries, in exchange for which Lafitte was given free rein on Galveston Island. The crown would not inquire into what kind of operation he ran there as long as he kept order, and as time had proved, Lafitte conceived a model of enterprise even more profitable than fencing plunder in New Orleans.

Bliven heard Ross's three raps on the door and rose from his study and entered the great cabin. "Come in."

Ross entered and saluted. "Dr. Berend is here to report, Captain."

"Send him in."

There entered a smallish older man—too old, really, to still be in the service—but, like Dr. Cutbush, whom Berend knew well, he had found a home and a useful life in the Navy, and no one was disposed to force a skilled surgeon to retire when the service was chronically short of them. Craighead Berend had a receding hairline behind which his tightly curled white hair tended to disorder. His skin was a Mediterranean sort of dark, marked with the keratoses of his age; his eyes were large, dark brown, and intense. He wore the coat of his surgeon's uniform, distinguished from the captain's by the single button and lace-fringed buttonhole at either side of the standing collar. And the fringe of lace at his cuffs was a quarter inch wide, as opposed to the captain's three-eighths of an inch.

They saluted quickly and shook hands. "Dr. Berend, how are you?" He stared coldly at Berend's dress coat. "Are you quite certain you are not dressing above your station? Here, let me see."

He stretched his arm next to Berend's and together they ascertained that the doctor's cuff lace was indeed just a fraction shorter than Bliven's. Berend erupted in laughter, revealing prominent front teeth and a missing bicuspid. "Can you imagine what kind of fop designed these damn things? I just don't know."

"There is no need to ask if you want coffee: Mr. Ross is already behind you with a cup. Be seated, please. Well, what do we have?"

Berend stirred a spoon of sugar into his coffee, omitting cream.

"Captain, you gave into my care nine Africans: five males—that is, three aged men and two boys—and four females—that is, three aged women and one young girl. I got them bathed and fed and treated them for lice, and other than the malnourishment one would expect in their circumstance, they seem to be in good health. They were apprehensive, of course, but a little kind treatment has gone a long way. Since the carpenter's men are working in the hold, I took it upon myself to have most of the sailcloth moved aft and I put the Africans in the sail room. I did not lock them in, but I put two of the marines nearby to corral them in the forward portion of the hold."

"Were you able to speak with the one who knows French?"

"A little bit, yes. They are of the Wolof tribe, who are the principal inhabitants along the Gambia River. They were captured by Mauritanian Berbers, sold to slave factors in Dakar, and put on the ship there. He believes they visited a couple of ports before you took them, but he does not know where. They had not seen light of day until you came along."

Bliven looked away and sighed in disgust.

"Oh, one other thing: I inquired into their religion, looking to the issue of eating pork. He said they are aware of the Mohammedans, and some of the Wolof have converted. But his village had not. His French was not very good, but I understood him to say that when the Berbers come riding through a village, chopping people down and selling others into slavery, and doing it in the name of religion, that is not a religion they want."

Bliven harrumphed. "Yes, we fought about that on the Mediterranean twenty years ago."

"The point is, they will be grateful for whatever you feed them. Forgive me, Captain, but you are going to have to make a decision what to do with them. You are aware of the new law?"

Bliven took a sip of coffee. "You are an educated man, Doctor, what is your opinion of the new law?"

Berend tossed his head. "It is a travesty, of course, there is no denying that. The only way to get a law through Congress was to give the South a say in draughting it. So now slaves captured on the open sea are to be turned over to the Customs Service. That sounds rather benign, but then the Customs Service is to sell them, give half the money to the finder as a reward, and the other half accrues to the Treasury to defray the expense of their so-called rescue. So the net effect has been to take a concept that was intended to protect these poor wretches and twist it into making the United States government the largest slave broker in the world. I may be a Virginian, Captain, but at least I am a west Virginian, and I don't mind telling you I am ashamed of this law."

Bliven sighed in sadness. "I wish to God I had never heard of slavery. Do our . . . passengers . . . know about the new law?"

"No. No, they believe they have been rescued."

Bliven hung his head. "God damn it."

"What are you going to do?"

Bliven chewed at his thoughts for several seconds. "On your honor, may I bring you into my confidence?"

"Yes, please."

"We know how perverse the new law is. Along the Gulf, it is even worse. There is a pirate named Lafitte holed up in Galveston in Spanish Texas."

"Yes, I have heard of him, of course."

"He has learned how to play this law. Lafitte has formed a partnership with a slave smuggler in Louisiana, some man named Bowie. They capture slaves at sea, or perhaps kidnap them from plantations and take them to sea to be 'captured.' They deliver them to the Customs Service and pocket half the money as a reward, then buy them in numbers for a discount before selling them on the block for full price. The ones that Lafitte takes to Galveston are given forged papers and marched through the swamps to sell on U.S. soil, thus even cutting the U.S. government out of the deal. We can't find Bowie and we can't touch Lafitte as long as he is a Spanish citizen. The new law is as you call it a travesty as far as the Gulf Coast is concerned."

"I did not know any of this," Berend conceded. "What are your intentions?"

Bliven looked at him until he was certain he had Berend's attention, and a smile of mischief spread over his countenance. "Read the law! It concerns slaves taken at sea." He pointed below to the hold. "Who owns those people? I don't own them. Do you own them? Who is to say if they are slaves?"

A matching smile spread across Berend's face. "I confess, I like your thinking."

"I know a man in Boston, a highly educated Negro, a teacher, a leader in his community. My intention is to take these people to Boston and entrust them to his care."

"And if he refuses?"

"He owes me his life, he won't refuse."

DURING THE COURSE of the evening the warm, humid east wind swung to the north, robust, drier, even with a chill. From where they drove the slaver into the Bay of Pigs, it was less than fifty miles south to the Cayo Largo, at the eastern end of that string of reefs and cays that extended east for a hundred miles from the Isle of Pines. Safely around the east side of Cayo Largo and into deep water, Bliven ordered west-sou'west for a day before due west—all of it a hard four-day pull to reach the center of the Yucatán Channel. There they loitered until a southerly wind blew up that shot them through into the Gulf of Mexico on the morning of the fifth day.

And after they spread more canvas to get into the Gulf before the wind could change again, Bliven heard Ross's triple rap at his door. "Yes, what is it?"

Ross entered. "The carpenter wishes to—"

Tall, gangling Fleming was through the door before Ross finished announcing him.

"Fleming! What do you know?"

"I believe we have found the source of our problem, sir. Will you please to come down?"

They walked quickly to the ladder amidships, down past the berth deck and into the hold, where Fleming led them forward to where a team of men were gathered around the light of five battle lamps. The stoutness of the *Rappahannock*'s construction was apparent from the extraordinarily narrow spacing of her ribs. These huge oaken timbers, eight inches broad and twelves inches deep to the hull planks, were spaced only sixteen inches on center, so that the spaces between the ribs were only eight inches wide. Thirty feet short of the stern compartments Fleming hopped down onto the ribs and, holding a battle lantern up with one hand, pulled up a large bolt of cotton cloth that he had used as a kind of blotter, and they saw in the space between the ribs a spread of water slowly cover the hull planks. Fleming pressed the dry side of the cotton blotter between the ribs and extracted it again, and the fast seep of water again covered the bottom of the cavity. "There she is, Captain."

"Does this leak extend to the neighboring ribs?"

"A little, sir, but very little."

"What do you propose?"

"As you see, Captain, it is not intruding under high pressure or it would be shooting over our heads. Yet there must be damage to the copper or it would not be coming in at all. I would caulk these seams with pitch, insert blocks of wood on either side of the leak, tight to the ribs on either side, to make a kind of coffer dam, except to keep the water in instead of out. Then I would plank tightly over the ribs and seal those planks with pitch, and see if that holds."

"Yes," said Bliven, "I see. Do as you suggest, only continue that operation to one more rib on either side for good measure. Do you see what I mean?"

"Clearly, sir. We will get right to it."

"Good work, Fleming, very good work. Let us hope this fixes the problem for now."

Miller had this watch, and Bliven could not wait to get on deck to relay the good—or at least the hopeful—news.

"So we are in the Gulf at last," said Miller. "Now you must make up your mind what to do."

"Yes, I must." The salt air was fresh and bracing after the must of the hold, and Bliven sucked it in deeply. "If we go straight home, we turn east-northeast through the Straits of Florida, and should do so quite soon. Fleming, however, believes that he can repair our difficulty, and I am disposed, having seen the leak, to believe him. Now, our orders for this cruise are to trouble the pirates and slavers. If we steer north, in a couple of days we will cross that line that runs from Havana to Galveston. If, as I suspect, Lafitte is picking up some of his slaves in Cuba, we may be able to interrupt his commerce somewhat. But if, as may be possible, Fleming is not able to safely manage our leak, two days' sail will place us within reach of the facilities at Mobile. I think that—"

"Deck! Ahoy the deck!"

Forward of the mizzenmast Bliven and Miller craned their necks upward. A new vessel, *Rappahannock* had been equipped with what they called a crow's nest, a lookout's platform encircled by a metal guardrail, newly devised by the Arctic whalers and such an improvement that Bliven had made certain to have one built as she was fitting out. It allowed lookouts to ride higher, above the topgallant yard, and in greater safety than they had been able up to that time.

It seemed impossible to even shout up to such a height. "What do you see?"

"Two sail, four miles, dead ahead!"

Miller cupped his hands at his mouth. "What is their bearing?"

"Northwest!"

They scanned the horizon ahead with their glasses but descried nothing. "Marvelous thing that the world is round," said Miller, "to see from up there over that tiny curve of the arc what we cannot see down here."

"Well, let's go have a look. The day is new; we may have some fun before dinner. Come to all sail, Mr. Miller."

"Set the stuns'ls?"

"Of course!"

"I think you are just in love with the speed."

"Indeed I am. Get to it!"

From the lookout's first hail the bosun had come close enough to be given his orders. "All sail, Mr. Yeakel. Set your stuns'ls if you please."

"Helm," said Bliven, seeing it was tall young Rippel who was at the wheel. "Come west-nor'west, aim to intercept them, but by all means keep the weather gage."

"Yes, sir."

Bliven cupped his hand at his mouth. "Lookout! Ahoy!"

"Sir!"

"Sing out when you see what kinds of ships they are!"

Again Yeakel's men were in the rigging, lashing fast the yards that held the studding sails, hoisting royal yards that forced the lookout to sit down in his crow's nest to see under the main royal.

As the full spread of canvas filled they raced ahead at what must have been twelve knots, such a speed as to get any young man's blood pumping. Clearly they were gaining on the two ships as fast as a strong man could walk.

"Deck! Ahoy!" It had been less than an hour.

"What do you see?"

"A large brig leading a barkentine! I see open gunports!"

"What do you think?" asked Miller. "A slave ship and an escort?"

"Very possible. But what are they doing down here? We must be a hundred and fifty miles from the sea-lane to Galveston." He shook his head blankly. "I have no idea. Well, beat to quarters, Mr. Miller." Miller turned to go, but Bliven caught him by the arm. "Except for actually loading the guns. Tell your gun captains they will load the guns only on your command. Have the boys bring up bar shot as well as balls, and grape for the carronades. Go ahead and load the carronades. Do you understand?"

"Aye, sir."

"Go, and come right back to me!"

Miller got the attention of the marine corporal standing duty at the head of the ladder. "Beat to quarters!" He disappeared below to arrange matters with the gun captains.

Bliven signed for the attention of one of the midshipmen. "No need for mystery: Hoist our colors from the spanker boom."

The ship flew into life as guns were loosened and limbered, and the dozen ship's boys shuttled powder and balls and bar shot from the magazine. The gunnery drill had simplified since Bliven's boyhood on the *Enterprise*, for the modern lanyards eliminated the linstock fuses and their attendant fuss. Gun crews rammed home the powder charges, but held off loading until they knew what shot to use. Within four minutes *Rappahannock*'s whole aspect changed from an elegant sailing vessel to a lethal, modern weapon of war.

Miller rejoined Bliven on the quarterdeck just as Ross appeared at the head of the ladder and came aft. Bliven asked him, "Is my cabin broken down?"

"Yes, sir, but I thought you would want this."

He handed him the sheathed jambia, which Bliven thrust beneath his sword belt. "Indeed, yes, good thinking, Mr. Ross. I do thank you."

Miller looked on, incredulous. "What the devil is that? Sir."

"For good luck," said Bliven quietly. He grasped the polished handle of rhinoceros horn and extracted it, to reveal its wicked, wide, curving ribbed blade, and handed it over. "When I was a midshipman on the *Enterprise*, we fought and captured a Berber brig, the *Tripoli*. I removed this from an Arab brigand who had no more need of it."

Miller turned it over, inspecting it. "Never have I seen such a thing."

Bliven accepted it back and sheathed it. "Well, not many Arabs in Pennsylvania, I imagine."

"Deck! Ahoy!"

"What do you see?"

"The two ships are separating! The barkentine goes north, the brig goes west!"

Even as his voice died away they felt the small concussion of a gun from the brig, and they saw a ball splash five hundred yards ahead of them. "What a fool," said Miller.

"No, it is interesting. He is challenging us, to cover the barkentine as she runs away, which means the barkentine is carrying valuable cargo—I am guessing human cargo. As with our friend Captain Hippomenes in Cuba, he thinks we will dash to save the poor slaves—if it is slaves. But if we come to starboard and chase down the barkentine, we surrender the weather gage to him, and he can come at us however he chooses. Now, listen carefully." He pulled Miller over near Rippel at the wheel. "Listen carefully, both of you. We are going to come up on his weather beam, classically, elegantly. Starboard gunports snap open smartly together. Broadsides across deep water, all that. Well, elegant naval battles are for novels. I want to take him down as quick as a fencing master. Mr. Miller, you will load your port twenty-fours with bar shot: Elevate to hit the rigging. Load your starboard guns with solid shot. Aim to hit between wind and water. Train your guns as far forward as they will go. If it looks like he is waiting to receive our fire, Rippel here will make a starboard turn at my command; Miller will fire at his rigging as his guns bear. Aim for masts, but ripping shrouds and canvas is also good. Then we will turn to port, and as we come abeam we will hole him with the starboard shot."

Miller gave him a lost-looking smile. "None of this was in any gunnery manual that I ever studied."

"Mr. Miller, *my* gunnery manual has not been written yet."

"What about *his* fire?" asked Miller.

"He can't mount anything heavier than twelves. He will get one salvo before I clear his deck with the carronades."

"What if he turns unexpectedly?"

"It won't be a fast or pretty turn if you do your job with the bar shot!" Bliven seized Miller's hand. "Now, below with you, and good luck."

"You, too."

"Mr. Yeakel!"

"Sir!"

Bliven held his arms straight before him, pointing them right and then left. "I am going to box him as I go in, starboard and then port. Be nimble, now. Be ready to brace up or ease off to match my turns."

"Never you worry, sir." He sprinted forward to relay the orders.

Then came the silence, the hair-rising silence before a sea battle, when all that was audible was the hiss of bows slicing through waves and the whisper of wind through the rigging. There was ample time for Miller to finish loading the guns. Bliven knew they were ready when he heard the starboard ports snap open and the carriage wheels squeal as they were rolled out.

The somewhat slovenly brig made no move; he could see that their guns were all on the weather deck—no surprise in a smaller ship, but convenient when it came to the effect that his carronades would have.

"Steady, Mr. Rippel, well done, now." They were eighty yards astern of the brig and off its port quarter; this course would bring them thirty yards abeam.

"Ready starboard, Mr. Rippel, starboard now!" The tall young lieutenant put all his weight on the great double wheel. They began to feel the bite of the turn, which really dug in as Yeakel braced up the yards to keep the wind behind them.

Bliven almost feared they had turned too far, when the twenty-fours beneath him one after another thundered to life, shaking the deck beneath their feet, and plainly they could see the brig's sails stretch and pop in spasms and they began spilling wind through the holes, as rigging snapped and curled crazily into the air. One lucky shot shivered the brig's mizzen, which lay slowly over, taking its spanker with it.

"Oh, what a godsend," roared Bliven. "Good for Miller! Hard aport, Mr. Rippel! Port, now! Mr. Yeakel, ease off your yards!"

Inexplicably, the brig made no attempt to turn or evade in any direction. *Rappahannock*'s bowsprit came even with the brig's stern but in her port turn was veering away so they could not fight beam to beam. "Bring your rudder amidships, Mr. Rippel! We—"

Bliven's voice was lost in a deafening roar from the gun deck beneath them. Their turn had brought all the starboard twenty-fours to bear at once; thus there was no rolling broadside, just one shattering salvo that holed the brig's hull, taking out chunks of railing and deck cabin.

"Carronades!" screamed Bliven. "Hold! Hold!" It was obvious that *Rappahannock*'s higher freeboard would send the grape whistling through the rigging, and he must wait for the down roll for them to have the needed effect. After several seconds they felt the port side lift in an oncoming swell, and suddenly they were looking down at the brig's deck. "Fire!"

They heard screams and saw men fall, but there answered back a salvo from three twelve-pounders. One ball missed forward; the second crashed into the starboard cathead, releasing the anchor, which dangled into the water without falling farther. The third crunched through the starboard railing and knocked a wheel off one of the three carronades' carriages, dislodging its barrel, which knocked the gun captain to the deck as it dropped onto his legs.

In a moment there was a second crushing broadside from the starboard battery, which caused the brig's port side to burst into a shower of wooden splinters. Without warning, her remaining sails came fainting down as the shrouds were cut and a white sheet ran aloft on its mainmast.

"Cease firing! Cease your firing! Marines to the deck! Get the wounded down to the cockpit! Mr. Ross, my speaking trumpet!"

In a moment it was in his hands. "This is United States sloop of war *Rappahannock*. Do you surrender?"

In a moment a similarly amplified voice came back. "Of course we surrender, you idiot. What does it look like?"

Miller was back beside Bliven and began to shake with laughter.

"What are your casualties?" Bliven shouted through the trumpet.

"Nine dead, six injured."

"How many are not hurt?"

"Twenty!"

"You, lower a boat and bring over your injured; we will do what we can for them." Bliven set aside the speaking trumpet. "Mr. Yeakel, lower the captain's gig: the marines will go over and take possession of the vessel. I claim her as a prize; we will all share in the proceeds. Send your bosun's mate over and start repairing what rigging you can. All her crew are to be placed in irons. Once their wounded are aboard, make all sail to chase down that barkentine."

Once they overhauled the barkentine, she dropped her sails without a protest, and proved to have forty-five Africans in her hold. It required until evening to place that crew also in irons and select a prize crew to follow them. Mobile was now a necessity, and there was no help but to turn the forty-five over to the Customs Service, after which they would meet their fate on the cotton plantations. But by turning over a fully laden slave ship, their attention would be diverted and there would be no need to know about the nine in his sail room. He would keep anchored far out in the bay and sequester the crew.

It was after dinner when Bliven held an examination of the pirate captain, a Frenchman, swarthy and theretofore not communicative. A table and chair were brought up to the quarterdeck. Bliven sat, with paper weighted before him, and an inkwell, and quill in hand, with Miller and Rippel standing behind and flanking him, and Dr. Berend to attest that the prisoner was not mistreated. He was led up from the hold, hands and feet shackled.

"What is your name?" asked Bliven.

"I am Henri Juchereau."

"What is your nationality?"

"Ha! I am Chinese! Haa-ha-ha!"

"Bosun, if you please, have the carpenter tie up a noose and cast it over the main course yardarm." Yeakel saluted, stepped away, and disappeared.

"All right, all right, I am French, but sailing in the service of Spain."

"Are you under the command of Lafitte?"

The Frenchman looked at him sourly. "Yes. He also sails in the service of Spain."

"What is your ship?"

"You have my ship. You know her name."

"What . . . is . . . your . . . ship?"

"La Belle Hélène."

"You are a pirate?"

"I am a privateer."

"Have you a letter of marque?"

"No."

"Why not?"

"It was lost in a battle."

"Why were you even in these waters?"

"Ah, American ships, they look for us, come from Mobile, maybe New Orleans. We went west to miss them. You came from the south. Bad luck."

"Why did you oppose me when all you had were a few twelve-pounders against my long twenty-fours?" There was an echo in his mind of having been asked a similar question after he lost the Tempest to the Java six years before.

Juchereau shrugged. "My life is over. It does not matter."

Bliven set the quill down. "Man, you look alive enough to me. What do you mean, your life is over?"

He sighed wearily. "If I fight you, I may die; my life is over. You catch me and hang me, my life is over. I cannot keep you from taking the barkentine and the slaves. If I escape and get to Galveston without them, the boss will mount my head on a harbor piling; my life is over. All comes to the same end, no?"

"We killed nine of your men and severely wounded six others. Did you have no consideration for them?"

"Their lives were over."

"Oh, hell, I'm not going down that road again. Monsieur Juchereau, your life may be over, but it will not be by my hand. I will take you to Mobile, and there you will be tried for piracy. Whether or not you hang will not be my affair."

*RAPPAHANNOCK'S* LEAK GAVE them no worse trouble during their northerly run to Mobile, but it gave them comfort to stay in company with their two prizes in case her predicament suddenly became dire. They entered Mobile Bay looking like a squadron, and as Bliven planned he anchored his sloop in deeper water, aloof, and conducted his business with the Customs Service from the deck of *La Belle Hélène*. After the slaves were taken off the barkentine, he handed Juchereau over in irons, but as he suspected from the lazy Southern drawl of the officer who took charge from him, he escaped within a few days. He might well have been finished with Lafitte, but that pirate's American partner, James Bowie, would surely find a job for him in one or another of his cutthroat enterprises.

In sum, Bliven could not be quit of Mobile fast enough. He registered his prizes, calculating that his share might be as much as four thousand dollars, which salved his feelings a little. Cautioning the slaves in his sail room to make no sound, he took on food and water enough to get home to Boston before the winter storms became likely.

November was half spent as *Rappahannock* eased into the familiar environs of the Boston Navy Yard. Bliven and Miller walked in silence to the port rail, their eyes wide.

"What in bloody hell?" gasped Bliven.

Miller pointed blankly. "Is that not the *Constitution*?"

"It is. Or at least it used to be." They drew closer and beheld the beloved frigate, her clean line now marred by the round humps of gigantic paddle wheels rearing above her midships.

Bliven and Miller washed and put on fresh uniforms, then descended into the captain's gig, to deposit Miller on the wharf. "Call first at Harvard College," Bliven suggested. "They will be the first to know of Jonah's whereabouts. But if that doesn't work, try the Unitarian Church. But do not fail to find him. When I finish my business, I will send the gig back to this spot to wait for you."

He was then rowed to the *Constitution*, and after receiving permission to board he was conducted down to the captain's cabin, where he was surprised by who greeted him. "Commodore Jones, how are you?" Bliven said. They advanced and shook hands warmly.

Jacob Jones was an anomaly in the American navy, not to say a marvel. He was a Delaware man, well moneyed and well connected. He had married the governor's daughter but was soon widowed; he never spoke of it, but there was a wide assumption that he joined the Navy to escape his grief. At thirty he must have been by far the oldest midshipman in the service, a station that would have humiliated any other man his age, but he learned his craft. He was a lieutenant on the *Philadelphia* when Bainbridge grounded her at Tripoli, and he spent a year in bondage with the rest of her crew. He rose to command the

*Wasp*, and in 1812 he captured two British vessels before, dismasted, he surrendered to a seventy-four, and after a prisoner exchange he commanded the frigate *Mohawk* on Lake Ontario. He was a heartily respected officer, and having once commanded a squadron was entitled to the honorific of "commodore."

"I am well, Captain Putnam, and your good self? Are you yet accustomed to hearing yourself addressed as 'Captain'?"

"Not entirely, but I find it agreeable." He gazed about the once-familiar environ of the *Constitution*, where he had known Preble and Hull and Bainbridge. "I somehow expected to find Hull still in command. Where is he?"

"He now commands the Navy Yard here. I am only recently brought over from the *Guerriere*."

"I see. Now, Jones, what in blazing hell have you done to your ship?"

"Not I, Putnam. Don't lay this on me."

They walked together back up to the weather deck, to where the port paddle wheel arced to twice their height above them as Bliven grasped the rail and peered over the side. The wheel had to be set out far enough to clear the ship's flaring tumble home. "Look at this: they must have taken out eight guns on each side."

"Ten," scowled Jones.

"But why, for heaven's sake?"

"Don't you know? As I understand, you were part of the reason."

"Never!"

"Well, you took part in the reason. Were you not serving on this vessel in 1812, when you were becalmed even as you were beset by a whole British squadron? You rowed and towed the ship, and then set kedge anchors and pulled yourself out of danger."

"True—" Bliven opened his palms upward in expectation.

"Well, the Board of Navy Commissioners took note of your narrow escape and made a decision to outfit the frigates with paddle wheels attached by gears to the capstan. By their dead reckoning—although not dead enough for my money—the ship can make a three-knot headway in no wind at all."

"But look there!" Bliven pointed down. "The drag they create must cost you three knots or even four when under sail."

"I know, I know! And clumsy to turn besides. But this was the decision of our vaunted Board of Navy Commissioners, and no one can tell them anything."

"But Hull is on the Board, and he was the one they chased! He would know better than this, surely."

"Yes, well, the Board has turned into a rather convoluted story. Hull and Rodgers and Porter are used to giving orders. They have had to adjust to placating politicians and making allowances for civilian contractors and awarding them deals to keep them away from the politicians."

Bliven threw his head back. "Augh! Well, that tells the story, does it not?" After the Second Barbary War, when the government decided to maintain a viable navy, the Congress could not be bothered to have its affairs overseen by its own committees, and instead created this Board of Navy Commissioners, which was not gaining fame for the strength of its foresight. The three officers that formed the commission were among the Navy's finest, but found themselves out of their depth, as it were, when out of the water.

"And this is not even the worst of it," spat Jones. "I hesitate to even *show* you the worst of it."

"No, I want to see."

"Come, then." Jones strode toward the after ladder and clattered down it, so quickly that Bliven had difficulty keeping up with him, past the gun deck and berth deck, which Bliven could only survey with the fastest glance, and on down to the orlop deck. They moved forward in a stoop, past the storerooms where Commodore Preble in former days had locked up the more precious of his foodstuffs, and down to the hold. "There, now." Jones gestured with ample head-room suddenly above them. "What do you think of these?"

Bliven beheld two huge iron containers, one to port and one to starboard, rising vertically inboard where they stood, but apparently conforming to the curve of the bottom. "What in the world . . . ? Are these water tanks?"

"Exactly. No more freshwater casks for us."

Bliven nodded slowly. "I have heard things are headed this way. Well, I suppose they do save the cost of a cooper making all those barrels."

"Yes. But how do you propose to limit the loss of water if one of them is damaged?"

"Oh." That was not the first contingency that came to Bliven's mind. "Oh, yes, I see."

Jones was not placated. "Yes, you see. Now, what do you not see?"

"I beg your pardon?"

"Look around you, man! What do you *not* see?"

Bliven peered into the recesses of the hold in the dim light of its scattering of battle lanterns. Nothing seemed amiss as he tried to re-member its configuration from previous years, and when the discrep-ancy finally came it hit him like a punch. "My God, where is your scantling? Where are your braces?"

"Gone!" shouted Jones. "Gone, to make room for these things!" He struck one of the tanks, which resonated deeply like a Chinese gong.

"Why, she will hog within two or three years." They both knew all too well that ships that were too buoyant amidships were pulled deeper at bow and stern, until her keel be it ever so stoutly made must snap and her back be broken.

"Ah, but no! Our Board tells us that the weight of the fresh water here will prevent that happening."

"But how will you replenish fresh water in the middle of the ocean? They cannot remain full at all times."

Jones folded his arms, done and defiant.

Bliven sank down to seat himself on a stray locker, and Jones sat upon the solid oak footing of the mainmast. "They've doomed her, haven't they? Jones, you may be the last captain of this ship." They sat together in the gloom of the lanterns for some moments. "Well, now, look here," said Bliven suddenly. "If they want to go all modern with paddle wheels, why not go all in with a steam engine, too?"

"They are not judged to be reliable."

"Nonsense. That Fulton fellow carried passengers up and down the Hudson for years on his *North River*. Steam power is well proven."

"Well, I wouldn't know about it. But listen, you had best get ashore: Hull is waiting to see you."

"What! Why didn't you tell me straightaway?"

"He knew you would have some opinions to vent about our 'improvements.'"

They headed back to the ladders. "He shares our opinions?"

"Oh, Lord, don't even get him started. He went out with us to test out the paddle wheels. Some of the words he used I'm not even sure what they meant."

"Ha! Good old Hull."

Jones emerged first onto the weather deck. "I think the game may be, at our next cruise, to just break up the paddle wheels and stow them in the hold. What the secretary doesn't know won't hurt him. But look here, now, tread carefully with Hull. He is laboring in heavy seas these days. I am certain he must regret letting himself ever get talked into shore duty."

"Good Lord, it's been"—Bliven paused to calculate—"six years or more. He has been ashore all this time?"

"Yes. Originally it was to help him clear up some family difficulty, as I understand. Now he can't wait to find his sea legs again."

"Where next for you, Jones?"

"Mediterranean Squadron." Jones grasped the rail and peered up the two hundred twenty feet of mainmast. "Several more months of fitting out, of course, after being in ordinary for a few years. You will find Hull on the receiving ship. He wanted his office there; he cannot be at sea, but at least in those surroundings he can close his eyes and imagine. Well, let us have the customary ceremony about this." The bosun had known to station himself nearby, and at a wave from Jones barked an order. Work stopped as the sailors within earshot stood at attention and saluted, as the bosun took the silver whistle that hung about his neck and piped Bliven off the ship.

The sailors in his gig rowed him over to the quay, which he ascended and then went up the gangplank to the roofed-over receiving hulk. He was announced and straightaway shown into the inner warren at once. Even as Bliven saluted, Hull rose and advanced to him, his hand extended. "Captain Putnam! Putnam, it is good to see you."

"Commodore, it is good to see you also. You look well."

"Come, sit, sit. The report that you sent from Mobile arrived safely. Congratulations on good hunting. Were you able to contain the leak that you reported?"

"Yes, sir, our carpenter isolated it and was able to wall it off. Apparently there was some deformation in the hull planking. The copper will have to be removed before it can be repaired."

"Yes, we will see to it." Hull took a deep breath. "Well, Mr. Putnam, there is something I must tell you."

"That is a remarkable coincidence, for there is something I must tell you also. You are senior, please continue."

The sloe-eyed Hull's expression went cold. "I warn you, you are not going to like it, so I am going to give it to you straight as whiskey. I have new orders for you."

"No, not right away! Surely I have some time coming with my family."

Hull waved it off. "No, not right away. Your ship is going into dry dock. The leak will be found and repaired, and she will be re-coppered as may be required. You will have at least a couple of months with your family."

"Good." That news at least made more palatable whatever the coming orders might be.

Hull leaned back in his chair and folded his arms. "Mr. Putnam, this is how it is. Up until now our naval affairs have been largely concerned with protecting our primary trade routes—the Mediterranean, the North Atlantic, the Gulf, and the Caribbean."

"Yes, sir."

"Well, our country is now at a stage where we are discovering just how big the world is. Certain of our merchantmen have been venturing into the Pacific for some years now. They carry our goods away to trade for . . ." Hull's voice trailed off as he thought for examples. ". . . pepper from the Indies, or they take on sandalwood from the Sandwich Islands, and sell it for silk and porcelain in Canton, which they bring home."

"Yes, sir."

"Our trade with Europe has been profitable, but that pales in comparison to the riches we might acquire by trading in the Pacific. However, our ship captains there have discovered, sometimes to their cost, that their trade may not be wanted. For instance, the king of the Sandwich Islands has granted trade advantages to England, to the detriment of other nations. Moreover, our trading vessels are learning that those waters are not any safer than the Mediterranean was twenty years ago, or the Caribbean now."

Bliven shifted in his chair. "That should hardly be a surprise."

"No, but it is not to be brooked. Mr. Putnam, we have received word that an American merchantman, the *Fair Trader*, Captain Saeger, out of Providence, was boarded and looted by Malay pirates in the Malacca Strait. The brigands then had the insolence to state that they let Captain Saeger and his crew live so they might harvest them now and then for more loot. Such insolence is not to be borne."

"No, sir."

"Now, the British, the French, and the Dutch have naval forces in the region, but they lack the instructions, not to say the disposition, to vindicate American honor in an area that they feel privileged to divide among themselves, to our exclusion."

"The Malacca Strait?"

"Oh, that's right. You are the geography student. There is British Malaya to the east, Dutch Sumatra to the west, the straits extend for three hundred miles, and in some places only twenty miles wide, lined with coves and islands for pirates to lurk in and pounce upon whatever low-in-the-water trading ship comes lumbering by."

"I see."

"A wooded gorge full of Iroquois Indians could not effect a better ambuscade."

"Yes."

"Mr. Putnam, your orders will be to proceed to the Pacific. You will punish the pirates in the Malacca Strait and open that sea-lane for our ships, but also to benefit the ships of all nations. You will also show the flag in the various native ports. You already have experience in conveying American friendship, expressing the advantages of trade with us as well as other nations, even as your presence in a sloop of war will convey the cost of disrespecting us."

"Dear Lord. How long will I be gone?"

Hull looked at him without speaking until Bliven's gaze met his. "A minimum of two years; that is the worst news. The United States is establishing an agent and acting consul in the Sandwich Islands, where our trading ships have been calling for nearly forty years—not as many as the British or the French, but the natives know who we are, most certainly. Now, one of the Sandwich Islands is called"— Hull glanced down at a small leaf of notes—"O-wha-hoo, and there is a harbor and town there called Honoruru. You may have your mail directed to the American agent there."

"I apologize, Commodore, my mind is still beached on the idea that I will be gone for two years or more. How can I tell that to my wife, and my parents?"

Hull breathed deeply. "Well, I doubt not that your farewells will be very affecting."

Bliven descended into a surly mumble. "So might my resignation, by God."

"What's that, again?"

"Nothing, sir."

"Oh, that reminds me . . ." Hull rose and began fishing through his desk. "We had word of you when you touched at Mobile and Charleston, and knew you would be coming home, so we did not forward this. Ah, there it is."

Bliven took the letter from him and recognized Clarity's hand in an instant. "Thank you, sir."

"Now, your orders will not issue officially until your ship is repaired and fitted out. So enjoy your time at home. You will receive half pay while off duty, of course, and I will keep you informed."

"I understand. Thank you, sir."

"Oh, damn me, I nearly forgot: What was it you wanted to tell me?"

Bliven had already risen and did not want to settle again. "Sir, may I trust in your confidence?"

Hull grew suddenly concerned. "Yes, I hope so. What is it?"

"I have heard you once bought a slave in order to free him. Can you tell me, please, if that is true?"

Hull had also risen. "It is, although in full justice it had partly to do with resolving a labor dispute in a Navy Yard. But, yes, I bought him and manumitted him."

"Then perhaps you will not judge me too harshly, one Connecticut man to another. When I chased the slaver into the Bay of Pigs, he cast off a dinghy with nine Africans in it, thinking that I would leave off pursuit of him to rescue them. I pursued him, but turned back after he reached Spanish territorial waters. I returned and took the nine into my care on the *Rappahannock*. Later, after engaging the pirate brig and taking possession of the barkentine with a full cargo of slaves, I did not include the nine when I took that vessel into Mobile as a prize."

"That barkentine full of slaves intended for market—you did turn them over to the Customs Service?"

"Yes, sir, but the nine slaves that I took on board at the Bay of Pigs I did not turn over to the Customs Service. Relying upon my own judgment, I determined that conditions along the Gulf Coast have perverted the intent of the governing law."

"You mean that slavery ring with Lafitte and his American accomplices?"

"I mean that precisely, sir, and in addition the customs officer in Mobile was a Southerner who I suspect had no qualms to send those slaves to the auction block. To turn over these nine that I had the power to save would have made me complicit in their operations, and this my conscience would not permit me to do."

"Where are they now?"

"Still on my ship. I have sent my first lieutenant ashore to find an influential and educated Negro that I know, to inquire whether he can take responsibility for them."

Hull nodded in thought. "I see."

"Nine luckless blacks I may be able to blend into Boston unnoticed," Bliven urged. "An entire hold of slaves I could not. I regret their fate, but I could not see how to save them."

Hull thought for a long moment before he spoke. "Well, Putnam, we have come to a hell of a pass in this country when an officer of your character must take into consideration what section his fellow officers hail from in trying to act with honor. I will tell you what: You make your connection with the African gentleman you mention. If he can help you, get the nine off your ship and into his care fast as you can. You have already made your report to me, and I see no need for it to go any further. I imagine that no one above my level will know or care to know anything more of the matter."

Bliven extended his hand. "We are conspirators, then?"

Hull took it. "That is a hell of a thing to have to be, but you and I can recognize that acting in honor has come to mean a different thing to an officer from the North than it does to an officer from the South."

"Yes." Bliven nodded sadly. "And I fear that such considerations will become more convoluted as time goes by."

"Captain Edwards is in charge of the dry dock. He will inform you when he is ready for you, but it won't be before four days' time. Get those poor wretches off your ship. Once you've got her high and dry, Edwards will take over, and we will sign you out to go home and visit your family. It will look well, of course, for you to come and inspect the progress regularly."

## { 4 }

## *Helpless*

Five mornings later Ross knocked at the door of the captain's cabin. "Enter," called Bliven from his berth, rising from where he had been reclining and entering the great cabin.

Ross entered, followed by a tall blond officer with raw and tightly drawn features. "Captain Edwards, sir," announced Ross, "master of the graving dock."

They traded salutes. "Michael Edwards, sir. Good morning." They shook hands. "We are ready for you. The tide will be at its height in midafternoon. It would be helpful to have you in position before then. Would that be satisfactory? Are you ready?"

"Yes, quite." Bliven found no need to tell him that his trunks and sea bag had been packed for two days, awaiting space in the dry dock. The nine black refugees in his sail room, his single great concern, had gotten safely off the ship. Miller had had no trouble locating Jonah. After depositing Bliven to meet with Hull, the crew of the captain's gig had rowed him around the peninsula and into the Back Bay, which they crossed. He left them at a quay as he hired a carriage to take him the two miles north to Harvard College. He needed inquire no further, for Jonah spent as much of his day there as he could. As Jonah explained to Miller, construction of the new Mill Dam had obstructed much of the Charles River's free flow, rendering Back Bay itself pestilential and stinking. He agreed to take the nine freed slaves off their hands, as Dakar had been the departure point for many in his community, some of whom he knew to speak the Wolof language. The first thing Bliven did after seeing them rowed away was to write to his parents that he would be home imminently. So, yes indeed, he was prepared for Edwards to get on with his duties. "What do you need for me to do?"

"Not a thing, sir. You may think of the dry dock as your harbor, and I am the pilot. Once we get you to the entrance, my crew will take out your bowsprit so you will fit easier. You appear to be about one hundred thirty feet between perpendiculars. Is that close?"

"Close? You have guessed it exactly. You have a practiced eye."

"Yes. What is your beam?"

"Thirty-two feet maximum, with a twenty-foot draught."

Edwards nodded. "Good. It should be easy enough to center you over the keel blocks. Do you have the architect's drawing plans?"

"No," Bliven said with some alarm. "She was built in Norfolk. Do you need them?"

"Not urgently. It would be useful to know what angle of bilge blocks to use beneath you to support the ship and not place too much weight on any one point. But we will discover that as we draw the water down."

"Well, then, I just stay on board while you perform your tasks?"

"Yes, sir, and once she is high and dry, you may disembark down a gangplank as relaxed as you please. Now, if you have never observed this procedure before—"

"I have not."

"Well, let me advise you: no ship enjoys the dry dock. She will groan and growl as she settles down, but think of it as you going to the doctor. You may groan and growl, but you endure it because it is necessary for your health."

"I understand."

"She will come out the better for it."

With the authority and sure hand of a pilot, Edwards had his own crew weigh anchor and set the topgallants, giving *Rappahannock* just enough headway to inch toward the narrow entrance of the graving dock. There, with block and tackle, the bowsprit extension was unlashed and stored on the spar deck, and after that the bowsprit was withdrawn from its footing and laid next to the extension. Then high tide lines were stretched forward, she was winched into the slip, and the huge gate was closed behind her.

Beams of equal length reached out to her port and starboard, centering her precisely over the keel blocks, and as the water withdrew, stout wooden stilts were braced under the hull, shorter as they approached the curve of her bottom, where finally a line of fat bilge blocks was placed under her.

It was Evans Yeakel, the bosun, who saw Bliven to the gangplank, which seemed like the edge of a cliff, so shocking was the sight of no water beside them. He held up the whistle that never left the leather string around his neck. "Shall I pipe you off, sir?"

"Ha! I think we can dispense with ceremony today."

"Do not worry, Captain: if any need arises I will send for you at once, and I will write you of the progress every few days."

"Very well. I leave her in your hands." Bliven glanced about the spar deck, then up into the rigging. He had every confidence in Yeakel. Officers came and went as they scaled the ratline of rank and command and influence. Bosuns, customarily, stayed with a ship, almost marrying the vessel. After a few cruises and changes of command, no man knew her as well as the bosun, her needs and her moods, how to coax her. The same indeed was true of the bosun and the crew, and his position was indispensable as a buffer, often an intercessor, between the officers, who were gentlemen, and the enlisted men, who were drawn from the lower social classes. No officer doubted that bosuns deserved a higher rank than they held, but if they wore the gold lace of command, it would sacrifice their credibility, their point of identification, with the crew. A bosun had to be content with his station and the knowledgeable appreciation of his officers.

Bliven hired a wagon to take his baggage to the stage depot, and he turned to regard *Rappahannock* in farewell. The sight alarmed him, even though he accepted that she was in good hands. There is something unnatural, something helpless, about a ship out of water. Whether powerful, or deadly, or capacious, or efficient, like a swan her beauty depends upon her being in the water. He saw *Rappahannock* supported on a very forest of spindly timbers that balanced her, held her up, and kept her from pitching onto her beam ends. To see her immobile, her big round belly exposed, was rather a shock, like seeing a large woman out of her corset for the first time. You might still love her, but you must see and acknowledge what she had been concealing.

Mr. Strait's stage line had long since passed away, replaced by others faster and more efficient. Public roads had begun to replace the private turnpikes, as there grew a popular clamor for internal improvements—canals most expensively, but straighter roads came in the bargain. In the two days, no longer three, it took to get home to Litchfield, it was impossible not to notice the changes also in the land. In the seventeen years since he first went to sea, the rural areas were even more thickly settled, farms crowded cheek by jowl as the landscape rolled by, forests confined to stream banks and hilltops. If firewood was dear before, it had become precious now, and Bliven told himself to make certain to provide for his parents before he departed for the Pacific—and how without imparting a shock could he tell them about that?

Although the company was more commercial and impersonal, the road north from New Haven still passed by his very door, and he prevailed upon the driver to halt long enough to deposit him. His mother as was her custom flew out the door to him, and Clarity close behind, whom he held long and kissed tenderly.

"Where is Father?"

"He has not been all that well. He is in bed but wild to see you. Come in, my son, and welcome home."

They let him enter the bedroom alone and could hear the laughter of their reunion. When he emerged, Clarity took him by the hands. "Dearest, I have a little something for you, a homecoming gift, as it were. Come back to our room." She pulled him through the hall and the keeping room, into the suite he had built on when they married.

From its place on her desk she lifted a book, not ponderous in size like a geography, but quite fat. "I think you might have an interest in this."

He read the title on the spine: *Fighting the Barbary Pirates, Or, The Liberation of North Africa. A True Novel of Adventure and Action.* Putnam. Partly he laughed, partly he gasped. "What on earth?" He opened it and curled the endpaper aside, and the frontispiece, and read the title again on the title page, then: *by Benjamin Putnam.* "What . . . ?"

Clarity was clearly enjoying his amazement. "The publisher told me that they loved the story, but the public would likely not accept it being written by a female. So your father kindly consented to let me borrow his name."

"Oh, my Lord! Oh, my Lord! You finished it? You are an author!"

"Authoress, if you please. As between us, we can accept a lady as a writer."

Bliven uttered such a whoop that it carried through the house as he picked her up by the waist and lifted her high, then held her tightly. "Oh, my love! I could not be more proud!" She knew he was telling the truth because she could see the tears in his eyes. "Whatever must the Misses Pierce say about this?"

She arranged her dress when he let her go. "Similar enthusiasm, perhaps less athleticism. And our young friend Harriet was suitably impressed as well. Since you left, she has confirmed her ambition to also be a writer, and I have been helping her with composition lessons. While she accepted my advice before, my credibility was surely augmented when the parcel of books showed up at our door."

"Ah, yes, Harriet. How is the young Miss Beecher?"

"Still precocious and gaining in self-possession now that the Misses Pierce have got hold of her."

He grew thoughtful. "But no prettier, I'll warrant."

"No, but we won't speak of that. She makes up for it with kindness, and joie de vivre, and my heavens, such a prankster you never saw."

"Still friends with my father?"

"Oh my, yes. It has been hard for her to see him confined, but her cheer when she comes to see him is unfailing."

"Well, then, God bless her."

* * *

THE PUTNAMS' BEDROOM off the parlor he found with the door open, and he entered without knocking and found his mother sitting at the bedside. "She finished it!"

"Yes," said his father. "We gathered that you learned of the news. Your shout made my window rattle. And what is more, they paid her for it. I warn you, you had best find some new battle to win, or her renown will begin to eclipse your own."

"Your cronies at Captain Bull's Tavern must have been right impressed to see your name on the book."

"Yes, well, they need not know all. However, I am seldom among them these days."

Bliven sat on the side of the bed. "You do not spend so many days in the great room, either, anymore."

"No. It is harder now to get that far, I'm afraid."

"May I ask, would you find it humiliating if I were to make it part of Freddy's duties to carry you there of a morning?"

Benjamin considered it. "I am comfortable enough for now, but as the days grow colder, yes, that would be very fine. I should like to spend my days by the fire."

"Well, then, leave it to me. I've got prize money coming from the two ships I took into Mobile. I can make it well worth his while."

As THE AUTUMN deepened, Putnam Farm accelerated into its fall activity, the twin tasks of reaping what had grown with such bounty and preparing for the winter. There was wood to lay in, workers to hire for the coming apple season, root vegetables to lay in the cellar. It was not yet time to slaughter, but Bliven made certain that his family would have preserved meats for the coming months.

He returned to Boston to inspect the work on the *Rappahannock*, and he almost wished he had not done so, for he beheld her belly ripped open as though some sea monster had taken a great bite out of her. It looked, as Captain Edwards informed him, worse than was its actual case. A growing deformation in her hull planking had pulled loose a seam in her copper bottom, laborious but not difficult to mend, and as with other nautical surgeries, closing the wound would be the easiest portion. In fact, work on her was close enough to complete that Hull handed him a letter instructing him to begin closing up his affairs at home and be ready for recall.

It was the morning after Bliven's return to Litchfield that Benjamin sat up in bed for his oatmeal and noted the quiet in the house. "Where are the children this morning?"

Dorothea looked out the window. "He has taken Clarity for a walk in the orchard."

"Oh, my, that does not bode well."

"No, it never does."

"Do you think he has been ordered back to sea?"

She sat on the edge of the bed. "I know he has, for he just told me. He has not wanted to spoil our time together while his ship was being repaired, but it will be a long voyage."

"Indeed?" He swept his hand out grandly. "Where bound, as they say?"

Dorothea tried to speak but her voice choked into a sob. "To the other side of the world," she managed at last. "To China, and the Indies. Oh, my husband, we shall never see him again, I fear."

Benjamin Putnam deflated almost visibly. "Oh, dear. Oh, dear.

This is a hard blow." He reached out to her hand. "But look you, we must not let him know how we are wounded. Such a parting will be as hard for him, and we must not make it worse."

"My love." Bliven wrapped an arm around Clarity's shoulders, looking gratefully through the now-empty branches of the orchard. He had inspected the books and it had been a good harvest, with good cider, and good sales both here and in the Hudson Valley. "The time has come for me to tell you some bad news, that it is time for me to go back to sea."

"How bad is your news, exactly?"

"As bad as you can imagine, my love. I am ordered to the Pacific. To the Sandwich Islands, and Canton, and the Indies."

"And how long will you be gone?"

"Two years, they think. More honestly, closer to three."

She stopped and then walked on with him. "I see. Yes, I see."

"You are taking this very calmly."

"Yes."

"I am proud of you, but I am amazed. I expected an absolute storm."

She stopped again and looked at him squarely. "Storms pass, glacial resolve does not. Do you imagine that I can do without you for three years?"

He held her tighter as they walked on. "But, my love, captains' wives are no longer allowed to sail with their husbands. And I must obey my orders or resign; there is no help for it. What can I do?"

She stopped again, looking first through the trees heavy with apples and then back toward the house. "My love," he said, tapping his finger above her ear. "I can hear your gears turning like a grist mill. What are you working at?"

"Dearest, it may be not a question of what you can do," she said quietly. "It is what perhaps *I* shall do."

"Would you leave me?"

She replaced her arm around him and they continued walking. "No, my captain, don't be ridiculous. I would never leave you."

"I am at a loss. What then would you do?"

"May I put you some questions?"

His surprise was frank. "Open fire."

"If you must operate in the Pacific for such a term of years, you will need some base of supply. I will venture to guess that Canton and the Indies are too far and uncertain to rely on. Is that a reasonable assumption?"

"It is. Most probably we will sail in and out of the Sandwich Islands. The government is establishing a legation there, and the consul will make it his business to be able to service American vessels."

"Yes. And apart from victualing your ship, I imagine a large part of his attention will be taken up with the missionaries, once they get there."

"Hadn't thought of that," he admitted. "But, yes, he must keep abreast of what they are up to. How many will there be, do you know?"

"Perhaps as many as twenty." They had reached the fence of split rails that separated the orchard from the field of pumpkins now thickly strewn with globes of dark orange. Bliven picked her up and set her atop the fence, where she balanced herself partly by clinging to his arm. "How often, do you think, would you call there to replenish and repair?"

He shook his head. "It's hard to say. Roughly, perhaps every six months."

"So, if—and I merely say if—I were there, in the Sandwich Islands, I would see you every six months, as opposed to waiting three years."

"Yes, but how would that be possible?"

"I don't know, dearest, but please! I am making it up as I go. Now, you remember our poor dear friend Henry Obookiah, who begged and begged the church to send missionaries to his Sandwich Islands? The church started the foreign missions school nearly two years ago, training people to preach abroad. Finally, now, after poor Henry is dead, they are forming up a company to convert those natives. He had the idea, not I, but he asked if I would go as one of them. He said that Mr. Beecher and the others were men of God but did not understand people, and that I—which I expand to mean the women in the company—can effect much good with people that the men cannot."

Bliven cast his gaze through the apple trees as though looking for help.

"Don't do that, dearest," she said. "You are trying to think of an argument against me. It has been in the back of my mind all these months, but I could not form it into a plan until now. And as I contemplate it, I realize it is what I must do."

"Beecher would allow this?"

"I think he will."

"But you know how he disdains the abilities of women."

"Oh, I have some points to use in leverage against him. He will see it my way."

"Why, for heaven's sake?"

"For heaven's sake, indeed, but that is my affair."

"You are intelligent and educated, but come down to it, you are still a woman and they will never let you preach."

"I would not care to preach, but I can spin, and weave, and they tell me that these skills are much wanted to teach to the native women. They say the women have no cloth except what they beat from tree bark, and that once they see our dresses they are near mad to be taught how to make them. It could be a great point of winning trust and friendship."

"Well! So women the world over like pretty clothes—even wild heathens."

Clarity smiled wryly. "Yes, well, God made us all the same, it would seem. And Lord knows I can teach many school subjects."

"Perhaps Miss Pierce can lend you her volumes of world history that she pieced together from news clippings and personal notes."

"Ha!" He helped her down from the fence and they turned back. "I doubt that world history will be the first subject they need to be taught."

"What about your mother?" he asked suddenly. "She isn't well. She might not want you to leave home."

"You could not be more wrong about her. She has supported the mission school from its inception. And she told me years ago how different her life would have been if she had not lived in fear of the unknown, of adventure."

"Ah, adventure. Have you any idea how long it takes to even get there?"

"Reverend Bingham, who is in charge of the mission, has said in his fund-raising appeals that the voyage might be six or seven months. I am willing." She laid her hands on his. "In what other way can I even come close to sharing your life? You cannot ask me to wait three years." When she saw he could make no answer, she went on, "But wait, there is another aspect to it all." She paused so long that he realized the thought was new to her as well. "With times turning bad, I took our money—which is in large part to say my money—out of land and mortgages. Keeping enough in cash to care for our parents, something must be done with the rest. For years now, Boston merchants have been making a fortune in Hawaiian sandalwood for the Canton trade. With me in the islands and your eyes in Canton, we can understand that business better than anyone, could we not?"

"You mean, establish friendships and get better terms."

"Well, yes, that too. Besides, the missionary board pays its people—not handsomely, but double what I could earn here as a teacher. By the time we come back, times here will have improved. We will still have the farm, and your parents can live well with Freddy looking after them."

"Let us not forget, I have prize money coming for the two ships I brought into Mobile. It will not be all your money."

"Fair enough. Only tell me, once, for all: Are your orders firm? I must know they will not be rescinded, for if I act, I must act quickly. The church's plans are far advanced."

Finally Bliven nodded, more in defeat than agreement. "Yes. I will be sent to the Pacific as soon as the *Rappahannock* is seaworthy and a crew assembled. That fact is unalterable."

"Then there is not a moment to lose, for the missionary company is packing even now. I will go see Reverend Beecher this instant."

"If you do this, it means you will leave before I do."

They hugged long and she smiled. "Well, then, I shall call it my revenge, for you have sailed away and left me enough times, God knows. It is well. Besides, I must live through something exciting for my next novel."

THE DISTANCE TO the Beecher house was faster to walk than to hitch a horse, but Clarity was breathing hard by the time she knocked on the door—not the front door but the one to Beecher's study. His face was instantly amazed as he opened it. "Why, Mrs. Putnam, come in, come in. This is a surprise."

"Well, Reverend, you have no idea what a surprise." She explained the nature of her errand and her request to be included, at the last minute, in the company of missionaries.

"But that is quite impossible," he said. "The Board has already resolved that only married couples may be included in the company."

What he meant as comforting she could only take as patronizing. "And yet, Mrs. Albright is going, as I understand."

"Mrs. Albright is an acknowledged master of the homemaking arts. It was felt that she has so much to offer the native women, she could help build friendships in ways that preachers cannot."

"As can I."

Beecher tried without success to stifle an exasperated splutter. "Mrs. Albright is past the . . . age . . . of temptation!"

"I beg your pardon!"

"No, no, no, my dear Mrs. Putnam. I do not mean to say that *she* could be tempted, or you. I say only that, with her years, she could not *offer* a temptation that would lead men into an . . . unhelpful state of mind."

Clarity regained her composure. "Well, still, that is not a very pretty compliment to *her*, is it! All right, Reverend. You and I are both New England folk, let us deal like it. Your fund-raising appeals have been unceasing in behalf of the coming mission to the South Seas. You do not have all the money you need, and you have been trusting God to provide."

"Yes, that is quite true."

"God is great, but God does not have an account with the Bank of Boston. I do."

"You would drive such a bargain, Mrs. Putnam?"

She raised her head with determination. "What is the cost of the company's passage on this ship you have chartered?"

"Well . . ."

"Don't shilly-shally; time is short. How much?"

"Two thousand five hundred dollars."

"And how much have you raised?"

"One thousand seven hundred dollars."

"You lack eight hundred dollars? You have paid for everything else—supplies, food, tools, gifts for the natives, that big house that you are taking apart and stowing on board?"

"Yes. All we lack is the last eight hundred dollars in passage."

"Very well. I will write you a draught for eight hundred dollars this instant, but you know my price."

"I have never known a woman to speak so." He raised his hands and shook his head. "The Board has met about this point and decided that single women are not to be commissioned to go abroad, Mrs. Albright being an exception. How will I convince the Board to accept you?"

Clarity pulled a blank bank draught from her purse. "How about this: Mrs. Albright will need a companion, someone to look after her on account of her advanced years, so she will not be a burden to the rest of the company."

Beecher's face went as slack as if he had died, as indeed he saw the hopeless nature of his position. "Why, yes. Yes, that would win the trick. But I must ask you this: your husband's orders for the Pacific are firm? There is no chance that they will keep him here or send him elsewhere?"

"He assures me that this is the case."

"And your mother supports this?"

"Whose money do you think I have handed you?"

"Very well, madam, you have your bargain."

FROM THAT DAY events so proceeded apace that there was barely time to pack. Bliven explained things to his parents, who received the news stoically, and he and Clarity were on a coach to Boston. Having reached the waterfront, he left her and all her trunks save one at the brig *Thaddeus* as he went on to the Navy Yard to inspect work on the *Rappahannock*.

With no one minding the boarding gate, Clarity went boldly aboard. It was a commercial vessel, with raised fo'c'sle and poop deck, and a well deck between them, most of which was occupied by a large hatch cover. She heard activity within the hold, and descended. At the foot of the ladder she saw workers. "Excuse me, you down there!"

A swarthy stowadore, sweating in the midday warmth, craned his head around, stepped up to a pass of decking along the keel, and advanced to ten feet from her. "Your pardon, madam. We are not used to feminine company down here. You must excuse our appearance."

"I will, if you will excuse my intrusion."

"How may we help you?"

"I wished merely to see that you have enough room for everything."

"Yes, ma'am, allowing for some clever stowing."

"And to have my trunks brought aboard. I will be taking passage." Clarity surveyed the hold. "You are placing the heaviest beams lowest down, for ballast?"

"Bless you, ma'am, so we are. You have cargoed many ships, have you?"

"My husband is a sea captain. I have assimilated some rudimentary knowledge."

The stowadore gestured into the hold. "I have loaded some unusual cargoes in my time, but this is the first time I have stowed an entire house, and a large, mighty house at that."

"Yes, well, where we are going, it will be easier to reassemble one than to take our axes and commence to chopping trees down, you see."

"Bound for the Sandwich Islands, as I hear."

"Yes."

"Well, if the winters in the tropics are as hard frozen as they are in New England, you will be well prepared."

Clarity straightened. "But we will repent our plan as we roast under the sun, if I take your meaning?"

The stowadore cocked his head to the side. "Oh, no, ma'am, not at all."

"Well, we shall see."

"You have chosen your vessel well. Captain Blanchard has made the voyage twice and not lost a stick of cargo." He gestured back to the hold to recover any offense he had given. "As you will see, we laid the sills and the joists on the bottom, alongside the keel, with the ironwork, and then the millwork in the open spaces. We saved the clapboards for last; they are the greatest amount of lumber. We will lay them athwart the heavier beams, and that will make you a kind of decking on which to store your personal belongings and such like."

"Clever man. I thank you for your trouble." She turned to ascend the ladder and he reached out to help her up. "No need," she said. "Thank you."

At the head of the ladder she encountered a middle-aged man, barrel chested and bearded, his whiskers ample but carefully shaved down the cheeks to shape his face. "I was not aware that we had taken on additional labor. Have you registered at the office, that you may collect your wages?"

Once Clarity mounted the last step of the ladder, she squared herself. "You have the manner of a captain."

He removed his cap to reveal a shock of graying auburn hair. "Andrew Henri Blanchard," he said, pronouncing his middle name in the fullest French manner. "Master of the brig *Thaddeus*."

"I am Clarity Putnam. I will be one of your passengers." She held out her hand, and he took it.

"May I come aboard?"

Blanchard turned to see Bliven standing at the boarding gate. "Come aboard and welcome, sir."

"Captain Blanchard, may I present my husband, Captain Putnam, United States Navy?"

"Oh, I have heard of you." He advanced several steps, holding out his hand. "Welcome indeed. It will be a pleasure to have your company on such a long voyage."

They shook hands. "Thank you, Captain, but I shall not be accompanying her, as my wife's business is quite urgent. I shall follow in my own ship when the repairs are done."

"Oh?" Blanchard's face fell. "I am sorry to hear you will not be with us. Ha! But I do see you casting your gaze about. She is eighty-five and one half feet between perpendiculars, twenty-four and one half feet in the beam, two hundred and forty-one tons burthen. We have been around the Horn twice together, and both of us the tougher for the experience. Have I anticipated your questions?"

"Indeed, sir, you have. I would not entrust my wife to just anyone."

"I have been reading of your exploits, Captain Putnam. There is a new book about you and the Barbary War. I do believe that everyone I know has a copy."

"You don't say so!" He and Clarity passed a knowing smile between them.

"Tell me, may I ask?" said Blanchard. "Is it true that at the Battle of Derna you fired ramrods from your guns at the Berber defenses?"

"Oh, God. How did— No one knows about that anymore. How—" He shot a sudden look at Clarity. "You didn't. Please tell me that you didn't."

"But, dearest, it was such an interesting part of the story. I could not possibly leave that out."

Bliven turned away and covered his eyes. "Oh, no."

She patted his shoulder. "I guess you have not read that far yet."

"Captain Blanchard"—Bliven turned and faced him again—"at Derna I was given a motley mix of Greeks, Egyptians, and Levantines to fire the guns placed under my command. They had no training, and, yes, one of the crews left a ramrod in a gun when they fired it. We were damned lucky it did not blow up and kill us all. I could have beaten them to death. So, yes, there is a grain of truth to the story, but I have not yet read the account that you are referencing." He glared at Clarity. "I cannot swear to its entire accuracy."

Clarity took his arm as they walked leisurely back to the end of the wharf. "Please do not be angry, dearest."

She felt his chest begin to shake, and looked to up see that he was stifling an eruption of mirth. "I am too proud of you to be angry. But mark now: we have let the cat out of the bag. At least one person now knows that your book was written by a woman."

"Well, that may not be a bad thing. Let a rumor start; let people wonder. In fact, let us buy one in a bookshop, and you can tell people, just a couple or a few. Not for the sake of my vanity, but it may be good for sales. The times are turning sour, and few people think of books as necessities of life. Talk can only help. Dearest, where is our carriage?"

"I sent it ahead to the hotel. I thought we might walk there; it is not far."

"Where have you arranged for us to stay?"

"You will see." He patted her hand that lay on his arm.

From Milk Street they turned into Liberty Square, then west on Water Street, and immediately upon turning right onto Congress

Clarity caught her breath. "Oh, my stars! Look at that!" Before them rose an enormous building, seven stories high and surmounted by a shallow glass dome. "What on earth is that?"

"That, my love, is the Boston Exchange, the largest building and perhaps the finest accommodation in the country. Let us go in."

They mounted a broad portico past a rusticated first floor, entered, and presented themselves to a receiving desk. "I am Captain Putnam," said Bliven. "I believe you have a room for us."

"Oh, yes, sir, we do. Your baggage arrived earlier today and was deposited in your room. Your key, sir. This gentleman will conduct you. Porter?"

Clarity allowed her gaze to be drawn to a rank of four easels standing on tripods beyond the registering desk. They bore simply framed portraits of seeming domestic couples, smiling, thoughtfully confident. Three of the easels bore two of the portraits, the fourth held one couple's portrait, with a similarly framed announcement. "Bliv, dearest, come look at this."

He bade their porter to wait a moment and joined her. In the rustic type of a handbill he read, "Our Christian Missionaries to Evangelize the Pacific Islands," followed by text describing the mission and inviting all readers to a great farewell blessing and service at the Park Street Church. "This is announced for last Sunday," he said.

"Yes, but as it says, there is still time to make a donation. Would you care to contribute?" He was glad she was playful.

"I am already giving them the most precious thing I have. They must be content with that. These are their portraits, the ones that are going?"

"Yes."

"Where are you?"

"Oh, I was an afterthought. The pictures had already been painted."

"Hm!" He read on, that the portraits were done in watercolor by the celebrated artist Mr. Samuel F. B. Morse. "Good Lord! Is he not the most fashionable portraitist in the city?"

"Surely," she answered. "One of the most, if not the very most."

"I wonder that they would spend precious money for such a commemoration."

"Oh, I doubt that he charged his full fee. And the public notice that has been taken surely earned back the cost. I am told that they raised a small fortune at that service."

Bliven took her arm and led her across the lobby. "Well, I still think your portrait should have been included. You are by far the prettiest of that lot."

She held his arm tighter but leaned her head to the side, askance. "Well, thank you very much, I think."

"How in the world did they find seven married couples who wanted to go?"

"Well, they didn't; they only found one. The other volunteers were single men. Reverend Beecher and Dr. Dwight and the others decided to send married couples rather than, forgive me, follow the sailors' example of being tempted by native girls on every island. So, except for the Chamberlains, who have several children, the young men had to go out and find wives quickly."

"Well, now, that is the damnedest thing I ever heard."

"It is not generally known, dearest, and best kept that way. Yes?"

"If you wish. You know these people?"

"Only a little." Clarity took in the lobby of the Boston Exchange, wide-eyed. Though she had graduated from Sarah Pierce's school, she had never been to Boston. She was too self-possessed to be overwhelmed but found it heady. "Such a dining room!" She pointed across the lobby. "Are we to eat in there?"

"Yes, in a bit. First we shall catch our breath and change clothes, then there is something else I wish to show you before dinner." Their suite was on the third floor, as well appointed as her own room had been at her mother's house. After she changed she gazed out the tall windows of the sitting room and the bedroom before he led her downstairs and into a waiting carriage. "Julien's Restorator, please," he said to the driver.

When they stepped down after a drive of a quarter of an hour, Clarity marked the house as very old, from Puritan times, for it had an overhanging second story with many corners and gables, all collected about a massive central chimney with numerous flues issuing from the top. "I thought," Bliven said as he opened the door, "you might enjoy to experience the finest oysters in the city. They tell me that Monsieur Payplat has been in business here for no fewer than twenty-five years."

Clarity peered about at the dining rooms and the throng within them. "The fare must be extraordinary: Look at all the people!"

She found the oysters and white wine exquisite, but they were not so many as to spoil the dinner to come. They returned to the Boston Exchange and ate courses of a supper centering around boeuf à la Bourguignonne. Although Clarity dined to the point of surfeit, and although it was late, she found herself not drowsy. Back in their room she closed the bedroom's window curtain, and as Bliven started to extinguish the whale oil lamp she caught his hand and became very serious. "Dearest, we shall not see each other for many months. Do not think me unladylike." Her breathing became shallow. "I want there to be light in the room. I want us to take off our clothes and see each other as God made us. I want us to have this in our memories in the coming months. I want us—" Her voice choked and he held her tightly.

"I know what you want, my love. I want it as well, and as much." It was as she desired. Not in the chiaroscuro of the night but in the colors of the light they made love passionately, sweatily, multiply. At the last she fell asleep, her face on his chest, his in her hair.

With all of love's joys spoken that night, there was little to say in the morning. The carriage took them to the wharf, where she discovered she was the last to arrive, for all seven of the missionary couples were assembled on the deck of the *Thaddeus*, and Muriel Albright standing among them was the first to see her, pointing, "There she comes." Her years were apparent in her old-fashioned dress, in her white hair pinned up tidy in a white bonnet, in the blue-gray circles beneath her blue eyes that had seen, and borne, the storms that life offered, and endured. She was, and was known to be, of that stock of New England women who grew old long before they grew feeble, women who, like old Dr. Dwight's wife, might well live to see her hundredth year.

All twenty-four of them—seven married couples, one couple with five children accompanying, the four Hawaiians, and Mrs. Albright—turned to see Clarity descend from the carriage. The leader of the expedition, Hiram Bingham, commanded their attention. "Let us leave our native land by singing 'Blessed Be the Tie That Binds.'" Their voices rose, not strong, not prominent, but curiously not out of place among the cries of seagulls and splash of chop among the pilings.

"Do not come aboard, dearest; I could not bear it," she said quietly. "Keep your seat; let us part now, as I invoke God's protection upon you, my heart, my husband."

"You have a good ship, my love. I pray a safe voyage for you, and I shall join you in that far ocean as soon as the winds will bear me." They kissed, and she saw the coachman attending to help her down. She walked to the gangplank and did not look back.

"Navy Yard, if you please," Bliven told him when he resumed his seat. He found the *Rappahannock* still on stilts in the dry dock, but with new yellow planking stacked around the gaping wound. Beside her lay thick sheets of shiny copper, ready to be hammered and shaped to the conformation of her hull. It was time to get himself back to Litchfield and order his affairs.

DOROTHEA WAS BUSYING herself about the keeping room when Bliven emerged from the rear apartment. He was immaculate, in dress uniform. About his waist hung the sword that the Congress had presented him at the conclusion of the Second Barbary War, four years before, and as he now habitually wore it his Berber jambia was thrust into his sash—not part of the regulation uniform, but no one begrudged this small portion of pride. He himself knew it to be his slowly swelling conceit and one day he must confront it, but for now he could call it pride.

Dorothea's floured hands flew to her cheeks before she could wipe them on her apron. "Oh, my son! You are not leaving so suddenly!"

"Oh, no, no. I am sorry to startle you so. Father wished to see me, and he asked me most particularly to come in full dress."

"Whatever for?"

Bliven shook his head. "I have no idea."

She motioned him on. "Well, your timing is good: he has had his breakfast and is reading over the last newspapers."

"He is not in here today?"

"No, he told Mr. Meriden that he would lie in bed today."

Even after a lifetime in their house, Bliven seldom had business in his parents' room, and the airiness of it always surprised him. It was spare yet comfortable, tidy yet amiably lived in, whitewashed but with sufficiently vivid colors in the corners to make it cheery.

The door was partly open, but he rapped three times anyway, not too loudly, just as he had Ross do on the *Rappahannock*.

"Ah, come in, my son. Yes, yes, that is very fine."

Bliven crossed the room, the hollow-sounding splat of his shoes on the wide pine flooring suddenly muffled as he crossed onto the braided rug in various shades of blue.

"Yes, come stand by me. Stand tall, now."

Bliven did as he was bidden, smiled, and opened his hands. "What is this about, Father?"

"You have asked yourself why have I wanted to see you thus?"

"Yes."

Benjamin paused to consider his approach to an answer. "You will be leaving us again, will you not, within a very few days?"

"Yes, I will."

"Well, this is how I wish to remember you. For, once you go, I think that you and I will not meet again in this world. Surely you have considered this."

Bliven felt the lump form in his throat. "Yes, I have thought on it, but you may yet regain some strength."

"Oh, my son." Benjamin waved off his patronizing. "Let us not pretend, not you and I. Look at me, lying here as helpless as a poor damned toonuppasog on its back."

Bliven sighed and sagged, and began laughing. "Yes, you are right. I see the resemblance." The image was an apt one, of the snapping turtles that lurked in their Connecticut bogs, warty and long clawed. For all their wiles in hunting and their sharp-hooked beaks, when you turned them on their backs they were as pasty white and crepe-skinned, as confused at their unaccustomed posture and diminished capacity as his father was, trussed up in bed.

Benjamin patted the side of the bed next to him. "Come sit with me, my son."

The Navy's dress uniform was not designed for comfort in sitting, owing to the tightness of the trousers, the width of the sash, and having to arrange the sword. One had to sit at attention even as one stood at attention.

Benjamin grasped Bliven's forearm firmly. "When I was your age, my father told me a thing. I did not understand it then, but as time has gone by I believe I understand it now. He said that when men get old they can feel when their time is coming—not all men, but oftentimes. It does not come down to a pain but to a kind of awareness. You cannot call it knowledge because there is no evidence, yet he knows."

"And that is where you are?"

"It is. Only do not tell your mother I said this. It helps her to think that I may yet regain my vigor."

"Do you believe that your uncle Rufus has been visited by this premonition of mortality?"

Benjamin rested his head back on his pillow, his eyes merry. "Haaa! That old fossil! He has made older bones than I ever shall, that cannot be denied. Have you read his letter?"

"I have. Truly he is a wonder of the age." In fact, Rufus Putnam was Benjamin's distant cousin, but he was addressed as "Uncle" because he was of the previous generation, a contemporary of his cousin General Israel Putnam who had been dead many years since. In the Revolution, Uncle Rufus had fought under both Horatio Gates and Mad Anthony Wayne, and when he might have retired to his comfortable home in Rutland, he led an expedition instead of other old soldiers to begin settlement of the Northwest Territories. Across the

Ohio River he had founded a town called Marietta, spent years fighting local Indians for those lands, and now at the age of eighty was a senior statesman of those western lands. He had lately written to the Connecticut Putnams to urge upon them the bounteous future and wealth to be had if they would remove to the West.

"Oh, my son." Benjamin squeezed Bliven's arm. "I am content that I have not caught this fever to pick up and go tame some wilderness. Would you rather that we had done?"

Bliven shook his head slowly. "Never."

"We have not done badly, your mother and you and I."

Bliven felt tears rise and issued the most terse command to himself that they should not spill.

"And yet"—Benjamin lifted his hand again—"there is something of your uncle Rufus about you. He is a fighter, an explorer, a man who cannot stand seeing a blank spot on a map. You are not unlike him."

"He reads history also, I believe."

"Indeed. And now you must to Hawaii, and China, and the Indies. I wish I could live to hear those stories."

"Perhaps you shall."

"Perhaps, but likely not. Now, when you read—*if* you read—that I have gone, you will likely be in some far corner of nowhere. It will be all right for you to mourn me." He raised a finger. "A little, for every man wants to be missed. But no terrible grief. I have lived long, and well, and I am content to answer the great God any time he shall call."

Bliven could hardly speak. "I am glad to hear it."

"And then I shall find out whether that too-loud Reverend Beecher was right about his little church being the only portal to heaven."

"Reverend Beecher takes a great deal upon himself." Suddenly, Bliven remembered saying good-bye to Dr. Cutbush back on the

*Constitution*—Cutbush, who was now nearing fifty and only last year was promoted to senior surgeon of the Navy; Cutbush who had shown him the importance of making a good end with someone. "But I will tell you this, that wherever I go in this wide world, I will always be your son, and proud to be so. And have no fear, I will never alienate our home and our farm. At the end of all things, this is where I will return, and we will all be together."

"I am content."

Bliven stood to his full height, posing, gripping the handle of his saber.

"I thank you, my son. Go on now, or your mother will think we are planning some mischief."

Bliven exited, crossed the parlor and hall into the keeping room, with the intention to steal by without speaking into his room to change, but his mother heard him coming. "Did you pass inspection?"

"Yes, I believe I did."

"Bliv, my dear, forgive my saying this, I believe that your father is dying—things, differences of degree that only a wife would notice. I have not spoken of it—I do not wish to distress him—yet, I believe that he will leave us before many more months have passed."

How perfectly sympathetic they were, he thought, each knowing the reality but unwilling to cause the other pain. "Well, Mother, being born and dying—those are God's province, are they not?"

"They are, to be sure."

He patted her shoulder. "Let us not preempt His work from Him, then, hm?"

THE MORNING BROUGHT to him another pressing aspect of his pending deployment: *What in hell do I know of China, or Malaya, or the Sand-*

*wich Islands, or any of these damned places?* The prospect of sailing into such a multitude of unknowns, hazarding not just his ship but bearing the responsibility of his country's standing while knowing nothing of the people and their customs and how best to represent the United States, was beyond daunting.

He was the first to rise, and in the kitchen rekindled the fire from the previous evening's embers and prepared coffee—thinking as he did so that he must write Sam and perhaps find a way to put in at Charleston, for he had not seen him now in many years.

At midmorning he removed a key from a ring, donned his cloak against the chill, and ambled the distance to the Marsh house. Such an early call would not disturb his mother-in-law, for she almost never ventured downstairs but was content to dwell on what had become her *piano nobile*, rather enjoying it that both servants and visitors must come up to her, as though she were in heaven already.

It was Becky who answered his knock, the same maid he had known since his first hopeful visit in his salad days, during his first flush of ardor for Clarity. "Captain Putnam, good morning! Come in this house!" She held the door wide. "Let me take your wrap."

"Good morning, Becky. How are you? How is your mistress?"

"We are all well, thank you. Mrs. Marsh is awake and having her tea. What brings you out on this fine crisp morning?"

"I need to search out a book, if I may."

"I will let Mrs. Marsh know that you are here, but customarily she does not receive callers before afternoon."

He was already entering the library. "Thank you. I won't disturb her unless she wishes to see me."

Some people were content to place a cabinet or two of books in a room and call it a library, but old Marsh had been assiduous in amassing his four walls of knowledge and enlightenment, studious and organized. When he and Clarity should finally come to sell the house, there would be no help for it but to retain this closed wonderful world that Marsh had built with his books, and that would require adding a library to his own home. Mrs. Marsh might yet live a long time, so that would not be imminent. Besides, the times indeed were souring, and even if the house was theirs to sell, they could not get a good price for such a large place until business improved. All was transpiring as Clarity's business manager had foretold; Bliven had seen signs of it himself in their family drayage and Captain Bull's Tavern, hearing men complain that banks had extended too much credit to people, largely to help them speculate on the empty Western lands. Banks that had encouraged clients to take out loans, and then willingly renewed them, now unexpectedly called in the notes. Their customers, now rich in land but bereft of gold, defaulted and were now ruined, and the banks along with them. What a pity that their former Secretary of the Treasury Mr. Hamilton had been killed, for it might be instructive to see how that champion of liberal banking in furtherance of unfettered enterprise might figure a way out of his system's collapse.

Clarity, God bless her, had written him that she had navigated the shoal with minimal loss. Acting on her manager's advice, she had disposed of Marsh's Western investments for gold before the trend of the times became apparent to all. She had sold at a loss, although a slight one, at a price that made the prospect of Ohio land worth a risk. Besides, she had reasoned, if her buyer actually moved west and improved the land, it could surely make him wealthy indeed. The only loss would fall on one who calculated upon reselling the land for a profit within a short time. Such a one, then, would be an even greater hoopoe than her father had been, and would deserve his fate. And beyond that, forewarned that the banks—local ones as well as the

Bank of the United States—might dissolve, Clarity kept the coins, now well hidden on Putnam Farm in a location known only to herself, Bliven, and his parents.

Alone in the library, Bliven found Marsh's shelf of explorations and travelogues. He went first to the large book of geography in which, in his youth, he had pointed out for Clarity the sites of his battles against the Berber pirates. For that sentimental reason alone he would not have wished to risk taking it with him to the Orient, but the question was quickly resolved when he found it so out of date and lacking in textual discussion that it was better left behind anyway. When he returned to Boston he would visit Carter and Hendee's bookshop on School Street and procure a newer one.

The most absorbing discussions he had ever had with Marsh had been on travel and geography, and in his youth it was from Marsh that he first learned the true story of Captain Cook, who had discovered the Sandwich Islands, where he would soon be bound. After Cook's death at the hand of Hawaiian warriors in 1779, at least twenty of his officers wrote memoirs that had the effect of lionizing him, and eventually of canonizing him. Those officers were hoping merely to earn some remuneration from Cook's fame, since their Royal Navy pay would give them no comfort in their old age, but ultimately they transformed Cook into a seminal myth of empire. Bliven had known of a couple of these books and acquired them to satisfy his own curiosity. It was Marsh who told him that of all those books, only one told the truth with no rouge and no powder, and that one was written by the only American who had sailed with him.

Bliven quickly laid his finger upon it and pulled it from the shelf. He sought out Becky to reclaim his cloak and, sending his compliments up to Mrs. Marsh, took his leave. Back in the quiet of his own study he opened it: *A Journal of Captain Cook's Last Voyage to the Pacific*

*Ocean.* John Ledyard was the scion of a wealthy Connecticut family who possessed youth, looks, money, and a curiosity to see the world before he must settle into some mode of living. Bliven found himself instinctively drawn to the story of this young man with whom, except on the point of wealth, he felt much in common. Ledyard's travels took him only as far as England, however, before he was snared by a press gang and forced into the Royal Navy. Any other man would have regarded this as a calamity, but given his lack of alternatives in the matter, the equable young Ledyard decided that it might serve his purpose of traveling the world and having adventure while at the same time saving him the expense of travel. Thus, when given the opportunity, he volunteered for Cook's third voyage of exploration and joined the contingent of marines on Cook's ship, a homely but rock-solid collier renamed H.M. Brig *Endeavour,* from which he would have a chance to see as much of the world as even he could desire.

What was now known, but that almost no one knew in Cook's time, for it was a deeply held secret, was that his new voyage had a dark purpose, to finally discover the mythical Northwest Passage, but to attempt it from the west where all others had tried to find it from the Atlantic via Greenland. Great trouble was taken to mask the true purpose of his errand; the story was put out that their intention was to return to his homeland a native of Tahiti who had been brought to England on Cook's first voyage and become a great celebrity. This Cook accomplished, and from Tahiti he sailed north unbeknownst to the world, with no thought of anything but open water between him and the northern polar latitudes. After crossing the equator, his stumbling across the verdant, volcanic islands that he named to honor his patron, the Earl of Sandwich, was the most improbable of accidents. He tarried only long enough to victual and water his ships before continuing his race northward, where he spent months trying to punch through the strait between Russia and North America into the polar sea.

According to Ledyard, Cook's failure to do this turned him hard and brittle and cruel. The smallest infractions among his crew were punished with the lash; when they complained of spoiled rations, he forced them to eat the foul-tasting meat of walruses. After months of frustration, and a growing pain in his own belly that gave every sign of cancer, he sailed south again, reaching the Sandwich Islands almost exactly one year after he left.

The women of these islands, like those of Tahiti and the other islands farther south, proved unstoppable in their determination to mate with this new race of what seemed to them godlike white men. During his northern run Cook, despite his greatest vigilance, had been unable to prevent such congresses from taking place, and upon his return in a year discovered that the venereal afflictions that his men had sown in their wake had spread like a wildfire through the entire chain of islands. Cook spent months mapping the islands, slowly circling each even as he had Labrador and New Zealand before—but denying his men, who were famished for the unashamed lust of a woman, any shore leave whatever.

This, wrote Ledyard, occasioned fierce grumbling among the men and nearly brought a mutiny down upon the captain's head. Cook's greatest faults, however, with which none of his officers tasked him and which Ledyard alone laid to his charge, were hubris and blasphemy. The natives of these islands, while possessing a complex culture and a stratified society, had never seen white men nor huge Western ships before, and naturally enough ascribed to them some divine origin. Cook inexplicably allowed them, king and chiefs and commoners together, to worship him. He suffered them to fall down before him, to heap gifts upon him, even permitting the priests to chew his food for him before placing it in his mouth to swallow. After weeks of this the *Endeavour* departed, but in a week returned to repair a mast broken in a storm, and at this the spell was broken utterly.

The natives taunted and stole from the English, especially any implements made of or containing parts of iron, for iron was unknown in these islands. At length they ventured to steal one of Cook's launches, to burn it down and salvage the nails. When Cook moved to seize the Hawaiian king and hold him for the return of his boat, the natives resisted and attacked Cook and his contingent of marines. When Cook was wounded and groaned, they realized beyond doubt that he was no god, and they fell upon him with knives of obsidian glass as keen as razors, and war clubs studded with sharks' teeth.

With Cook's gruesome end Bliven laid the book down to reflect on what lessons were to be gained. These events had happened forty years before, at which time the islanders were primitive but not stupid. They had doubtless become much more accustomed to Western people and ways, and certainly Clarity's native friends whom he had come to know somewhat showed none of this ferocity, although they allowed that it still existed. The missionary effort would not be without danger, yet piety, humility, helpfulness, and the intercession of the Christian natives would go far to ensure their safety. But as for himself, he must take care not to repeat Cook's arrogance and be sure to mark the boundary between upholding the dignity of his country and indulging his personal conceit.

# ❧ 5 ❧

## *Seasick*

The *Thaddeus* stood out from Boston on October 23, 1819, with the passengers gathered in the well deck, clutching the last parcels of their belongings, sitting on the last-minute trunks they had not previously consigned aboard. They heard the pilot order the topsails and fore staysail set, and felt a surge of excitement, that electricity of adventure begun, as she edged away from the wharf.

Clarity had not considered how one settled aboard a vessel to get accustomed to months at sea. She spied a young man with curly auburn hair, healthy and vigorous in every respect, in an officer's uniform who seemed to be more or less in charge of the embarking, and she walked over to him, conscious of the ship's first gentle roll in the harbor swell, thrilled to feel for herself for the first time what Bliven had called finding her sea legs. "How do you do?" she asked, and held out her hand.

He saluted in that easy merchant-sailor manner and then took her hand. "James Hunwell, first officer. You are Mrs. Putnam, I believe?"

"Yes."

"Your trunks arrived earlier and we placed them in your cabin. You are aware that you will be sharing accommodation with Mrs. Albright?"

"Could you take me there, please?"

They walked aft, and he passed first up the ladder to the poop deck, not in rudeness but to take her hand and help her up the last few steps, then held open the door to a main cabin that held a large dining table, the compartment lined with doors every few feet down either side, much as Bliven had described to her the officers' berths on a warship. He had told her in years past how spare those accommodations were, but she was not prepared for the cell that she entered. It was scarcely wide enough to accommodate her lying down. Her trunks were lined down one bulkhead, two holding her own clothes and belongings, and three with assorted bolts of cloth, a disassembled spinning wheel, carefully nested cookware—everything she could think of to demonstrate American methods of home keeping to the natives, even as she admitted to herself that somehow those people had, evidently, managed to feed and shelter themselves for unknown centuries quite without American assistance. Her trunks were arranged so as to make a smooth platform on top, on which was laid a thin mattress and bedding.

"Forgive me, my dear, I did not hear you coming. I was resting." Clarity had not thought to turn and regard the opposite bulkhead, which was arranged similarly, with Muriel Albright stretched atop that mattress, her stockings just protruding from beneath her black dress.

"Oh! You are Mrs. Albright. We have been aware of each other only distantly up to now. I am Clarity Putnam. How do you do?" She extended her hand and Muriel took it.

"Not yet seasick, thank the Lord, although I am somewhat appre-hensive of what is to come. Pray, sit with me." Muriel raised herself to recline on one arm as she edged herself the remaining inches against the confining bulkhead, and Clarity seated herself on the edge of the mattress. "You must be the young lady who wrote the book I have heard of. You are becoming rather famous."

"Truly? I wonder at it, for my name is not on the book."

"No, but Captain Blanchard has taken much amusement in telling others that you seem to have written more history than your husband would have wished."

"Ha! He will recover, I'll warrant. He is being sent to the Pacific for a span of two or three years. I joined the missionary company to be nearer him, as well as to help in the effort with the natives."

"Ah. I was aware that your name was not in the original company. And I will guess that you had to face down the good Reverend Beecher and his opinion that women are not capable of much outside of being led by a man."

"Oh, my." Clarity in her time had often been charged with frank-ness, but she was unprepared to encounter it in one from the previous generation. "Well, yes—actually, I did."

"I suspected so. How much did he make you pay?"

Clarity stared at her, thunderstruck, then burst into a laugh. "Eight hundred dollars."

"Oh, my dear, you should have driven a harder bargain. I only had to pay five hundred, and they will get far more use out of you than from me."

Clearly this was a sage woman who knew more than she spoke. "Yes, but in fairness they were out of time to raise money; that was the sum they needed and they could not sail without it. And you? How did you convince them to let you come?"

"It was not difficult, really. I am a widow, I have no family left alive, I have some reputation for my housekeeping skills, and I am not without some taste for adventure." She cocked her head almost coquettishly. "I let them believe that I am past the age of temptation. And, well, I read to them those verses in the Bible showing that it was women who financed our Lord's ministry, that it was women to whom our Lord first announced his resurrection, and also that it was the women of Thyatira to whom Saint Paul turned for shelter and support."

"Oh, good for you!" They held hands for a moment, chuckling together, cementing an alliance that was sure to prove its worth.

The pilot ordered the sails furled and the anchor dropped off Boston light, where the *Thaddeus* received a lighter of last-minute supplies, and the passengers who had penned last letters home pressed them into the pilot's hands as he wished them well and descended to his vessel. They sat, immobile and rocking, awaiting a favorable wind to make the fifty-mile skirt down Cape Cod as Clarity became better acquainted with the other missionaries. As she had imparted to Bliven, of married couples in the Congregationalist Church who heard the call to evangelize, only one husband and wife, Daniel and Jerusha Chamberlain, were of compatible minds to take their five children and raise them far from their homes and friends. The remaining men had volunteered to the journey as single men and been denied unless by a certain deadline before the sailing they were able to find, court, and marry women with a similar spirit for Christian adventure. This set off a scramble of wife hunting, and a few had been man and wife together for scant days.

Their leader, Hiram Bingham of Vermont, was a week short of his thirtieth birthday, and Clarity found him one of the most beautiful men God had ever created, with a square brow, Nordically high cheek-

bones, a jutting chin, and piercing dark eyes beneath fashionably un-
kempt dark hair. Bingham had been promised to one young woman,
but he broke his engagement when she could not share his call to convert the heathen on the other side of the world, and for all she knew
end her days floating in a cauldron with carrots and potatoes. Nor was
she the only entanglement that Bingham had thrown over in casting
off his home ties: he was the fifth of seven children, and the one on
whom his parents had pinned their hope of support in their old age.

Accepting his call to the cloth, he was ordained at Goshen on September 29, which was the first ceremony for a foreign mission to take
place in Connecticut. At that ceremony he made the acquaintance of
Miss Sybil Moseley of that environ, who made apparent her interest
in the Sandwich Island enterprise, and they were married on October
11, only twelve days prior to the start of their journey.

While that marriage might have seemed remarkably hasty to out-
siders, within the church it was regarded as a holy union formed in
zeal to get on with the Lord's work. To Clarity this match made sense
for a different reason, for Miss Moseley was a lady of near-epic plain-
ness, as homely, in fact, as if human features had been rendered on a
large grape. There was no other conceivable circumstance in which a
woman of her looks might land a man of his beauty, except to cast her
lot to this enterprise in which only a select few women were willing
to risk their very lives.

Bingham's best friend and closest confederate as a missionary was
his classmate from Andover Seminary, Asa Thurston, who was but
two years older. On his arm was his wife, the former Lucy Goodale;
they had been married for eleven days. Bingham and Thurston were
the two ordained ministers; the other missionaries, as Clarity came
to know them, had been cleverly selected for their various talents:

Daniel Chamberlain with his angular, almost pointed face and wisps of thinning hair, was a farmer, a humble occupation for one who traced his line to an ancestor who was court chamberlain to King Stephen of England in the twelfth century. With him were his wife, Jerusha, careworn though not unattractive, and their children, sons of twelve, ten, and five, and daughters of eight and a babe in arms. Clarity could not help but wonder whether, as the only family on board, they were meant as a lesson on the benefits of a large brood when it came to tilling the soil—a point on which so many Putnams had succeeded but she had been so tardy. Jerusha maintained a hawk-like vigilance over her children; from that and from her general bearing of suspicion and apprehension, Clarity wondered what inducements it had taken to persuade her participation.

Thomas Holman was a doctor, and his wife, Lucia Ruggles, was sister to one of the two Samuels who were teachers: Samuel Ruggles and his wife, Nancy, and Samuel Whitney and his wife, Mercy. And then there were Elisha and Maria Loomis; he was a printer. Perhaps his inclusion was premature, for they had not been able to procure a printing press to bring aboard. But as the Lord had provided money, and Clarity with it, perhaps He would provide that as well.

A raised poop deck occupied the after one-third of the length of the *Thaddeus*, whose central cabin and its ten tiny compartments exactly accommodated the seven couples mostly new-married, one for the Chamberlains' children, one for the four Hawaiians, and one for Clarity and Muriel Albright. The central cabin contained a long table at which they met for prayers and for meals.

On October 24, Blanchard weighed anchor and rounded Race Point as his passengers lined the starboard rail and pointed to its squat new white lighthouse of which the locals were known to be so proud. The *Thaddeus* beat eastward and then flew south in a stiff wind as those in the missionary company who had never been to sea discovered the effect that wind and wave had on the stomach and equilibrium. "Do you see, ladies and gentlemen?" Blanchard shouted at them from the wheel abaft the great cabin. "This is how we are meant to sail! Ha! Cleavin' the water at ten knots. By God, this is sailin'!"

As the others sought the refuge of the great cabin, Clarity joined Blanchard by the wheel, steadying herself on the binnacle. "Captain, I fear this will take some getting used to before we can share your enthusiasm."

He regarded her fully. "Aye, that's true for the others, maybe. But not you, you have the look about you. You are neither seasick nor frightened, are you, lass?"

With the courses set she could not see ahead, and the beaches of Cape Cod slid by to starboard. Clarity squinted out to the open sea to port. She took a deep breath of salt air just tinged with spray and said, "No."

"Well! It is a captain's wife you are, and no mistake. I'll be proud to tell your husband so, next I see him, by God."

"As a captain's wife, Captain, I do not mind your language, but may I entreat you, for the sake of the others and their delicate sensibilities, perhaps you could imprecate the Almighty a little less often? Maybe you could save it for moments of genuine emergency, to give greater effect to your instructions."

Blanchard threw his head back and roared in laughter. "Just as you say, ma'am. But look you, now. Come here, take the wheel, see how it feels."

Clarity did as she was bidden, grasping hard the dowels of its spokes, nudging it ever so slightly to port to judge the strength needed to steer a ship. She saw no need to hide the keenness of her interest and how she was enjoying herself.

Blanchard took the wheel back. "Aye, it's a captain's wife you are, indeed."

AFTER BREAKFAST AND prayers in the great cabin, Bingham gave the table over to Thomas Hopu to begin what was intended as daily drill-ing in the Hawaiian language. Elisha Loomis was prepared, and from his stores provided paper and pencils to everyone to take notes for their later practice.

As he stood, Hopu seemed to adjust with ease to the rise and fall of the deck from the port quarter. "My first thought," he said, "is for our friend Opukaha'ia, whom you called Henry Obookiah. We all here owing to him, his zeal, his faith. He has gone to sleep in the Lord, but I know he looking down on us now and is pleased and giving praise. First word he would teach you, some of you know already, is *aloha*. You say it, please, aloud."

"*Aloha*," said the company in unison.

"That pretty good. Second syllable longer. *Aloooha*. This is word for greeting, and parting, but deeper. Mean, my love to you, mean, share breath together. Now, somebody say *aloha* to you, you say thank you. 'Thank you' is *mahalo*. Say it, please: *mahalo*."

The company's voice filled the cabin with more confidence. "*Mahalo*."

"Yes, good. Now we expand the greeting. Thank you very much. 'Very much' is *nui loa*. Say this, please: *nui loa*." After they complied Hopu said, "Mrs. Putnam, you will please greet Mrs. Albright, and she will thank you very much."

Clarity turned and nodded at Muriel. "*Aloha*."

Muriel nodded in return. "*Mahalo nui loa*."

"Yes!" crowed Hopu, and he pointed at Kanui and Honoree and Prince Tamoree. "We understand that! You sound just like us!"

When the general mirth died away, Hopu turned serious. "One day you will meet king. Word for 'king' is, *moi.* Say like two words: *mo-ee.* Word for 'Majesty' is *Kamahao.* You meet king, you bow, or curtsy, say, '*Ka mea Kamahao, ka moi.*' Mrs. Chamberlain, rise, please."

Jerusha pushed back her chair and stood.

"Curtsy, please. Say, '*Ka mea Kamahao*—'"

"*Ka mea Kamahao,*" she repeated.

"*Ka moi.*"

"*Ka moi.*"

"Very good! You may sit."

Mrs. Albright next to her raised her hand. "What is your word for 'queen'?"

"We have no word for 'queen.'"

"Huh! That does not seem so very enlightened."

"No, no, queens very powerful, and much respected. We have no word for 'queen,' but we say 'king-woman.' Word for 'woman' is *wahine.*"

"Well, that is all right, then. I see."

"Mrs. Albright, rise please, and curtsy. Say '*Ka mea Kamahao.*'"

"*Ka mea Kamahao.*"

"*Ka moi wahine.*"

"*Ka moi wahine.*"

"Very good! You may be seated."

Chamberlain raised his hand. "Mr. Hopu, I do not know that this is a prominent word in your language, but I fear that it is becoming a word of some importance among us. What is your word for 'seasick'?"

Hopu flashed his brilliant white teeth and hooted in laughter, his white eyes and teeth contrasting with the darkness of his face. "*Poluea*. Everybody say '*po-lu-way-ah*.'"

"*Poluea*," they echoed.

"Everybody say 'Mr. Chamberlain is *poluea*!'"

"Thomas?" Bingham raised his hand. "Can you tell us something about your king?"

Clarity thought it remarkable, how Hopu's visage changed as suddenly as a shutter closing over a window, and he pondered darkly for several seconds. "You all remember," he said at last, "what happened to the parents of our dear Henry Obookiah. They were killed by soldiers of King Ta-meha-meha."

"They were cut down while pleading for mercy," said Clarity, but she could tell instantly from Hopu's expression that he wished she had not spoken.

"Ta-meha-meha is a great king," he said haltingly. "And, like all great men, perhaps sometimes, for state reasons, he has had to do regrettable things. That is all I should say, maybe."

"I am not afraid to speak," said Tamoree, who was instantly the focus of attention. "My father is king of Tauai. Ta-meha-meha tried to conquer my island, but my father's soldiers defeated him, drove them back into the sea. When Ta-meha-meha failed at this, he had to make peace with my father. Then he told his own people they failed because someone broke the *kapu* by eating forbidden foods. He found three men and tortured them to death. It is true that Ta-meha-meha is a great warrior. He has conquered all the islands but mine. He is also a liar and a bully and a killer. I can say this because I am his equal in rank. Hopu must not say this, for if he were found out, he could be killed. That is how things are."

Jerusha Chamberlain sank in her chair. "My God, what have we let ourselves in for?"

No one felt like studying further, and there would be months of lessons, so Bingham dismissed the company to rest, or read, or take exercise on the deck, as they wished. But Clarity did not mistake the looks exchanged by the two preachers, Bingham and Thurston, expressions of shock and worry that after years in the West, and years of studying the grace of Jesus Christ, it took only the mention of a rival native king for Tamoree's ferocity to resurface, his hauteur, his senses of entitlement and superiority—all of which were anathema to their cultivation in him of the spirits of meekness and service. When he reached home at last, what might they have unleashed? How could they bring the light of the gospel to these islands if they brought a new war with them?

IN HARBOR, RIO DE JANEIRO
DECEMBER 20, 1819

*My dearest Husband,*

*I write you this in the manner of an experiment. For our letters to reach each other, with only one of us running about the world, was enough of a wonder. But, with both of us crossing latitudes and longitudes, who can say how the mail shall work out between us? My intention is to leave this with the American consul here, and advise him that you will follow in several weeks' time, and if he should hear of the arrival of the United States Ship Rappahannock in the harbor, he must endeavor to place this in your hands. However, if six months shall pass, he should forward it to the American consul in Honoruru, in the Sandwich Islands.*

*From Boston we have been at sea now just short of two months, at first riding the shore currents so as not to be opposed by the Gulf*

Stream—waters that you know well, my dearest. Once we entered more tropical waters, while we were sometimes in sight of isles of the West Indies, we felt ourselves more on, and of, the ocean. I realize now what isolation one feels when there is nothing but water from horizon to horizon, and how you must bond with your crew to avoid feeling that you are alone in all creation. Occasionally we speak a passing vessel, and inquire where she is bound, but more often we see them pass at a distance and are left to wonder what is their business. Our little band of missionaries, while all of differing temperaments, have become allies and even friends in this endeavor. This is indeed fortunate, so as to make bearable our accommodations. Our cabins on the Thaddeus are so tiny that I fear when I come to die, I will not know what to do with all the space in my coffin.

And now, dearest, it is a queer feeling to tell the great news that I must do, for although the issue is undecided at this moment, it will in all probability be decided by the time you read this. For several weeks out of Boston, many of the company suffered from the sea sickness. I, indeed, suffered very little, until we entered the tropical latitudes. At that time my symptoms became very acute indeed, to the point that I was ill even when the others were not. When this became apparent my companion Mrs. Albright, in the privacy of our cabin, ventured to ask me questions of an intimate and womanly nature. When I made answer, she sent straight for Doctor Holman, who examined me as closely as propriety would allow, and at the end announced his belief that I am with child.

Oh, my dearest! You can imagine the wide pot-pourri of emotions attendant upon such a discovery. To be enceinte, not just far from home but upon the limitless blue ocean, is a hazard to one's health not in perfect times to be wished for. But, Holman is as good a doctor as one could find at home, good enough that the church sent him to represent our system of medicine to the heathen savages, therefore let us be content to trust in him, and in God.

Rev. Bingham, of course, is most seriously unpleased, and shocked that such an indelicate circumstance could arise. Indeed, he quite despaired, and asked me how such a thing could happen, and I told him I presumed it was a result of the sheer passion of our leave-taking. I thought the poor man would faint and fall overboard. No doubt, he and Mr. Thurston, who is the other ordained minister, serve a high purpose, but I swear such young men acting like such little old ladies you never saw.

In sum, above, beneath, and surrounding it all is my joy—absolute, and unbridled. Dearest, we have succeeded. By the calendar, I should be safe ashore in Hawaii with two months to spare, and now that the news has spread to the entire company, Hopu assures me that there are doctors in Hawaii, and even if they are not resident, I shall have my choice of surgeons among the visiting ships, for now their harbors are almost never empty.

I must close now, for the lighter will soon depart and I must consign this to the consul. Moreover, Reverend B. has called a meeting of the company to discuss a matter of the utmost gravity—whether to celebrate Christmas! I know you remember my parents' opinion of the matter, which is still held by Rev. Beecher, so I must listen with the greatest attention what arguments have perhaps been advanced that might persuade our New England understanding of it to relent, and join the rest of Christendom. With my wishes for your safety, and many blessings, my dearest—

Clarity Putnam

RIO DE JANEIRO
DECR. 20, 1819

*My dearest,*

*The boat has not left yet, so I break the seal to add just a*
*postscript—there was a great debate upon this evening, and a vote*
*was taken. By 5 to 2, the women present but not voting—the decision*
*was made for observing Christmas as is done in the other churches!*
*Their reasoning was, that the purpose of our mission is to bring the*
*Lord to these far islands, and to waste energy attacking Christmas*
*with the Catholics, Anglicans, and what not, would be a distraction.*
*They also voted not to send notice of the same home to Cornwall. I*
*wonder why! (I hope Reverend Beecher does not hear of it, it might*
*prove fatal.)*

*C.P.*

FIVE DAYS LATER, with fresh supplies taken on at Rio de Janeiro, the
women of the company produced a Christmas feast of roast beef and
vegetables, with fresh bread, and butter not yet grown rancid. The
strange thing, apart from them celebrating Christmas at all, was to
do it in the heat of summer, an inescapable reminder of their having
reached nearly thirty degrees south of the equator. At the dinner's
conclusion it was Sybil Bingham, homely and all but chinless, who
emerged from below bearing a succulent-looking pudding and set it
before her husband, who headed the table. All stood as Bingham said
grace a second time, but he was not too pious to wait for all to resume

their seats before he began cutting slabs of the pudding and letting them fall onto the pewter plates.

"Well, now," he said eagerly, "it has long been said that the proof of the pudding is in the eating."

"Yes," said his longtime friend Asa Thurston, "but are you referring to the pudding or the wisdom of keeping the holiday?"

"Either way," Bingham rejoined with unaccustomed ease, "let us all now take our first bite of it together!"

In a few moments Blanchard rose, resting a knee on his chair against the unpredictable roll. "And now that you are enjoying your dessert, there is something of which I wish to apprise you all at once, for I must make a decision. In a few weeks' time we will be at the latitude of the entrance of the Strait of Magellan. That is one way to the Pacific. Or, we can continue on for another two days to the Strait of Le Maire, and round the tip of South America on the open sea. The Magellan Strait is shorter, and more sheltered from wind and wave. It is also tortuous, and wickedly narrow, with rocks, lethal rocks close by both port and starboard. Also, the Atlantic tide is ten times or more the force of the Pacific tide, and as it enters the channels it cannot be resisted. The Strait of Le Maire, if we continue on, is a hundred times wider, and leads to the open sea, the Drake Passage, and so round the tip of the continent, with no land posing a hazard. There is room to maneuver, but in winds and seas of such terror you cannot imagine. However, weighing the wind which I can see against the rocks which I cannot, this is what I propose to do. I hope you can agree that this is the safer course."

He resumed his seat, and Bingham waited a moment to see if there were any comments before speaking for the others. "Mr. Blanchard, you are the captain, and yours are the orders to give. We are grateful that you have told us, and we are confident that you will make the right judgments."

For four days coursing past Patagonia they felt the seas grow higher, the wind behind them stronger, as though they were being sucked inexorably into some mighty and mortal vortex. Mariners had never written about Cape Horn in such a way, that its pull reached out as though it were some giant whirlpool. Blanchard assured the passengers that it was the coincidence of an approaching tempest but all knew the reputation of that dangerous passage.

Their fears were not eased when, on January 29, Blanchard assembled them in the large cabin and announced that this was the day they would enter the Strait of Le Maire. The *Thaddeus* was already pitching like a toy boat on a freshet. "Sometimes," he said, "the seas will collide and rise higher than our masts. It is not likely, but if such a sea were to come over our stern, this cabin and everyone in it would vanish in a twinkling. For this reason, my crew have prepared a place for you in the hold, where you will be safer. There is a lamp, and pillows, and food and water, and for you, ma'am"—he looked at Muriel—"a backed bench nailed well down. Sometimes a ship must tack back and forth for days, awaiting a favorable wind to enter the strait."

Just as he said this a great sea slammed their starboard quarter, causing Blanchard to catch himself on the edge of the table to keep his balance as the rest caught their tumbling bowls of pudding. "You see my point. Now, we have the coincidence of approaching the strait with the perfect wind hard at our backs, and my intention is to shoot straight through as fast as I can. So, by your leave—or really without your leave—I will ask you to gather what is necessary and descend to the hold."

In their cabin Clarity and Muriel looked over their things, gathering a change of clothes should they be confined longer than they hoped. "Well," ventured Clarity, "whether we stay up here and get washed over the side, or hit a rock and drown in the hold, I rather think that my mother's gold locket will not provide much comfort in either case. We might as well leave our keepsakes here."

"Yes, my dear, but I do not believe that things will come to such a pass."

They gathered again in the great cabin. "It is not raining at the moment," said Blanchard, "so let us take advantage. Come." He led them out and stood at the head of the port ladder down from the poop deck. He grasped each firmly by the hand and helped them halfway down, where they were taken by James Hunwell, the first mate, who saw each safely onto the well deck. They repeated the procedure from the well deck down into the hold, seeing chairs and a parson's bench arranged on the flat stowage of clapboards for their house, and amid chests of tools, and bolts of cloth as gifts for the native women.

Once they were all together in the hold, they were startled to hear the hatch cover being slammed down and battened into place. For the duration of the day and night they felt the vessel by turns sit back on her haunches like a great bear and then suddenly lurch forward and down until her bow knifed deep into a trough and lifted back again—either with or without a sickening thirty-degree roll. Their whole space was ill lit by a single thick-glassed battle lantern. Bingham stood, one hand clinging to one of *Thaddeus*'s ribs, the other gripping Sybil's chair until the blood was squeezed from his fingers. She sat grimly upon it, clutching the seat, determined that she would drown where she sat before suffering the indignity of being pitched off it. The Thurstons and the Chamberlains sat cross-legged on the clapboards with the children, from which lowness they could not be pitched anywhere, and close enough together that if one started to tumble away the others could catch him.

Clarity was frozen to a trunk, her hands gripping the edge so as not to be thrown off. Only once—when the ship shuddered at the top of a mighty sea and then fell down and to the left so long it seemed she could not recover—she cried out, not a word, just a syllable. It escaped her lips before she could check it.

In her nailed-down parson's bench, elderly Muriel Albright sat in her plain black dress and white cap, leaning passively with the attitudes of the ship. She gazed evenly at Clarity until their eyes met, and she patted the small space on the bench next to her. "Come sit next to me, dear."

"I am not afraid, truly," protested Clarity.

"Indeed, you are not. But come keep an old lady company."

Clarity waited until the ship buried herself up to the catheads and was steady for a second, and she lurched across the hold and reached the bench next to Muriel before the vessel's coming massive lift could vault her across that space. Muriel took Clarity's hands in her own and held them as the ship rolled several more times. It became obvious from the ferocity of Clarity's grip that, contrary to her protest, she was indeed scared half to death.

Muriel shook her hands for a second as though they were first greeting and inclined her head toward Clarity, who thought for a moment that Muriel would lead her in a prayer, and leaned in close as well. "Do you believe in God, my dear?" Muriel almost whispered.

The question wounded her almost to the core. "Why, yes!"

"Yes, girl," she whispered, "but do you trust God, truly?"

"I should hope I do."

"Then there is no need to fear this. My dear, our very being here is an act of trust, and faith. There is not one thing that any of us can do at this moment to alter whether we are going to live or die. See how completely we have put ourselves in His hands? If the dear Lord wishes us to reach these Sandwich Islands and bring the light of the gospel to those suffering people, we shall attain that object in safety. But if the Lord in his wisdom should call us unto Himself even in the next instant, we would stand before Him humbly, but justified. It is in God's hands."

Clarity's lips twitched almost to a smile. "Well, yes, but let's not count Captain Blanchard out of it altogether."

"Ha! Yes, he may still have a say in the matter."

Clarity leaned over and kissed her cheek. They sat together for two hours more, until shortly before sunrise, when the wild vaults and plunges ceased, transformed into a deep, steady roll. Some lurched to the mattresses that the crew had spread out for them; others, exhausted by terror and seasickness, drowsed where they sat. Clarity awakened at the sound of the hatch cover being removed, her head on Muriel's shoulder as brilliant morning sunlight streamed in, illuminating the dingy chaos of the hold.

"You may come out now," called Captain Blanchard, "but mind the deck, it is still slick."

They emerged cautiously from the ladder, Clarity thinking about Socrates and the cave, wondering whether once they saw the world above they would scuttle back down to the familiarity of their darkness. But what they saw astonished them.

It was just as she had read about the Strait of Magellan, for from the terror of Drake's Passage they had entered the Pacific—the pacified ocean. They found themselves in a heavy swell and running before the wind, stiff and following. The sunlight was brilliant; the sea glittered. The sails were set up to the topgallants and they raced as though God Himself were filling the canvas with His breath.

The women tightened the chin straps of their bonnets until they bit into their jowls, but still the bills and ruffles whipped and snapped around their faces. Muriel came with some effort up the ladder and steadied herself on Clarity's arm. They strolled to the starboard rail, where they shielded their eyes from the brilliance of the sun, equally blinding from above and from glinting off the rolling swell. Muriel was seized suddenly with a fit of laughter, and supported herself on the railing.

"Muriel, what is it?" Clarity smiled at her quizzically, wanting to share in the mirth.

The elder lady closed her eyes and howled in laughter until she lost her breath. But her face was shining and she held out her arms to the limitless ocean.

Clarity feared she might be hysterical and put an arm around her. "Yes, we are safe now. Can you see? We are quite safe?"

She waved her off. "Oh, no, my dear. That is not it. I laugh for my name's sake."

Clarity's face went slack. "Your name? Muriel?"

"Yes! It is Irish; it means the bright sea! Oh, I was meant to be here! I am—" She began to calm down. "I am where I was meant to be." She maintained her voice loud enough to be audible above the wind and creaking timbers, and she said, "Do you not see, dear Clarity? He was testing us. He does mean for us to reach those islands."

"Yes!" Clarity shouted back. "It seems He heard my prayer to speed us there quickly, too!" They held hands tightly and watched the sails pull against the masts, the standing rigging pulled taut to take the strain.

That was not, however, the true meaning of the Pacific Ocean. This they discovered a month on, as they reentered the tropical latitudes and were becalmed, with no breath of wind, on a sea of blue glass, sweating under the February sun. Four of the men said they could swim, and stripped to their trousers and shirts, enjoyed a frolic in the ocean. For fifteen minutes they whooped and splashed, when First Mate Hunwell ordered them back aboard.

"Why?" hallooed Ruggles. "Do you see a great mighty wind coming?"

"No, but I see, as you do not, a great mighty dorsal fin cleaving the water two hundred yards out. So unless you wish to be luncheon for a shark, you will hie thee back aboard, and be quick about it."

The word "shark" brought the women crowding to the rail, searching the water until it was seen, and then they jumped up and down, shouting, and urging the men to haste. After the last was safely aboard, Clarity walked up to Hunwell. "Are sharks good to eat?"

"Yes, the flesh is very good, although the innards are poisonous."

"Well, if he came around to find some lunch, perhaps you could catch him and he could be the main course instead."

"Well, by God." He stared at her. "By God, maybe." From below deck he produced a set of heavy tackle and a wicked, heavy six-inch hook, which he baited with a pound of rancid pork, and flung the line out as far as he could in the shark's direction. It was the best sport imaginable, the whole company quietly urging the beast closer to it, as though they were betting on a horse race, encouraging him to come back when he turned away, as his circles drew tighter. When it took the pork and ran, Blanchard grabbed Hunwell by the seat of his pants to keep him from flying over the rail, and together they pulled the line. Clearly they saw the fish in the crystal water thrashing against the side of the ship. "There is a pistol in my cabin," Blanchard shouted. "Somebody get it! Bring it to me."

It was the moment of truth when they pulled it out of the water: the hook might bend, or the rope break, or he might wrench himself free. "Stand back, everyone!" They pulled mightily and the fish flew over the rail and landed on the deck with a *whump*. It was eight feet long, twisting left and right in that space bounded by the hatch cover and the ladders to the poop, a trickle of blood coming from the hook embedded in the corner of its mouth, files of curving, serrated teeth visible within the awful crescent of its mouth.

But for all the violence of its thrashing, it was helpless. When it was still for just a moment, Blanchard advanced and fired into the back of its head, causing a violent spasm, then stiffness, then limpness. None of the company had seen a shark before. They had grown accustomed to leaving a lantern on the deck at night, and feasting the next day on the flying fish that launched themselves onto the deck by morning. But this was new to them.

Lucy Thurston advanced as close as she dared. "All my life I have heard of the terrors of the deep. Now I understand."

"Behold the work of His mighty hand," said Bingham.

"Ah, posh!" waved Blanchard. "He is just a baby. I have seen them three times this size."

The four older of the Chamberlain children evinced a keenness to touch it. "Children!" cried Jerusha. "Get away from there!"

Hopu and his Hawaiian fellows watched the proceedings from the fo'c'sle, staring dully but saying nothing. At length Clarity approached them. "Hopu, are you upset about something?"

He framed his words. "In my country, the word for spirit, for power of spirit, is *mana*. The word for shark is *mano*. We have great respect for sharks."

"Oh, I apologize sincerely if we have offended you. We didn't know. You don't eat them, then?"

"Yes, we eat them, excepting one kind, but we do so with reverence."

"Is this shark of the kind your people do not eat?"

"This one would excite no comment. We know now, the Bible says that such matters are of no importance. My thought is for how such a thing could make your mission more difficult, when you are ashore."

*How much we have to learn about these people*, she thought. "Dear Hopu, how important you are to us. Will you teach us about sharks at our next lesson?"

Hopu nodded. "Most surely, if you wish it."

One thing that they all agreed upon was that the steaks cut from its flesh were delicious. In the following days, some of *Thaddeus's* crew dried its gritty skin into razor strops and presented them to the men of the company, and made keepsakes of its teeth, which they distributed to all. None suspected that this would be the most excitement they would enjoy for weeks, for the hot calm doldrums they had entered before encountering the shark intensified to such an extent that they wondered the ocean did not steam beneath them. After two more tortuous weeks of the sea as smooth as glass, with not a breath of wind to break the heat that grew more oppressive, Clarity approached Captain Blanchard as he took his noon sextant reading. "Is this normal?" she asked.

"Oh, yes, ma'am," he answered. "It is a known feature of this ocean in this latitude. We will drift out of it eventually. I shouldn't worry before we spend another month in it. The trick is, to not let it drive you mad first."

"Indeed." She looked out at the horizon, then up at the limp rigging, and shook her head. "I rather believe we should have brought more books."

AFTER MOTIONLESS WEEKS that tried the tempers of all, they drifted into a trade wind that carried them, gently at first but then with more vigor, toward their goal. "Five months out," said Blanchard at lunch on March 29 after taking the noon reading on his sextant. "We have made excellent time despite our delay in that long calm—almost record time. It should be right there." He pointed ahead, northwest. "We should sight the island almost at any time."

"Oh! Oh, please," cried Kanui. "Will you let me be lookout? See farther from up there!" He would not be dissuaded, and he and the other natives stormed out of the cabin and into the rigging. Within half an hour they began screaming. "*E ke Mauna Kea! E ke Mauna Kea!*"

At once Blanchard was out on the poop deck. "Well, I'm damned. There must have been a mist that lifted."

The company streamed out to join him. Clearly above a string of clouds they saw a mountain peak capped with snow. Lucia Ruggles put her hand over her eyes to see it more clearly. "Why, I would have thought these islands were small. That mountain is gigantic."

"Yes, ma'am," said Blanchard. "This island is not tiny; it is almost exactly the same size as your Connecticut."

Through the afternoon they drew closer, able to see green jungle on the flanks of the mountain, and waterfalls, and eventually houses along the shore. When they saw canoes being launched, Blanchard had their ketch lowered. Ruggles had volunteered to ascertain what welcome or hostility might await them, and he was rowed by Hopu, with Tamoree as insurance for their safety, for as a prince of the country he could vouchsafe their protection.

The company waited three hours for them to return before the *Thaddeus*'s ketch glided up in the small chop. Not waiting for the hooks to lower from the davits, Hopu and Tamoree gesticulated wildly for Kanui and Honoree to throw ropes down to them. When the missionaries heard the commotion, they gathered on the well deck at the head of the ladder. The four natives chattered in a staccato of their native language, much too rapid and advanced for any to follow; they began jumping up and down while hugging, laughing, and brushing away tears.

Hiram Bingham came to the fore. "Hear, hear, now. What is this? What has happened?" They all looked down at the ketch as the lines were being hooked to its eye bolts, and they saw Ruggles smiling broadly.

"Oh, Reverend Bingham!" cried Hopu. "Oh, such news! Oh!"

Bingham laid his hands on Hopu's shoulders. "Slowly, now. Take a breath, Thomas. Slowly, now, tell us."

Hopu's chest still heaved up and down. "Old king dead! Old religion is no more! Queens declare no more *kapu*, no more sacrifices. Some priests fight. There was a war. Queens win the war and pull down temples. Wooden idols with shark teeth, and all graven images, piled up and burnt."

Clarity gasped. "Just as Henry said he wanted to do!"

"Hopu." Bingham looked at him intently. "What do you mean, 'queens'? How many are there?"

"Many, all widows of old king, but two of importance. Kepurani is mother of new king, very high born, not often seen but people must fall on the ground when they see her. Working queen is Kahumanu, stepmother of new king, rules with him, has greatest power. Ending *kapu*, and making war, was her doing."

The davits creaked under the weight of the ketch, with Ruggles seated in it, and as he gained the height of the deck he pulled away a cloth to reveal a tumble of baskets in its bottom—a cornucopia of bananas, coconuts, breadfruit, large, fat fish, sweet potatoes, sugarcane, other fruits they did not recognize.

Bingham's hands flew to his cheeks. "What is this?"

Ruggles had overheard as he was winched up, and he stepped onto the deck. "A gift from that working queen."

Chamberlain laughed. "Did you greet her correctly, as we were taught?"

"I most certainly did."

"What did she do?"

"Do? Why, she held out her hand and she said, 'How do you do, Mr. Ruggles.'"

The company exploded in laughter. "What was she like?" asked Bingham.

"Well, she is huge; she is a giantess; she is the largest human being I have ever seen. But then, that seems to be a feature among these people. Those of the ruling class are twice the size of the common people. Just see with what she has gifted us!"

Bingham shook his head. "Can all this be true?"

"Every word," said Ruggles somberly. "It is a miracle."

After a stunned moment more, Bingham looked up, as though finding some confirmation from the firmament. "Let us kneel and pray."

Clarity helped Muriel to her knees. "Yes," she whispered, "let us kneel before we fall over from shock."

Bingham's voice, often pompous, was quiet now, genuine in the awe of the moment. "Our great and powerful Lord, Thy scripture hath said, 'Every valley shall be exalted, and every mountain and hill made low. Make straight in the desert a highway for our God.' Let us doubt not that this marvel is Thy doing alone, that Thou hast destroyed the false gods of heathen darkness and prepared the way to bring Thy light to this forbidding land." His voice nearly broke with the reality of it all, as though heretofore he had been merely playacting at being a missionary until this intercession, this staggering coincidence that seemed to be the very hand of the Almighty, only now made it real to him. "Let us not fail Thee, O God! Speak through us, act through us, that Thy will be done. Amen and amen."

Hopu rose and called, "Captain Blanchard?"

Blanchard clattered down the ladder from the poop.

"Queen say: Please to continue on to Kawaihae. She will receive us there."

Clarity helped Muriel to her feet. The older lady straightened her dress as she said, "So apparently it was not a wasted lesson for us to learn how to address a queen."

"It would seem so," Clarity answered and recited, *"Ka mea Kamahao, ka moi wahine."*

"Oh!" cried Hopu. "Listen, everyone! There is a word I forgot to teach you. I am sorry! It is a very important word. Say it now: *luau."* He extended the first syllable and rather barked the second. "Say it now!"

*"Luau,"* they chorused.

Hopu spread his open hands over the wealth of fresh food and shouted, *"Luau!"*

The company cheered, *"Luau!"*

It was Clarity who asked, "What does that mean, Thomas?"

Hopu gazed greedily at the bounty. "It mean, a feast!"

## { 6 }

## *Festina Lente*

His and Clarity's parting had left Bliven in such a stew of emotion that all he could do was postpone considering any of it, and he instructed the carriage on to the Navy Yard. He spied *Rappahannock's* grounded masts from the entrance and directed the driver to her, feeling as he approached the graving dock an almost spousal anxiety for her well-being, even for her modesty, as she appeared undressed without her elegant bowsprit and with her surprisingly large round belly exposed, supported by the forest of stilts.

He was cheered, however, to see that her bottom had been scraped until the copper shone penny-bright, a kind of gigantic repoussé hammered to match her curvature that would make her sleek through the water, proof against shipworms, and beautiful as well.

He had the driver continue right up to her and deposit his trunks at the foot of the gangplank, and paid the fare. He could look straight down into *Rappahannock's* wound, through her ribs like a surgeon looking into a patient. He saw four new ribs showing bright yellow-brown against the bilge-stained umber of the original construction, and he was struck anew at her excessive engineering. She lacked the sandwiched layers of oak that made the frigates all but invulnerable, whether to enemy cannonballs or even to the rocks at Port Mahon that had been unable to sink the *President*. But in compensation was the extraordinary density of her ribbing, shaped timbers eight inches broad laid sixteen inches on center, and the knees above them angled like scantling, that made her class the heaviest and toughest sloops in the world.

Satisfied with his first look, Bliven boarded and found the spar deck deserted, but upon descending to the gun deck and entering his great cabin he found Alan Ross exiting one of the guest compartments in some apparent embarrassment. "Captain, good morning! I was not expecting you today."

"Yes, I see you were not. Do I gather that you have taken up residence in my cabin during my absence?"

"I confess, sir, the guest berth is more comfortable than my own, but more to the point, it is located farther from the noise below."

"Oh. Well, that is sensible; indeed, it occurs to me that you may be able to manage your duties more efficiently if you station yourself there whenever we are not providing passage to guests."

Ross was plainly embarrassed. "Truly, Captain, I did not intend to presume any familiarity."

"I did not suppose that you had, Mr. Ross. But in exchange for your improved accommodation, you will be able to answer my call at any hour without my having you come trotting up from the wardroom."

"Sir, that is a very fair exchange. Thank you."

"Besides, I will not be sorry for your company. Is Mr. Yeakel aboard?"

"Yes, sir, I believe he is below."

"Very well, my trunks are on the dock, if you would bring them aboard."

"Right away, sir."

Bliven exited and strode forward, thinking as he did so it would be a long time before he saw the gun deck so quiet, so orderly, again—screws, sponges, and ramrods all on their hooks, lanyards perfectly coiled. He reached the ladder, the one feature of the *Rappahannock* that caused him worry. The frigates had ladders fore and aft, which was sensible, because there were magazines fore and aft; but there was the additional advantage that if one ladder became obstructed by fire or wreckage, the lower decks were still accessible through the other. The sloops were considered smaller enough vessels that one ladder amidships was thought sufficient. As a matter of naval architecture it was defensible, but Bliven regarded it as a point of vulnerability that would always lurk in the back of his mind.

He descended to the berth deck and then into the hold, unaccustomed to seeing it so brightly lit as it was by the hole in her side. The hold of any vessel was always a warren of nooks and crevices; to view it so illuminated was something he had never seen before, and in it he saw his bosun kneeling, his feet on an original rib and his knees on a new one, inspecting its joinery onto the keel. "Mr. Yeakel, good morning."

Yeakel got stiffly to his feet and stepped up onto the decking, saluting as he did so. "Good morning, Captain, I did not know you were back aboard."

Bliven returned the salute. "Have you been living aboard all this time?"

"Yes, sir, rather than have to rent a room somewhere."

"Have you been satisfied with the work that has been done?"

"Yes, sir, but I have not been the real test of it. Commodore Hull comes regularly to inspect, and he keeps Captain Edwards and his men on their guard."

"Is that so? Well, we can be grateful for such close attention. Tell me, Mr. Yeakel, have you laid in all the line you will need?"

"Yes, sir."

"I have been thinking it won't hurt to store more, as much as you can find room for. I have a mind, once we reach the Sandwich Islands, to lay over and reset the rigging."

"Yes, sir, I understand. Considering how long we will be in tropical waters, that would be a wise precaution."

Standing rigging put up in the Boston chill could go dangerously slack in tropical heat. As a young captain, the great Preble himself had nearly lost the *Essex* for want of such foresight, and the *Congress* was nearly lost when her stays and shrouds became so lax that her masts snapped from the pull of the sails. Samuel Barron's seamanship passed into legend when as a young lieutenant he saved the *United States* by resetting her rigging even while under way. As the American fleet became more international, the concern would become chronic.

"Captain Putnam, good morning. Welcome back aboard."

Bliven turned to see the dry dock's master approaching. "Captain Edwards, good morning." They traded salutes and shook hands. "You have done a very great deal of work, I see. Did you find so much damage as to require such an extensive repair?"

"In point of fact, we did not, but Commodore Hull has been emphatic in pressing upon us the length and importance of your coming mission, and he has insisted that every trace or possibility of defect must be made good before you sail."

"Well, I am off to see him now. I shall pass along how diligently you have been at your task. Mr. Yeakel?"

"Sir?"

"Where has Fleming gone to, do you know?"

"As it happens, sir, I do. He lives in Roxbury."

"Well, take the day, dress up, get yourself a horse, and go see him. He knows the ship better than anyone, save yourself, and I don't want to sail with a different carpenter. If he resists, overcome him."

Yeakel smiled, for Fleming was easily twice his size. "I'll do my best, Captain."

Bliven made his way down the waterfront to the receiving ship, that hulk that he grieved for every time he saw her—or it, for she hardly seem fitted for the feminine pronoun anymore. He was admitted as soon as he presented himself, and Hull rose and greeted him with some surprise. "My word, Putnam, but you are prompt to respond to our call. Do sit down. How is your family?"

Bliven arranged himself in a Windsor chair on the opposite side of Hull's desk. It always caused him to look closer, how well kept Hull was for a man approaching fifty, his handsome sloe-eyed visage settling now into a distinguished-looking affability, heavier, his hair combed upward into that Regency fashion of affected tousle. "Thank you for asking, Commodore. My wife is very well, and strong-minded as ever. My parents are growing old, I fear."

"Damn, Putnam, when I saw you last, I hope I did not give offense when I said that your parting would be touching. If I sounded dismissive, it was my own discomfort at how terrible it is for all seamen to take leave of their families for certainly years at a time. I regretted having said it almost immediately."

"I understand, sir. They did their best to make it easy for me. In that way they are more courageous than I. My mother is a perfect Stoic, and my father would shoot himself before he would try to make me feel sorry for him."

"God bless them for that, but now that you have said good-bye, it would likely be too much for them if I send you home again."

"What? How do you mean, sir?"

"The fact is, Captain Putnam, you need not be in too great a hurry to sail, for we have no powder or shot for you. It seems that while the government has made the decision to show our flag in the far corners of the world, someone forgot to tell the armories. If we can't find you something in the coming weeks, you may have to put in at Gosport or Charleston to take on armament."

"I see. Have you written to my other officers to return for duty?"

"Yes, we have. Lieutenants Miller and Rippel will sail with you again: the third lieutenant surrendered his commission rather than commit to such a lengthy deployment, as did your chaplain." Hull suddenly pointed his finger at him. "And your purser. You are very hard on pursers, and I wish you would not be."

"Only because I expect them to be honest."

Hull sighed and rolled his sleepy eyes. "Oh, for the Lord's sake, here we go again."

"Commodore, when we established our navy, we had the opportunity to correct one of the worst abuses—apart from forced impressment—of the British Navy. We could have made our navy responsible for supplying the needs of its own seamen, with pursers given the duty of distributing shoes and clothing and sundries as they are wanted. But no, instead we copied the Royal Navy in making pursers of independent merchants, who use their own suppliers and charge their own prices, which run sailors into debt just to keep clothes on their backs, and their pay is remitted to the purser to discharge the debt. This would be so easy to correct!"

Hull leaned forward, his eyes suddenly energetic. "I admit everything you say, except that it is surely not easy to correct, because to effect it, the Navy would have to tie up millions to fill the storerooms, and they don't have it. They save themselves this money by engaging pursers as contractors, and regulate the prices they may charge and the profit they may take."

"*Distantly* regulate the prices and profits, sir."

"Perhaps."

"*Loosely* regulate the prices and profits."

"Putnam, that is the system we have, and no one is going to change it for you. If the pursers were not allowed to make a fair profit—yes, as they define it—no one would do it."

Bliven waved his hand. "Well, if there is no profit in their honest operation, that rather completes my point for me, sir, but never mind."

Hull leaned back and glared. "You are a damned fine captain, sir, but, by God, sometimes you are a trial."

"Well, you will find somebody. If you can't tell me that he's honest, at least find me someone who is well connected to ready suppliers."

"You can hunt around, too, Putnam. Perhaps you can find someone who can withstand that frightful moral squint of yours."

Bliven recognized the admiration buried in the criticism, and laughed. "That is fair enough. Where has my surgeon gone to? I need to write to him."

"We have written to him, so you needn't bother. We have as yet no answer from him."

"No, I need to contact him on another matter, anyway."

"Well, then, you can write him through the Navy Yard at Gosport. I suppose once we get you afloat again it will be time enough to round up some sort of a crew."

Bliven considered the disadvantages of breaking in new men on such a difficult undertaking; of advantages, there were none to consider. "Evans Yeakel is as fine a bosun as can be found, I shall just have to trust him to get the men settled and working. But I at least want men who have been to sea before. I do not want to suffer disillusioned shirkers deserting me on the other side of the world."

"I will do what I can," Hull agreed. "God knows, there will be men who bolt when they reach someplace that they imagine answers their definition of 'paradise.' But, come down to it, your situation in that event would not be altogether dire. Most vessels that put in at the Sandwich Islands have no trouble filling in the missing ranks with native fishermen. Their reputation is that they are fine sailors, they work hard, and they follow orders to the letter, for they are grateful to get out of such a terrible place. Ha! It seems it is only a paradise for our sailors."

Bliven's blood froze. "A terrible place, sir?"

Hull shrugged. "Unending war and mayhem, human sacrifice . . . one even hears of cannibalism. Surely you have heard of this."

"Only distantly, sir. My wife is connected to the church that is presently to send missionaries to those islands."

"Is she, now? I have been hearing of them. In fact, one could not fail to learn of it in this city, with all the drumbeating and psalm singing in recent days. According to the newspaper, their church service of fare-thee-well drew upwards of five hundred of the curious, over and above the faithful. Well, I hope they enjoyed their send-off, because I do not expect we will see any of them again."

Bliven raised his head. "My wife has gone as one of them."

"What!" Hull turned pale, his forever sleepy-looking blue eyes flung open, and then just as suddenly squinting. "Damn you, Putnam, you led me on!"

"Not intentionally, sir, although I am glad to have your honest assessment."

"Well! I—" He spluttered some unintelligible syllable. "Of course, I cannot be certain about the cannibals, you understand. That is, merely what I— Why in God's name would she do such a thing?"

Bliven laughed softly. "In God's name, exactly: that is just what she said. Over the years she became friends with one of the natives who led the missionary effort; you know the one whose death spurred creation of the mission school that is supported by our church in Litchfield. When I told her that I was ordered to the Pacific, she positively declined to do without me for three years, and she got it in her mind to go with the expedition to the Sandwich Islands. She does have many useful skills, and despite the church's preference to send married couples, she changed their minds by paying up their deficit in chartering the ship. Her plan is to get to see me every few months when I put in at Honoruru, depending upon it that you will not order me to a different base of supply."

"No, we won't, and let us discuss that point. Honoruru is still the best port from which you may operate. The old king has been friendly with the ships of all nations, as well he might be for they have made him rich enough. I do not know that you can victual and water your ship in Surabaya or the other ports in the Indies. We are friendly, officially, with the Dutch, but they are very jealous of their spice trade and are not overly welcoming of other countries. Now, the British have just signed a treaty with the Sultan of Johore . . . Here, wait, this will be easier."

Hull rose and riffled through a store of rolled charts from atop a large commode behind his desk, and selected the one he wanted. He unrolled it, weighting its edges with a book and his inkwell. "We just received this from them; it is a chart of the passages into the Strait of Malacca. It is up to date and I believe we can rely on it—we shall have to in any event, for we have no other. Now"—he waved his hand over the central part of the chart—"the whole of the Malay Peninsula is divided up among a crowd of tinpot little rajas and sultans. This southern extremity is Johore, which is one of the largest and most powerful. There is a British gadfly in that area"—he closed his eyes and tossed his head in the haughtiest manner he could manage—"Sir Thomas Stamford Bingley Raffles."

Bliven threw his head back and laughed.

"He's been there about ten years, trying to siphon off some of that spice monopoly from the Dutch. The Dutch are furious, but there isn't much they can do about it, because the British Navy is about thirty times the size of their own."

"Ha! That sounds familiar, doesn't it?"

"Yes. At least they are not shooting at each other anymore, or at least it takes a long time for shots fired in the Asian jungles to be heard in Europe." Hull lowered his head. "If you take my meaning."

"And apply it to myself, yes, sir."

"Well, Raffles at last word was the governor of a fortified British enclave on Java. From there he saw that, here, on the very tip of the Malay Peninsula, there was some chaos to exploit. The legitimate sultan was ousted and exiled by his little brother—"

"My God, just like us in Tripoli?"

Hull paused. "Yes, a very similar circumstance. Yes, I hadn't thought of that, except here the British are treating the rightful sultan to five thousand a year, plus another three thousand to the local raja to stay out of it, and they have backed it up with a battle line of seventy-fours. The sultan—at least, the one recognized by the British—leased them a trading concession and the right to build a port here, on the island of Singapore. That would have been over a year ago. We will be curious to hear your assessment of what they have done to create a harbor and perhaps fortify it."

"Fortify it? Against the Dutch, in case they get ambitious?"

"Yes. Only take care that whatever you do, remember that the United States is strictly neutral and has no interest in that disagreement. Do not allow yourself to get caught between the British and the Dutch."

"Wait, sir, forgive me." Bliven studied the chart for a moment. "The British are on Malaya, and the Dutch are on Sumatra, with the Malacca Strait between them?"

"That is correct."

"And I will be ordered to engage pirates in the Malacca Strait?"

"Yes."

"But not to get between the British and the Dutch?"

Hull realized the thrust of Bliven's questions and smirked. "The irony is not lost on me, Captain. But more than that, you must identify in whose employ those pirates are operating. If they work for the sultan of Johore, there won't be much you can do, because we don't want to complicate things for the British." Hull's finger tapped northward up the map of the peninsula. "But if the pirates belong to the sultans of Malacca, or Perak, or somebody else, then you are to let them know that American ships must be let alone. Teach them a lesson if need be."

Bliven ran his fingers through his hair. "Operating on the principle that guns fired in the jungles, or jungle straits, will likely not be heard elsewhere."

"Somewhat. We don't know the exact state of the alliances; you can learn more when you are there."

Bliven leaned back and sighed. "Oh, for heavenly days."

"Yes, I know. On your way to the Sandwich Islands you might make a friendly call at Valparaiso. The British usually have ships there, and you might learn more."

"Why would there be British ships at Valparaiso?"

"Oh, did you not know? Admiral Cochrane has gone down there to take command of the Chilean Navy, at their invitation."

"What? Commodore, are you joking with me? I knew that Cochrane had been brought down, of course, but I'd no idea what became of him."

"No, it is quite true. As soon as the Chileans heard that he was cashiered from the Royal Navy, and the fact was confirmed when he was expelled from Parliament, he lost his knighthood, his banner was thrown out the front door of Westminster Abbey—total degradation—"

"God, how could they be so stupid?"

"That is a topic for another day. But once the Chileans knew of it, they snapped him up. By heaven, I admire them. Any new Latin country that puts an Irishman in command of their army and an Englishman in command of their navy is damned serious about their independence. I wish them well."

"Indeed, yes."

"At any rate, Valparaiso is all bustling with the commercial trade—all the whaling ships stop there now to provision—and sympathetic English captains visit to butter him up, because they calculate that he will return in glory once there is a change in government. And whoever is in power, it is still in Britain's interest to destroy what's left of the Spanish Empire in South America."

"Still annoyed about the Spanish Armada, perhaps." They shared the laugh. "Who is the American consul? Can you give me a letter of introduction?"

"No, in fact we do not have a legation there. Chile has been functionally independent for three years now, and no doubt we are headed toward recognizing them, but we have not attended to that formality as of this date."

"No, that would be too much to ask."

Hull's sympathy was evident. "I realize this is a complex set of affairs to keep handy in your head. I will reprise it all in your orders."

"What can you tell me about this American captain who was raided by pirates in the Malacca Strait?"

"His name is Saeger—Jakob Saeger, Dutch ancestry, from New York. Not connected to the Dutch in the Indies at all, but no doubt has used his bloodline to try and cultivate a good commercial relationship. He has been in the Canton trade for about ten years, shipping out tea and porcelain, most recently selling off sandalwood from Hawaii there. He seems to have made a pretty hard name for himself in those parts, but we don't know any details."

"What is the pirates' strength?"

Hull shrugged. "Like pirates anywhere, small ships, lightly armed. I'm sure they are of some local design, no doubt very exotic looking, being the Orient. You can learn more when you get there."

"It seems I will have a great deal to learn after I get there."

Hull peered up at him evenly. "That is why we are sending you. You have a . . . a sensitivity for foreigners and their ways that other officers might not, dating back to your experience in Egypt and all."

At last Bliven understood why he had been selected for this mission. "I had best return to my ship. I have much reading to do. Allow me to thank you for giving her your close attention while undergoing repair."

Hull stood. "Certainly. And here, the charts are yours: Take them with you. You will find one for Canton and one for Singapore: Pay particular attention to it, for the waterways leading to the settlement will appear to you to be nothing but creeks coming out of the jungle. The charts of the Sandwich Islands are based on those made by Captain Cook himself, for he was such a careful cartographer that they have found no room for improvement. You will use your discretion, of course, but I expect you will want to visit all of the anchorages where trading ships call—Honoruru, mainly, but also Lahaina, and Kairua. Learn all you can of the general situation and how American affairs lie—and of course you can look in on your missionaries. Then continue on to Canton and talk to all the American and British traders there that you can, then to Singapore and meet Raffles, if you can get an audience, and make a patrol in the Malacca Strait. Of course, report back everything you learn, as we will be sharing it with the State Department. That corner of the world is a blank slate to them."

"You will keep me advised about the powder and shot?"

"Of course, but as I say, you may have to put into Charleston for them."

BLIVEN WALKED LEISURELY detours about the Navy Yard in the October sun, the charts under his arm—a sad look at the *Constitution*, now bestridden with her ugly paddle wheels, and further around the curve of the harbor he espied the unmistakably elegant lines of a frigate under construction. He regretted that Boston had not been chosen to build one of the new American ships of the line. That would be a sight to see—American ships the equal of Nelson's *Victory*. Perhaps if he put in at Gosport for ammunition he could sneak an inspection of that monstrous new *North Carolina*. Surely Boston would have a turn; perhaps when he returned from Asia he would see one looming over the waterfront. He smirked to think of how, when they launched the *Constitution*, she got stuck in the ways twice before finally taking to water at her third christening. Maybe someone felt that the two thousand tons of a ship of the line would never leave the builder's yard in Boston at all.

He indulged himself a few disgruntled moments at the shortsightedness of the American Navy, already made manifest in the *Constitution*'s side wheels and water tanks. If they had any sense, they would follow the British model of launching only smaller vessels from slipways. Their great ships of the line they built in dry docks, floating them free when they were ready. The United States had no dry docks of sufficient size, but rather than look to the future of ever-larger ships, and construct such a large facility—which would thereafter be as useful for maintenance as for construction—no doubt they would spend much less money on a large slipway. If a new vessel got stuck on one again, well, they would figure something out.

Then, too, they allowed their disdain for the British to cloud their judgment on matters of the greatest practical moment. *North Carolina* in their hubris was to be mounted with forty-two-pounders, in haughty disregard of costly British experience. The English had already tried those gigantic guns and discarded them. They were simply too big to handle, and the muzzle blast was so powerful that they damaged the ships' upper works. But, nothing would do but the American Navy must have the biggest guns, and never mind whether the recoil should sink the ship that fired them.

It was past noon as Bliven walked up *Rappahannock*'s gangplank, and he spied smoke issuing from the ten-foot stack forward on the spar deck, and caught the aroma of fish, and baked beans, and then fresh bread. With no crew and no cook, he suspected Ross, who he knew was a capable hand in the galley. When he returned to his sea cabin he found the silver service steaming with coffee on the table, with the large lunch fully set, and shot a quizzical look at Ross.

"Saw you coming, sir. I thought you would be hungry."

"You thought rightly." As he ate, Bliven looked around the great cabin and saw that Ross had him unpacked, books in place on the double shelf with its spindled rails to keep them from tumbling off with the ship's roll. When he was alone he looked into his berth and found his clothes organized in the bureau drawers, his coats hung up, his hat and looking glass on their shelf.

He had resumed his meal when Ross returned. "Can I get you anything else, Captain?"

"Mr. Ross, tarry a moment. Do I remember correctly that you are twenty-six years of age?"

"Yes, sir."

"Yes. You know, you have served me well, and I am glad to have you with me, but have you taken any thought for your future? Are you ambitious to do anything?"

"Sir?"

"The world is not a comfortable place for old men who are poor. I am just curious what you mean to do for yourself."

Ross laughed in a nervous way. "Like what, sir?"

"Well, for instance, you might make a success as a ship's purser. You would be the men's storekeeper and you would make something off everything you sell to them."

"Oh, bless you, sir, but that takes capital. I could never post that kind of bond. And from what I understand of the factors who do post those bonds, I would not care to be connected to them, if I may speak so freely."

"Quite right, Mr. Ross. Your honesty does you credit." He should have considered that more carefully, how often pursers were so hard on the men because the lenders who supply their capital were so hard on them.

"You will allow me to thank you, Captain, for taking an interest in my affairs. The fact is, I am not well educated, and after the Navy, if I enter service in the house of some well-off family, that would not be a bad life for the likes of me."

"Such a family would be lucky to have you."

"Well, only if you cast me off, sir."

"Ha!" Seldom had Bliven heard a bid for permanent employment so artfully put forward.

After Ross had cleared away the lunch, Bliven unrolled Hull's charts on the large table, weighting their edges with books so the curled paper would begin to relax. He placed the Malacca Straits on top and stared at it almost dumbly, the jumble of names he would never be able to pronounce. He read and studied through the afternoon and through supper, at last spreading open the chart of the Sandwich Islands. They were anchored in the southeast by the great island of Hawaii, a hatchet-shaped triangle, perhaps a hundred miles north to south up its western side, the northeastern and southeastern angles of sixty or seventy miles each. Halfway up its western face was the bay of Kearakekua, which he knew from reading Ledyard was where Captain Cook landed, and a year later landed again, and met his death. They called it a bay, but on the chart it was hardly enough of an indentation in the coast to give any shelter from the ocean. Twenty miles north of there was Kairua, also with almost no harbor, although it was the royal capital.

North and west from Hawaii island lay a scattering of half a dozen other islands, each of four or five hundred square miles. First was Maui, whose roads at Lahaina were a gathering place for ships of all nations, then Molokai, and then the most promising, Oahu, which had the only real harbor and safe anchorage for ships at Honoruru. Ready for bed at last, Bliven stood and surveyed the whole. "Clarity, my love," he whispered, "where have they taken you?" He must learn much, much more.


IN THE MORNING after breakfast he strolled through that part of the city near the waterfront, which he had come to know well, until he stood before a tall red-brick building with a Dutch gambrel roof at the corner of Washington and School Streets. It was of two full stories, with a third story contained within the vast roof and an attic yet above that in its upper angle, the entire appearance showing it to be that sort of business whose first floor was for the commercial enterprise, and whose proprietor and family lived above it. The sign hung over the door read CARTER AND HENDEE, BOOK SELLERS AND PUBLISHERS. A bell dingled from a spring as he opened it, and he found himself in a shop whose shelves were as lined with leather-bound volumes as old Marsh's library, books whose leather and ink and fine cotton paper permeated the air with that unmistakable scent of the book room. Bliven had long since concluded that if knowledge had this aroma, he could spend his life breathing deeply of it. The building had formerly been an apothecary shop; he had not been here since this change of tenancy, and he felt satisfied that Clarity had chosen her publisher well.

As soon as the bell rang, a young man emerged from a rear room to greet him. He appeared to be about twenty-five, of a spare build, dark-complected, with dark eyes and rather bushy brows, conveying immense intensity for one so young. "Good morning, sir," he said. "How may we be of service?"

"Good morning. I am Captain Putnam. I have come to see either Mr. Carter or Mr. Hendee."

The young man's manner lightened several degrees as he erupted,

"Oh, my God, of course you are! I should have recognized you from the engraving in your wife's book. I am James Carter. Please, may I take your hand?"

"You are gracious, Mr. Carter." They shook hands. "Tell me, how on earth did a man of your youth become so established already in such a successful concern?"

"To tell the truth, I come from a bookish family. My parents are both teachers, and indeed I tried my hand at teaching in the common schools; but a classroom holds so few, I realized that publishing books would reach a larger audience."

It was impossible not to compare Carter's situation with that of Ross, for whom he had just had similar thoughts. Carter had education, which Ross lacked, but also ambition, which apparently Ross also lacked. Advancement in life must require both, failing family money and influence. "Wait. Are you that Carter fellow who tried to start a school for seamen at Cohasset?"

"I am, sir. I hope that does not make us adversaries. I mean, I realize that if all seamen were well educated, they would likely find other employment."

"Ha! Perhaps in the future we will compete for them, but, for now, there are enough slothful ignoramuses in the country to keep the Navy well supplied."

"Oh, Captain, I am sorry that I am alone in the shop today. Mr. Hendee will be deeply grieved that he missed you. Have you come for copies of Mrs. Putnam's book?"

"No, in fact. Now, Mr. Carter, you may be aware that my wife has departed for the Sandwich Islands with that company of missionaries from the Congregationalist Church?"

"Yes, sir. We corresponded very recently about what she might write about for her next book, for truly we must follow up such a success with some adventurous topic that will capture the public's imagination. She wrote us that this was what she had determined upon. There was no time to gainsay her intention, for I myself could not have encouraged her to such a lengthy and . . . well . . ." It was apparent that he was searching for a discreet word.

"Dangerous," said Bliven.

"Well, yes, dangerous enterprise. When I suggested an exotic locale for her next story, I fear that I may have planted the germ of the Sandwich Islands in her mind."

"Well, then, set your mind at rest: you did not originate her plan of action. She did not undertake it until after I was compelled to tell her that I and my ship were ordered to the Pacific, possibly for a term of three years. Her decision had more to do with staying nearer to me than wanting to supply you with an exciting adventure tale."

Carter's head fell back slowly as he took a deep breath. "Oh, I see. Oh, my dear captain, what a mix of emotions, not to say contradictory emotions, that must arouse in you."

Bliven nodded. "Yes, you have pretty well grasped it. You must yourself be married, Mr. Carter?"

"No, but I am almost engaged, as I fondly hope."

"Is she a strong-minded woman?"

"She is, very much so."

"Ah, then God help you. But I will tell you, what I need of you is a modern geography. My father-in-law left us a large library, but his geography is going on twenty years old. I am sailing into waters and ports that are barely known in this country, and I desire to have some source that can prepare me at least to some little degree for what I am to encounter."

Carter nested an elbow in one hand and pulled at his chin with the other, resuming that penetrating demeanor that Bliven first saw. "Yes,

I understand." In a few seconds Carter pointed emphatically into the air. "I believe we can help you. Will you pardon me one moment?" Before Bliven could respond, Carter turned on his heel and withdrew into the second room of books, returning with a leather volume remarkable not for its height or breadth, but for its thickness. "This one is only a few years old, by the celebrated Dr. Jedidiah Morse."

Bliven took it, and cracked it open to the title page, which read *A Compendious and Complete System of Modern Geography*, with subtitles that went on for line after line.

"If you will permit me to show you"—Carter left the book in Bliven's hand but peeled a few pages further on—"you will see that it opens with an alphabetical index of all the place names discussed, so you don't have to waste time searching and searching for a location of particular interest."

"Well, then, I shall test it." They huddled together while Bliven searched through this index and found entries, with their corresponding page numbers, for Canton and Malacca and Malaya and the Sandwich Islands. There was no entry for Singapore, which was no demerit, because it had only existed for a year or so. "Oh, yes, I believe this will just do."

"You will see it is not an atlas per se, but there are maps of the various regions on the pages that fold out."

"Yes. I'll take it."

Carter backed away a step. "There is one other thing. If I remember correctly from your wife's book, although I do not know if it is factual or if she invented it for purposes of the story—one can never be certain when reading historical fiction—I believe you were a midshipman on the schooner *Enterprise*."

"Indeed I was. It was my first time at sea."

"And you served under a lieutenant named Porter?"

"Oh, he was and is a very real officer, and a very fine one."

"Yes, one moment." He went to a nearby shelf and returned with two matching volumes. "Do you own a copy of his book?"

"His book?" He took them, opening the one whose spine was stamped Volume I, and Bliven's mouth fell open by degrees as he read: *Journal of a Cruise Made to the Pacific Ocean, by Captain David Porter, in the United States Frigate Essex.* "Why, Mr. Carter, I am amazed. I knew of course that Porter had taken the *Essex* to the Pacific during the war, but of this book I had no cognizance whatever. I have never seen nor heard of it. How is that even possible?"

"Well, sir, you are yourself at sea for long months at a time, and then so soon as you return you are on the first coach for your home in Connecticut. Perhaps it is not so surprising. Also, as I think on it, it was published in New York, and so was not seen so prevalently hereabouts."

"Well, I must have it. Its value to me could be inestimable."

"Then it is yours, sir, along with Jedidiah Morse."

"How much do I owe you?"

"Not so much as a half dime, Captain Putnam. You must have them with our compliments."

"Oh, you need not—"

"Yes, sir, we do need. Listen to me now: your wife's effort is thrusting us into the front rank of Boston publishers. This is the least we can do to express our gratitude and warm regard."

"Then, sir, I thank you." Bliven extended his hand and Carter took it.

"I am sorry you will be away for so long. You would be welcome here often."

"And I am sorry I cannot take you with me." He looked once more around the chamber. "You and your books."

Carter laughed. "It is probably a bit premature to think of opening a bookshop in the Sandwich Islands. Besides"—he grew more thoughtful—"I have not so adventurous a nature. I fear that some of us are fated to be but mental travelers. But God speed you, Captain Putnam, and bring you and your lady safe home."

Bliven departed the bookshop light of foot, and marveling how a man of only five-and-twenty could have come to such a facility with books or such elegant manners. It was impossible not to compare him to the rootless or uprooted vagabonds who so often volunteered for service in the Navy—over a veritable parade of whom he would soon have to pass judgment on whether to allow them to serve on his *Rappahannock*. Young Carter gave him hope for the coming generation.

Back aboard the *Rappahannock*, he leafed through Morse's nearly seven hundred pages of geography, but he was consumed by curiosity for Porter's journal, especially on the point of Porter's governing his crew when they were among the Pacific Islands, with their legendary enticements of native women. He remembered Porter as a strict disciplinarian but fair, insofar as the Navy understood "fair," and one who tried to obviate trouble with his crew by anticipating their desires and, to the extent compatible with good order, accommodating them.

Bliven quickly discovered that Porter's journal was fronted with a summary of contents by chapter, and upon seeing that the first volume ended with his visit to the Galápagos Islands, realized that the information salient to him must open the second volume. But first he allowed himself to smile that Porter, like grizzled seamen before him who had taken pen in hand, felt compelled to deprecate the quality of his literary effort, and aver that he had written his book—his massive book of five hundred pages in two volumes—only at the insistence of friends, and for the education of his son, who he hoped would grow up to become himself a creditable naval officer.

After the Galápagos Islands, Porter made straight as an arrow for the Marquesas Islands and hove to at Nuku Hiva, the largest of that group. A quick reference to the Morse geography made Bliven believe that he was on the right trail for what he wanted to learn, for that was an island of some one hundred thirty square miles—it would take six or seven of them to equal his own Litchfield County—but crowded with as many as one hundred thousand natives, and thus might stand in as a substitute for one of the Sandwich Islands, thickly populated with islanders of a similar race and customs.

After establishing a shore base from which to repair the *Essex*'s accumulated damage from her passage around the Horn and extensive action, Porter indulged his crew by allowing a quarter of them to spend the night ashore, each quarter in turn. "All was helter skelter," Porter wrote, "and promiscuous intercourse. Every girl the wife of every man in the mess, and frequently of every man in the ship." This open-ended idyll, however, did not come without cost. No larger an island than Nuku Hiva was, it was divided between two chiefs who were bitter and deadly rivals, with lesser chiefs being forced to choose between them. By luck, the women who Porter's seamen enjoyed came from the dominant tribe, and after a few weeks of serial abandon, their chief made it clear that he expected these powerful new white men to assist him in subjugating his enemy. To this Porter acquiesced, but then, when it was time for the *Essex* to be on her way, Porter found his men reluctant to leave. This was an experience well known to British ships, whose captains did not hesitate to resort to brute discipline to extract obedience. This tactic had provoked a famous mutiny in the spring of 1789 on HMS *Bounty*, formerly a small merchant vessel that the Royal Navy purchased to attempt the transplanting of breadfruit trees to the West Indies.

Porter's account was consonant with everything Bliven had read about the Sandwich Islands. So far as anyone knew, venereal diseases had once been unknown among the Hawaiians, and Captain Cook's determination to keep his chancred seamen away from the native women was founded not in cruelty to his men but in his desire not to infect these healthy if lusty people with the burden of English licentiousness. After his initial discovery of the islands, and just before continuing north to the polar regions, Cook had sent a watering party ashore on the tiny island of Niihau, at the northern end of the chain, to return immediately upon filling their casks. Opposing winds and rearing, booming surf forced them to stay on land for two days, and Cook knew what the result would be. When he returned after a year, the *Endeavour*'s surgeon inspected the eager women as they boarded her, and discovered that genital sores had become as sure a mark of imperial claim as planting their flag. Cook was dismayed, but on this second visit, with both his men and the local women equally afflicted, threw up his hands and allowed all to have their pleasure.

With the Sandwich Islands' active trade with the West, Bliven's hands would be tied in the local quarrels between chiefs, but medicine, at least, had advanced to a point where the diseases of love could be treated—albeit painfully and over a long period.

BOSTON
30TH OCTOBER, 1819

*My Dear Dr. Berend,*

*I have conferred with Commodore Hull, on the subject of the Rappahannock's coming dispatch to the Pacific, to establish an American naval presence in the Sandwich Islands, and Canton, and* to make contact with the new British establishment and enclave which is to be called Singapore. Part of our assignment is to face down and if needs be fight the pirates who have long infested the Strait of Malacca, and who have recently committed depredation upon our country's shipping.

You have perhaps received Mr. Hull's letter to you requesting your return to duty, with the advisory also that the voyage might be of as much as three years' duration. I hope you will not object to my adding, I do not wish to undertake such an arduous duty with anyone other than yourself as the surgeon on board my ship. We must operate in a portion of the globe largely unknown to our country, with, we may expect, local diseases and afflictions equally unknown to us.

Certainly, there are many who would decline such a duty, and all would admit that a man of your years has earned the right to some leisurely posting. But frankly, sir, it is precisely to your years—that is to say, your broad experience—to which I appeal. Into such a far corner of the world I am loath to lead my men without feeling certain that they shall have the best medical care that can be given. And after the retirement from sea duty of our esteemed Cutbush, I consider that to be yourself. Therefore if you are in good health, and you have still no family connection to keep you land-bound, I do most keenly hope that you will come. Miller sails with me, and we shall have many fine dinners in the tropical climes!

And touching upon the point of medical care, Doctor, I need not tell you that the Pacific Islands are a very popular port of call for all sailors from the Western world, in no small part owing to the extreme amorous nature of the native women. This has been well known since the earliest discoveries. In the Sandwich Islands, particularly, from all accounts, the sexual aggressiveness of the women has in the past extended so far as to actually chase down white sailors and verily pull them into their huts to have carnal relations with them. To such a course, naturally, most seamen have not the least objection, but as a consequence the various species of the Diseases of Venus are rampant, and we must prepare accordingly. I doubt that such a moral place as Boston has enough of the proper medicines in the whole city, as may answer our need. Without implying that Virginia is any less moral a place, may I advise you? Round up all you can of the mercurous chloride, or any new formulations of mercury as have been found effective, before you come, and then see what you can find here.

Finally, allow me to forward a message from the bosun, Mr. Yeakel, that the efficacy of your treatment of the sail room must have been devastating to the pests therein, for when he opened the compartment some days later to inspect it, and restock the canvas, he says that the remainder of the fumes nearly put his eyes out. He begs me to say further, that if any vermin survived this onslaught, it is not because your effort was at all deficient, but that they must be immortal beings.

In closing, let me urge you to haste, if you can come, for like the great Dr. Cutbush, I know that you would prefer to inspect and examine those who volunteer and aspire to our crew, and winnow out those who are weak of limb or constitution.

> This letter, Doctor, comes with
> the great respect and friendship
> of Bliven Putnam, Capt. USN

DR. CRAIGHEAD BEREND, USN
NAVY YARD, GOSPORT

There were other letters to write, and in the absence of a purser, Ross procured a stack of stationery from the ship's stores, noting the withdrawal meticulously in the records so that the new purser, when they acquired one, could account for the discrepancy. Bliven wrote to Commodore Hull—he could easier have just told him, but he desired the record in writing—directing his share of the Mobile prize money, when it came, to his wife's business manager; and he wrote to that manager, instructing him to convert the Navy's draught to gold and silver. He was not to deposit it in any bank, nor entail it in any investment. He was to keep it secure, keeping himself informed of his parents' needs as well as those of Mrs. Marsh, whose longtime advisor he was, and use the money to supply their wants. He wrote to Sam Bandy that he expected to be in Charleston within a couple of months and hoped that they could stage a reunion. And he wrote to young James Carter, thanking him again for the gift of the books, and instructing that the royalties from Clarity's novel should also be kept paid current to her manager.

Every day that passed of the next two weeks seemed to crawl by, and made Bliven the more anxious for the open sea. Closing up the *Rappahannock*'s hull slowed as he won Hull's approval to have Edwards's crew wall off a safe powder handling room lined with copper and lit by lanterns through thick glass, after it became likely that the powder he took on in Charleston would be bulk, in casks, and not premeasured in silk bags, as was now standard. And he wanted a bigger gun room for small arms, because he requested and was granted an amplified contingent of marines, given that pirates Eastern or Western relied on boarding ships for hand-to-hand combat, since they stood no chance in a duel of heavy cannon. James Carter took it upon himself to acquire a few further books with information on Malaya, mostly in memoirs of the minor English nobility recounting their adventures in foreign service. Bliven was reading one so dutifully in the late morning that he started when he heard Ross's three raps on the cabin door.

"Enter."

"Excuse me for intruding, Captain, but there has been some news I thought I should tell you. It is probably nothing, but I feel certain that you will want to hear it."

"What is it?"

"As I say, it is probably of no moment to you, but, well, I was ashore to purchase some supplies, and I heard tell that a merchantman, a Boston brig, has foundered off Cape Hatteras."

To Bliven it felt odd that such instant terror could manifest itself in such outward calm. He was aware that his breath was shallower and his senses heightened, but his voice was measured. "There is no word what vessel?" Surely Clarity's ship had had time to clear those shoals before this could have happened, but still—

"No, sir. I heard it in the market. Two men who I learned are clerks on the receiving ship were speculating about it, but when I questioned them they knew no particulars. Sir, I do not see how it could be your wife's ship."

"Thank you, Mr. Ross, I quite agree. Nevertheless, if you will fetch my hat and coat, I shall endeavor to learn what I can."

He paced off the distance to the receiving ship with purpose. So this was what Clarity must have felt like when he was months at a time at sea, every time she heard of some unidentified calamity—the emptiness in the pit of her stomach, her hands sweating beyond control, the blotting out of any other thought, the hopelessness of incomplete information, and the desperation for certain news. When he saw her again, he assured himself, he would acknowledge what he had put her through and how much she must love him to have endured it. And now in addition he must raise additional topics, plausible topics, to raise with Hull so as not to appear hysterical.

"I wonder if I might see the commodore for a moment?" Bliven asked Hull's aide when he reached the office.

"I shall let him know that you are here."

As he rose Bliven asked, "By the way, what is this I hear of a ship wrecked off Hatteras? Do you know what one?"

"Yes, sir, a merchantman, the *Berenice*, carrying fish and iron works. Apparently she struck bottom close inshore, and there were survivors."

"Ah. I am glad to hear it." He dared not betray the tidal wave of relief that was breaking over him.

The aide ducked in and out of the inner chamber. "The commodore will see you."

"Putnam!" boomed Hull as he rose. "By God, sir, your timing is impeccable. I am hungry, and I want good food, and to be waited upon. I have in mind some of that roast duck they serve at the Exchange. Everyone here must work. Will you come with me?"

"Most happily, Commodore, thank you."

Outside, Bliven was struck afresh with the perquisites of command, as Hull had only to raise a finger for a barouche to appear with a young sailor at the reins, and they were rolling easily across the bridge that became Washington Street, toward the central district. "Well, Putnam, what was it you wished to discuss with me?"

"Sir, my ship will soon be ready for fitting out, and to take on a crew. We cannot readily do that until we have a purser aboard, so I was wondering if you had found someone suitable."

Even in the mid-November chill, Isaac Hull faultlessly lifted his bicorne to acknowledge the salutations of strangers who had so noted his passage. "You are not going to assault me with more of your reform ideas?"

"No, sir, on that front I am beaten, for the present."

"I am glad to hear it."

"Besides, I am counting my blessings that you did not take it into your head to saddle my ship with any of those damned metal water tanks."

"Ha!" Hull cleared this throat. "I thought about it."

"Considering the nature of the defect in my hull, it might never have been found beneath one of those things. I am certain that occurred to you."

"Putnam, don't abuse me or I will give you paddle wheels."

They arrived and entered the Boston Exchange, busy in commerce at the height of the day. Turning toward the restaurant, Bliven noticed that the watercolors of the missionary couples painted by the celebrated Mr. Morse had been taken down.

They were shown to a table in a quiet corner. "What shall we do for a chaplain for your crew?" asked Hull. "Do you know anyone?"

"No, sir, I was rather hoping you would."

"I see." Hull looked up when the waiter appeared. "Roast duck, if you please, and some good ale until it comes. Now, these missionaries that your wife accompanied to the Sandwich Islands—they are of the Congregationalist bent, as I remember."

"Yes, sir."

"Well, given that they will be the first American presence in those islands, do you think perhaps it would be helpful to choose you a chaplain of the same strain?"

"Oh, God, no! In truth, sir, the leaders of my wife's church are so strict and strident, I fear that they will make more enemies than converts, whether among the natives or among residents from other nations with a more conventional religious background."

"Yes, I see your point."

"Moreover, Commodore, I have been reading in Captain Porter's journal of the *Essex*'s cruise in the Pacific—"

"Oh, damn! I forgot to ask if you had that book or if you would find it useful. Glad you've got it."

"Yes, sir, a very helpful clerk in the bookstore put it in my hands. Porter wrote quite frankly—no, very frankly—of the seductive powers of the native women and the needs of a crew half a year or more at sea. I fear that a chaplain of the Congregationalist faith would find scant following as he preaches on the heavenly virtues of purity."

"Ha! Yes, I see what you mean. Well, perhaps we could find you a nice Unitarian. Some of them can be rather open-minded."

Bliven exploded in laughter as tankards of ale were set before them. "Oh, good God, would that not cause the mighty Reverend Beecher to drop dead as a stone? Oh, well, how about an Episcopalian: they don't insist on very much."

Hull nodded. "Yes, but I don't know of any who are available. And these new Methodists are a bit extreme as well. Come, now, let us think on it. The regulations are so lax about chaplains, put the right coat on any man and give him a big dark book that looks somewhat like a Bible, he would pass muster as far as the Navy is concerned. Wait—how about just a simple Deist?"

Bliven was struck quiet. "Well, yes." He considered their tenets. "They believe in God, and in Christian principles, but accept the different avenues that people find to Him. A Deist would serve very well. Do you know of any?"

"I know of two, actually. They have rather fallen from public favor among the more competitive creeds." Hull raised his pewter tankard. "Leave it to me. Here's to Deists!"

"And to God, however you find Him."

"I am glad that is settled," said Hull. "Now, Putnam, one thing more."

"Sir?"

"Did you truly suppose that I might learn of some mishap that could even conceivably involve the safety of your wife and not send for you?"

Bliven blushed to learn that Hull had guessed his true business straightaway. "No, sir," he answered meekly. "My steward had just this morning heard of it in the market but could discover no detailed information. Naturally, I—"

"Never mind, Captain. But be assured that I am as watchful for my officers' well-being here as ever I was on a quarterdeck."

"I am glad of it, sir. Thank you."

# { 7 }

## *Strange Shores*

At the northern tip of Kohala, the usual trade wind had disappeared in the face of a strong westerly ripping through the Alenuihaha Channel. Captain Blanchard knew it would not last, and he judged it better to tarry at anchor in the lee of the landmass than to struggle their way through in a wind that blasted against them. On his previous visits he had known vessels to labor for four days in rollicking wicked seas to beat a passage between islands when, on a favorable day, one would blow like a leaf straight to the destination.

From the tip of the island he retreated six miles and anchored in Waipio Bay, intending to introduce the missionaries to the islands with this sight of the valley, flat as a floor, winding like a labyrinth back into the interior between jungle-sloped mountains a thousand feet high that intersected like herring bones more and more distant until they rose to five times that height and disappeared into a pearl-colored mist. From the top of a rearing plateau, a waterfall shot itself into thin air and fell the full height to thunder on the black lava rocks of the shore.

The *Thaddeus* hove to, furled her sails, and dropped her anchor, with the entire company surrounding Blanchard at the wheel on the poop deck. Muriel Albright made her way to the rail facing the beach, one hand grasping it and the other holding Clarity's hand. "Look at this place," she whispered. "Oh, never did I imagine it to be so beautiful." They all watched the sun set behind the mountains before adjourning to the great cabin for a rich supper of fish, sweet potatoes, boiled *kalo* leaves, and fruit that the queen had sent aboard in welcome. Hopu used that evening to call a final lesson after the dishes were cleared. The missionaries scurried to their compartments and returned with their notebooks and pencils.

"Few more important words," Hopu said. "Sorry, don't know days of week. My country, we not need days of week. 'Time to go catch fish.' Why, because Tuesday? No, because hungry! Don't need days of week."

Even the dour but beautiful Bingham began to shake from mirth.

He grew serious. "But you bring word of God, and God say, 'Worship on Sabat.'" He winced at his mispronunciation and repeated the last word, emphasizing the final diphthong to the point of making a face, sticking his tongue far beyond his teeth. "I mean, Sabaththth." He panted, feigning exhaustion. "My language, we have no sound for *ththth*. Thththank goodness!" Sated with the fresh feast, the missionaries roared in laughter. "We like end words with nice little vowel. So we say, 'Sabati.' You say now."

They echoed, "Sabati," and wrote it down.

"Very good. Now, God say, 'Keep Sabati holy.' Word for 'holy' is *lani*. Mean sacred, also mean royal, because king is sacred. You say *lani*."

"*Lani*."

"Very good. Holy Sabati, *sabati lani*. You say."

"*Sabati lani*."

He opened a book he had brought, and held up a lily he had pressed the previous Easter. "Flower. Say *lei*."

"*Lei*," they repeated, and wrote in their notebooks.

"Easter lily is sacred flower. Sacred flower, *lei lani*. You say."

"*Lei lani*."

"Very good."

The evening sped by. "Such good pupils," said Hopu at last. "Thank you. Many months now you listen to me. *Mahalo nui loa*." He looked around quizzically. "Of course, you had no escape, either. Well, never mind. Now, have treat for you. Captain Blanchard, please to send for cook." From the heavy pine sideboard Hopu extracted pewter bowls, returned to the head of the table, and set one short stack before Clarity at his right and another before Bingham at his left. "Now, in my country, we have very important food. Most important food. When plenty other food, we still like it; when nothing else, we depend on it, maybe all we have. My friends, Kanui and Tamoree and Honoree, we have not eaten it for many years, but I make free to show cook how is done. So we wait one more moment."

Blanchard returned, holding by two towels a small kettle with a ladle visible above its top and setting it before Hopu. At once he began ladling into the bowls a thick lavender-colored porridge. "We call it *poi*. You say *poi*."

"*Poi*," they chorused.

"Nobody begin yet!" He continued portioning the gruel into the bowls until all were served. "Now, when we ashore, queen will have feast for you. What is word for feast?"

"*Luau!*"

"Very good. There will be many bowls of *poi*. Important that you like it. If you not like it, say you like it! God will forgive your little lie. Now, let us begin." As they ate they reached a consensus that it did not taste bad, it merely did not have much taste at all; and given that it was the island staple, they concluded that when among themselves it would serve best as a kind of sauce over the other dishes, whether meat or vegetable.

Daniel Chamberlain rolled it around in his mouth to assess its texture. "What is it prepared from, Thomas? Is it gathered or grown in a garden?"

"Ah, is good question from brother Daniel, our farmer. *Kalo*, you boil leaves and eat like spinach, and *poi* is made from roots; grind up and boil. Almost everybody have garden of *kalo*."

Chamberlain nodded his thanks; Bingham had excused himself so discreetly that few noticed he was gone until he returned and remained standing. "Brother Thomas, will you rise?"

Hopu looked in surprise at his three fellow islanders and pushed himself up from the table.

"Thomas, for five months now you have taught us beyond value about your language and your life, the life of the islands. No one asked you to do this; you have undertaken it out of your own goodness, and above even that, you have made our lessons more enjoyable than any theater. We know that you have done this for your love of the Lord, but the Bible tells us that the servant is worth the wage of his hire. Therefore, with the consent of this company, we have made up a purse of money." He handed Hopu a small cotton sack closed with a drawstring.

"Is heavy." Hopu tried to laugh through a deluge of emotion.

"We hope that this will help you reestablish your life back here in your home."

"Thank you. Thank you so very much. My heart is too full; please excuse me."

The company sat approving of Bingham's action and its effect on Hopu, when Tamoree spoke suddenly. "Reverend Bingham, forgive my speaking."

"Yes, Brother George?"

"I speak as I begin to remember what it is like, to be a prince among my people. What you have done was in the best way of what we call *ho o pono*. That means, to settle with honor to make good account. You did not know that, but I guess that to act well in a dealing has words in any language."

Bingham bowed his head, moved. "Thank you, George. What you have said means a great deal to us. And now, may I suggest that we retire to prayers and rest?"


"THAT WAS RATHER nice, wasn't it?" asked Muriel Albright as she slipped beneath her covers.

"Yes, but . . ." Clarity had begun to remove her shoes but instead left them on. "I'm just going to take a walk around the deck and see if Thomas is still out there. I am a little worried about him. He seemed quite overtaken."

The rear door of the great cabin opened onto the very stern, by the wheel, and finding no one there she walked forward on the starboard side, down onto the well deck, past the hatch, and then up to the fo'c'sle. Right above where the bowsprit was inserted to its footing she found Hopu, curled up and weeping copiously. "Why, Thomas!"

He started up as though kicked, reclining on his hip, supporting himself on one arm as his other hand brushed the hair out of his face.

"Mrs. Putnam! What are you—I am sorry, you should not see me like this."

"Nonsense." She knelt by him and placed a hand on his shoulder. "Can you tell me what is wrong?"

"Is too hard, is too many things."

"Well, I'm afraid now you must try." She sat down close by him.

"Is not the gift of money," he said.

"No, it was generous, but not *that* generous."

"Is not the five months on the ship. Is not even the two years in mission school, but is all ten years since we came to America. In ten years, this is first time anyone speak to me as if I worth something."

The incoming small swell rocked the ship rhythmically and gently. "But, Thomas, has anyone ever been mean or cruel to you?"

"No, no! People always kind, everybody kind, but everybody kind in way of charity, kind to lost little hungry boy. Always I try to earn keep. I become funny little black man who makes good jokes. They pat me on head and say, 'What nice little ignorant black man. See, we can train him to love the Lord.' I—we all—work hard to learn, but we not belong, and we must not have feelings. Feelings not allowed."

"Thomas, what do you mean? You are not allowed feelings?"

"Do you not see? Beecher, Bingham, preach, preach, preach that all men equal before God, but little black men from Hawaii should not feel anger, should not feel sad, should not love, at least not like they do. We are young men, we have feelings of all young men, for young women. But that is not permitted. Cannot see or speak or touch young women. Not good enough to touch white women. And now I am so happy to be home, happy to be where people not better than me. So it made me cry."

She replaced her hand on his shoulder. "Thomas," she said quietly, "what I am going to say may surprise you."

He looked into her eyes, no longer caring that she saw tears streaking his cheeks.

"Thomas, I cannot defend everything about your life in America. Dr. Dwight, and Reverend Beecher, and Mills, and the others—I believe they are good men, as are Mr. Bingham and Mr. Thurston. But there are limits to their understanding, just as there are limits to what all men can understand. They never meant for you to feel that you are inferior."

"Henry felt these things, too. Opukaha'ia loved you. Did you even know that?"

Without thinking she drew back. "No! No, he never said anything."

"Yes, he did. He told Mr. Beecher that he loved you and was punished."

"Oh, poor Henry. Poor sweet, innocent Henry." At last she understood why Beecher had so consistently warned her against too warm a friendship with him.

"Do you not see? In my country, white men take our women whenever they want. We have come to accept this, because in our country love is freely given. In your country all is tied up, and ashamed, and nobody may speak. You say slavery is wrong, but black people serve you all the same. So really, yes, Mr. Beecher and others do not want us to feel inferior, so long as we do not act like we are their equal. Can you understand this?"

Clarity felt the years of her friendship with Henry weighing on her like chain mail now that she understood the weight he had carried. "Thomas, do you know the meaning of the word 'hypocrisy'?"

"Oh, yes, we know it very well."

"I will not deny that some of our care of you and your friends has had an element of hypocrisy about it. But we did not mean for it to be so."

"I believe that."

The chill of sitting close above the water was dispelled momentarily by a breath of warmth that issued from the valley. "Thomas, let us say that you found a girl in America. Let us say that you married her. Do you really believe that now—now that you have come home— that she could ever really be happy so far from her home, so far from everything she has ever known?"

"I do not know," he whispered. "And yet, you came here."

"Yes, but when my husband goes home, so shall I. You know, when I got married, I left a life in which I had everything money could buy to one where I had to take a share in cooking and cleaning and doing for myself. That was a very hard change, and I moved only a mile away. But to the other side of the world?"

"And yet, you came here because you love your husband."

"That is true."

"Can not a woman love me so much?" Involuntarily he sobbed.

"Oh, yes, Thomas. A woman could love you, but it would be much, much easier if she shared a similar life, perhaps if she were Hawaiian, like you. May I tell you a secret?"

"Yes, I shall keep it faithfully."

She leaned forward, shaking her head as she whispered, "We did not like your *poi* very much."

Hopu's belly shook as he wheezed, then harder, until he bellowed in laughter that reverberated around the bay. "Very well, now I can marry a woman who likes *poi*!"

"And now you are home again." She squeezed his shoulder. "You will find that wife, and you will be a splendid husband and father. And with this great difference, too: you are making your country a better place. The old religion—what do you call it?"

"*Kapu*."

"*Kapu* is gone, and you are bringing the love of God to your people. You and your friends have been highly blessed among all the people of these islands. Try to not forget that."

As THE SUN rose, the trade wind resumed its natural course, and within an hour of Blanchard giving the order to weigh anchor they were abreast of the northern tip of Kohala. There the full press of the trade wind took them, and all felt their westward surge until he turned south down the western side of the island. By degrees the coastal jungle diminished to groves of palm trees on the shoreline, but with the uplands beyond them remarkably parched, dominated by an almost desert scrubland.

The whole company was gathered on deck, watching the coast as it slid by, crescents of forested beach separated by the rocky headlands of lava flows that had reached the sea, and behind them the gray-brown brush streaked with green about the hollows and stream beds, where, they surmised, there was at least occasional water. "This is as if we are in a different country than the one we woke up in," said Bingham.

"That is the trade winds, Reverend," said Blanchard from the wheel. "When they hit the mountains it makes rain, but the mountains take all the rain, and there is not much left for this side of the island. All the islands have a wet side and a dry side."

"Indeed, I never imagined."

Jerusha Chamberlain left her children in a clot at the port rail except for the baby, whom she cradled in her arms. She rarely spoke at all; thus Blanchard was attentive to her as soon as she approached. "Captain, may I ask you a question and be frankly answered?"

"Of course, ma'am."

"Can you assure us without doubt that there is not some kind of trick behind all this? How can we know that we will not all be killed once we get ashore?"

"Oh, ma'am, this is not so primitive a place as you imagine. The upper class, the lords, have been getting rich for years on foreign trade. They would never do such a stupid thing. Moreover, I know of my own experience that the Hawaiians have a peaceable and loving nature. Common crime is low where nature supplies food and shelter, where love is free, and ambition is thus quenched."

Her eyes proclaimed her doubts. "But have we not been told that they spend most of the year at war with each other?"

"Yes, but they fought only because the chiefs forced them to. But once the old king conquered everybody, there has been no war, and that was ten years ago. Common murder would hardly occur to them, except on one small point." Blanchard's eyes twinkled. "It is said that they have an uncommon skill with poisons. They are not a violent-natured people at all, but if they were sufficiently provoked, that is how they would do it."

Jerusha stared hard at him, clutching her baby tighter.

"I am sorry, ma'am, you asked for a frank answer." She made no reply but stalked back over to her family.

"Captain, how do you know where we are going?" asked Muriel Albright. "Are you guided by latitude, or landmarks, or do you know the place?"

"Oh, I know the place very well, ma'am. But you shall know it, too, for there is a sizable village, because it is the royal pleasure resort. There is a little harbor where you shall see many canoes; most of all there is a hill behind the town on which is a great hulking fortress temple of red stone. Only a blind man could miss it."

In three hours more they raised the place. Blanchard shortened to a single topsail and the spanker, gliding forward until Hunwell called out ten fathoms beneath them, some hundred yards from the beach. "Drop your sails! Let go your anchor! Ladies and gentlemen, we have arrived, and I hope you hold that our charter is fulfilled."

Bingham advanced and shook hands with him. "Captain, you have been all that we were assured you would be."

Those of the company who brought telescopes raised them to their eyes to survey the town, but their attention was arrested where, on the nearest part of the beach by a promontory of lava boulders, they saw a large native woman sunning herself, as naked as the day she was born. She was of middle age, with a large belly, her pendulous breasts falling to the sides. She was attended by two men, both as naked as she, who were anointing alternately her and themselves with some kind of unguent. They studied the three not in lust but a kind of morbid fascination. "Children!" snapped Jerusha. "Go wait in your cabin! Go quickly!" She scooted them inside.

"You can't protect them forever, ma'am," said Blanchard with evident sympathy. "What does your own Bible say? 'What came ye into the wilderness to see, a man clothed in fine raiment?'"

"Well said, Captain," announced Bingham. Then he smiled sardonically. "You have shown no evidence that you know the Bible. Brothers and sisters, it is well that we see the scope of the labor before us." The offshore wind brought the sound of splashing and laughing, as they saw the beach, alternately hidden and revealed by the surf, thronged with people reveling in the sun and spray, most as naked as Eden.

Dr. Holman raised his arm. "Look! Here comes someone to meet us."

The saw a high-prowed canoe knifing toward them, rowed by a dozen men, with three more standing in its waist. Hunwell helped them tie up alongside as Blanchard and the missionaries came down the ladder to the well deck to receive them. Two young men came up and through the boarding gate, followed by a middle-aged man of stunning self-possession. He was at least six and a half feet tall, tremendously broad and powerful, with voluminous, curly black hair that fell to the middle of his back. His eyes and ears were remarkably small, his nose tiny and pugged, but his lips full-fleshed, with a distinct downward turn at their corners. His chest and back were covered in tattoos, his feet large and calloused, and wrapped about his waist was a stenciled cloth garment of a kind Clarity had never seen before but took to be the native cloth that Henry had told her was pounded from the bark of mulberry trees.

From such a fierce appearance they were astonished at his perfect English. "You are the brig *Thaddeus?*"

"We are, sir," answered Blanchard.

The imposing figure raised his hands. "*Aloha!* In the names of His Majesty the King, Reho-Reho, now reigning as Ta-meha-meha the Second; of his royal wife, the queen Kamamalu; of their sacred mother, the queen Kepurani; and of the *kuhina nui*, the queen Kahumanu, I bid you welcome. I am Karaimoku, advisor and first minister to the royal family."

"I have heard of you, sir." Blanchard advanced, saluted smartly, and they shook hands. "Welcome aboard. Are you not he who the English call William Pitt, in honor after their own first minister?"

"I am the same. When you first arrived on the windward shore, we were surprised that you brought some of our native people home to us. They informed us that you did not come to trade but to share knowledge of your religion. Is this true?"

"It is," said Blanchard. "May I present the Reverend Bingham, who is the leader of the company of missionaries?"

Karaimoku nodded at him and Bingham nodded back. "We know of your religion. I am myself a Christian." A murmur of surprise and approval moved through the company. "I was received into the Holy Catholic Church last year, on board the French man-of-war *Uranie*, Captain Freycinet."

Clarity watched Bingham intently lest he launch immediately into a doctrinal dispute at this first exchange, and made up her mind to faint if he did so to disrupt the conversation. Instead he said, "We are very glad to hear it, sir," and she felt much relieved.

"You have brought women, and children."

"Yes, sir, for it is our intention to live among you and teach you what we know, as in return we learn about your life."

Karaimoku's eyes widened. "White sailors come here to get drunk and ravish our women, and they bring rum and whiskey for the king. Have you brought rum and whiskey?"

"Sir," said Bingham, "we have brought the word of the living God, and gifts for your people, and tools to help them build better lives. We have no part of whiskey."

"Wherein do you make a profit?"

"We do that which is pleasing to our God. That is our reward."

"No money?"

"Our church will give us enough money to buy what we need, so that we do not burden you."

"But why would you do this when you get nothing out of it?"

"Because, sir, our holy book says, 'Go and preach the word of God to all nations.'"

"And you have brought your *ohana* here to live?"

No one made a response, but Clarity knew the word from Henry. "Our families, yes."

"Well!" It was apparent that Karaimoku was equally flummoxed

175

for a reply. "That is a horse of a different color. You may not land without an invitation from the king, but I will tell him of your intentions straightaway. I must tell you, he was expecting rum and whiskey, but I will do what I can for you."

"We are most grateful, Mr. Karaimoku."

"Now, then"—he recovered his bearing—"it pleases Her Majesty, the *kuhina nui*, to say that she wishes to visit you upon your ship on this evening. Can you be prepared to receive her suitably?"

"Our cabin is very small," said Blanchard, "but we can bring chairs and lanterns on deck and spread a sail over the hatch cover to set food upon."

Karaimoku nodded slowly. "You have had a long journey. I shall send food out to you, that you may receive her properly."

"Most kind, sir."

"One thing more. There is no dignity for the queen to come up your ladder. Have you a bosun's chair to lift her aboard?"

"Indeed we do, sir."

"It is well. Now I will take with me Tamoree, who is prince and *alii* to his people, for Their Majesties are most anxious to greet him. And the one called Hopu, who came ashore earlier and can answer their questions as to his life in America, and why you have come."

As the canoe diminished in sight, Muriel leaned over to Clarity. "Well, they do seem to have queens all over the place, don't they?"

"Yes, now we're up to three, and we had better get busy if we want to make any impression at all." The men of the company formed a chain to pass chairs from the great cabin down to the well deck as Blanchard sent a man below to return with a clean sail that they spread over the hatch as a great tablecloth. The women descended to the galley, set water to heating to boil *kalo*, and to make coals in which to roast sweet potatoes. In thirty minutes Karaimoku's canoe returned and his men handed up fish, vegetables, fruit, a huge, beautifully worked wooden bowl of the mauve-colored poi, and finally, cradled in an enormous basket, an entire pig roasted through and of such an aroma that they could not forbear sampling it and pronounced it the finest pork that any had ever tasted.

As the light faded, Blanchard had his crew round up all the lanterns on the ship, light them, and string them on a line that they ran between the main and mizzen, about ten feet above the well deck.

The canoe that they saw sweeping toward them was in essence an enormous barge consisting of two canoes each as large as Karaimoku's with a deck lashed between them, decorated with palm fronds, proceeding in such state that it made Clarity think of Jesus entering Jerusalem. At last they could make out Hopu and Tamoree standing with Karaimoku on either side of a huge woman in early middle age, attended by four pages in English officers' coats, and four ladies-in-waiting. All the women wore dresses in the old directorate style, the one they took for the queen in pink silk tied and trimmed in dark green, her attendants in white.

Hopu and Tamoree were first up the ladder, followed by the pages, who spread lengths of the native tapa cloth along one side of the well deck. It took six of Blanchard's crew to hoist the queen up and onboard. She took Clarity's breath away: she was much over six feet tall, and massively huge; she could not have weighed less than five hundred pounds. Yet she stood easily, almost gracefully, from the bosun's chair. She extended both her hands to the captain. "*Aloha*, Andy Blanchard, you have come back to us. It is good to see you."

Blanchard stepped toward her but stopped and bowed before he took her hands. "*Aloha*, my queen, thank you. You are looking very well."

"How is your pretty wife?"

"Ma'am, we came straight to answer your call. I have not yet been home to see her."

"Heh! Then you are a better subject than husband, it seems. And these are the gentlemen who are bringing us the word of God?"

The men followed Bingham's lead in bowing as he recited, "*Ka mea Kamahao, ka moi wahine.*"

Kahumanu nodded. "Well, we shall discuss it and see about it. And these are your ladies?"

They curtsied in unison.

"What are these dresses that they wear? Is this a new fashion?" She strode over among them, taking each by the hand until she had greeted them all. "Your dresses are very pretty, and more modest." She circulated among them, noting accurately the lower waistlines, more ample sleeves, the addition of rustling petticoats, and other changes since the last time she had examined Western clothing. "Oh, I wish I had such dresses."

"In that case, ma'am," said Clarity, "may we show you?" She raised the lid of a sea trunk to reveal bolts of bright print cloth in a rainbow of colors. "We have brought this material for Your Majesty, if you would be pleased to accept our gift."

"Oh! You can make me dresses of this cloth?"

"We would be honored to do so, ma'am."

"Oh! Heh! Oh! Ladies, you will understand that because of my station, I must restrain my emotions, but you have pleased me very well. Now, then, let us eat the food before it gets cold, this food that"—she pointed to herself—"you have provided me, which"—she pointed around the deck—"I have provided you, to provide me—but never mind! Heh!"

They gathered around the hatch cover, but before they could sit, Bingham said loudly, "And now let us give thanks to the Lord for his bounty." Kahumanu and her suite looked on curiously as the company bowed their heads during the brief grace, which ended as Bingham commended the queen to God's mercy.

They ate in the style of the *luau*, with everyone reaching freely for what they wanted.

"Captain Blanchard, I am surprised," said Clarity. "You never mentioned that you had a wife."

"Mrs. Putnam, you never asked."

"Where does she live?"

"When we rounded Kohala, you saw an island on the northern horizon. That is Maui. The next island beyond that is Molokai, and that is my home."

"How charming! What is her name?"

"Ha! Her name has about thirty-five syllables, and I cannot pronounce it, so I call her Lucy."

"You have a native wife, then?" A glance across the cargo hatch revealed Hopu eavesdropping with a look of something like vindication.

"I do. I hope that does not bring down your New Englandish disapproval."

"On the contrary, my only thought is to wish you great happiness."

After half an hour the gathering fell silent at the issue of a scorching eruption from the queen, directed at Karaimoku, who was seated by her. He seemed to shrink within himself, and Clarity was dumbfounded by the change that came over the queen. Where all had been perfect amiability there sat a quarter ton of immovable, implacable harpy pouring out a torrent of invective in the native language, too fast for them to catch, on her first minister, who answered softly and in few words.

The storm passed, but the queen said nothing more to Karaimoku until she departed, lowered with a wave in the bosun's chair as her attendants climbed down the ladder. Karaimoku was the last to leave, not before Bingham made his way to him. "Mr. Prime Minister, we are greatly distressed that we might have done something to offend the queen. Please, can you enlighten us and tell us how to repair the damage?"

"No. No, no." Karaimoku paused at the boarding gate. "It was not about you at all. The queen invited my brother to join us. He said he would come in his own canoe, but he did not. You must understand that my brother is the high chief Boki of Oahu. He is, as one English officer described him, the black sheep of the family. He has no love for the queens, nor they for him. He did not consent to the end of the old religion, but he did not fight because he knew that side would lose. He dislikes Europeans, he is cruel to his people, but he is powerful because he is close to the king, whom he supplies with rum and whiskey, which he buys of the Europeans." He gave Bingham a moment to take all this in. "Did you really think you had arrived in paradise?"

Bingham harrumphed with a smile. "I thank you for your candor."

"It will be a few days before you may land. There is much to prepare. And now I must take Hopu and Tamoree with me again. The queen will question them more about you."

For a week the *Thaddeus* rocked at anchor, kept in food by natives who rowed up to trade, which was itself a hopeful sign that they had not been forbidden to do so. Blanchard had a tarpaulin rigged over the well deck for shade, from where the company observed sea turtles paddle by, and occasionally spied the blow of a whale out to sea.

When Karaimoku came back, it was a morning of light rain show-ering down, never heavy nor constant. He was dressed in a tidy black suit, with white shirt and cravat, as though he might have been a banker or lawyer, with the single exception that his feet were bare. What they took for native artlessness, the company realized might ac-tually have been by design, for after the canoe tied on he ascended the boarding ladder far more nimbly than he could have done in shoes.

Blanchard shook hands with him. "We are glad to see you, Mr. Pitt. We began to fear you had forgotten us."

"Not at all. Their Majesties have been much occupied with state affairs. Chiefs have come from many islands to make their allegiance to the new king, and matters must be discussed with each of them. However, it is their pleasure to receive you on this evening."

"Oh, good gracious," erupted Bingham. "No more notice than this?"

"More rain is coming. May we speak in your cabin?"

Karaimoku stood at the head of the table, Captain Blanchard sit-ting close by, and the entire company crowding the compartment. "I tell you in honesty there has been difficulty. Some people are talking against you, that you will bring strange ways that we will not like, and that you are dangerous. Boki my brother is one, and he is against all foreigners, but there are others, even other white people like your-selves. Some of them have spoken against you."

Blanchard waved a hand in the air. "Well, hell, I know who that is. I'll bet it's old Johnny Young, is it not?"

Karaimoku looked at him in surprise. "It is he. Do you know Mr. Young?"

"Who does not? I would have thought he would be dead by now; he must be about eighty. Folks, the story there is that Mr. Young was an English sailor taken captive by the old king over thirty years ago.

He was given a choice between teaching the king about modern military tactics and weapons, most especially cannons, and training his army, or be taken into a temple and sacrificed to the gods. Being a sensible man, he chose the former. His tutelage is the main reason that old Ta-meha-meha was able to conquer everybody else. The old king rewarded him with land, power, and high-ranking wives, over all of which he is as jealous as an old dog over a soup bone. The prime minister will correct me if I have done him an injustice."

"He fought well for the king and deserved his rewards, but I know also that he tells things his own way. And it is true that he promotes the English interest over the American. He knows better than to lie to the king or his minister, but his truth is British. But all this aside, it has pleased Their Majesties to receive you on this evening, at court."

"I say again, this is rather sudden," Bingham protested. "Am I expected to make them a sermon, a reasoning for our faith and our mission?"

Karaimoku raised his hand and shook his head. "You will not speak, but I think you will be told a day when you can speak. It will not be a *luau*; eat your dinner before I come for you. Wash yourselves, and wear your best clothes. Have a mind what you will say if you are called upon. Do not approach until you are recognized and beckoned by the king, at which time I will present you. I will come back for you at sunset."

As soon as he had gone, the women set water to heating in the galley, enough for a basin of it in each cabin. In their berth Clarity and Muriel scrubbed vigorously. "Well"—Muriel smirked—"the suddenness of it all may prove a blessing if Mr. Bingham has not the time to work up a mighty sermon."

Clarity agreed, but they were interrupted by raised voices from the

Chamberlains in the next berth. They could not hear distinctly but understood that Jerusha was refusing to take her children ashore.

The bay was calm as glass when the sun disappeared over the horizon, leaving in its wake strands of orange and violet clouds; they saw the bright twinkle of torches ashore and through their glasses observed that an arbor had been raised and people were gathering. Kara-imoku reappeared, this time in a double canoe with a deck lashed between them, and accompanied by Hopu and Tamoree, now bare of foot and chest and wrapped in tapa.

Bingham was the last to descend the ladder and stared at them as though he had never seen men's nipples before. "Gentlemen, I am sorry to see you thus clad."

"On this night, Reverend," said Tamoree, "it will be better for Hopu and myself to stand with you as one of them, not as though we have forsaken our people and become one of you. A little humility on your part will also have a good effect."

Hidden in the folds of their dresses, Muriel reached out and squeezed Clarity's hand, certain that the rest of the company shared their amazement at Tamoree's transformation into a lord of his people and heir to an island kingdom. "It is well," he continued, "for Kanui and Honoree to be dressed as you. Among us we can show the bridge between our two worlds."

"Yes," Bingham agreed. He was uncertain at how to react at having been set so straight, but trusted in Tamoree's guidance. "I am glad that you have thought this through."

The great double canoe shuddered as it slid up onto the beach; a wide plank was raised up to it to allow the company to descend to the sand without getting their feet wet. Sybil Bingham, who seldom spoke, took steps small and unsteady. "Gracious," she swore, "the land is not moving! I feel as though I am still swaying with the ship. How very queer and unsettling. Captain Blanchard?"

He laughed loudly. "Remember, ma'am, this is the first you have set foot on dry land in over five months. It will take a while for your sea legs to get accustomed, but they will."

Karaimoku led them up the beach to the line of green grass and into the scent of flowers that were new and strange to them. Under the arbor of palm fronds were lined up three chairs in the style of Louis XIV. There was a sort of clearing before them, with a throng of people standing in an irregular circle, one or two of whom came forward into the royal presence when called to receive a greeting or answer a question.

"These are all chiefs and persons of quality," said Karaimoku.

"No common people?" asked Bingham.

"Commoners do not come to court. Now we wait. You see the king on the center throne." It was apparent even from their distance that the one he referred to, who was wearing an English officer's uniform, was intoxicated almost to the point of fainting dead away. He laughed at everything in a high, rasping cackle, seeming insensible to the various representations made to him, which instead were answered and disposed of by Kahumanu, who sat at his left. "On his left is the *kuhina nui*, whom you know. On his right is his queen, whose name is Kamamalu."

"And what a queen she is," breathed Clarity. "My word!"

Karaimoku overheard her. "English officer measured her once. Six feet, seven inches tall, and very strong. Behind the king you see my brother, High Chief Boki, whose absence caused the row last week on your ship. By him you see his wife, Liliha."

"Yes," said Clarity. "Remarkable." They would have stood out at any gathering, she thought. He appeared to be in his mid-thirties, brown-skinned but almost Western in his features, even handsome in a self-possessed, haughty way. At intervals, when different people came forward to transact with the king and queens, Boki would lean forward and whisper something that would amuse the king, and three times while they waited, Boki signaled to a servant to come forward and fill the king's silver cup from a bottle with the long neck and round bole that even the missionaries knew to be rum.

Liliha beside him, her hand threaded through his arm, leaning on him, was much younger, perhaps twenty, and whereas the royal ladies wore Western dresses, she wore a skirt of native tapa, her breasts exposed, large and round and full, and Clarity saw in an instant how she held her shoulders back to show them to their best advantage. It was well that Karaimoku called her Boki's wife, for in any gathering she would have been seen as a courtesan, and a successful, laughing one.

"Wait here." When there seemed to be no further business, but still the king gave them no sign, Karaimoku strode into the clearing before the gilt chairs, speaking out of their hearing to the royal persons. Karaimoku stood aside even as it was apparent that the king had nodded off to sleep. After an embarrassed moment it was Queen Kamamalu who took the initiative. She reached over, took hold of and raised her husband's limp arm in greeting, and bending his elbow beckoned the missionaries forward. She let his arm fall in his lap as she whispered some witticism in his ear that made him giggle in his sleep, and she paid him no further mind.

"*Aloha*," intoned Kahumanu. "You are welcome, you who bring the word of God. Mr. Bingham, it is our pleasure that on next Sunday you and your company shall come to this *lanai* and preach to us the message you bring."

"We are grateful for such an opportunity, ma'am."

"Do not be grateful yet. I do not promise that you can stay, only to hear what you have to say, and then the chiefs will discuss it."

"I understand, ma'am."

"Your ladies, however, may stay to make me the dresses they promised." There was a ripple of laughter. "Later on this night they will have my permission to measure me. Now, Hopu has told me that one of you has come with a special purpose. Mrs. Putnam, come forward!"

Clarity was surprised and apprehensive, but now was no time for timidity. She approached and curtsied. *"Ka mea kamahao, ka moi wahine."*

*"Mahalo.* Mrs. Putnam, no doubt you have been told that we are a savage people."

The flash of fear and uncertainty must have been plain to read on her face.

"Tut-tut, woman. Do not be afraid; you may speak freely."

"That has been the opinion of some, Your Majesty, but I learned early in life not to believe everything that is told to me."

"Heh! A very wise doctrine. Now you have met us, what is your opinion?"

This was her first close look at the queen in state, and her attention was drawn to a thick braided necklace of what appeared to be human hair. "Ma'am, I think that the delicious food you have provided us, and your gracious hospitality, speak eloquently that you are not at all savage."

"Heh! Well done. Now Mrs. Putnam, I am told that you have come with these others on an errand that is different from theirs."

"Majesty?"

"Hopu and Tamoree tell me that, at your home, you had a friend from our islands who grew sick and died. He asked of you if you would visit his family and tell them that he loved them and was thinking of them."

"Yes, ma'am, his uncle and his grandmother."

"Hewa-Hewa, step forward!" Advancing two steps from the crowd of courtiers appeared an old man, his hair white but ample and wild, his nose hooked, and dark eyes fierce, and his neck hung with amulets that dangled in the hollow of his chest. "This is the chief priest of the old religion, who has consented that it should be put away. Your friend Opukaha'ia, whom you called Henry, was known to our priests. Hewa-Hewa tells me that this uncle, who was *kahuna* to the storm god, fought in the battle to keep the old religion and was killed. But his mother, who is the grandmother to Henry whom you seek, does still live at Kearakekua. Kapiolani, step forward!"

There advanced from the crowd an ample, middle-aged woman, whom Clarity recognized as the one the company beheld sunning herself on the rocks a few days before. "This is Kapiolani, High Chiefess of Kona. We give her our commission to conduct you to the grandmother of your friend. This is a journey of three days, and three days to return. Mrs. Putnam, will you agree to undertake this?"

Such an adventure, so soon after landing, was almost too much to have hoped for. "Oh, yes, ma'am, with all my heart." She faced the chiefess and curtsied, but not so deep as to the queen. *"Ka mea ki-eki-e,"* she said, using the term for highness, short of majesty.

"How do you do, Mrs. Putnam."

"I believe we saw you a few days ago, ma'am, at the beach."

"Ha!" Kapiolani straightened herself and tossed her head a little. "Well, I beg your pardon, I was not dressed for company."

Clarity burst into a laugh, at which the chiefess laughed, showing white, even teeth. "Good!" boomed the queen. "You shall be friends. But, Mrs. Putnam, Hopu has told me that you are with child, and that such a journey might not be wise. Do you feel able to undertake this?"

"Majesty, I am grateful for your concern, but let me assure you that I am able, and indeed eager, to visit Henry's grandmother."

"You are very tiny. Can you have a child?"

"Ma'am, the women in my family are more resilient than we appear."

"Where is your husband?"

"My husband, ma'am, is a captain in my country's navy. He will be here soon in his own ship, to bring you America's greetings and goodwill."

"Heh! Mr. Bingham brings us the love of God, and your husband will bring us the love of your country. We feel well beloved." The queen harrumphed deeply. "Well, Mr. Bingham, you see the way of it. Do you approve that Mrs. Putnam shall make this journey?"

"Mrs. Putnam's zeal for the Lord, ma'am, is equal to anyone's. If she feels able, I can but wish her godspeed."

"Wonderful! Then it is settled. Get off, now. Come see me when you return."

## { 8 }

## *Missy La Laelae*

As Clarity and Kapiolani left the court together with Blanchard, Clarity turned over in her mind how the queen as well as Karaimoku must have learned their English from British sailors, for it was sprinkled with their slang: "tut-tut," "horse of a different color," "You see the way of it . . ."

"I have horses," said the chiefess, "and guesthouses, and servants. You will not find it a difficult travel."

"Chiefess Kapiolani, I gather you wish to leave at once?" Blanchard asked.

"Yes. It is not so far to my first house. It will not be too late when we arrive."

"Then, ma'am, while you are putting your train together, I can take Mrs. Putnam back out to my ship and she can gather some things she will need."

"That is very helpful, Captain, thank you." As Blanchard and Clarity descended to the beach, she looked over her shoulder a few times to see no fewer than a dozen horses brought together and packs and parcels began to be apportioned among them, and she realized what state a high chiefess traveled in. By the time Blanchard brought her back, the train was packed and waiting on her, with one horse only lightly burdened so as to receive her portmanteau.

From the palm-fringed shore at Kawaihae, the chiefess's steward took the lead of her lengthy caravan. Kapiolani and Clarity rode immediately behind him in the finest English sidesaddles, followed by two female servants.

"You are very well attended, Chiefess," said Clarity.

"In your language," said Kapiolani, "I think you call them ladies-in-waiting. Why are they called that? Is it because they must wait for me to tell them what to do?"

"Not exactly, ma'am. In English, the word 'wait' has two meanings. One is to wait for, as in 'to wait for me to return from the ship.' The other meaning is to wait upon, which means to serve. Ladies-in-waiting means ladies who serve."

"I see. Thank you."

The ground rose by degrees away from the sea until they reached the foot of a high hill that was crowned with the enormous stone platform that marked Kawaihae from the sea. She judged it more than two hundred feet long, with walls perhaps twenty feet high and what appeared to be a watch tower at the near corner. In the dying sunlight the edifice glowed deep red against the darkening sky. "What a remarkable structure," said Clarity. "Is it a fortress of some kind?"

The train turned south to follow along the foot of the hill. "Do not ask this just now." There was a telltale change of timbre in her voice.

"Chiefess, are you all right? Is it the sight of that old ruin? What is it?"

"Look well upon that pile of rocks, and I will tell you when we are away from this place."

"I am very sorry to have upset you, Kapiolani. I should not have asked about it."

"No, Mrs. Putnam, your question was natural. You shall be satisfied anon." The night deepened, relieved by torch bearers preceding them and following them. After an hour they reached a small compound of *pilis*, the native grass houses, at Waialea Bay. As soon as Kapiolani dismounted, her retainers went into what seemed like a well-rehearsed routine, lighting a fire, arranging mats to sit on, and removing baggage into a couple of the houses, which surrounded a small and irregular courtyard. Clarity observed her own portmanteau being carried into a subsidiary house next to a very large one. The chiefess herself helped Clarity off her horse and said, "We shall have tea, and some supper, before we retire."

From the large house emerged a matronly woman of perhaps fifty, wrapped in stenciled native cloth, who advanced and embraced Kapiolani warmly. "Mrs. Putnam, this is my friend Kinoiki. She maintains this one of my households for me."

"I am so pleased to meet you." Clarity extended her hand and the woman took it.

"*Aloha*, Mrs. Putnam, you are welcome here. We have prepared this guest house for you, if you would care to refresh yourself before supper."

"That is most needful, and timely. Please excuse me, and thank you." In it Clarity found the ground laid with straw mats, and it was furnished with a small table with a basin and pitcher of water, a ceramic chamber pot with a lid, what looked like a Hepplewhite chair, a rack on which to hang her clothes, and a bed on a low frame made up with sheets and a blanket.

By the time she returned, she saw that mats had been laid on the ground before the fire, and a mahogany table set nearby laden with a tea service in chased silver. She observed Kapiolani pouring tea through a strainer into the pot, and then in a practiced way pouring tea into a cup of bone china and placing the cup in a matching saucer and a light yellow tea cake on a plate. "Please be seated," said the chiefess, and handed the tea and cake down to her.

Clarity sampled it. "Great heavens! How did you acquire such excellent tea? And tea cakes?"

Kapiolani heaved a great sigh as she eased herself onto the ground with her own tea and cake. "Ah, the tea cakes are easy. I am, as you would say, very rich. As you see, we live simply, but no fear. I can buy anything I need. Our climate is not good for growing wheat, but my stewards purchase flour from traders who call."

"I see."

"Are you rich, Mrs. Putnam?"

Clarity laughed at her artlessness. "Yes, I guess I am, but I left most of my money at home, to care for my mother and for my husband's parents."

"Good. That is well done. Now, the tea—that was another matter! The English brought tea with them, and of course they trade in China for it. But once we acquired a taste for it, they did not want us to get accustomed to the best kinds, so they sold us only the lesser quality."

Clarity nodded. "Yes, I understand. Our experience was, they felt the same way about our political rights."

"Ah, yes," laughed Kapiolani. "I have heard this. But once we bought good tea from others, and bought no tea at all of the English, they changed their view."

"Quite right! Good for you."

"My chiefess," said Kinoiki, "I believe you will wish to know the news, that *kahuna* who caused you so much pain at Kawaihae, he is now an old man, and he has just come to live in this district."

Kapiolani's face changed to a stony intensity, the same almost alarming flexibility of expression that Clarity had noted in the queen. "Why did I not know this?"

"Chiefess, he lived at his temple until this year, when the queens, and you, and the other high chiefesses put away the old religion. Only since then has he come to stay with his relations here. Why do we not end this discord now, and send for him?"

"Yes!" she snapped. "Send for him right now. Bring him to me." Clarity saw Kinoiki give an instruction to a runner—one of her own household, not Kapiolani's, for he would know where the old priest would be found.

It was tension that needed to be broken until he arrived. "Chiefess, may I ask you something?"

"Yes."

"It is about how you put away the old religion. When I was in school, I studied a great deal of history, from all periods of time. Sometimes one country will conquer another and force people to change their religion, and sometimes a new idea will come about and start a new religion. But never until now have I heard of people just saying, 'We are tired of this, we have had enough.' Can you tell me how it happened?"

"It is a long story. More tea?"

"Yes, thank you very much." She held out her cup.

"Our religion, the old gods, were very ancient. We brought them with us when we came here centuries ago."

"Where did your people come from?"

Kapiolani shrugged. "It must have been from Kahiki or those other places south of here. There is nowhere else to have come from. The *kahunas* ruled our lives for centuries. To break *kapu* was death; there was no other punishment, at least for the common people. Then, when white Europeans came, and then more and more of them, we saw that they broke *kapu* all the time. Nothing happened to them. No idols came to life to kill them, no tidal wave swept them away, no volcanoes swallowed them up. The great queens saw that *kapu* was of no benefit to the people, that it was all silly."

"I see."

"The *kahunas* all supported the old king, but when he died the queens made Hewa-Hewa, the chief priest, agree that its time was passed, and they announced it at the installation of the new king. Most chiefs and priests accepted this, but some few made ready for battle. They were led by the old king's nephew. If he won and Reho-Reho was killed, he would be king instead. His wife also fought; she was the sister of Karaimoku."

"So, in one sense, the battle was about religion, but really it was about the same old struggle for power?"

"Yes. There was a terrible battle. Karaimoku led the queens' army. Hundreds of the rebels were killed, including his sister."

"That must have been very hard for him."

"It was. But since then we have freedom of religion. People may respect the old gods, or worship the Christian god, or have no god. We do not interfere."

"That is very surprising; that is the last thing I would have expected to find here. In my country, we are very proud of ourselves for having freedom of religion, and here you know all about it already!"

"Yet, you have come to preach the new religion."

"To preach, yes, but not to force or compel people to accept it. Christianity is a religion of love and service. In past centuries, some Christian kings and leaders forgot themselves and forced obedience, but they were wrong to do so."

"It is a brave and good thing to admit when a religion goes wrong. That is why I have so much respect for Kahumanu. You have not met the queen mother, Kepurani?"

"No, not yet."

"I am not surprised. She is so high, few people are allowed into her presence." Kapiolani pushed herself up to her feet. "And now—no, keep your seat—I am going to see how Kinoiki is doing with our supper."

When she returned, during the hour that it took the runner to return, they visited, and Clarity learned that Kapiolani was married to a powerful warrior chief named Naihe, that she governed her own lands, but her union with him made them a formidable family. As a woman with her own means, she also had lovers whom she felt not the least embarrassed to include as part of her household. Similarly to Henry Obookiah, but some years earlier, she was a toddler when she was nearly killed during Ta-meha-meha's war of conquest. Family servants left to care for her were routed in a raid and threw her into a clump of bushes as they fled. She was left for dead but rescued by an aunt.

"Truly, Chiefess, your story says a very great deal about life on this island in those old days. I am sorry that you suffered so much."

Kapiolani grew thoughtful. "I have not understood how chiefs of my rank, who have all they need, who govern hundreds or even thousands, can be greedy for more. Some are cruel to their people, such as the brother of Karaimoku, or even Karaimoku himself in earlier days. Surely we have a duty to care for those beneath us."

"That is part of the message we have come to share." Clarity also noted that the chiefess, though kindly disposed to her commoners, did not question her right to govern over them, but realized that was not a point to question so soon.

"And now, Mrs. Putnam, you asked about the temple on the hill above Kawaihae and why it distresses me. The old *kahuna* who is now coming was the source of my distress. You will not understand what we talk about unless I tell you of it. Our old religion was called *kapu*. That means forbidden things."

"Yes. Henry Obookiah told me a little about it."

"Yes. Many *kapus* forbade things to women. One was that for a woman to eat a banana meant her death."

"He mentioned that as well. But I never understood why!"

"When I was a little girl, four or five years old, I was curious about the same thing. How could a banana be evil for women but not for men? I had a pageboy, a sweet boy, who lived in our household to serve me, and one day I ordered him to bring me a banana. He obeyed me, as he was bound to do, but he was followed, and I was discovered. The *kahunas*, the priests, were very angry. They went to my parents and said I should be killed, but because of my young years and high rank, they would spare my life. But I must lose my wealth and become a servant, and must never marry. All this unless my parents gave them someone from their house to sacrifice in my place." Her voice became soft and strained. "So my parents gave my pageboy to the priests. He was my friend and my playmate, but the *kahunas* took him away and we never saw him again."

"How terrible! Do you know what happened to him?"

She shook her head. "No."

After a long silence they heard footsteps, and Kinoiki's runner entered the light from the fire. "High Chiefess, I have brought the man you sought." He was followed into the yard by an old man, a mass of wrinkles but still straight in posture.

"What is your name?" asked Kapiolani.

"Chiefess, I am Po-ele-ele-nui." Clarity understood the name to mean Great Darkness.

"Hmph! How appropriate. Do you remember me from when I was a little girl?"

"Yes."

"I had a pageboy, name of Mau, whom you took from me for my

sin of eating a banana. We never saw him again. I want to know, at last, what became of him."

"High Chiefess, I must tell you that he was taken into the temple at the Hill of the Whale. He was tied to the *kapu* stake and strangled in sacrifice to Kuka-ilimoku."

Kapiolani did not sob, her voice did not shake, nor did she betray any other sign of emotion except for tears that traced their way down her cheeks. "It is as I have always suspected. Mrs. Putnam, that high hill we passed when we left Kawaihae is called the Hill of the Whale, and that great stack of rocks that you took for a fortress was the temple to the war god. Kawaihae is a beautiful place, but I have never taken any pleasure in it, for this reason."

"Perhaps," said Clarity quietly, "now that you know the truth, you can mourn for your friend and let it pass away."

"Kinoiki, stoke up the fire, please, for we are not done."

"What could we do, Chiefess?" protested Po-ele-ele-nui. "Those were terrible times. We were under the command of the king, and it was his order that *kapu* be enforced, to keep the people in subjection."

Kapiolani's glare pierced him. "So you knew that the gods were false even then?"

"The priests have known this always, Chiefess. The old religion was merely a way to control the people."

"And make a handsome living for yourselves!"

"To make them serve the king, and the chiefs, such as yourself."

"Then I am sorry for my part in it. Mrs. Putnam"—she turned to Clarity—"despite what you may think, that you are the first to bring news of your God, that is not the case. We learned of Him through British chaplains and French priests on their ships. We have learned enough to know that if we wish to be forgiven our sins, we must forgive those who have sinned against us. Is this not so?"

"Truly yes, ma'am." Their circle began to be more brightly illuminated as Kinoiki had added logs to the fire.

"Then, Po-ele-ele-nui, I wish you to know that I forgive you. Here is supper coming. Please, sit with us and eat."

"I thank you, Chiefess." Po-ele-ele-nui remained standing. "I have already eaten."

That dark ferocity came over her again. "Wicked old *kahuna*, you will sit, and you will take food, and you will eat with us."

In a flash Clarity remembered, as Obookiah had told her, that under the old religion the sexes eating together was an unthinkable sin, then realized that in her forgiveness Kapiolani was also exacting her revenge, strangling out his last attachment to *kapu* as surely as they had strangled the life out of her little page. Both the weight and the subtlety of her stroke were breathtaking.

Po-ele-ele-nui stared at the ground as he sank to a mat, a space apart, and accepted a plate of pork and sweet potatoes with a small bowl of *poi*. With every bite he chewed she could see his sense of defeat deepen, his certainty that he was betraying everything he had lived for. Kapiolani ended his anguish and dismissed him after forty minutes, and suggested that they all retire.

"Mrs. Putnam, the light from our fire out here should allow you to do what you need," said Kinoiki. "You will understand that we do not encourage the use of candles in houses made of grass."

Clarity's eyes opened wide. "Yes, I quite approve. Thank you for your kind hospitality." She curtsied to Kapiolani. "*Ka mea ki-eki-e.*"

"Pleasant dreams, Mrs. Putnam."

SHE AWAKENED TO a tray of bread and jam and tea. In getting dressed she noticed an itch at the top of her stocking, and upon inspection saw a number of tiny red blisters just at the point where her skin was exposed. She scratched one, causing it to itch and burn more. She determined to not disturb the others and inspected the edge of the bedding where it had touched the ground. She would not have noticed the tiny black dot on the quilt if it had not moved a tiny space and then disappeared. "Fleas?" she whispered. "Oh, my God."

She made her toilette and dressed as quickly as she could, shaking out each garment vigorously, including a shawl that she wrapped around her shoulders against the morning chill. Upon entering the courtyard she discovered the horses already saddled. Kapiolani exited the large house in a fresh new dress. "Good morning, Mrs. Putnam, did you sleep well?"

She curtsied. "Very well indeed, thank you, Chiefess."

"Well, let us be up and doing. Are you prepared to resume?"

"Of course." As she mounted she looked back and saw a man carrying her portmanteau to a pack horse. She resolved to die before she would mention the fleas. "Kapiolani, may I ask you something?"

"My, your curiosity also awoke well rested, but this is a good thing. What is it?"

"When my friends and I first arrived, we saw the other side of the island. It was green; there were streams and waterfalls, and mountains of jungle. Why do so many chiefs gather here, where it is hot and dry?"

"The chiefs are all from different places, but they gathered here to honor the new king. But to answer your question: You saw the forest and the streams?"

"Yes. They were beautiful."

"Yes. And where do you think the water comes from, for those streams and the forest?"

"Well, the rain, I suppose."

"Ah! And in what activity was I engaged when first you saw me?"

"Um, you were sunbathing, ma'am."

"Correct! And how enjoyable would it be to lie out in the rain?"

"Ha! Yes, yes, I see. Well, may I say? I am sorry that last night it must have been painful for you to speak to that man."

"It will pass. It is better to know what happened."

As on the day before, the steward led their train as they continued southward. By degrees the ground inland to their left rose higher until Clarity realized it was the shoulder of a great mountain; the morning sun had not reached its western slope, and she pulled the shawl tighter around her. "Does this mountain have a name?"

"Surely. It is the volcano Hualalai."

"Volcano? It isn't going to erupt, is it?"

Kapiolani turned in her saddle. "No. I have given instructions."

Kapiolani's expression was just droll enough to show she was joking, and Clarity laughed heartily. The path widened as they entered a grassy vale, and they rode abreast. "But there is still something that I do not understand, from what we spoke of yesterday. For what reason would it have been forbidden for women to eat bananas? It seems so trivial; it makes no sense to me."

"The *kapu* was so ancient no one remembers, but in my opinion you have noticed that bananas look like that part of a man which is his great pleasure."

"Oh, my!" Instantly Clarity regretted having put the question to her.

"I think maybe, in those older times, men saw women eating bananas and became frightened of what else they might want to bite off."

"Oh, for goodness' sake! Well! All I can say is, only a man would think that a woman would think that it looked good to eat."

When the chiefess made no reply, Clarity looked over and saw her shaking so hard, she was holding her saddle pommel with both hands to keep from falling off, until finally she inhaled deeply and shrieked in laughter, and the valley they were riding through rang with it. At length she regained her composure. "Well, surely we are from different worlds. I know that my race are more frank about such matters than your race. You may find that my people are more willing to give up their gods than their pleasure."

Full light of day found them riding through a dry forest and then down through another sun-spattered dell that resounded with flute-like bird calls. "This is remarkable," said Clarity at last. "I have never been so far from home that every tree, every bush and flower, every bird and its song, I am seeing and hearing for the first time. Your country is beautiful."

Kapiolani was clearly pleased. "We think this also."

"These large trees that we see: some grow straight and tall, some have branches that are gnarled and twisted. What is it called?"

"That is the *koa*; it is our boldest tree, and the word means fearless or warrior. The great bowls in which our *poi* is served is made from its wood."

"Yes, I have seen them. They are beautiful, as much works of art as serving bowls. Tell me, where are the sandalwood trees, which have become such an article of commerce?"

"They are deeper in the forest, but there are not so many as there once were."

"Yes, that would follow, wouldn't it?"

"Some chiefs have cut all they have, so there are places where there is no sandalwood left at all."

"You have not done this?"

"No. Before he died, the old king saw what was happening and laid a *kapu* against cutting the small sandalwood trees, so that there would always be more growing. After he died, the new king and his retainers, such as Boki, have cut all that they can to get all the money they can. The ship captains have advanced them great amounts of money to deliver sandalwood in the future, but more of them have none left, and they are greatly in debt with no way to pay."

"I see. So then sandalwood would not be a wise investment for a newcomer."

Kapiolani reined her horse to a dead stop and stared at her. "I thought you came here to share the word of God."

"I did, and to be near my husband, who is coming on his ship. However, I believe that being kind to the poor is a virtue. Being poor is not a virtue."

"Ha! That is true enough." She flicked her reins and they walked on. "There may still be enough sandalwood for a small venture, but do not depend upon it. And take care, Mrs. Putnam, that your people do not become like sandalwood."

Clarity pondered this for a moment. "You mean expensive and fragrant?"

Kapiolani smiled. "No. Come, I will show you." She gave orders to one of her retainers, most of which Clarity did not understand, and he galloped ahead of them, into a patch of forest higher up the mountain slope than they were.

He led them to a tree perhaps twenty feet tall, with a bush-like crown of leaves that were thick, waxy-looking emerald-green ovals, and a trunk surprisingly thick for being so short. Next to it, sprouting seemingly from the same square foot of ground, was a *koa* tree of about the same size but desiccated and almost leafless.

"Do you see?" Kapiolani pointed. "The sandalwood gets its start by sucking off the life from the larger tree, which must eventually die. The sandalwood grows by killing that which gives it life."

"I believe I take your meaning, Chiefess. Thank you for showing me this."

It was another day to reach Henry's grandmother in her village on the bay of Kearakekua, among the bushes and low trees that found root in the crevices of a lava shelf that lay as flat as a wharf at the water's edge. When they arrived, Kapiolani led her onto it, to a white stone with a cross chiseled into it. "You may be interested," she said. "This is where the great Captain Cook fell."

"Really?" Clarity looked about a mile across the bay to a similar brushy forest, but with the addition of a beach, and looked high up on her left at a looming cliff a thousand feet high. "Isn't that beautiful?"

"You see beauty," said Kapiolani. "I see the place where they cast off women who ate bananas."

"Like poor Henry's aunt?" She grew faint at the thought of being pushed from such a height.

"This was the place. Listen, now. When you meet his grandmother, do not enter her house, and do not sit on her mats. I have stools for us to sit on."

"Why? Is that considered rude?"

"No. I am sorry to tell you that the common people are all infested with lice. It will be well to take her by the hand, but do not embrace her."

They returned to the village, and as they approached the *pili* Clarity saw that it was tiny, the whole house smaller than her bedroom in Litchfield. Everything about Henry's grandmother when she came out evinced her poverty: the dirty tapa in which she was wrapped, the cast-off blouse with which she covered her wizened dugs. But there was a kettle by the fire, and some tin cups, and she served them tea as Kapiolani's steward unfolded the stools for them to sit on.

With Kapiolani helping her still-elementary Hawaiian, Clarity explained Henry's life in America, the beloved place that he made for himself there, his brilliance in translating the holy book from the ancient language straight into their own, to share with them. To all of it the old woman listened with what Clarity believed were the softest eyes she had ever seen, eyes that shed tears as she described the serenity of his death. At length Clarity produced a small case, which she opened to reveal two silver cuff links, with a design engraved on them that she explained was the initial of the name he was known by, Henry, and gave them to her.

Clarity was certain that she recognized the tea, and realized that Kapiolani had sent it ahead so that Henry's grandmother might have something to offer them. And when they left, she heard the chiefess instruct her steward to make sure that Henry's grandmother had enough to eat, and to maintain her.

Word of their return to Kawaihae preceded them, and Reverend Bingham met her at the beach. "Sister Putnam, I am rejoiced at your safe return. How was your journey?"

"Useful in so many ways, thank you."

"Did you meet Obookiah's grandmother?"

"Yes. She was touched deeply that we sought her out."

"Well, nations are won to the Lord by such small steps." Clarity looked out into the bay and saw the *Thaddeus*, which had not moved a yard. Bingham continued, "Mrs. Putnam, I must tell you that progress here has been mixed. I preached a sermon to the chiefs, which they heard respectfully, and they questioned me closely about its meanings and our intentions. They have agreed to disperse us among the various islands, in the care of the chiefs; you, and Sybil and I, Mrs.

Albright, and the Chamberlains and the Loomises are to go to Honoruru, where you may await your husband."

"Oh, thank goodness!"

"However, we reached a positive impasse on the subject of preaching to the common people. I surmise that the chiefs are accustomed to having the best of everything, and intend to keep heaven to themselves as well. I have not been able to overcome this as yet, but even they are so intrigued at the possibility of eternal life, they are allowing us to stay for the time being. Come, the queen has ordered to see you immediately upon your return."

They found her sitting in the palm frond lanai, attended by her four ladies and Kapiolani already with her, and Blanchard and George Tamoree. Boki and Liliha, strangely, were also in attendance. "Aloha, Mrs. Putnam," called out Kahumanu. "The high chiefess Kapiolani has reported to me that you carried through your duty with the grandmother of Opukaha'ia with grace and kindness. This pleases me very much."

"I thank Your Majesty." She approached and curtsied. "I was glad to meet her and have the opportunity to tell her what a fine man, what a kind and brave man, her grandson grew into, and that when he came to die he was in perfect peace, and was thinking of her and how good she had been to him."

Much affected, Kahumanu swallowed. "Did she weep?"

"Yes, ma'am, she did weep, but I believe that sweet tears were mixed in with the bitter ones."

"Tell me, what did you learn from this?'

Clarity reflected for a moment. "Perhaps I learned that when someone we love has left us, the loss is easier to bear if we learn how much he loved us in return."

"Mrs. Putnam, has Mr. Bingham told you of our pleasure to send you to Honoruru to await your husband, and minister to the people there?"

"Yes, ma'am. Thank you."

"It is our desire to keep Dr. Holman and his wife with us for the time being. However, we lords come to Kawaihae for rest and pleasure. Before he died, my husband had two capitals, this and Lahaina, but because Honoruru has the most trade and the best harbor, he determined to make that place his one capital. It is our determination to move the court to Honoruru to govern our foreign relations, so as your time draws near to have your baby, Dr. Holman shall be at hand for you."

"You are most kind, Majesty."

"Not so kind: you can continue making dresses for me of your Boston chintz!"

Clarity laughed easily. "I will be happy to, ma'am."

"We have given Captain Blanchard our commission to return Tamoree here to his home on Tauai. You will sail with him, and Mr. Blanchard will leave you and the others at Honoruru as he passes by. Boki and Liliha bear my command to see to your comfort and safety." Liliha still evinced the shifting posture of a seductress, clinging to her husband's arm as the badge of her office, taking amusement in the foreigners who stared at the breasts she refused to cover, and that in itself registered all of her opinions about God and missionaries. "Boki is the brother of our trusted prime minister, and high chief on Oahu. We have made him responsible for your safety and well-being."

*And he is also the black sheep of the family,* Clarity remembered darkly, but she had the presence of mind to curtsy to them. *"Ka mea ki-eki-e."* Boki looked at her impassively, but Liliha nodded to her.

"Mind you," the queen said clearly, "we do not know how long you may stay. Your visit is . . . they tell me the word is 'probationary.' You may have been told that Mr. Bingham and I had a lively talk about who may hear this preaching. We lords are responsible for the happiness of our people; thus we govern what they may learn, and keep from them what may upset or disquiet them. Mr. Bingham has said they must hear the preaching also."

"Yes, ma'am, I have heard that you had a disagreement."

"What do you think about it?"

"Majesty, all men and women are equal before God, and God commands that His word be told to all. But this does not mean that all men and women are equal. Some men are great warriors, and some are not. Some men, and indeed women, have the intelligence to lead a nation, but most do not. Those who lead nations well deserve the love and obedience of their people, but all people high and low have the right to be treated with justice and kindness. That is the law of our religion, and it is well known to your people also. Kapiolani showed this. Henry's grandmother is very poor, and when we left Kearakekua she told her steward to see that the old woman had enough food and did not want for anything. When I told Kapiolani that this was the very heart of our religion, she was surprised; she said this was the duty of the chiefs to take care of the elderly and the poor. They did not need to be told to do this, for a chief would be ashamed not to do it. Much of our religion you practice already, and I believe it will only strengthen your position to allow the word of God to be heard by everyone."

Kahumanu leaned back and shifted her weight. "We might also say, Mrs. Putnam, that some women make better preachers than men. We will consider all that you have said. Now, since you left us, I have had long talks with your friends Hopu and Tamoree. They tell me that your given name is Clarity, and that Opukaha'ia turned this name into Miss Clear Day, and that this became an endearment between you."

"Yes, ma'am, that is true."

"Henceforward, then, that shall be your name in my court, as my endearment to you, Missy La Laelae."

HONORURU, SANDWICH ISLANDS
MAY 15, 1820

*Dearest Harriet,*

*With fondest greetings, my young friend, your correspondent once again set foot upon land upon the opposite side of the world, after a passage of one day more than five months.*

*This was six weeks ago, and I take advantage of the departure on the morrow of the brig Viper, William Rea, to write and apprise you of events since our parting. She will be bound home, to Providence, and Capt. Rea has promised to forward this so soon as she drops anchor there.*

*Oh, Harriet—is not the vastness of God's creation almost more than the mind can take in? To think, that you are half a year older since I left, and will be another half a year older by the time you read this, and I a year older from today by the time I can read a reply! If these Sandwich Islands were more forsaken, I should feel myself very isolated indeed, but in fact, there are at any time two or three ships in the bay, so there are always new people to meet.*

*Here in Honoruru I have been given a house, which, and you may wonder at this, was built in the native style, of sheaves of grass stitched together. If the Bible tells us that a house built on sand cannot last, can you imagine a house made of grass? Its advantage, however, lies in its very impermanence. The storms and tempests that occasionally strike these islands, they say, are of such force that even* the strongest stone house of New England could not stand against them. Their perfect answer to this is to build houses of such a temporary nature that if one blows away, it can be rebuilt in a day or two.

My nearest neighbor here is a Mr. Marín, a Spanish immigrant who came to these islands many years ago, and has made a place of honor for himself. It seems, he is no less than a wizard in the arts of agriculture. He is beloved of the King for his aptitude in distilling rum and brandy, for which he is made a captain in the royal household. He also brought grapes from Europe and has a small winery, although I cannot attest to its quality. He has introduced fruits new and wonderful to the people here, such as oranges, and a delicately flavored melon called a mangoe. Several years ago he was the first to grow pine apples, a fruit that you know from the carvings on the corner posts of your bed right there in Litchfield, which have come to symbolize hospitality. But my dear, the taste of the real thing is beyond description, and pork roasted slow in its juices will make you imagine the joys of Heaven!

We cannot know how long we are to remain here, for our presence is probationary only. The Queen who holds the most power, whose name is Kahumanu, and her prime minister, who is a mighty and forceful soldier named Karaimoku, are receptive to the gospel—indeed they are baptized Papists, for the French preceded us here. But, they are suspicious what its effects might be upon the common people, who are still recovering from the evils of their native religion, under which many were sacrificed to the pagan gods. Of this I shall write more at a later time.

I expect that our Capt. Putnam is even now on his way to the Pacific, sailing in my very wake, as I hope—for if he does not hasten, he will find me prepared with a very great surprise. This will be news to you as well, that in three months' time, God willing, I shall become *a mother, and our Captain will find our child in my arms! Now Harriet, you must have no apprehension for my safety. One of our company of missionaries, Mr. Holman, is a physician of good education and experience, and many ships that call have surgeons on board, so I shall be as well looked after as if I were at home.*

*Oh, Harriet! Here is something for you to do. I know you will wish to convey this happy news to your father. By all means may you do so, but when you do, tell him not of Dr. Holman, whom he knows, but tell him that I have made the acquaintance of the most charming native sorcerer, who has assured me that he will see me safely through the enterprise. (I should like to see the Reverend's face when you do.) Then you may tell him the true case of the matter. If he scolds you, you may show him my letter, which will admit that I put you up to it. He may also gratify his curiosity by reading its entirety, if he pleases.*

*After the success of my novel about the Barbary War—at which I do still rather blush, but you know me well enough to know that too great modesty from me would be suspect—the publisher was inquiring previous to my departure what I might give him for an encore. Knowing this, you will excuse the inordinate length of this and my future letters to you, which I pray you to keep safe for my return. Then, with you having read and, as I hope, enjoyed them, you may return them to me to refresh my memories of the facts and events for use in my next opus.*

*To the common people we are objects of the greatest curiosity. We must walk a quarter of a mile to a stream in which to wash our clothes, and going and coming, the native women gather, and laugh, and often ask if they may touch us. One scrubbed at my arm quite hard, and I am certain she was curious whether we are painted white, and if our color would rub off! They are shrewd, however, and mischievous, and I can tell you they know how to drive a bargain. We* are always in need of firewood, and when one comes to our door with an arm load of wood, he can act very put out that we offer the going price, and not more for his kindness and trouble. Nor is it any rare occurrence to find ourselves being baldly cheated, no doubt because they believe from our pale skin that we are "pale" of mind as well! When they are found out, though, they laugh and take it in good part, and I am certain the same is expected of us.

The government here is one that any European would recognize. Just as in England, where the king is over the dukes, and the dukes are over the earls: here, the king is over the high chiefs, and the high chiefs are over the chiefs. Until quite recently there existed this one great difference: there was no right of succession. Whenever a king died, there was a general fracas of everyone fighting everybody, until one was left standing. This as you can see made for a very bloody country to live in, indeed this was the circumstance that claimed the lives of our dear departed Henry Obookiah's family.

The last King, whose name was Ta-meha-meha, ended this awful cycle, not by negotiation but by conquest, and he becoming King of all the islands, and his heirs are recognized by all. So, only in the few months preceding our arrival, this became a much safer place in which to live. His victories made the throne safe for his son the new King, whose name is Reho-reho, but he is a drunk and a wastrel whom even his advisors admit is incompetent beyond help. Yet, deposing him would throw the country back into civil war, so his ministers hide him as much as possible, make excuses for him, govern for him, clean up the messes that he makes, and hope for a better future. May God grant that our country should never be in such a condition!

Foreseeing this, the old King placed authority in the hands of Queen Kahumanu. Or more accurately, she was the favorite of his wives who, it is commonly known, numbered nineteen, and she rose to preeminence by being the funniest and most hospitable, but also and most importantly the wisest counselor. Reverend Bingham recognizes the dark side of her nature—she is greatly carnal, she loves having power and can be ruthless in her exercise of it, but he also pronounces her, in her policy and forecast, the equal of the best politicians that Europe or America can offer.

The royal family, and the high chiefs and chiefs, live in great luxury. Their houses may be mere grass, but they are furnished with the most expensive goods that come on ships from Europe, and now from the United States, and they are paid for in a singular way. These islands, while beautiful, possess no coal or iron or other minerals that other nations would trade for. In the forests, however, there grows a tree, the sandalwood, whose wood is beautiful and fragrant, and the ship captains reap a huge profit from selling it in Canton, and they buy as much as the chiefs can whip their people into cutting from the forests. For every chief I would guess that there are a thousand commoners, so you will surmise accurately that sandalwood is the backbone of the Hawaiian economy, much as rice is to our Carolinas.

The people themselves see none of this profit, and live on a subsistence of fruits, and the roots and leaves of a plant called kahlo; for meat they have pork and fish, and—I hesitate to tell you of this but if, as you are considering, you accompany your father to Ohio, you will find it to be true of many Indians as well—their diet extends to the consumption of dogs. None but two of our company admit to having tried the meat of a dog, and they pronounce it palatable if you think not upon its source. I confess that I am not yet up to such an experiment. Mr. Loomis, who is our printer as yet without a press, is one who admits to having tasted this delicacy. When Mrs. Chamberlain asked how he found it, he thought for a moment, growled, and then yapped quite happily! She grew so discomposed that she had to retire from the group. Poor Mrs. C, I cannot imagine a woman less suited to the rigors that we have undertaken. She and her farmer husband were sent here to Honoruru also, I imagine so that he can assimilate the local agricultural arts from Mr. Marín.

Dearest, I must close this first chapter of my Letters from the Sandwich Islands. I will subscribe it in a way to surprise you. The Queen has taken a great liking to me, and when Hopu told her of Henry Obookiah's name for me—Miss Clear Day—she was much delighted, and has bestowed the same name upon me in the native language. And so, farewell from

Your devoted friend,
Missy La Laelae

MISS HARRIET BEECHER
LITCHFIELD, CONNECTICUT

## { 9 }

## *Far Shores*

Bliven found no great joy in spending the winter aboard the grounded *Rappahannock*. He would have thought that the contractors who supplied the Navy with building materials, and who deposited their draughts, would have escaped the effects of what people were calling the Panic of 1819. However, it became a sobering lesson to him on the interconnectedness of the economy that ruin anywhere back up the line disrupted the activity of their carpenters and coopers and coppersmiths.

Michael Miller returned aboard shortly after Christmas, saucy and eager for adventure, giving Bliven someone with whom to share his impatience. Not until the middle of February was the graving dock flooded and the freshly painted sloop of war rocked free of her supporting timbers and eased back into the harbor, high in the water for want of ballast and stores. With her rigging still down, it would have been convenient to push and tow her to space at a wharf, but when those facilities were built the Navy had not calculated upon ships of her twenty-foot draught, and now the bed could not be dredged without undermining the wharf itself. Thus she was towed out to anchorage as close as a falling tide would allow, with a boat always in the water to shuttle to shore. A boat crew came aboard, who would be taken into the crew, so the berth deck was no longer deserted. And then tall old Fleming came with his trunks of tools and a helper, and began turning his attention to building a stock pen in the hold, and a cage to confine chickens, and an extra compartment in which the purser when they got one could sort and store the slops from which the men would buy their clothing. He also at Bliven's order constructed simple sheds over the heads on either side of the bowsprit, not from any consideration of privacy, but if it were true that one could catch one's death of cold, then exposing one's naked privates to the elements at nearly sixty degrees south latitude, where they were bound, only invited disaster.

The growing crew made desirable the acquisition of a cook. In a full crew this was a job that went to some partially disabled old tar, perhaps lamed by a hernia or a sprung back, whose main accomplishment was not to poison the lot of them. Bliven made a point of dining ashore with Miller in different restaurants, and after they consumed a fine dinner at one place or another they would request to pay their compliments to the *chef de cuisine*. Eventually they conversed with one who confessed to both financial and domestic discomfiture, a skilled cook to whom two or three years at sea was an opportunity to seize, and who, importantly, could provide one level of sustenance to the crew but also prepare genuine food for the officers. His name was Burnam, with curly, sandy hair and fair complexion, and round of figure, which was a good sign in a cook. He was articulate and decisive but respectful and, best of all, eager to come.

It caused Bliven and Miller a few seconds' regret to steal him away from his hapless employer, but his willingness eased that, and then his assurance that there was another in the kitchen who could take over for him dispelled their qualms entirely.

The day after she anchored, Edwards's men came aboard. *Rappahannock*'s eighty-foot bowsprit was inserted back to its footing and made secure, and the topmasts replaced. Bliven scrutinized this operation with Miller and the bosun at his side, greatcoats pulled about their shoulders against the cold and bicornes tight down to their ears. "What do you say, Mr. Yeakel? Does she not begin to look like a ship again!"

"Aye, sir. But, Captain, you have mentioned this before: it might be well to wait for the weather to warm up a bit before setting the rigging. There will be less of a difference when we hit the tropics."

"Yes, yes, quite right." Slowly the ship came to life. Hull sent out a chaplain, a Deist from Virginia named Mutterbach, spare of frame with a tightly drawn but pleasant face, and blue eyes that conveyed interest, attention, concern. He shared a dinner with the captain and first lieutenant, who found him intelligent, humble, kind in nature, and educated in the scriptures, but possessed of no dogma. They were unanimous that he would do admirably, and Miller showed him his compartment in the wardroom, between his own and that still-empty one to where they hoped the surgeon would return.

That question resolved itself the day after tall, blond young Lieutenant Rippel came back aboard. Bliven was reading alone in his sea cabin. Three small sharp raps, and Ross entered. "Excuse me, Captain, you will want to know this. Dr. Berend is here." *Rappahannock*'s surgeon followed him through the door without waiting for admittance.

"Dr. Berend, what on earth? We've had no letter." Bliven came around the table and they shook hands tightly.

"Captain Putnam, I will tell you the truth, by the time I decided I should come, my letter would have been slower to arrive here than my person."

"I was just working over tea, but this calls for some celebration. Would you take some sherry, or Madeira?"

Berend waved it off quickly. "Oh, no, no, much too early in the day for that. But I would love some tea, if you have any left."

In his excitement Bliven fumbled the saucer onto the top of the sideboard but it did not break. "Sugar?"

"Ah, yes, please. It is good to be back; I feel suddenly confirmed in the correctness of my decision. By the way, here, take these. The chief quartermaster asked me to bring these out to you: he sends the flags of countries where you may call—Brazil, Argentina, Chile. The European flags of the vessels you may encounter you have already." He handed over a bundle of colored silks, each tagged with the name of its country.

"Brazil has a flag?"

Berend laughed, revealing that he had lost a couple of teeth during the preceding months. "Yes, well, they are in something of a mess, are they not? To be annoyingly precise, this is the flag of the United Kingdom of Portugal, Brazil, and the Algarves; it has been good for maybe three years. But in the state of things just now, they may be independent and have a new flag at any time."

Bliven shook his head. "People are so touchy. If we salute a port and raise the wrong flag, they are like to open up on us, and not in salute."

Bliven handed him the cup and resumed his seat. "I am delighted to see you, but I am surprised that I was able to talk you into leaving what must have been a comfortable situation."

Berend smiled, but it was sad and wan. Bliven was distressed to see him older, his hair thinner and coarser, his liver spots more pronounced. "I thought much the same, but upon reflection, there was little to keep me there." He took a long sip of the sweet tea. "It is a queer estate, to outlive one's family. I do not recommend it for those with sensitive constitutions."

"I can understand that, but I know you, and you must have friends lined up outside your door wanting your society. Not to mention congenial widows who must be keen to entertain a proposal from you."

Berend nodded. "Yes, I have friends, I have been blessed with friends. But when one's family is gone, those affections that had been directed to them must find some new repository, and that naturally bends toward one's friends. But they already have families, and while they like you, they do not return that affection in kind. It is an inequity under which I began to chafe. They like me well enough, they like me warmly, but they do not need me. A man should go where he is needed, and you gave me to believe that I could be needed here."

"And so you are, Doctor, and very much wanted. And now tell me, touching upon this matter of certain medicines that I suggested you might acquire for when we reach the Pacific: Were you able to procure a store of them?"

"All in my baggage. I do think I have brought enough mercurous chloride to cure the whole Pacific of venereal disease. I also had the chance to procure a supply of quondams, but the Navy refused to approve of it. They said that to remove the likelihood of infection was tantamount to giving the men license to vent their immorality with no consequences."

"Well, they have a point."

"No, they don't."

Bliven stared at him in shock.

"Forgive me, Captain, I must remember that I am back in Navy harness. My only business is with the men's health, and you and I both know that seamen cramped aboard a ship for half a year must have relief."

"I suppose."

"The commodore told me that your wife will be waiting for you in the Sandwich Islands, gone there with missionaries."

"That is true."

"Very fortunate for you, but two hundred and forty or fifty men under your command will not have that to look forward to."

"Very well. Where was your request disallowed, Gosport or here?"

"Gosport."

"I will write the purser of the Navy Yard here on your behalf, but do not raise your hopes. Even if the medical benefits are admitted, quondams are so expensive, the Navy will say, Why not just offer the men rooms in the finest hotel for their trysts?"

"I would thank you to write such a letter, and speaking of the same, when I came through the receiving ship I saw your new purser there. You will meet him soon."

Bliven rolled his eyes.

"Now, he didn't seem like such a bad sort. He is in it for the business, of course, as they all are, but he does not seem any more predatory than the rest."

On its next errand the boat brought a third lieutenant, Lennox Jackson, with an alarmingly slight build, straight raven hair over brilliant blue eyes, freckles, and a boyish enthusiasm that made him seem much younger than his twenty-seven years. As Bliven interviewed him he saw out his stern windows a large cutter sweeping toward them crowded with marines in their blue jackets with yards of gold cordage and their tall hard hats. In a few moments Ross rapped his three and entered. "Your lieutenant of marines is reporting, sir."

"Send him in."

The youth that entered was a shock: Bliven had seldom seen such a large young man, over six feet tall and broad in proportion, but of gentle features, with dark blond hair and hazel eyes. Bliven rose to meet him. "Welcome aboard, Lieutenant—"

"Horner, sir, David James."

"Well, Lieutenant Horner, I am mortified that the Navy has not provided you a ship to match your proportions."

He laughed easily. "None of them do, sir."

"My third lieutenant, Mr. Jackson." Those two shook hands. "Do let us sit down before you knock your head on the beams." Bliven had read of the tsars of Russia employing giants as bodyguards; this one would do splendidly.

"My orders, Captain." He handed them across the table.

"How many are you?"

"A reinforced company of fifty, sir, plus two corporals and a sergeant, and myself."

"God Almighty, we are embarrassed for accommodation, Mr. Horner. The berth deck is already going to be packed tight as a barrel of mackerels. I hope you will not mind if we house you forward on the gun deck. It, um, also has the most headroom."

"I appreciate that, sir."

"Where are you from?"

"Salem, sir."

"I see."

"No, sir."

Bliven had been reading his orders and looked up in surprise. "No to what?"

"We have not burnt any witches in some time, sir." He smiled. "Most people ask."

"Ha! On the contrary, Lieutenant, where we are going, I might have found it useful to draw on such experience."

When the purser came aboard, he proved to be a New Yorker of English extraction named Erb, by profession an importer of luxury goods whose business had declined with the times, but whose connections in that world made him widely known and his credit accepted. Bliven reconciled to having him aboard, and told himself to thank Hull for supplying him officers who seemed capable and agreeable to his command.

"Mr. Ross, would you fetch Mr. Miller and ask him if he has completed his list of stores we shall need?"

"Right away, sir."

It took only a moment for Miller to enter and be introduced. "I have finished the requisition for victuals, Captain. I have reckoned on the crew of one hundred and eighty-six officers and men, and fifty marines, for nine months." Miller handed over the paper, and Bliven read through the list: 64,800 pounds of ship's biscuit; 110 barrels each of beef and pork; 35 barrels of flour; 4,250 pounds of cheese; 950 pounds of butter; 108 bushels of beans; 54 bushels of peas; 100 sacks of rice; 250 pounds of raisins; 425 gallons of vinegar; and 3,096 gallons of whiskey.

Bliven looked up at him. "Three thousand and ninety-six gallons of whiskey?"

"Yes, sir."

"Have you calculated this exactly enough? Are you absolutely certain we will not need three thousand and ninety-seven gallons of whiskey?"

Miller consulted the page of figures that he had kept in hand. "One hundred eighteen pints per day for two hundred seventy-three days. Won't do to have a tipsy crew, Captain."

"Hm!" he muttered. He signed the requisition and handed it to the purser. "And so to work, Mr. Erb. Now, I don't know that we can find rice just now."

"Yes," said Miller, "but if we put in at Charleston for powder and shot, we can take on rice there."

"That may be." He had already written to Sam, but he could write again. To purchase a hundred sacks of rice could help him considerably.

With Dr. Berend aboard, crewmen began to arrive daily and submit to his inspection, gauging the clarity of their eyes and soundness of their teeth, trying their muscles. He turned away many that Bliven might have found acceptable, but Berend was able to choose the ablest, for in such trying times there were many who needed work, even a sailor's pay. Yeakel began to set the rigging, and as the web of sheets and lines grew denser, Bliven's pride in the ship swelled. Lighters began tying up, their crews hefting up boxes and crates and packets of slops bought on the new purser's credit: trousers and shirts and shoes by the hundreds; tobacco for smoking at those limited times and locations where it was allowed, or more commonly chewing. Then there were holystones for scrubbing down the yellow pine decks; and chocolate and brandied cherries, liquor, and toiletries for the officers. Alan Ross saw all these come aboard and wondered if he had been foolish to decline this situation when it was offered him; a provident man could probably live out his life on the profits that Erb would reap from this one voyage.

They took on twelve tons of ballast below the hold's decking, and Hull sent them a sailmaker. With studding sails out the *Rappahannock* set some forty-two thousand square feet of canvas, nearly an acre if laid upon the ground, thirty-three discrete sails, each of them cut exactly, hemmed, and punched through with metal grommets. With them were thousands of yards of blank canvas to repair or replace them, for the gales of Cape Horn were famous for making tatters of the finest sailmaker's handiwork. As they feared, they took on neither powder nor shot and were directed to put in at Charleston.

In drawing twenty feet, the sloop's hold was almost as capacious as an orlop, and Berend was satisfied with the roping off of a cockpit, should they get into a fight. Fleming had even built him a table on which to operate, since they would carry only two midshipmen and, in naval tradition, operations were performed on a table formed of midshipmen's trunks. "Gentlemen," Bliven told them while they were below, "it occurs to me that we are a greatly overpopulated ship. You will see that when we take on swine and fowls, we will keep them down here. Fleming has built them stout pens forward there."

"You do know, Captain," said Miller, "on most ships the fowl are kept topside in the fresh air. Besides," he added, "if we get into a battle, perhaps we can have our very own fighting gamecock."

Bliven smiled and considered it for a second. "No, I would not wish for Macdonough to think I am trying to outdo him."

The officers laughed lustily. All knew the story of Macdonough at the Battle of Lake Champlain. When British ships on the lake sank both the vessels under his command, the indomitable Macdonough responded in a matter of weeks—an almost impossibly short time— by constructing a powerful 700-ton corvette, the *Saratoga*, in which he renewed the fight. The first British salvo from the brig *Linnet* broke open the chicken coop, whose resident cock, rather than seek shelter, fluttered from rigging to gun slide and back again, crowing and flapping and scolding defiantly. *Saratoga*'s sailors took such heart that they defeated the *Linnet* with their starboard battery, and then with that side shot to pieces swung at their anchor and defeated HMS *Confiance*, a thirty-six-gun frigate, with their port battery.

"Captain," asked Berend, "have you given any thought as to who you shall designate as the duckfucker?"

Another gust of laughter erupted, the men recognizing that it was an old tradition in the Royal Navy for the seaman who was given care of the ship's fowl to be known by that rude sobriquet. "As I think on it," said Bliven, "I believe I shall defer to the quartermaster's judgment. He can select some man who comes from a farming background."

"Oh, are you not a farmer yourself, sir?" posed Miller.

"I am. However, I have never in my life fucked a duck, and I wish to God I could as solemnly affirm the same about my officers."

Their spirits rose still higher as a sailing day approached. Hull gave Bliven a thick sheaf of orders, in which he kept his promise to repeat the complicated political chessboard of the Pacific, and explain his freedoms of action when left to his own judgment.

It was on April 10, 1820, months after he wanted to be away, that the bars were inserted into the capstan and the anchor was hoisted from only eight fathoms down and made secure to the catheads. As the pilot boat glided by them, Bliven called out, "Mr. Yeakel, set your tops'ls and stays'ls."

"Aye, sir."

Bliven took the wheel himself, cleared the harbor, and, after the pilot turned back, stood out east-southeast for Race Point and then southerly by degrees down the well-known beaches of Cape Cod.

He found himself of two minds about the wind. After sitting so long in port, his natural desire was for one full and following, but if they had to beat down the coast it would not be a bad thing, for Yeakel could begin forging the crew into a unit with the repetition of bracing and wearing. For now, he was content to have the wind at his back. In a voyage south down the whole curve of the globe, it was hardly farther for him to angle across the Atlantic to the African coast—he had always wanted a look at Dakar to see for himself how slaves were stored and embarked—and then cross again the relatively short distance to Brazil, but the necessity to put in at Charleston removed that possibility.

Soon to exit his thirty-fourth year, he had left Boston many times, but never with such a feeling of change coming over him. Departing as a midshipman of fourteen was one quality of emotion; being a lieutenant and knit into the fabric of a crew was a different sensation. This was not the first time he had left as captain of a vessel, yet it was not the same. With the passage of time and the impending death of his father, somehow Connecticut exerted less pull on him, but at last he realized that the great change was that this time he was not leaving everything behind; he was sailing toward something, and the faster he could urge his vessel forward, the sooner he would be reunited with his wife, and everything about his affections and future that she embodied.

Owing to the duration of the cruise, they took on board only two midshipmen, Evarts and Quarles. Most families would not countenance giving up their prepubescent sons to three years of hard life at sea unless they were driven by the ambition to have a latter-day Preble or John Paul Jones among their relations. Or else, and Bliven had to satisfy himself against this point, they might merely be incorrigibles who had to be gotten out of the house. The same could be said, in a smaller way, of the bare minimum of eighteen ship's boys that he carried, bunking far forward on the berth deck where the surgeon and bosun could keep an eye on them, keep them out of mischief, and better secure them from seamen of dubious morals.

Their first morning out, he saw that Rippel had the midshipmen at the taffrail, and drew near enough that they snapped to attention and he bade them carry on. "Now, young gentlemen," lectured Rippel, "it is vital for a crew at sea to be able to measure their speed in order to reckon their position. After today this task will be entrusted to you."

*As far as they know.* Bliven looked away so he could smile upon his memories.

"Mr. Evarts, I hand you this sandglass. In it are precisely twenty-eight seconds of sand. Mr. Quarles, I hand you this length of line. You see at the end of it is a wooden float, and you will see that a knot has been tied in it every eight fathoms. You shall drop the float over the rail, and the instant it hits the water, Mr. Evarts will turn the glass over to mark the time. You shall pay out the line until the sand is exhausted, at which time he will call, 'Mark!' When he does so, you will stop paying out line, and haul the float back in, counting how many knots had gone out, and you will report that number to the officer on the deck. Do you understand?"

"Yes, sir," they said together.

"Very well, let us try it. Mr. Quarles, have enough line in hand that the float can fall all the way down. Mr. Evarts, turn the glass the moment it hits the water. You may proceed."

Quarles cast the line gently, and the wooden chip made a tiny splash, at which Evarts snapped the sandglass on its head.

After a few seconds Rippel shook his head. "No, no, no! You must pay out the line more quickly, otherwise you are merely towing it, and that will show slower than your true speed. Haul it back in and try again."

"I am sorry, sir," said Quarles.

"No matter, I did not make it clear enough. You will get it right this time. Evarts, turn the glass back up."

When the upper part of the glass was drained and ready, Quarles cast it again, paying out line to such slack that the float disappeared rapidly behind them. When the last of the twenty-eight seconds of sand dropped into the lower basin, Evarts called out "Mark!" in his voice that had not yet changed.

"Lieutenant, sir," said Quarles, "do I start counting the distance from where the line was wet from the water, or from what is in my hand now?"

"A very pertinent question, Mr. Quarles, you show aptitude. Count from what is in your hand, for the line extends not straight down, but astern and counts in the distance to be calculated. Continue." Quarles hauled in the dripping line until the float came over the taffrail. "Well, gentlemen, how many knots were betwixt you and the float?"

"Eight, sir."

"And was there a significant length of line paid out until the next knot would have appeared?"

"Yes, sir, about thirty feet. Is that enough to consider half a knot?"

"How far is eight fathoms?"

The boy thought for a moment. "Forty-eight feet, sir."

"It is. Thus our speed is eight and a half knots. Do you see what officer has the deck?"

"Mr. Miller, sir."

"Well, then, go and report our present speed to him." Ordinarily this was one of the quartermaster's duties, to log their speed every hour, but they had discussed it and thought it well for the midshipmen to build a rapport with the lieutenants before resuming the regular order.

The boys advanced to where Miller had a hand on the binnacle. "Mr. Miller, sir?" They saluted, and he returned it gravely.

"Gentlemen?"

"We wish to report our present speed at eight and one half knots, sir."

Miller removed a square of paper from his breast pocket, with a pencil, and wrote it down. "So noted, gentlemen. Thank you."

Rippel had come up behind them. "Now, get you below to your books, both of you. Well done."

"You know, Mr. Rippel," said Bliven, "when I was a midshipman on the *Enterprise*, most of my instruction was entrusted to a lieutenant named Curtis. He was as sorry a waste of humanity as ever drew breath. I took an oath to myself that if ever I rose to command, the ancient practice of abusing cadet officers to indoctrinate them into the Navy should never, not ever, take place on my ship. I hope I may count on you and Mr. Jackson to sustain me in this determination."

"Of course, Captain. Did you feel I was too sharp with them?"

"No, not a bit. Now, Mr. Miller here will be largely occupied with his executive duties, so you and Mr. Jackson may discuss between yourselves which of the midshipmen's courses of study you each feel the better to take charge of."

"Yes, sir."

For days southward, they stayed inshore of the Gulf Stream, riding coastal eddies, and without event turned into the confluence of sloughs that formed Charleston Harbor. Bliven had been devising excuses to remain in port long enough to meet Sam, if he could come, but upon calling at the Navy Yard he knew from the brevity of the note waiting for him that they could not meet.

ABBEVILLE, S. CAROLINA
15 FEBY., 1820

*My Esteemed Friend Putnam,*

*I thank you for your recent favor of correspondence. As much pleasure as it would give me to see you, I regret bitterly that I doubt it will be in my power to do so. I have not received a reply to my letter to you, sent to Boston, and so send this separately to Charleston. If you*

*must lay over there for long, let me know of it and perhaps something
can be managed, but as it seems now, affairs here are at such a pass, I
cannot look away.*

*Remaining yr friend through all,
Sam'l. Bandy*

BLIVEN PUTNAM, CAPT. USN
COMD'G
US SHIP RAPPAHANNOCK
C/O CHARLESTON NAVY YARD

From the Navy Yard Bliven took a stroll into the town, turning
over in his mind what Sam might have meant by remaining his friend
"through all." That answer came with surprising swiftness as he discovered that if the attitude toward the federal uniform had been cold
when he was here during the War of 1812 it was now, if anything,
hostile. He knew of course that John C. Calhoun, that preening
rooster of Southern pretense he had encountered as a boy at the same
social where he met Clarity, had risen to serve three terms in Congress. There he became a thorn in the side of everyone who did not
bend the knee to South Carolina as a mighty and sovereign nation.
After six years of forging a pugnacious alliance of Southern extrem-
ists and making enemies of everyone else, he became Secretary of
War, an office he occupied even at this hour.

Bliven had to wonder whether having a Southern extremist in that
office had anything to do with the fact that Northern armories seemed
stripped down to their echoing bare walls, while those of Charleston
strained to hold all the powder and shot diverted to them, but at least
now that would work to *Rappahannock's* advantage, for powder and

ball and grape and canister were stocked in plenty, and loaded in two days. Before committing to their long voyage, Bliven anchored off Fort Moultrie and staked floats every hundred yards away from the ship to mark the range, and used the opportunity to test the powder, which he found excellent and consistently effective to a thousand yards, and also to verse the men in the exercise of the great guns. This was simpler than it was in the days of linstock fuses, and there were enough seasoned hands in the crew to apportion them as gun captains. If he should find himself in a battle and the gun captains did not show great aptitude for gunnery, he would have the lieutenants point the guns.

As *RAPPAHANNOCK* PLOWED her stately way south, past the Caribbean islands and down the coast of Brazil, Bliven took some superior fun in directing the visit of Neptune and his "wife" as they crossed the equator. So many of the crew had never done so that he decided to make it more a day of rest, with singing and fiddling and jig dancing. In a twist unheard-of in the Navy, he saved a little mild abuse for the junior officers, for of the lieutenants only Miller was a veteran of crossing the line. Rippel and Jackson had the men stripped and doused in a barrel of water; his own joke was that as they braced to be dunked in cold sea water, Bliven had had the cook prepare it with hot fresh water, and slipped them a cake of soap to make it worth their while. Lieutenant David James Horner—Bliven noted that he always introduced himself using both his given names—also had never crossed the equator, but Bliven judged his character too fine and grave, and too easily embarrassed, to inflict any indignities upon him. When some of the more crusty sailors cast eager eyes in his direction, Bliven decreed that Neptune's authority extended only to seamen, not to marines.

Only his steward Ross was aware that Bliven began having trouble sleeping at night. He had sailed the South Atlantic before, lost the *Tempest*, and then in the *Constitution* played his role in defeating the *Java*, but as they cruised past the twenty-fifth parallel it weighed on him that now he was entering waters new to him. At length he realized that what unnerved him was the prospect of making his first rounding of Cape Horn, that graveyard of ships, that terror of all sensible seamen. Dr. Berend, he learned, had traversed it once but had no part in plotting its navigation; indeed, he had spent the passage below, ostensibly to comfort the sick but in truth, as he now admitted, avoiding being topside from his own terror, for it was from his account an uncommonly fraught passage.

After two and a half months at sea, their water turning foul and rations rancid, their fresh meat long since exhausted, it began to press where to make port to provision and water, for Rio de Janeiro was in political upheaval. In his lack of sleep Bliven had begun rereading Captain Porter's account of his voyage in the *Essex*, in whose long-vanished wake they were following. Indeed, if it had not been for Porter's memoir, he would not have thought to put in at Santa Catarina Island and its congenial little town of Florianópolis.

Brazil was vast, and this was part of it, but far enough removed from the turmoils of Rio that the people, to all appearances, were left content to live their bucolic lives. It lay at nearly the twenty-eighth south parallel, a temperate land of plentiful vegetables and fruit, and Porter had taken special trouble to describe their water as excellent. He even noted the soundings of the harbor and where a ship of deep draught could anchor in safety.

Before pushing on, Bliven called the officers and warrant officers into the great cabin to consider the hazards of the coming weeks. "Gentlemen," he began, "no one knows from one day to the next, even from one hour to the next, what the conditions are in the southern straits. We should prepare for some eventualities now. I want the extra spars carried down and stowed on the gun deck. Take the bow chasers off their carriages and lower them into the hold. Take the carronades off their slides and do likewise, only make sure in the hold to lash everything down very securely. We want all the ballast we can put down there, but it wouldn't do at all to have it break loose and roll around."

That procedure when completed would remove at least seven tons of weight from their upper deck and locate it where it would do the most good.

"Now," he continued, "once we get near to the straits, we will dispense with the morning routine of stowing hammocks in the netting. All that would accomplish is to make the men's bedding cold and soggy. I can stand the extra clutter for a few days if you can, and I believe it will have a good effect with the men."

Bliven went back to studying Porter's experience and was discomfited to learn that he had chosen the rock-lined defile of the Strait of Magellan, narrow as an attic hallway, over the longer but broader passage of the Le Maire Strait. It was an opportune time to consult with his trusted bosun, whom he called to the quarterdeck. "Mr. Yeakel, have you made the rounding of Cape Horn before?"

"Yes, sir. I was bosun's mate on a commercial vessel."

"And how did you find it?"

"Like Jacob and Esau, sir."

"I am not such a religious man, Mr. Yeakel. I do not follow you."

"Captain, I was a smooth man on the day before, and a hairy man on the day after."

"Ha! Walk with me." They advanced slowly forward on the spar deck. "Did you take the Le Maire Strait or the inland passage?"

"We followed Magellan himself, sir, and not to tell you your business, but I would be a happy man not to do so again."

"Upon what considerations?"

"Well, first, it is a longer passage than it seems because it is in the shape of a great S. Some of it is wide enough, ten miles across in places, but there are two narrows that are just as tight as a garden gate, and the smallest miscalculation will ground you on the rocks. Except the winds do not allow for calculation. Sir, imagine yourself in a doldrum, and following the cat's paws on the water to detect how the breeze varies from all over the compass. Now imagine that times a thousand, being slapped left and right and behind so fast, you don't know what direction you are facing. That is just the wind; the current is worse, and the tide worse than that. If it comes with you, you must ride it like the flood of a river; and if it comes against you, it will spin you around and set you into the wind before you can haul in the sails. Quickest way in the world to lose your masts."

"Is that all?"

"By God, sir, it is bloody well enough, at least for me."

"Hm." They had reached the bow, and were looking down at the catheads. They were in a rolling seaway, and where the anchor was tied up its lower fluke disappeared into the water as the bow buried itself in a trough. "If we can catch an opening in the conditions, I want you to secure the anchors tighter. The last thing we need is to lose one when we might need it, or even worse have it come partly loose. I hate to think what damage a four-ton anchor could cause if it starts bashing into the hull."

"Yes, sir."

"We shall be utilizing the Le Maire Strait, you will be happy to hear.

Once we enter our run, I will want you topside during the most peril-ous times, and your most able seaman with you to assist."

"And what of the bosun's mate, Captain?"

"He will take over when you are resting. You and he will not be on deck at the same time. I want him kept safe in case anything happens to you."

Yeakel's eyes opened wide. "Well, I suppose I am not indis-pensable."

Bliven waved it off. "Don't feel picked at. I am taking the same pre-caution with myself and Lieutenant Miller."

"Yes, sir."

As they passed the Punta Desengaño they discovered how the Roaring Forties gave way to the Furious Fifties, with three hundred miles yet to go to the Le Maire Strait. The sea took on a leaden green hue, which Bliven was expecting, for Porter wrote that it prompted him to begin sounding, although he never found bottom.

From the last position he was certain of, he needed to make south-west for the Cape of San Diego which he should like to starboard, and the Isla de los Estados to port, with twenty miles of open water be-tween them that formed the Le Maire Strait. This lay at the fifty-fifth south parallel, with another hundred miles to go before rounding the Isles l'Hermite that formed the actual Cape Horn, near to where the Furious Fifties blended into the Shrieking Sixties.

He stalled, tacking with little forward progress, hoping for a wind that would favor him. He was on the quarterdeck with Yeakel, and he had requested his massive young marine lieutenant to take the wheel on the possibility that he might be the only one strong enough to hold it, and turn only as he was directed.

Then for ten minutes a gale roared over their stern from the northeast—the prevailing direction, or at least the direction from which the wind came for the greatest percentage of time, for it came from all directions with equal force. "I wish I could depend on this!" he shouted right into Yeakel's ear. "It is wild, but she rides well enough. If it would last we could shoot right through."

The spray was blinding, the rain frigid. "I know, sir," Yeakel shouted back, "but you can't depend on it. It could stay behind us the rest of the day, or turn against us in the next instant."

"You're right, I know. Double-reef your courses and we will trust to the tops'ls." The royal yards they had dropped long since.

"Don't be angry, Captain, but I did that already!"

"Ha!" Bliven pounded him on the back. "Good fellow!"

It lasted for three hours, with Bliven more and more thankful; then, between the rain and mist, and darkness falling, they could hear breakers off to starboard but could not see them, nor see land. "I believe we have favored a bit too much to the east, Mr. Yeakel. Mr. Horner, come southwest by south. Do you know what that means?"

"Yes, sir."

"Do you need a rest?"

"I don't know, sir. I cannot feel my hands. Does that mean I need a rest?"

"Oh, my Lord! Get you below for some hot coffee! Mr. Jackson, you and Mr. Rippel take the wheel together. It will take you both to match his strength. Thank you, Mr. Horner, well done."

In the Southern Hemisphere they were approaching the shortest days of the year, so first light did not come until midmorning. They must have been making ten knots during the night, and thus Bliven could calculate that they were past the latitude of the Isles l'Hermite and ordered a westerly course, but with double lookouts aloft in case he was wrong.

But it was the last they heard of land, and the next day he risked a turn to west-northwest, wagering that they would begin to see the outermost of that terrible labyrinth of mountaintop islands that form the southern coast of Chile. This proved correct, and in two hundred miles more they passed the point of Desolation Island, marking the exit of the Magellan Strait, which for all the buffeting they had suffered, he was still glad they had not chosen.

With the worst of the danger past, Bliven excused himself, turned the deck over to the watch, and retired to his sea cabin. "Mr. Ross, bring me coffee in thirty minutes, if you please."

"Very good, sir."

He retired to his compartment, where he closed the door, lay down, wrapped himself in blankets, and shook for the next half hour. With the coffee Ross brought a basin of very hot water, with which he washed himself as he changed clothes, composed himself, and returned to the deck to discover sunshine and a panoply of mountains to the east.

Behind the coastal foothills, the snow-swept peaks rose to heights that were utterly astonishing. Bliven had been up into Vermont and had seen the Green Mountains, with Lake Champlain on his left and the forested heights rising to a difference of near four thousand feet. But here, these Andes that he saw rearing in the distance must have been five times so high, and then the depth that the sea plunged to must have been inestimable. They were on their northerly heading well within sight of the coast, yet the carpenter's mate consistently called out soundings of no bottom.

From the Horn to Valparaiso had taken Porter a month, but now it was August and in this equable season, coming out of their rainy months and the coldest part of the year, riding the Peru Current, Bliven thought he might shave off some of that time.

In three weeks the terror of their subpolar passage had mostly passed for the crew, who felt some pride that they could claim to have rounded the Horn. That was one phrase used by seamen that even the most hopeless landlubbers knew and respected.

Miller came on deck at the change of watch and saluted easily. "Good afternoon, Captain."

"Mr. Miller." He saluted back. "How are things?"

"Sir, I just made a sweep, and everything is in order. Dr. Berend sends his compliments and asks me to tell you that he has assayed the crew, and there is not a sign of scurvy anywhere."

"That is good hearing, after nearly four months at sea."

"Apparently, your taking on half a ton of onions at Saint Catherine's has had its good effect among the crew."

*Good old Porter,* thought Bliven. If he had not read Porter's memoir so closely, it would never have occurred to him to take on onions at Saint Catherine's as a prophylactic against scurvy. "I am very glad to hear it."

"Of course"—Miller clasped his hands behind his back—"their breath could drop a bull sea elephant stone dead."

"They can detect a difference?"

"Actually, sir, I am somewhat serious. Thinking not just about onions but the stench generally, it might be well to rig a wind sail and get some fresh air down to the berth deck before we get back into the tropics and it gets any worse. This would seem to be a good day for it."

The wind was strong over the port quarter, and not too cold. "Yes. Yes, you're right. Round up the bosun and the sailmaker. Have Mr. Yeakel take in the mizzen stays'l and funnel a wind sail down to the ladder to the berth deck. That should air things out nicely, thank you."

Miller saluted and turned to leave. "I will tend to it now, sir."

After two hundred miles of steering north-northeast, the sweep of the coast altered their course to north and had the lookouts alert for the first of two big tongues of headlands. Miller had the deck as they passed the first and he altered to the northeast. He had just determined to send down for the captain as he came abreast of the second headland, where after an easterly turn would lie Valparaiso's capacious, north-facing bay.

"Deck! Deck ahoy!"

"What do you see?" called Miller.

"Ships, sir! Coming around the headland, a whole God damn fleet, sir! Jesus!"

"Can you count them?"

"No, sir. Some are obscured by others! At least two dozen!"

The commotion brought Bliven, Rippel, and Jackson onto the quarterdeck, still buttoning their coats and snugging down their bicornes. Bliven strode over to his first lieutenant. "What do we have, Mr. Miller?"

"Captain, I was just going to send down for you. We are about to raise Valparaiso, but the lookout sighted a large squadron standing out of the harbor."

As soon as Bliven saw what lay ahead, he spied the bosun at the hatch, awaiting orders. "Mr. Yeakel!"

"Sir!"

"Shorten sail, reef your courses. We'll give them time to get by us."

"Aye, sir!"

In a flash, Jackson was eight feet high in the mizzen ratlines, peering through his glass. "Captain, it must be Cochrane! It has to be!"

Bliven, Miller, and Rippel had walked over to the starboard rail and raised their own glasses. "Cochrane," said Miller softly. "By God, I would give two months' pay just to meet and have a talk with him."

Bliven leaned on the rail. "I know. So would I."

"Sir," Jackson called down, "I make three frigates in the van, a corvette, five brigs, and maybe fifteen transports."

"Cochrane," breathed Miller again. "After Nelson, there was no greater legend in the Royal Navy. Napoleon himself called him the Sea Wolf."

"And they broke him and drummed him out over that stock market business." Bliven shook his head. "Maybe the single most stupid thing the English have done in the past century."

"And that is a high bar," agreed Miller.

"Mr. Jackson, you may come down from there; he can't see you. Miller, I wish my wife were here. If she wants to write novels about someone, there is the man to write about. Somebody will one day, I'll bet."

Jackson rejoined them, breathless. "Just think, if we had gotten here a day earlier, we might have met him."

Bliven laughed, lightly and tolerantly. "And what would you have said to him?"

"That I think he was innocent, sir. His trial was a political sham."

"And I believe that about half of their Admiralty would agree with you. But that is what comes of being a prickly and disagreeable officer. Remember this, Mr. Jackson: when you make enemies, being brilliant atop that makes you a target."

Jackson leaned on the railing. "Nevertheless, he is a great man."

"Well, calm yourself. I imagine this is about as close to such greatness as we will ever approach."

Miller smirked. "About a mile and a half?"

"Ha! Yes, more or less." Bliven noticed that it was Midshipman Quarles at the wheel, looking small and nervous. "Mr. Quarles, would you like to take us into port?"

"Yes, sir!"

He made certain that both Rippel and Jackson were listening. "Well, then, when we are well clear of the headland, begin a starboard turn, slow and stately. Mind how close the shore is. Keep about a mile off. Do not turn too tightly or you will run us onto the beach, and that would not make a good impression."

"No, sir!"

"Mr. Miller, beat to quarters, prepare a salute, twenty-one guns. Have the quartermaster prepare to run up the Chilean colors."

They stood quietly as the coast slipped by them, until Valparaiso's fort loomed into view. "Officers to the starboard rail," said Bliven. "Execute. Gentlemen, hats up." They removed their bicornes and held them high as the Chilean tricolor with its three white stars ran smartly up the foremast, and far forward one of the twenty-fours boomed with its concussion, followed at ten-second intervals by twenty more, which almost made the round of the gun deck. "Hats on."

As soon as the last report of their twenty-fours echoed off the facing hillside, smoke jetted between the crenellations of the fort's parapet, and three seconds later the concussion and boom smacked their ears as the fort answered, gun for gun.

Bliven's uncertainty of how to open an inquiry into Pacific matters was quickly resolved, for they discovered two American whalers riding at anchor in the bay, their crews on deck to witness the sloop's arrival, and Bliven made to keep them company, anchoring fifty yards away.

*Rappahannock*'s officers regarded the city, which though very old had only recently come into importance as a stopping place for whaling ships. There was a long, arcing crescent of a beach from which extended a single jetty. The buildings were a jumble backed by a

confusion of low hills, and behind them three mountains, almost coni-
cal. Whatever the native names or Spanish names had been, mariners
had taken to calling them Fore Top, Main Top, and Mizzen Top.

Bliven spoke the nearer of the two whalers and was invited aboard,
and he and Miller were lowered in the captain's gig and rowed across
at once. His inquiry as to what the whalers knew of Captain Jakob
Saeger and the *Fair Trader* was met with consternation.

The captain, M. Edgerton, of the whaler *Naumkeag*, was a New En-
glander, barrel-chested and bluff, with a squared beard and piercing
eye. He received Bliven and Miller in his cabin, joined presently by
the captain of the second whaler, the *Penobscot*, New Bedford. "We do
know Captain Saeger," Edgerton said, "although not well. The best
that can be said is that he is a hard man. He has been in the Pacific
trade for about ten years, he is known to make hard bargains, and he
is hard on those he deals with."

"How shall I know him?" asked Bliven. "Can you describe him
to me?"

"He is quite old, and very tall. Thin white hair, head shaped like a
tall apple, blue eyes, tiny mouth, crooked and cruel, bad teeth."

*A seaman poet,* thought Bliven. "What was his business here?"

"After the pirates lightened him of one cargo, he went to Canton
for another, and then came here to sell Chinese trade goods to the
merchant class, which is growing. Then I'm damned if he didn't take
that money and buy surplus guns of the English. They sold him four
small nine-pounder carronades that they didn't have any use for, with
powder and shot—mostly grape, as I was told."

"Do you know where he would be now?"

"From here, he would make for the Sandwich Islands for a cargo of
sandalwood, then to Canton. If he has a good load, he will recoup his

losses. I imagine he will go home at some time, but my guess is he will make that run three or four times to lay in enough money to retire to a life of leisure before he goes home finally."

"Has he a family?"

"He had a son, sailing a second ship, but they were lost at sea. Doubtless that added to the sourness of his mind."

"What is his ship?"

"The *Fair Trader*? Large schooner, two masts, about three hundred tons burthen. We are curious, Captain: What business could you have with such a man?"

"My business is more with the pirates who attacked him. The Malacca Strait must become a waterway of great importance, and the United States is interested in doing its part to make it safe for our commerce."

"So you are bound for some hot action?"

"We shall see."

"Har! Given a choice of who to fire upon, I am not sure whether I would point my guns at the pirates or Saeger! For my part in the business, the pirates can have him."

"Do you yourself have any experience with Malay pirates?"

"I, sir?" Edgerton harrumphed. "My business is whales, and for the present there is a plenty of great fat whales in the waters west of the Galápagos."

"Indeed. Are you outward- or home-bound?"

"Homeward bound, sir, with a hold full of sperm oil, which will make a great profit for the owners and our share. And I tell you, I cannot get there fast enough to collect, for at the present moment we are broker than the Ten Commandments."

Bliven's laugh was full and sudden. "An expression I have not heard before, Captain. Perhaps, if I were to send over my purser, you would be willing to sell him some barrels of sperm oil for some ready cash?"

"By God, sir, you are a gentleman! He will be most welcome, most welcome."

Miller and Bliven had started to descend to the gig when another officer approached them, unseen by his captain. "Farrell, sir, first mate. May I have a word?"

"Certainly." He and Miller paused at the boarding gate.

"I am sure you will realize, sir, that no sea captain relishes speaking ill of another."

"That was not obvious," said Miller. "Your captain seemed quite eloquent."

"Captain, beware Jakob Saeger. He is a mad dog."

"You don't say."

"Being humiliated by native pirates, it did something to his mind. He was a hard man before, but now I swear he lives for vengeance, and not just against those who robbed him. His hatred extends to natives generally. It is as if in the fever of his dreams he imagines his hatreds to be the equivalent of spreading civilization. He makes complex agreements with them; he will advance them cash for their sandalwood, at an interest, which is a concept completely foreign to them. When they learn the extent of their debt and cry that they have been cheated, he congratulates himself on having made a shrewd bargain. The name of his ship is a misnomer, sir, for cheating and extortion to him are on an equal plane with fair dealing."

"This is not pleasing to hear, Mr. Farrell," said Bliven, "but most useful, and I thank you for taking the trouble."

Farrell made his respects with a touch to his hat in the British manner.

"By the way," said Miller, "was that Cochrane making the sortie this morning?"

"It was, yes. He is bound for Peru to help them win their independence."

"Really? Why? Of what interest is that here?"

"Chile, sir, is newly independent herself, and her government calculates that they will never be truly secure as long as the Spanish have a toe on the continent, leave alone next door. The Spanish in Peru find themselves in a vulnerable moment, so now is the time to strike, if strike they will."

FROM VALPARAISO, BLIVEN determined to duplicate Porter's route, nor'-nor'west to the Galápagos Islands, where perhaps they could take on some of those gigantic tortoises, which were said to make an estimable soup. The engraving of them in Porter's journal piqued Bliven's curiosity whether any such reptile could attain the size depicted in the book's engraving. Indeed, throughout Porter's journal his observations of natural history were dispassionate, written dryly, with only occasional hints of curiosity or amazement. But when he came to the Galápagos, he was almost lost for how to describe such desolate weirdness, such incongruity of creatures, and as the days passed Bliven thought he must die of sheer anticipation before the lookout finally called "Land ho!" down to the deck as they approached Santa María Island. Two hours later they entered the Isabela Channel, and while taking constant soundings slid by Santa Fe Island to starboard, seeing Santiago ahead of them, with the long, skinny spine of Isabela to port.

He knew to avoid the tortoises of Santiago Island, for Porter had noted their foul taste, giving him to speculate that despite their physical similarity to the tortoises of the other islands, they must be a distinct species. Instead, Bliven accompanied a victualing party when they found a suitable beach at Isabela's pinched narrow waist, and what he saw ashore sent his mind into a spin.

He had known, distantly, of a growing argument between prelates of the Christian churches who claimed that God's creation was now as it had always been, and a small but growing rump of scientists— people like Cuvier, who had unearthed a skeleton of a giant, flying creature in Bavaria; of Mary Anning, who was continuing to dig up huge, extinct reptiles on the south coast of England; and there was a whole coterie of dissidents who published scientific papers that hearkened all the way back to Xenophenes of Colophon, who realized two centuries before Aristotle, from the presence of fossil fish in the mountains, that they must once have been underwater. All of which pointed to the possibility that the earth was infinitely older and had undergone tumultuous, cataclysmic changes over a vast stretch of time.

But what to make of this place? Of desolate, volcanic shores washed in a cold ocean current; of tortoises with shells like cauldrons; of cormorants that could not fly; of laidly lizards with serrated backs sunning themselves seemingly from every rock. It was easy to believe that this was how the earth must have looked at an earlier time, as indeed Porter had speculated in his book.

It became apparent that the victualing party had miscalculated. They figured on the tortoises weighing perhaps two hundred pounds each—not up to half a ton. Such huge creatures could only be got out to the ship one or two at a time, not in a couple of trips, as they had imagined. Additional seamen were eager to go ashore and help, enchanted in the volcanic weirdness, while Bliven, Miller, Horner, and a platoon of marines scaled the island's divide to have a look at its western side. They found the heights covered in thick scrub and cactus whose leaves consisted of thick waxy pads, which they discovered one of the tortoises eating.

"Captain!" called out young Lieutenant Horner. "Over here, sir!"

Bliven and Miller approached the sound of his voice, and found him in a shallow vale near the summit of the island's divide. They realized that Horner had deployed his platoon into a line of flankers, which seemed like a pointless exercise until they found him standing over the remains of a campfire, its coals still hot beneath the dirt recently kicked over it.

Whoever it was, it was apparent that they had seen the *Rappahannock* approach and stood not, as Shakespeare wrote, upon the order of their going.

Bliven and Miller traded a knowing look. "Pirates, even here." These islands pocked with hidden coves were well known as a haunt of the last remaining buccaneers. They hurried to the ridge and saw off the western shore a small barkentine just dropping her sails; the longboat in which men had made their escape was tied on and being towed, not taking time to hoist her up.

Miller rested his hands on his hips and shook his head. "Mediterranean, Caribbean, the south of Asia now. Damned pirates everywhere you look. The oceans seem to be lousy with them."

Bliven nodded in agreement. "Well, this was their lucky day."

"Shall you not pursue them, Captain?" asked Horner.

"No. It would take hours to get everyone back to the ship and beat around the island to the west side. We shall have to save them for a later day."

In the evening, the pen that had formerly lodged the pigs, long since consumed, was now crowded with ungainly tortoises, walking its circuit, climbing each other's backs.

Dominating the others was one that seemed a third larger than the rest, with wrinkled eyes that appeared as old as time. Bliven had ordered a bin filled with the cactus pads on which he had seen them feeding, and reached into it, being careful to avoid the spines, and held one in front of that largest tortoise. Showing no fear, the reptile cocked its head and studied the pad before opening its massive horny beak and biting a V-shaped slice out of it. Bliven looked up and saw Miller observing with amusement.

"You know, Captain, it is said that these tortoises can live for a year without eating."

"Yes, but have you considered how that might affect the flavor of the meat?"

"Ah, yes, you make a good point."

"This large fellow here, though—I think that he is not for the table. I should like to take him home to show as a curiosity. Have the carpenter paint a white dot on his shell," said Bliven. "He reminds me of someone. I think I will name him Beecher."

"Aye, sir."

From the Galápagos they stood west into the vast, empty Pacific— empty except for the New Englanders working the sperm whale grounds, encountering three to five every day for two weeks. And then it took three weeks more across the trackless deep, daily referencing their chronometer, before the green mountains of the Sandwich Islands rose over the horizon. The very sight of them, and the knowledge of what awaited him, made Bliven's heart pound. Matching what they saw with what was shown on the chart, he reckoned that they had raised the islands at the north shore of the one called Molokai, which could not have been luckier, and he congratulated himself on his navigation, and avoiding having to spend days in coasting the islands that held no interest for him until he should raise Oahu.

By degrees slow and agonizing it grew larger until they found themselves almost in its shadow. "You may muster hands, Mr. Miller."

It was a command that was almost obeyed already, for as *Rappahannock* cruised under easy sail toward the Kaiwi Channel, most of the crew who were not engaged in duties gathered at the port rail to stare at its cliffs, their beetling heights in shade, that vaulted from the sea and shot into the air for a vertical half mile. None had ever seen such a thing. When all the officers had joined him on the quarterdeck, Bliven advanced, steadying himself on the binnacle, surveying his crew crowded onto the weather deck.

"Men, we have been at sea for six months. You have performed your tasks admirably, and I am proud of you. Many adventures lie before us, but I am confident now that I can rely on you for anything that I may reasonably ask of you. But now I am going to ask something of you that may not be reasonable. Or rather not I, but your ship's surgeon. Dr. Berend, will you address them?"

Berend was unaccustomed to public address, and squared himself self-consciously. He was unused to raising his voice, and was somewhat surprised to discover that he had no natural projection. "Now, men," he began, "we have been together for some months, now. I have lanced your boils and trussed your ruptures; some of you I have raised your heads and given you broth when you were too sick to move. I think I may be believed when I tell you that I have your best interest at heart.

"Now, this afternoon, we will anchor in a port that is famous throughout the world for its women, who are said to have no equal in pleasing a man."

The cheer that drowned him out was loud and lusty.

"But men, I must tell you, the English got here first, forty years ago, and spread their venereal diseases among these women, and now from the natives' own amorous nature, hear me now, these are the most diseased islands on earth, and an almighty discouragement to venting your passions here.

"In Captain Cook's time, those who became infected were doomed, but today there are medicines that can help."

Berend was interrupted by a lusty cheer and more laughter.

"But hear me now as you love your life! The treatment of this disease will cause you such agony as you never imagined. When I must squirt a solution of mercury deep up your cock, the burning will be like a coal of fire shoved inside you, and it will not be a single treatment. It is required for months, sometimes for years. There is good reason for the adage that you can spend one night with Venus and the rest of your life with Mercury.

"And now therefore I warn you: if you are so weak of self-control that you succumb to your passions, and become afflicted with these diseases, I will treat you, and I will do what I can for you, but you will have none but yourself to blame, and I will not feel sorry for you."

"May we ask a question, Doctor?"

He could not see who asked it, but it did not matter. "You may."

"Mr. Erb has passed the word among us that he has quondams to sell to us. Is that not a sure solution to the problem?"

Bliven skewered Erb with a glare. "You never spoke to me of this."

"No, Captain, I did not." He shrugged. "Nor did I tell you of every hat and shoe. Why would that have been necessary?"

"Dr. Berend, are the quondams a sure proof against disease?" Bliven asked.

"No. They help, but their efficacy is not certain."

"Explain it to them, then!"

Berend raised his hands. "Men, listen to me carefully. Here is the truth about the quondams. They can come off, and you will be infected.

They can break, and you will be infected. A woman's juices can come in around its edges, and you will be infected. Further, if you buy one, do not accept it, and pay for it, until you blow it up with your breath and see if it leaks. If it has holes in it, and this often happens because of the chemicals used to treat and soften them, you will be infected. If you buy one and it contains your issue without leaking, wash it well, and use it again, but always test it before you use it. You must understand, your life depends upon this."

Bliven was as angry as he could ever remember. "Mr. Miller, dismiss the men. Mr. Erb, for how much money are you selling the quondams?"

"Two dollars, Captain."

"What! Where will a common seaman find two dollars after he has paid you for his common slops?"

"They will have some money, after you pay them when we drop anchor and give them shore leave."

"Dr. Berend, come here. For every seaman who reports to you with a venereal disease, despite his having used a quondam, you will charge Mr. Erb two dollars, which you will refund to the man in question."

"I understand your feeling, Captain"—Berend smiled sadly—"but I fear you would be exceeding the regulations."

"Then take it up with the Department of the Navy, Doctor. They are the ones who declined to issue quondams to you for free, as I remember. So, Mr. Erb, I suggest you take it upon yourself to remove their wrappings and inspect them for defects before you sell them." Bliven turned on his heel and stalked forward to the ladder and went down.

"Tell me something, Doctor," said Erb.

"What is it?"

"If a man bought and wore two quondams, would that not increase his safety?"

Berend hated it, but it was true. "It would." The sure circumstance was that a seaman would hand over four dollars—a princely sum to him—for two quondams, put them both on at the critical moment, and be so dismayed at feeling nothing through the two layers of pig's intestine that he would take them off and indulge without them.

The commotion had taken so much time that when Bliven emerged in a fresh uniform they had raised Koko Head on their starboard bow, and it was almost time to make the turn around Diamond Hill. The Honoruru anchorage was not hard to find, for they had only to follow a New Bedford whaler, the *Abigail*, through the reef and into the harbor. It was curious—there was no fort to salute—and though there were enough houses visible to discern the presence of a town, they appeared like so many haystacks. Indeed, he was not certain that they *were* houses, and it was a relief when people began walking down to the shore, a mix of white and native. He studied them through his glass, his heart pounding, until he spied a tight gathering of the little grass houses with a clot of three black-clad white men and four women standing before them, and he saw her, a telescope to her eye, pointing with excitement.

Bliven decided that he and Miller should go ashore first. The captain's gig was not large enough to ferry all the officers to the single low wooden pier that extended out from the beach. He knew these were the missionaries, but they were Congregationalists and his chaplain was a mere Deist, and that might prove an unneeded distraction.

Six seamen pulled at their sweeps, at the tiller a helmsman, who reached out at a piling at the end of the pier and made them fast.

Bliven hardly heard his own footfalls on the hollow-sounding planks, for he saw her at the end of the grass just beyond the remarkably narrow beach.

"Oh, dearest," she tried to shout, but her voice came out as barely a breath. "I so prayed that it was you. I had Reverend Bingham come out with his field glass to see, and when he smiled and handed it to me, I knew. I read the name of the ship and saw you on the deck." She sobbed, but just once. "Oh, thank God, you are here and safe."

He heard all this as he approached her, but for all her spoken greeting, and as Bliven rushed forward to seize her, he froze at the sight of her carrying a baby in her arms. "What in the world?"

She was beaming. "Captain Putnam, may I present to you your son?"

## { 10 }

## *Honoruru*

"What! What?"

Clarity pulled the cotton kerchief that shielded him from the ferocity of the sun from his face to display him, but did not hand him over, for she had never once seen Bliven hold a baby.

"When?" He touched the infant lightly and ran his finger down his cheek.

"Born nine months to the very day from our last night together in Boston. Like his father, he likes to be punctual."

"Are you all right?"

"Perfectly."

"Is he well? Is he strong?"

"He is a little ox."

"Oh, my love, my angel!" He placed his hands on her shoulders and kissed her, leaning across the baby but careful not to press him. "What is his name?"

She cradled the baby in one arm and threaded her free hand into the crook of his arm. "Come, let us return to the shade. I must tell you, I resolved from the first that if we had a boy, you would name him, and if it was a girl, I would name her. Up until this moment his name has been Baby. Therefore, sir, the privilege is yours. How shall we call him?"

"Oh! Well! How would it be, Benjamin, for my father, and Samuel, for my friend?"

"I think it will serve very well."

"Where are we going?"

"To the mission station, so we can collect the others, and then to the queen's house."

"Just up there?"

"Yes. As soon as the queen heard it was an American warship, she assembled the court. I recall that you met the king of Naples once, so this should not overwhelm you."

"I shall gather my courage, my love. Oh, I am so sorry, I would like for you to meet my first lieutenant, Michael Miller."

Miller touched his hat. "A great pleasure, ma'am."

"How do you do, Lieutenant?"

"Mr. Miller," said Bliven, "we did not expect to be presented immediately upon our arrival. If you please, go back out to the ship, fetch Rippel and Jackson, and Dr. Berend and the chaplain. Be sure to bring the gifts."

Miller saluted and returned to the pier at a trot.

She led him to a row of grass houses, where waiting outside were the Binghams, the Chamberlains, Muriel Albright, and the Loomises. He was quickly introduced, after which Bliven pointed to the beginning of an ambitious construction: a cellar dug, stakes driven into the ground with string stretched between them, sills and joists laid for a foundation, and a great stack of lumber covered by a canvas sail.

"What is this?" Bliven asked.

"Well may you ask!" huffed Clarity. "We left Boston with all the materials needed to reassemble a house big enough for the group of us, but no one asked whether anyone knew how to put it back together! We have been relying on visiting ships' carpenters to get us this far."

Bliven looked over at Bingham, who shrugged. "We are better evangelists than carpenters, it seems."

"Should that not be part of your vocation, when Jesus was a carpenter?"

"There you have us, Captain!" laughed Bingham. "Such an argument might carry some force!"

"Well, I will send Fleming, my carpenter, to you. He will know just what to do."

"We would be so grateful."

Bliven's lieutenants, chaplain, and surgeon were spied walking up in a group from the shaky wooden pier to join them, giving Clarity a moment to draw Bliven aside. "Dearest, you have no idea the good you have done. Reverend Bingham has not laughed these last two months. It has been a bit of a stressful time.

"Well! Are we ready?" Clarity inclined her head in the direction of a low hill nearby, surmounted by a large grass house surrounded by natives. "We oughtn't keep the queen waiting." She went three steps to lead them there but then stopped when she noticed confused glances among the men. "Oh, my Lord, you don't know! Gentlemen, listen carefully. The old king Ta-meha-meha died a few weeks before our arrival. The new king is a drunkard and his stepmother, the old king's widow, runs things. Many in the court are nominal Catholics, owing to the visit of a French frigate last year, and most of them speak at least some English. Most importantly, the old religion of wooden idols and human sacrifice was brought down before we landed, so we have been living here in perfect safety. So, please, do not act superior or as though you are suspicious of their savagery or any such, because it hasn't been like that."

As they neared the structure the well-uniformed officers were greeted with smiles and waves and cries of *"Aloha!"* at which they raised their hats and nodded.

"Shout *'Aloha!'* back to them," said Clarity softly. The officers complied and saw the response of eager but respectfully distant goodwill.

"I am glad they haven't eaten you, but still," said Bliven, "the queen lives in a hut?"

Miller appraised it. "Yes, but it is an almighty large hut."

Clarity hushed them. "Their architecture is far better suited to the weather than our New England house will be, as Captain Blanchard and others have found amusement in telling us. This is her audience hall; she actually lives in another nearby, but wait till you see the inside."

All had to stoop to enter. Light came in this front door and also a rear one for the queen to enter privately from her residence. Located well away from the walls to avoid any possibility of starting a conflagration, stands held torches that lit the interior with a flickering sufficiency. "Good heavens!" whispered Bliven. It was true the walls were of grass, and the light from torches. Otherwise they might have been in an English drawing room, tastefully appointed with mahogany furniture, gilt mirrors, and a large and fine carpet spread upon the ground.

The assemblage parted for them and they advanced, and as had been the case with the missionaries earlier, it was all Bliven could do not to gasp at the sight of the queen. Seated on her low dais, all five hundred pounds of her, she held the room with easy command. She was flanked by courtiers, and behind her stood two lackeys—Bliven's impression of them was as Roman lictors—each holding a pole more than ten feet tall and topped with a broad cylinder of feathers like an enormous bottle brush. They held the poles out at an angle, making a high, feathered arch above the queen's head. Behind all, the wall of the *pili* was hung with a kind of tapestry of native yellow-gray tapa decorated with geometric stencils in blue and red.

"Missy La Laelae!" boomed Kahumanu as they entered, her voice at least as deep as Bliven's own, but with greater sonority. "Come up to me."

"Wait here," whispered Clarity. She advanced with a firm step until she was five paces from the dais, where an ornate stand held a shorter, five-foot pole topped by a gilt ball nearly a foot in diameter. She stepped back and dropped into a deep curtsy. *"Ka mea Kamahao, ka moi wahine,"* she said. Bliven's jaw went slack; he had no idea she had acquired such a facility with the language.

The queen was dressed in a Boston frock of yellow and green cotton print, and held out her right arm. "Come, Missy." Clarity mounted the dais as the queen extended her right leg, and Clarity sat upon it as the queen embraced her and laid one enormous meaty hand on her back and with the other lightly stroked the swaddled infant. "How is your baby today?"

"He is very well, I thank Your Majesty."

"Tell me now some good new thing today about our Lord Jesus Christ."

"Well, one thing that I most love is that He sees every kind thing that we do. Whenever you act with mercy, or give out true justice, he is pleased, and when we each come to our own day of judgment, he will remember all those things in our favor. Our Lord said, 'Blessed are the merciful, for they shall receive mercy.'"

She laughed deeply and shook her head. "So much better than old gods." She looked up to the far side of the *pili*. "Who are they?"

"My husband, ma'am, and the officers of his ship."

"Heh!" the queen thundered. "Bring him!" She pushed Clarity off her lap. "Bring him!" She gestured to the courtiers who had been gathered at the side. "Hopu, come here."

As Clarity approached Bliven she whispered, "This is formal, so I won't take your arm. Gentlemen, you are not expected to bow, but salute very smartly."

Clarity returned as far as the *kapu* stick. The religion had been brought down, but the tradition of placing one before the throne to create a sacred space was so ancient that it was continued. "Majesty, may I present my husband, Captain Bliven Putnam, and the officers of the United States sloop of war *Rappahannock*?" The six marched forward, Berend, Mutterbach, and the three lieutenants cuing their steps to match Bliven's, their bicornes in the crooks of their arms, and they followed his lead in snapping to attention and saluting.

"*Aloha*, Captain Putnam," said the queen. "You are welcome. It is considerate of you to come in a ship with a name that we can say easily. This is not true of many ships that visit us. *Rapahanaki*. This we can pronounce."

"I thank Your Majesty. It is the name of the river where our first president, George Washington, was born."

"Heh! It is good to receive information, even when it is not solicited. Gentlemen, you are welcome. Hopu here can say my English for me if I falter."

"Forgive me, ma'am," said Bliven, "your English seems quite as good as our own."

"You are forgiven, but it is not for you to correct me. I will know when I make a crooked job of something." She laughed, and the gathering then knew they were permitted to laugh as well.

"I know Hopu," said Bliven. "We are old friends." He extended his hand and Hopu took it eagerly.

"Will you meet also my prime minister, High Chief Karaimoku?"

Karaimoku stepped from the crowd and shook hands with Bliven, nodding pleasantly to the other officers. "The English often call me Mr. Pitt, for the obvious reason."

"Ha! I am certain that such an accolade is well deserved, sir. Would you prefer me to call you Mr. Pitt or Karaimoku?"

"Mr. Pitt, I think. It is easier for you to say."

"What message do you bring us, Captain Putnam?" asked Kahumanu.

"Your Majesty, my mission to your part of the world is manifold. Many months ago, a trading ship of my country was attacked by pirates near Malaya. These pirates have made that sea-lane dangerous for the ships of all nations. My government has sent me to investigate what happened, to find and if necessary to fight the pirates who committed this crime, and to clear them from that waterway. Being aware that I must pass by your country, my government asked me to pay a call and to express their friendly and respectful interest. My orders to that effect are contained in this letter from our president. Ma'am, it is addressed to your late husband, King Ta-meha-meha, because the sad news of his passing had not yet reached our country."

"Thank you, Captain." She made a graceful gesture. "Karaimoku will receive this letter. And what is your first impression of our country? They tell me of your saying that first impressions are lasting."

"I think first, ma'am, that it is the most beautiful place I have ever seen."

Kahumanu pointed at him suddenly. "Quite a widely held opinion!"

"Indeed! Second, my wife has already told me of the kind and generous treatment that she and the other missionaries have received since they arrived. I shall report this to my government. They will be very gratified. They have sent to Your Majesty a few tokens of their desire for friendship, if I may present them?"

"Yes, of course."

Miller, Jackson, and Rippel laid their parcels in front of where Bliven stood; Clarity suppressed a smile as they reminded her of the Three Wise Men. "First, ma'am, you see a portfolio of drawings showing scenes from around our country, which you may look over at your leisure. Second, they send you a silver desk set, with pens and an inkwell, in the hope that it will open many years of friendly correspondence between our countries. And third, they send you the seeds of various crops that grow in our country, in the hope that you will find them useful and enjoyable."

"That is very kind, Captain. We have a Spanish farmer here, Mr. Marín, who has introduced to us many foods that we had not known before. We will entrust your seeds to him. If they can be made to grow here, he will spy out the way to do it."

"Really? I have been a farmer myself, ma'am. I should be very pleased to meet Mr. Marín and learn his methods."

"Heh! We will see if that can be arranged." Without warning the queen stood, and at once a broad aisle opened before her to the entrance. "And now, gentlemen, while we have been talking, food has been laid out for us, and entertainment for you." She swept before them with her ladies, and then Karaimoku, who guided Putnam by the arm, with Clarity, followed by the officers, and they arrived at a grassy lawn near the shore.

When Bliven thought of a beach he necessarily thought first upon Cape Cod, two miles wide on average and stretching for thirty miles or more; here the beaches were beautiful but intimate, no wider than the common town lot and lying in arcs of fifty to a hundred yards between small headlands.

Thirty feet from where the grass gave way to the sand, they saw mats of native cloth spread on the ground, laden with bowls and baskets and platters of the most sumptuous-looking foods. Bliven was stricken with the terror of not knowing the etiquette, when the queen tapped him on the shoulder. "Captain Putnam, do you know of the *luau*?"

"No, ma'am, I fear that I do not."

"Be at ease; there is no ceremony. Gentlemen, find a plate; take and eat what you will. Be seated. Some of our young warriors have competitions for you to enjoy."

The officers loaded their plates with the likeliest-looking foods. Clarity took her seat next to Bliven. "If you think this is informal," she said, "at your average *luau* everyone eats with their fingers. This is a royal event, so you see the silver serving pieces and forks."

Karaimoku sat at Bliven's other side. "Tell me, Captain, do you not find that sitting upon the ground is a great leveler of rank and pretense?"

"My heavens, I do think it must be!"

"Servers will come with rum or water. I will sit by you and inform you of what you shall see."

Bliven had already noticed strapping young men in grass skirts and anklets of dark green leaves depositing perfectly round boulders upon the ground to their left.

"This is a contest," said Karaimoku. "The young men balance themselves on these round rocks of lava, and roll them with their feet as they race across the course. This trains them for coordination in warfare."

"My word!" Bliven was astonished at their agility, and joined in the laughter and applause when one would lose his balance and be sent flying. They watched several heats until one was hailed as the champion.

He then saw two warriors face each other about seventy feet apart at the edge of the beach, flexing and shaking themselves. One took hold of a spear that must have been ten feet long and tipped with a blade of obsidian so sharp that its edges were translucent. He found just the right balance and, taking careful aim, hurled it at the other.

Bliven gasped, his hands flying to his mouth as the intended victim coolly measured its approach and at the last instant dodged aside and snatched the spear in mid-flight out of the air. Taking equally careful aim, he hurled it back at the other, who similarly evaded and caught it out of the air. The process repeated until one man failed to catch the spear but only knocked it aside, at which there was laughter and applause among the court, and good sportsmanship between victor and vanquished.

"My God!" cried Bliven.

"No fear, they practice with blunt spears," said Karaimoku.

"Those are not blunt spears. Is this not terribly dangerous?"

Karaimoku shrugged. "Once in a while, one is a little slow. Obviously, he does not win."

"Wait a minute. You are a chief; you have led men." Bliven pointed, his finger tracing the flight of a spear back and forth. "I gather that you yourself have mastered these arts?"

Karaimoku grinned. "I am quite good, actually, but as chief I no longer compete."

This spear-snatching contest also proceeded through several rounds until one reigned supreme. Quickly Bliven learned to ration his breathlessness or else faint dead away. As night fell torches were lit, and Bingham led the missionaries in paying their respects to the queen and praying around her, which she seemed to appreciate. They waved and called good night to Clarity and the officers.

"Are they not retiring quite early?" Bliven asked her as he waved.

"Ah, therein lies a tale, dearest. The dancing is about to start. They do not venture yet to criticize it, at least not vociferously; they register their disapproval by retiring from the scene so they do not have to watch it."

"Is it that bad?"

"Um, you will see."

As the missionaries moved away, more of what Bliven took to be the common people began to emerge from the surrounding shadows, keeping a respectful distance from the chiefs and the feast. It began with a call, a kind of guttural, bawling, cadenced chant, with a thunder of drums that Bliven found hair-raising. The men and women performed their choreography in unison, like a Greek chorus, the women's chests as bare as the men's above their grass skirts and anklets of leaves, by turns graceful and expressive, or violent, or thrusting and lewd. In its changes of mood it was as nuanced as ballet, and it was soon no mystery why it must have overwhelmed the New England sensibilities of Bingham and his followers.

"It is called *hula*, Captain," said Karaimoku. "Your missionaries do not like it, because they think it is done to entertain, and to stare at the bodies, but they are wrong. Every step of the *hula*, every line of the chant, tells the story of our people. You read your *molelo*, your history, in books. We have *hula*. Your people of God do not see this. It pleases me to see you paying such close attention to me!"

"Well, then, that part of the dance where they seem to be, well, mating with each other—what is the purpose of that?"

"Some *hula* is history, some *hula* praises our land, some *hula* praises the king and the chiefs. That part was to honor the king's cock, which is very large."

Bliven's mouth fell open. "Oh, my God!" When he recovered himself he added, "It is all so new and strange."

"But look now, you have not seen your wife for a year, and it is time for your little one to go to sleep. No one will be offended if you wish to steal away."

"Yes, it is time to go." They stood and shook hands. What a heady brew it was to feel himself bonding with a tattooed island chieftain, half again larger than himself, with an enormous fall of plaited black hair, with his button-small eyes and pug nose, who spoke perfect English and could exercise great influence over the direction his government would take. "Will you come visit my ship tomorrow?"

"Yes, most happily, but not early. In the afternoon?"

"That is perfect. Gentlemen," he said to the officers, "take your ease, enjoy yourselves. I am remaining ashore tonight. Send my gig to the pier after breakfast and we will prepare for the prime minister's visit."

They stood as well. "Good night, Captain," said Miller. "When you return to the ship in the morning, we can arrange shore leave for the men?"

"Certainly. We need also to set Mr. Yeakel to the rerigging and get Mr. Erb with the American agent to see about victualing. Work will resume."

"Come, I will show you the way." Clarity took his arm, leading him east, past the compound where the missionaries lay sleeping. "You know, dearest, I do believe that the queen took more enjoyment out of watching you and your officers than she did in the athletics."

"Ha!"

"This was a very successful evening. You fellows made a fine impression."

"We are heading away from the town. You do not live in that compound with the others?"

"No. I did for a while, but when the queen learned that my husband was coming, she provided me a separate house where we can have some privacy and be a family. It is a little west of here and near the beach. It is a pleasant walk." She took his arm, and he let her lead the way. "Mrs. Albright has been living with me, but she will be staying at the compound while you are in residence." The moonlight on the white sand made the path easy to follow.

"Forgive my saying so, but that was a very great deal of sweaty flesh for you to have to see. Were you not offended at such a display?"

Clarity burst into the huskiest laugh he had heard in years. "Oh, my gracious, Bliv! We have been here for over half a year. If we became disjointed at every unchristian thing we see, we would never get anything done. One can only get thrown off a high horse so many times before staying on the ground. But make no mistake, these are good people."

Their walk lengthened to nearly a quarter of a mile; they passed beyond the shelter of the harbor, and they heard the small dull boom of the surf on their left. "You and Mrs. Albright have had no qualms about living apart from the others?"

She laughed. "None at all. These are wonderful people, quick, intelligent, funny, hospitable. That was quite a little tête-à-tête you had with the prime minister during the games. Did you learn much?"

"He is a highly interesting fellow. He was the old king's right-hand man, and apparently he is even more indispensable to the queen. He has accepted an invitation to visit the ship tomorrow."

They reached her *pili*, in a clearing looking out upon a small private beach. It was longer than it was wide, divided halfway down its length by a matted bamboo partition into a sitting room and bedchamber.

They undressed by the light of two candles in their glass globes.

"That was an interesting name that the queen had for you. What was it?"

She laid the baby in his cradle. "Ben. I shall like calling him Ben." Clarity freed herself from her shoes and was unlacing her bodice. "'Missy La Laelae.' It is a play on my name. Do you remember our poor friend Henry used to call me Miss Clear Day? Hopu told this to the queen, and explained to her the meaning of my given name, and just as quick as anything she called out, 'I shall call her Missy La Laelae!'"

"Where, then, is the witticism?"

"Well, you see, in the romance languages, 'la' is an article, similar but more specific than our word 'the.' But in Hawaiian 'la' is a noun; it is their word for 'day,' or 'sun.' Their adjective for 'clear' is based on the same root as 'day,' since daylight makes things clear, you see? Their word for 'clear' is 'laelae.' So 'Missy La Laelae' is simply 'Miss Clear Day' rendered in their own tongue. The fact that it sounds so musical is just an accident of the language, but you may trust me on this, they are keenly aware of the beauty of their language."

"Well, the queen does seem like a good-hearted sort, although perhaps not very sophisticated."

"Oh, ho, don't you underestimate her, she has a backbone of strap iron. She understands how she came to power and what she must do to keep it. I was at court one day when she sentenced someone to death, and I would not care to cross her on such a day."

"Really!"

"Reverend Bingham knows her better than anyone, and he compares her to the emperor Constantine."

"Truly? In what way?"

"He says it was Constantine who made Christianity the religion of the Roman Empire, but in exchange he required absolute loyalty from the Church. He would let God be the lord of heaven, but only if God would let him be the lord of the earth. And Mr. Bingham is right, Kahumanu has a very similar understanding of things."

She removed her chemise and draped a shawl over her shoulders before lifting Ben from his cradle to nurse.

"Why do you cover yourself to give Ben his supper?"

A troubled look flickered across her face.

"What is it, my love? Tell me."

"Bliv, dearest, I know that you must know that having a baby, well, changes a woman. She will knit back together, sort of, after a time, but for a while she is not the most appetizing sight in the world."

He could see her hand moving beneath the shawl, stroking the baby as he nursed. "Oh, dear Lord, you don't think you're pretty anymore!" Bliven exclaimed. "And all this time I thought it was the most natural thing in the world, and as hard as we worked for it—aside from being my fault. I mean, I am the one who did this to you."

She stood, smiling, letting the blanket fall from her shoulders, revealing her breasts, larger than he remembered, a net of blood vessels converging upon the nipple he could see, swollen and discolored. Ben continued undisturbed at the other.

In a moment, he pulled his shirt up over his shoulders and draped it over a chair, leaving him naked, his long months of deprivation quickly apparent. "This is rather where we left things, is it not?" he asked softly.

"Yes," she answered, then added slowly: "And you see in my arms how that turned out."

His face went slack, until she grinned and he saw her mischief returning.

She sat on the edge of the bed, nursing until Ben refused any more, and with the least rocking went to sleep. "He is such a little man: eat, sleep, soil his linen, 'Thank you very much.'" She laid him in his crib and stretched out beside Bliven.

"I also," he whispered. "I do not know but I have heard that having a baby makes some women not desire their husbands for a time. Are you—"

She laid her fingers over his mouth, then kissed him. "Never doubt how much I want you."

Their passion grew, and when he mounted, indeed it was different. "I am not hurting you?"

"No, my dearest. I have waited for so long."

They continued, rocking in bliss and rhythm, when he stopped suddenly. "What was that?"

"What?"

"Shh."

The silence hung heavy for several seconds, then there came from beyond the bamboo partition the tiniest snort, and titter, and then the sound of feet running out their door.

"What the devil!" he hissed.

She cried out as he withdrew, covering herself as he snatched up his sword and ran out the door after whoever had been spying. When he came back he was swearing lividly, and cast his sword into the chair.

"Be careful with that thing! Never know what you might cut off." She covered her face with her hands and shrieked in laughter.

He cast himself onto the bed.

"Did you find anyone?"

"No. Couldn't get very far like this."

"Oh! I am certain that you gave them an eyeful. Oh, my heavens. We are a long way from Connecticut, are we not, dearest?"

He started to say something but gave it up, let out his breath, and shook his head.

"Well, don't make an issue of it. I will take it up with the queen and see if we can do anything about it."

IN THE MORNING a young Hawaiian woman arrived and built up a fire in front of the house, where she prepared a breakfast of pork, eggs, bread, tea, and slabs of fresh golden pineapple, a fruit that Bliven pronounced the most wonderful thing he had ever eaten. He and Clarity were up, washing and dressing as soon as they heard her stirring about. "*Aloha*, Missy," the young woman said as they moved chairs outside to eat in the open.

"*Mahalo*, Keikilani. Bliv dearest, this is Keikilani; she helps me around the house."

"So there are servants in paradise?"

"Yes, well, what you saw last night were the chiefs and courtiers. I am afraid that not many of the joys of paradise extend down to the commoners. Life for the *kanakas* is very hard."

"How so?"

"Think of the *ancien régime*: 'Let them eat cake.' It is the little people who catch the fish and raise the pigs and grow the *kalo*, then hand most of it up to the chiefs for the privilege of living on the chiefs' land. They have done it for so many centuries, they have no idea of a different way. The chiefs who are so nice to you and me have little regard for them. Reverend Bingham was almost thrown out for wanting to preach to them. The first thing the queen said was that if the word of God is a good thing, it belongs to the chiefs, not the country people. That is the dark side of missionary work, dearest, helping the least of these. Nurse them when they're sick, give them some basic tool they are lacking—yes, employ them, for even a little money gives them some independence."

"I didn't know," he said after a moment.

"Keikilani there found herself with child, and after it was born, Mr. Chamberlain discovered her digging a hole in which to bury it."

"It was born dead?"

"No." She looked at him sternly until she was sure he understood. "But many of the *kanakas* have so little hope, they can't bear to bring more children into the world. Mr. Chamberlain took it up with Reverend Bingham, and they gave her the means to keep and raise her child."

"Dear God, they kill their own newborns? Is this a common occurrence?"

"More than we can generally bear to talk about."

"Oh, my love, you did not bargain for this back in Connecticut."

"No. We are inured to their cruelties, but now we know better why God sent us."

Bliven shook his head sadly. "Well, if you were one of my officers I would cite you for gallantry. Speaking of which, I must get out to the ship. For the coming days you may think of me going to the office in the mornings. There are a hundred things to be done before we go on."

He found his gig waiting at the pier, the helmsman holding the rope that kept them at the pier. "Good morning, Captain."

"Good morning, Briggs." The helmsman cast off and the sweeps began to pull through the calm harbor water. "You are behaving very discreetly."

"Sir?"

"You must be dying to ask about shore leave. Ease your mind, we are going to attend to it today."

"Yes, sir."

The bosun saw them approach and, as Bliven topped the ladder, piped him aboard with his silver whistle, causing all on deck to snap to attention and salute. "Thank you, Mr. Yeakel. Please have the officers assemble in my cabin at once."

"Aye, sir."

"Mr. Yeakel?"

"Sir?"

"I think it is time to undertake your big job. Can you commence with the rerigging?"

"At any time, sir."

"Sooner begun, sooner finished, Mr. Yeakel."

Bliven was no sooner in his sea cabin than his officers entered one by one. "Well, gentlemen," he told the group, "I think we learned last night that we have landed on a congenial shore, and we may begin apportioning shore liberties among the men. Unless someone has a better suggestion, I think we can send them ashore by the messes. The men in each mess know and will look out for one another, and with one mess ashore each evening, two will remain on the ship, and every man will get one night in three ashore. Now, I think this quite liberal. Mr. Erb, you will pay each man one half of the wages owed him, less what you have debited for his slops and supplies. This will prevent any man from ruining himself with gambling on his first night ashore. Warrant officers who tend their duties by day may have shore leave any evening, and by day with need and permission. Officers have the freedom of the shore except when one has the deck, with night watches to be divided among the lieutenants one night in three. Does anyone have anything to add?"

"Captain," said Miller, "a few of us went ashore to investigate the town earlier this morning. We were told that since the whalers began calling here there has been talk of providing a seamen's bethel and lending library, but it is not yet a reality."

"Oh, good God! Somehow I do not think that a chapel and reading room are the first needs that our men will address. No offense, Reverend Mutterbach." The chaplain smiled and raised his hands in surrender. "Does Honoruru have enough of a commercial district to entertain a third of our crew without being overwhelmed?"

"Yes, sir," said Jackson. "Once word spread of the growing number of ships calling here, there was a busy district of bars and cafés."

"A more serious matter, sir," said Erb. "I have spoken with the American agent, who tells me that the incoming amount of ships' provisions have not been well able to meet the demand from the growing number of vessels calling here. He can supply us some salt meats and biscuit, but likely not enough to fill our needs."

"Captain," said Miller, "are we not going to Lahaina from here to inquire further after the abused Captain Saeger? More ships call there than here. It seems that we could take on what we can here and top off there."

"Yes, that is how we shall do it."

At noon Bliven took his gig back to the pier to await Karaimoku, who emerged from the royal compound just as they tied up, as though he had been waiting. This day he wore native dress that revealed his tattoos and powerful chest.

They exchanged pleasantries on the pull out to the *Rappahannock*, and then Bliven said, "Mr. Pitt, may I ask you something? You need not answer if you find it too personal."

"What is it?"

"I know that the English and Americans call you Mr. Pitt, but I am curious: What does your real name mean?"

"It means Sacred Ships."

"How fascinating! Do you know why you were given this name?"

Karaimoku nodded. "At the time I was born, it had to do with a ceremony in the old religion. We had a year-end festival, and at its end a canoe was laden with our finest foods and sent to sea as an offering to Lono, the storm god. I believe I was named for that. But when the ship came bringing your missionaries and the word of God, I took it as a sign that I should help them however I could."

"I see."

On board, Karaimoku evinced curiosity about everything, beginning with their figurehead of Mary Washington. Westerners always pointed out that Washington's wife's name was Martha and always had to be corrected that as the ship was named for the river of Washington's boyhood home, the figurehead was of his mother. Karaimoku was well aware of the difference between long guns and carronades; in the hold below, after a moment's demoralization at the sight of Beecher the giant tortoise, he paid the strictest attention to the close ribbing in the hold and the diagonal knees that held up the berth deck. The largest vessel that had been built in the islands was a barge for the king, but it was apparent that Karaimoku was taking careful note of *Rappahannock*'s improved construction.

It took three days before Kahumanu convened her court again, and Clarity repaired there as soon as she heard of it. When the queen saw her at the edge of the circle, she called out. "Missy La Laelae! Come to me, we are glad to see you." As Clarity approached she added, "How is your baby?"

At the foot of the dais Clarity dropped into a curtsy. "He is well, ma'am, thank you for asking. He is with Mrs. Albright."

"Come to me." The queen patted her thigh, and Clarity sat upon it. "What will you tell me today of our Lord Jesus Christ?"

"Our Lord, ma'am, knew well those parts of the holy book that were written before he came down to earth to live among us. Part of that holy book is a collection of wise sayings that are good advice for everyone to live by; they are called the proverbs. One that I like is 'Who can find a virtuous woman? For her price is far above rubies.'"

Kahumanu shook her head slowly. "That is not a general principle such as those you have been telling me. What is the meaning of this saying?"

Clarity's search for words was apparent in her halting speech. "Ma'am, in a place like this, it is hard for a woman to maintain her dignity when there is no privacy, when anyone may look in upon her at any time."

"Missy, something is on your mind. What is it? You may speak plainly."

It took all her courage to say it in front of the whole court. "Ma'am, I had not seen my husband in a year. He will be here only a short time. A few nights ago, we were watched while we were . . . together."

The queen appeared to ignore the titter that rippled through the court. "Perhaps they were curious. Many have heard that missionaries do their mating in a strange way." She gave herself away by almost laughing.

Clarity blushed to deep crimson. "But, Majesty, how would you feel if you discovered that someone was observing you at such an intimate moment?"

Kahumanu considered it, and then her eyes lit up and she looked up at her ladies. "I don't know. Is he young and handsome?" The court erupted in laughter, with which Clarity had no choice but to join, then covered her face. The queen patted her back. "There, now, Missy. Is it not better to laugh at such things than burn ourselves with shame?"

She sighed. "But very well. Hear me, everyone! From this time I lay a new *kapu*. No one may approach the houses of the missionaries closer than twenty paces except you announce yourself with a greeting, that they may know you are coming. Place *kapu* sticks twenty paces from their houses. See to it that the country people learn of this. Disobey this command at my displeasure."

"A *kapu*, ma'am?" Clarity gave her a searching look. "I thought the old religion was dead."

"The religion is dead, but I am still the law. This will preserve your dignity in future." The slight pressure at her back told her it was time to dismount.

That afternoon brought the arrival of a sleek schooner, the *Albacore*, flying the American flag, and with her home port of Boston painted across her stern. She was particularly welcome, both for her cargo of salt pork and for being laden with letters addressed via the American agent, who dispatched a large packet of them to Bingham to distribute among the missionaries.

It was evening before Bliven arrived at their *pili* and sat reading by a lamp lighted with whale oil, a sure advantage of living in a port town at the edge of the whaling grounds. "Good Lord!" he said, shattering the quiet.

Clarity was startled in the bed where she lay, reaching aside to gently rock Ben's cradle. "What is it, dearest?"

He held a letter out at arm's length. "There is a letter from Brazil. You are going to have a baby!"

"Mercy! If the posts move any faster, they will begin telling our fortunes."

Bliven's visage fell as he regarded the next letter and broke its wax seal.

LITCHFIELD, CONN.
JULY THE 17TH, 1820

My own dear Son,

This letter, I presume, will reach you in some "Pacific" place, which I hope will betoken not merely the geographical location, but describe a peaceable cruise in that far place. My dearest boy, it is my duty to convey to you that sad news which we have long been expecting, but hoping would be forestalled for as long as the dear Lord would allow. Your excellent father departed this life one week ago. Over time, his slumbers had become deeper, his speech softer. I was sitting with him when he opened his eyes and looked at me, took his last breath, and went to heaven. He did not suffer. That I who loved him so much was the last thing on this earth that he saw, I attribute to the immeasurable blessing and mercy always shown us in our long life together.

I believe he felt his end coming, for he took care to tell me, that when I wrote to you, to remind you not to mourn him too deeply, that he was content to enjoy my company and cooking, but equally content to answer the great God whenever He should send for him.

Your good mother-in-law provided space for him in the Marsh burying ground, and in fact settled that we all shall sleep at last with her and her husband's family, which I allow is a more honored place of rest for us than I would ever have expected. Reverend Beecher was not here to disapprove of this, for he has gone visiting to Ohio to spy out the chances of leading the new seminary at that place. Before he died, your father said that he hoped the good Reverend would encounter your uncle Rufus in the woods of Ohio, so that wherever he *went to shout his hosannas, he would be nettled by Putnams—so you see, my angel, that he was saucy to the last.*

*Oh, how I shall miss him, but my Dear Son, you are not to worry about me. I am greatly saddened, but I am well looked after. Mr. Meriden manages the farm very well, the tavern and the livery both turn a small profit, although the times have been hard, and the prize money from your captures is safely stored—therefore I judge that in a little time I shall become one of those good-doing widow women who become so esteemed in a town.*

*Mrs. Marsh no longer leaves her house but she is not ill, and she joins me in sending love to dear Clarity. She said at our last visit that she had dreamt of her, teaching French and water colors to half-clothed native girls, but realized upon waking that this is likely not what occupies her!*

*Farewell, my dearest Bliv, may the Lord's mercy continue me to see you again.*

> *Your Loving Mother,*
> *Doro. Putnam*

> BLIVEN PUTNAM, CAPT. USN
> VIA AMERICAN AGENT,
> HONORURU
> SANDWICH ISLANDS

Silently he rose and handed Clarity the letter. "I shall be back in a few moments."

She read it carefully, and then from the door of the *pili* saw him sitting at the line where the grass met the beach. After several minutes she checked on the baby and walked out to him, and the moment she sat down he extended an arm around her and drew her close. She thought it better to let him speak first, and rested her head on his shoulder.

"He told me to mourn him only a little," he said at last. "Do you know, I have spent my Navy life overhauling and fighting wicked men? It seems that I took it for granted that some men in the world are so deeply good."

"You told me that you parted well. He knew how much you loved him." She could almost feel the heat radiate from his face as his tears fell silently, and he nodded. "Well, dearest, you will have a lifetime to tell your son what a wonderful man he was."

Bliven stood, pulled Clarity to her feet and kissed her, and they walked slowly back to the house. "You lost your father some years ago," he said. "I have not known the feeling. It is a little like walking through a door and knowing you shall never go back and walk through it again."

"Because we only get older, Bliv. We never get younger."

## { 11 }

# *Old Story, New Language*

Only once did Bliven actually walk the lanes and closes of that district in Honoruru where seamen went for their pleasure, which lay inland from the warehouses of the trading merchants. He did not study closely the men ambling down the dirt streets, as he did not wish to know which of his men—or worse, his officers—might be making use of Erb's two-dollar quondams. The few native women that he saw on the street were poorly clad, yet were still closely assayed by seamen with cash to spend, and he understood how Clarity's servant must have come to get pregnant, and for how little money.

While there were a few traditional *pili* houses in this warren, most were built of sawn lumber, but their construction bore little merit. They were almost uniformly built so shabbily and so close upon one another that the whole section seemed to beg for the single match that would burn the entirety of it to the ground. A passing merchant officer, hale and swaggering in confident middle age, noted him casting his gaze curiously about and offered guidance if any were required.

"I thank you," responded Bliven. "I am just idly rambling. However, I am curious on one point: Why are there no buildings of brick?"

"Ah, that is a point upon which I can gratify you. The clay in Hawaii is not suitable for making bricks. It is, however, marginally adaptable to make adobe. Those are the buildings you see of that smooth, plaster-looking material."

Bliven pointed. "Such as that one? I have noticed that they are thicker at the bottom than at the top. Is that the style in which they are commonly built?"

"Not intentionally, but the climate here is not the best for adobe. It melts a little whenever it rains; thus you get these clots and clods about the bottom over time. And you will see readily that they require maintenance more or less continuously."

"Yes." He extended his hand. "I am Captain Putnam, United States sloop of war *Rappahannock*, now in harbor."

"Captain Ward, whaler *Cassandra*, twenty-three months out of New Bedford. How do you do?" They shook hands cordially. "Is this your first look at these islands, then?"

"Indeed it is, but you sound as though you know your way around well enough."

"I should hope I do. This is my fourth call here."

"Then there are likely other points on which you can enlighten me, if you are so kindly disposed. Is there a place nearby where I can buy you a drink, Captain Ward? Have you the time?"

"Lord, yes! In this vicinity you are never more than twenty paces from such a place. Take my towline and we shall indulge our own private gala." Ward led the way across the dirt street to a building of framed lumber twenty feet wide, with a plank door in its center.

"No windows?" noted Bliven.

"Oh God, no. Glass here is far too dear to have to replace after every brawl. Seamen come to these places to get drunk, get in a fight, and screw. The order in which these are accomplished is of no consequence, but little establishments such as this provide relief at least to the first two needs." Inside there were a dozen small tables, and beyond them a rear door to an outdoor area, to which Ward pointed. "Let us sit ourselves in the *lanai*. I crave fresh air."

On their way through Ward acknowledged the proprietor behind his counter, a ruddy, closely whiskered Englishman in an apron. "Good day to you, Francis," he hailed. "A whiskey for me, and for this gentleman . . . ?"

"Do you have wine?" asked Bliven.

"Bless you, yes, sir, we have wine."

"Wine, then." They passed through and seated themselves beneath a thatched arbor. The bartender emerged with a full glass in each hand without benefit of a tray. Bliven thanked him and took the glass from his hand, and sampled it. The liquid was reddish purple and looked like wine, and it rather smelled like wine, but the taste ate through his tongue like acid. "Jesus God in heaven!"

"Sir?" Francis looked at him. "Is it not to your liking?"

Bliven sucked in deep breaths. "Oh, it will do nicely," he said, "but where in the world did you acquire such a distinguished vintage?"

"From Mr. Marín, sir, the Spaniard, by special warrant gardener and vintner to the king."

Bliven's face went slack. "The king drinks this?"

"No, sir, the king is more a brandy man, as I understand. That will be a dollar for the two of you."

Bliven fished the coin out of a pocket, handed it over, and nodded to dismiss him, and when he was gone looked at Ward in something like shock.

"Do not feel badly, Captain," the whaling master said. "I understand that he keeps a funnel beneath the bar, and returns to the bottle the portions that men leave in their glasses."

"I have had bad wine before, but this is truly epic."

"I have seen men drink it and live."

"Then they have astonishing constitutions! I would say, there is one point on which you could help me. Can you point me to the American consular agent? I believe his name is Mr. Jones."

"You have come to the right place, then." Ward leaned back in his chair and stretched his legs in enjoyment of having a fellow captain to talk to. "Mr. John Coffin Jones, Junior. Like you, he is new to the islands, but unlike you he comes to this district with far different matters in his mind. He is a randy little switch of a boy, twenty-three or -four, maybe, nice looking, devil-may-care, loaded with money. Went to sea as a cabin boy, lives to fuck; you will see him with a different native girl every day. He has been here a few weeks now, so he must have settled into his consular duties in some way."

"Where is his office?"

"They have not gotten around to naming streets here yet, but if you inquire after him at the Marshall and Wildes warehouse, they can direct you. His father is a partner in that firm, and you will see they have the largest warehouse in the waterfront. All the chiefs owe them money."

"Truly? How so?"

"Well, as you must know, the competition among the trading companies is very fierce to get their hands on sandalwood to sell in China. That company was the first into the field, and they locked up much of the market by giving the chiefs fortunes in money and lavish furnishings—"

"Yes, I have seen some of their furnishings."

"—on the promise that they would deliver sandalwood in the

future, and deliver it only to Marshall and Wildes, you see? Then, as it turned out, there is not so much sandalwood in the forests as was previously supposed, which has left the chiefs in a scramble for how to pay their debts, and the interest."

"Interest? I have heard before of charging them interest. What in flaming hell do natives know about interest?"

Ward waved it off impatiently. "Well, if they do not understand it, they should not have made a bargain on that basis, should they? At least, that is the position of the younger Mr. Jones. When he is not spreading his seed about the waterfront, he is showing the account books to the chiefs and asking how they are going to make good on what they owe. And then, if they cannot pay it he will probably be willing to take an equivalent value in their land."

"Is all this not in some conflict with his duties to represent the interest and goodwill of the United States?"

Ward's face went blank with honesty. "Oh, yes, I daresay it is. But his father is very well connected. There was some politics involved, I imagine. But what about you, Captain Putnam? What brings you and a big sloop of war to this part of the globe?"

"I was ordered to Malaya to announce our presence in the Malacca Strait, to let the pirates there know to leave our ships alone. So here I am provisioning, and looking in on that shipload of American missionaries that arrived here last year."

"Ah, yes, the missionaries!" Ward took a draw at his whiskey, seeming from the face he made to almost relish its badness. "Bless their souls, there are plenty of seamen who do not want them here, let me tell you. And your young Mr. Jones is first in that line. Never misses a chance to speak against them to the king and the chiefs."

"I was not aware that many people got a chance to speak to the king."

Ward's speech slowed. "Hm! I detect that you know more than you have let on. Well, I will tell you, if you don't know already, the king is a drunkard and a lecher, so those who are most responsible for the government—"

"And that would be the queen mother and the prime minister, Mr. Pitt?"

"Stepmother, but yes, exactly. They keep the king happy, usually out fishing, where he can't cause any harm."

"The queen and Mr. Pitt, and at least some faction of the chiefs, seem to have welcomed the missionaries, and have become Christians, is that not so?"

"Oh, yes, but there you have uttered the important word: 'faction.' Now, it seems to me that these Hawaiians have a more spiritual bent than other primitive peoples I have encountered. For them to believe in something lies deep in their nature. When Kahumanu and her side suppressed the old religion several months ago, there was nothing with which to replace it. Your missionaries arrived just in time to fill that void. But the queen does not punish those who still respect the old gods. In this she is quite modern, but it has allowed that other faction to grow, which resents the new god being foreign."

"Interesting. I have never heard of another case where people put aside their religion with nothing to take its place."

"Nor I," Ward agreed, "and your missionaries came along at the critical moment."

Bliven stood. "Well, I must see if I can track down Mr. Jones. I thank you for your time, and I hope we meet again."

Ward kept his seat and toasted him with his remaining whiskey. "Fair sailing to you, Captain Putnam."

"By the way, you have been plying these waters for many years:

Have you made the acquaintance of a Captain Saeger, schooner *Fair Trader*?"

"I have. In fact I found him anchored at Lahaina Roads not two weeks ago; he had taken on a full hold of sandalwood for Canton. He seemed quite eager at the prospect but was in no hurry to leave. He was spreading money merrily around the dives, at least the ones that were still open, for the missionaries there have influenced the high chief to close down the whorehouses. He was not happy about that."

"You saw him in Lahaina two weeks ago?"

"I did."

"Well, now, that is good hearing. His trail grows warmer! Tell me about him."

"Don't know him well, but then, I don't think anyone does. His vessel is a fine big tops'l schooner, quick as the dickens. Motley crew, though. Why do you ask?"

"I am bound for Malaya to inquire into pirates that attacked him a few years ago. I understand he has a hard reputation."

Ward let his head fall from side to side. "Well, yes and no. He is a hard man, to be sure, but it is a hard life trying to trade sandalwood when the big companies have bought off most of the chiefs. Of course, it would help if he didn't hate natives so much."

Bliven sat again, at the edge of his chair. "What has he got against them?"

"Oh, not just Hawaiians, mind; he hates all dark little people. He used to have two ships, the *Fair Trader* and a smaller vessel captained by his son. He was killed years ago by Boogis pirates in the Indies. They got it in their heads that he had some gold hidden somewhere on his ship, and they tortured him—cut off his fingers one joint at a time, and worse. It was Saeger who found the body, and I think that turned his mind over into somebody else. Don't know what he was like before."

"I see. You are schooling me, Captain Ward. I confess I have never heard of the . . . was it Boogis pirates? I have fought buccaneers in the Caribbean and Tripoli corsairs in the Mediterranean—"

Ward's eyes opened wide. "Oh, that is where I know your name! Now I really am glad to have met you. If you are Malaya-bound, you will encounter them. What course do you propose to get there?"

"At present I am thinking of Canton first, then down the coast of Indo-China to Singapore."

"Safe and sensible. But if you want to learn about the Boogis, you will bear south of the Philippines, through the Sulu Sea and along the Borneo coast. All those little islands you see with houses built on stilts out over the water, those are Boogis of one kind or another, different tribes, but they are all sea people. Watch out for them, though: they are a heartless lot."

Bliven rose again and offered his hand. "I am in your debt, Captain, and I thank you again."


IN THAT BUSINESS section west of the missionaries' compound and the royal enclosure, Bliven found a few sound buildings of lava or coral blocks, but most again of framed lumber so closely built together that they hazarded fire. Closest to the waterfront were a rank of warehouses, giving way to mercantiles and hotels farther away. The firm of Marshall and Wildes he easily found; in fact, he would have seen it from where his ship lay anchored, but it faced a street running away from the beach. He found young Jones working at a large table whose papers appeared organized, with a writing desk behind him with its pigeonholes labeled and with folded papers sorted among them.

It was a better impression than Bliven expected to receive after what Ward had told him, but the young man appeared efficient at his duty—whether to his firm or his country was another matter, and the question of what women and how many he rogered in his spare time was his own affair. However, it was impossible not to imagine the slew of diseases surely now stewing beneath his dark blue trousers and picture him writhing in the tortures of mercury on his visits to the doctor, if he sought treatment. Bliven placed letters into the post, condolence to his mother, encouragement to Sam, and a brief account of his arrival and pending departure to Hull, with the assurance of a full report upon his return.

From the business district he made his way back to the east, down the beach path to Clarity's *pili*, which he found empty and, for want of a door, standing open. He found by the fire some tea in the kettle left from breakfast, and moved a chair outside to take his ease until she returned. When he saw her coming along the path, she seemed light of heart, carrying the baby, wearing not a dress but a tapa skirt wrapped around the bottom of a trimmed cotton blouse, carrying a kind of knapsack over her shoulder. As soon as she saw him, her countenance brightened even more, and he rose and embraced her before they sat together.

"How have you been occupying yourself today?" he asked.

"I have been with Mrs. Albright, teaching sewing to some of the women, and of course we work in little Bible stories as we do it. And in exchange, look at this: they showed us how they make their material. They do not spin and weave; they pound it from the bark of the local mulberry trees. It is actually quite soft but not very flexible."

Bliven stood but winced as he did so.

"Are you all right, dearest?"

"Just a bellyache. I met a whaling captain in town and I bought him a drink to visit with him. I got hold of some wine that was quite dreadful; that is likely what it is."

"Perhaps, but from observing your meals, I might have another idea. You have cramps in your belly?"

"Yes."

"And have you perhaps become worried, well, about your stool, in a way you have not spoken of?"

It was shocking to hear her address such a subject. "Well, I—"

"Black and greasy?"

"Yes, in fact."

She shook her head. "Don't worry about it. That, dearest, betokens too much pineapple. Avoid it from your diet for a couple of days, and then eat it only in moderation. You will be fine."

"Well, thank you, Dr. Putnam."

She stood and enjoyed letting him hold her. "Why don't you leave your surgeon here and let me ship out with you?"

"No, I couldn't. He needs the job. But, my love, it is time to tell you that we must leave soon. The bosun has finished the rerigging, we have taken on all the provisions we can here, so we will take on more at Lahaina, and then into the sunset."

"Singapore?"

"Singapore, and its straits, and then to Canton, then back here."

She buried her face in his shirt, motionless, until he said, "Are you regretting your decisions? Are you sorry you came so far away?"

Clarity pulled back and looked deep into his eyes. "No, not a bit, not for a moment. I will see you more often than I would had I stayed home, and I am having the adventure of a lifetime. I wish you could stay longer, but I am . . . if I said I was content, you would know I was lying, so I will say I am *reconciled*. You won't sail tomorrow, surely."

"No, no. Four days' time, we think, that will be next Sunday. My aim heretofore has been to spare you mounting pain. Would you rather I tell you of such things further in advance?"

"No, I think not. You are right, it might bring a cloud over our remaining time together. Besides, there is some little degree to which I can sense it coming. If I should ever require to know more certainly, I shall ask. Of course, come Sunday you may not leave until you come to church and let them pray over you."

Bliven considered this, and nodded. "Happily, the tide will not flow out until afternoon, so that will be well. I suppose I can stand that. May I bring Reverend Mutterbach? He is just a Deist, but he is very nice."

He had been to one of their Sunday services before, held within the grass-walled church, with the chiefs seated in chairs, and the Louis XIV throne for the queen. It was still a shock to him, however, how large these people were, so that the chairs had to be spaced widely, as though this chiefly class were a separate, perhaps conquering race. He judged the sermon—delivered partly in English and partly in Hawaiian, expounding upon the verse that those who would be first in heaven must be the servants of all—well suited to its hearers. But he had never before stayed for the second service, conducted outside for the commoners, seated on tapa mats in a mixture of Western and native clothing. He did not know the subject because the sermon was preached entirely in Hawaiian, but the audience listened respectfully and seemed pleased with what they heard. He was surprised how many there were, filling an extended lawn before the church and causing Bingham to raise his voice beyond what seemed comfortable for him. What drew Bliven's closest attention were the hymns that they sang, tunes that were familiar, but babble to him for being sung in the native tongue; what was more, the people sitting on the grass sang in full voice, without music, apparently having memorized the verses.

Bingham was quite hoarse by the time he greeted Bliven and Mutterbach afterward, and shook hands with them. "We are sorry to learn that you will be leaving us, Captain, Reverend. Will it be soon?"

"Presently, I fear," said Bliven. "My wife has her brave face on as she walks us to the pier."

"Godspeed to you, then. And we will miss Mr. Fleming as well. As you see, he has brought us along with our house, and even more usefully has shown us how to finish it ourselves."

"He has been invaluable to me as well," said Bliven. "In fact, when we left Boston, I sent my bosun to Roxbury to kidnap him if necessary. I could not do without him. But tell me, what on earth is going on over there?" He pointed perhaps fifty yards away, to an excavation of dimensions as large as any lecture hall in Boston.

"Oh, dearest," said Clarity, "the grass church that you see is temporary. That is where the new church shall be, a great edifice of coral rock."

"That is very well, but do you really need it to rival St. Paul's?"

"I take your point, but for the permanent church to convey to the natives some impression of the glory and permanence of God will not be a bad thing."

"I see."

"The ground has been donated to us by a chiefess named Ha-o," added Bingham, "who has come to be a believer. You see it has a spring of fresh water, which she very sensibly said can be used for baptisms. Our intention is to name the church The Waters of Ha-o, after her and the spring. Building it will be a labor of years, though, likely decades."

"Perhaps when I bring Mr. Fleming back . . . ," he said to general approbation.

Bingham gestured out to the harbor. "The natives dive down to the reef and cut free great blocks of coral, and haul them up here by hand."

Bliven nodded. "Like the medieval guilds building the cathedrals in Europe."

Bingham stared at him, astonished. "You know about that? Captain, you surprise me."

"Architecture has long been an avocation of mine."

"Dearest, let us leave Ben with Mrs. Albright and save him the long walk. Ben, can you say good-bye to Papa?"

Bliven leaned down, kissed the top of his head, and said seriously, "Take good care of your mother," to a ripple of laughter. "Ah, you good people think I am joking, but when he is older and I say that, his obedience will be second nature to him!"

Clarity hid her rising anguish as they walked to the waterfront, seeing Mutterbach and her husband to the captain's gig, which was waiting for them. She had learned to take some pride in the New England stoicism of her farewells, and she gave away her emotion only in removing her bonnet and letting the wind lift her hair as she walked back up to the mission.

Muriel Albright hugged her as she handed over the baby. "Would you like for me to come back and stay with you, my dear?"

"Yes, I would, very much. But not today. Today I intend to indulge myself in being an emotional derelict, and I want no witnesses."

"I will move back soon, then."

When she came, in three days' time, it was not as Clarity expected, for she was riding on a wagon, sitting beside the Spanish farmer and now a chief by marriage, Francisco de Paula Marín. He clambered down first, stiffly, for he was nearly fifty. He was strong and swarthy, as Clarity had imagined all Spaniards must be; the wagon had a step, but Marín placed a box underneath it that so that Muriel would not have to strain. After moving the pieces of a bed into the *pili* and setting it up, he joined Clarity for tea at the fire as Muriel unpacked. "Oh, did you not hear?" he said. "There was a big scene between Kahumanu and the chiefess Liliha. The queen pressed her hard to give some land she owns in the town to start a school. The chiefess refused at first, but the queen worked her over and got her way."

"Liliha?" Clarity was amazed. "Everything about her, every move, every gesture, proclaims a strumpet."

Marín shook his head sadly. "I understand your feeling, but perhaps you should not judge her. You do not know her story. I believe she is—how do you say?—more sinned against than sinning. Did you know, her name means 'heartbroken.'"

"By all means, then, exculpate her. What is her story?"

Marín stretched his legs, and Clarity realized it was not a simple explanation. "She is very highborn, one of the few women in the kingdom high enough to defy Kahumanu, even though she's only twenty. Her father's father was one of the twins who founded the dynasty; her mother's father was the king of Maui, who many people think was the father of the old King Ta-meha-meha."

"What do you mean, 'they think he was the father'?"

Marín held up a finger in explanation. "Ah! After he became king, Ta-meha-meha claimed a higher descent from somebody else, and made it punishable by death to say he was the son of the king of Maui."

"Well, I have to admit, that's power when you can create your own facts!"

"Yes. Well, Liliha was married very young to a nephew of the old king."

"Wait! If she was the niece of the king, that would make her husband also her cousin, if I follow you."

"Oh, Mrs. Putnam, that's nothing. Among the nobility here, the most desirable circumstance is to marry one's brother or sister."

Clarity looked down into her tea. "Oh, my."

"Yes, but they are raised by different families, so it does not seem immoral. It is complicated. Just look at the present king's wife, Kamamalu. She is not just the king's wife, she is also his half-sister, and his cousin, and his aunt, too, as I believe."

"They sound like something out of ancient Egypt."

"Similar customs, yes, like the pharaohs. Well, Liliha seems to have actually loved this husband. But then enter your friend Karaimoku, whom you missionaries look to as such a friend and benefactor."

"Indeed? What has he to do with it?"

"Karaimoku was a great favorite and advisor to the old king. Another of his favorites stole Karaimoku's favorite wife, which sent him into such a rage that he burnt down most of Honoruru looking for her. Failing to recover her, he stole a wife from his younger brother, the chief Boki."

"The one that Karaimoku calls the black sheep of the family?"

"Well, yes, as the pot said to the kettle. That put Boki in such a rage that he stole Liliha from her husband, who was *his* nephew."

"But wait—he was *Ta-meha-meha*'s nephew."

"Yes, he was nephew to both of them."

"Heavens, Mr. Marín, you are making my head hurt! I cannot begin to fathom such a prevalence of incest!"

"It is their custom. But to conclude: Liliha seems content to stay with Boki, because his lands are some of the richest on the island, and they are on the north shore, as far from Kahumanu as one can get, and separated from here by a high mountain range. Much of it is very thick jungle, with lots of sandalwood, which has made them very rich."

"I see," said Clarity. "Although I understand that sandalwood is becoming increasingly difficult to find."

"That is true, but he still has it. This is not widely known, but he allows the practice of the old religion in his lands. The priests there have been known for many years to be fierce, and devout to the old gods. Boki has given them the land surrounding their temples, and laid a *kapu* against disturbing the forest. These priests are the ones who killed Captain Vancouver's men many years ago. He landed a watering party, but to the *kahunas* it was a sacred stream, and the men were captured and sacrificed. Those forests have never been cut for sandalwood."

"So he has established rather a bastion against the missionaries?"

"Quite so. I have heard it said that some of the priests who lost the war to preserve the old religion escaped the battle and sought refuge there."

Clarity took a deep breath. "Dear me. That sounds like quite a forbidding place."

"It is, but in fairness to Boki, he is not completely against Western ways, because he knows how much of his wealth comes from them. Perhaps you will think less of me when I tell you this, which as a gentleman I would regret but it is not a large matter because I do not think it is a vice: Boki buys the wine from my vineyard, as you would say, wholesale, even in the years when it is not a fine vintage." Marín leaned forward to impart a confidence. "He says it is good enough for the likes of foreign sailors."

"Ha! No doubt there is some element of truth in that."

"Liliha is loyal to him politically, but she eases her loneliness by taking for lovers whomever she fancies."

HONORURU, KINGDOM OF HAWAII
17TH OCTOBER, 1821

*My dearest Harriet,*

*Well, I suppose that the Age of Miracles has not entirely ended, to discover that you received my letter of a year ago, and your reply is just now come to hand, courtesy the brig Randolph, Capt. Grubbs.*

*I regret extremely that Captain Putnam is not here to share your letter, having some months ago taken his ship to Malaya, and China, and to what adventures may God protect him. I did not know when I came here, that it is twice as far from these islands to China, as it is back to North America! The scholars tell us that the world is some twenty-five thousand miles around, but oh! nowhere could one gain more of a sense of what that means than in the isolation of this tiny country in the middle of the Pacific.*

*Your announcement that your papa has decided that a move to Ohio would be premature at this time is one that I welcome, and I think that the Reverend has exercised wise judgment. While I know you to be a young lady of courage and resourcefulness, Ohio as yet is a raw frontier, and labor there for the Lord's cause must be thought of as more in the nature of missionary work than ministry to a civilized people. I sympathize with the disappointment that you express, and I acknowledge your adventurous spirit. Such is your spirit that I think that you would not shrink from the requirements of missionary labor among people only barely touched by civilization.*

*I recently received my neighbor Mr. Marín, who deposited my elderly friend Mrs. Albright to stay with me while the Captain is away, and she is very welcome both for her company and in looking after the baby, who is becoming a handful. Mr. Marín brought, in addition to some welcome fruits and vegetables from his farm, news of court intrigues that made me reflect anew upon what different people these are from ourselves.*

*Now, dear Harriet, I am going to write you a second letter anon, with news of the mission and its doings, and that letter you may share with your father. But herein, Harriet, I am going to write to you as a young adult and my equal, in your zeal to get out there and do some good in the world. You must know at once the kinds of things you may be up against. So, I am going to tell you some things, not to shock you, although they will, but to give you an idea of what awaits one at the pale of civilization.*

*The families here are mostly small, first I imagine because the diseases spread by visiting seamen have affected the ability of women to conceive, but secondly because the common people, the kanakas as they call them, have so little to live for. Most of what they harvest or catch or raise, they hand up to the chiefs, who do no work and yet live in comparative luxury. Infanticide is not rare among the commoners—such a shocking thing to say. Future generations will have difficulty believing that this could have ever been, just as you express the hope that the people yet to come will find the notion of slavery beyond their comprehension.*

*Families among the chiefly class are also small, but for a different reason: the chiefs, while they typically marry, as a custom prefer to lavish their attentions on young boys, whom they court with expensive gifts even to the humiliation of their wives. In our own* society, women often marry for money, without love, looking to their future security; even so, here such boys who are the objects of the chiefs' affections accept this station as a means to advance into the chiefly class and own property, which the commoners, being mere serfs, may not do.

And these are just some of the moral considerations: the general health of the people is appalling. The population has begun to decline, from diseases unknown here before the discovery of the islands—smallpox, measles, etc.—and also from lung afflictions such as consumption. Skin diseases are everywhere; more people suffer from scabies than do not.

Now it would be helpful, while we seek to alleviate the sufferings of such people, to have some sympathy or cooperation from our government—by which of course I mean our American government, not the queen. Under our Constitution, it may not legally involve itself in religious causes, but from our standpoint we could easily believe that they work against us and seek instead to take advantage of this unfortunate population.

When the United States appointed a consular agent to the Kingdom, we might have expected a man of experience and good judgment. Instead, I believe that Mr. Jones arrived here principally as a debt collector for his father's firm, and that his father used his influence to win him the post of consular agent so that their company would seem to have the force of government behind them. His chief skill seems to be putting the screws to their clients.

It is discouraging to think that in future, people will look upon the American presence in Hawaii as one of expropriation and cruelty, and we missionaries will be linked to them as by a chain, and no one will know how mortified we are by them.

*I cannot bear to end on such a note of selfishness from one horizon to the other, so I will tell you one further truth—that the mission must be counted a success. Services are heavily attended, and conversions are many, evincing a deep spiritual strain among these people that, if anything, yearns to be reached and nourished.*

*Word reached here very recently of an occurrence in which I take especial joy. The High Chiefess Kapiolani of Hawaii Island, who became a dear friend to me before I removed to Honoruru, has converted to the Christian faith, and more than that has performed an astounding act of devotion. She became upset when she learned that many commoners on her land were reluctant to abandon the old gods, owing to the presence of an active volcano, called Kilauea, which they hold to be the home of Pele, their fire goddess. This highborn woman walked barefoot, in pilgrimage, to this volcano, and descended into its very crater. She stood at the edge of a lake of fire and lava, and cast rocks into it, insulting Pele, daring her to come do her worst, if she existed at all. Local pagan priests fled in terror. Of course, nothing happened—but because of her courage and devotion, opposition to the gospel has collapsed as flat as the walls of Jericho before the blast of Joshua's trumpet. Such a thrill of admiration I have seldom felt for anyone.*

*Farewell, my dear girl—keep practicing your writing. If what you one day produce for publication shows the skill and acute expression of your letters, success awaits you!*

*Ever your loving friend,*
*"Missy La Laelae"*

MISS HARRIET BEECHER
LITCHFIELD, CONNECTICUT

\* \* \*

FROM HONORURU, WHICH suddenly required the hiring of a pilot because that had suddenly become an emolument within the gift of the
crown, the *Rappahannock* stood down to Lahaina, dropping anchor as
near to shore as the sounding would allow to finish taking on victuals. Jakob Saeger, however, had embarked two days before for Canton. Bliven decided to conclude his Malacca business as quickly as he
could and see if he could overtake him at Canton to get a full account
of what had befallen him, and a list of his losses for which reparation
could be sought, which had never yet come to light.

Upon leaving Honoruru it was discovered when roll was taken
that a half dozen men had deserted the ship, lured by the climate and
easy sex, preferring to lose themselves in that maze of prostitutes'
hovels, in the suicide of untreated chancres and insanity, than continue in their duty. It was in his power to send Horner and the marines ashore to hunt them down, but he concluded that to have them
and their discontent, and probably their disease, back aboard was not
to be preferred when Miller easily made up the balance with derelict
merchant seamen eager to work to get home.

Within a week of leaving Maui, Bliven decided, measuring each
day's progress by the chronometer and the casting of the knotted line,
and looking at how far they had yet to go, that no one crossing the
Pacific for the first time had any conception of the true expanse of the
globe.

None of his officers, he discovered, had ever heard of Boogis pirates any more than he had, but together with Miller concluded to
disregard Captain Ward's advice on making for Singapore via the Indies. If these "sea people" were indeed the root of piracy in these waters, then for a single American sloop of war to thread the passages

through those myriad islands and islets and reefs and rocks and atolls and sandbars would do more to put them on their guard than to cow them. From Ward's description of their ruthless nature, they were likely not a people to be easily cowed.

Instead, they made generally due west for a month, and then west by south for a month, until they rounded the north coast of Luzon, then southwest through the South China Sea, along the Indo-China coast, slowing, minding the charts carefully to pick through the island-studded shallows to the southern tip of Malaya. Indeed they did begin to see the shores obscured by houses built on pilings over the water, and they were approached by native fishermen in their curious-looking proas, but never too closely. Always the American flag of light silk but the size of a mizzen topsail fluttered from their spanker boom, and they wondered if it was the sight of a theretofore unseen ensign that prompted them to keep their distance, or was the sight of a fifteen-hundred-ton warship itself enough to ward them off?

In all it was just under three months before he saluted their battery and dropped anchor in Singapore Roads—roads, for there was no bay, or harbor. Sir Thomas Stamford Bingley Raffles, whose name they had often chuckled over, he discovered, was not in residence, but was occupied in strengthening his fortifications on Java. Ashore, Bliven discovered that Raffles had left in his wake detailed town plans for how Singapore was to be laid out, in quarters according to race— European, Chinese, Malay, and Indian—and he wondered if that re-flected any experience that the different nationalities could not cordially assimilate. Truly this would become a crossroads of the world—so far from America that he learned those who knew the name only from reading it were pronouncing it incorrectly. It was not "Sing-apore" but "Sin-gapore." And he got his first look at an elephant, a gigantic bull with long, straight tusks, nearly ten feet tall, six or seven tons of him, painted blue and crimson and gold, with a howdah on his back, carrying some prince or other down new-named Bridge Road, all of which details he noted to relay to Clarity.

The authorities that he did find in the Royal Navy office were helpful. The ship was watered and victualed, for Erb produced letters of credit from British banks, as a well-connected purser should be able to do. Bliven also found them helpful on the question of pirates. Not all Boogis were pirates, they told him, but certainly they were the focus of what piracy there was. Their influence, which was to say their extortion and their hiring themselves out to local potentates, was felt from Siam across the Indies to the Philippines, for they were the most populous race in that part of the world.

With Raffles absent, the administration lay with his longtime assistant, whose title was "resident commandant": Thomas Travers, whom all acknowledged spoke for Raffles on all things. Travers was familiar with the pirates' depredation upon Saeger's ship, and although he did not know about the murder of Saeger's son, he expressed no surprise. As long as the interests of Britain and their client, the sultan of Johore, were not affected, and Johore employed no pirates at that time, he gave Bliven full license to assert American power against them.

Boogis pirates, Bliven learned, operated from proas of the kind he had observed casting fishing nets but larger, some large enough to mount a swivel gun or six-pounder. The Boogis depended upon their quarry being unarmed, and massed their proas six or eight at a time to mount an attack and swarm a victim. All this he seemed to have heard before. After his third call ashore he decided he had heard enough. Word came in even as he was taking his leave of Travers that pirates in the service of the sultan of Malacca had raided the coastal town of Sitiawan some one hundred fifty miles up the peninsula that belonged to the sultan of Perak. To spread terror among the citizens, the pirates rounded up the city governor and wealthiest citizens, and publicly executed them by what Travers described as their local embellishment, the Chinese *ling chi*, the so-called death by a thousand cuts. The Chinese template had its mercy of sedation and early death, with continuing mutilation; the Malaccan pirates had kept their victims alive as long as possible. By the time Travers finished his account, Bliven found himself sick at his stomach, and made his farewell.

The morning after that third call, light began to come through the open stern windows, seeming as olive-colored as the water they were anchored in, the air as dank and muggy in the morning as when they had retired. Ross had prepared a bed in the window seat, where Bliven now reclined, as yet unshaven, coffee and soft biscuits on a serving cart beside him. There were three raps at the door. "Enter."

"Lieutenant Miller, sir."

He strode in as Ross held the door open. "Good morning, Captain." Then he checked his steps. "Good God! Forgive me, sir, but you look like hell."

"Yes, Mr. Ross has already apprised me of that fact." Bliven beckoned him to come around the table and sit by him. "I feel like hell, too, and now I get to look at you, come barging in here looking fresh as a colt. Mr. Ross!"

"Sir?"

"I would like for you to find the bosun, the purser, and the carpenter and bring them to me."

"Right away, sir."

"No, not in too great a hurry. Bring them in thirty or forty minutes."

"Aye, Captain."

When they were alone, Bliven pointed to a packet on the table.

"There you see my orders for this cruise. I wish you to read them, in the event that you must assume command."

"Are you quite well, sir?"

"I am not sick, but I fear that may not be the same thing. Michael, I have been lying here, trying to puzzle out how it is I woke up this morning, overcome with the most complete sense of revulsion for this duty. I woke up feeling I hate this, I loathe it, and I want out."

Miller moved a chair from the table to where he lay. "Oh, I am so sorry to hear that. Was it something I said?"

"Ha!" Count on Miller to try to lighten the moment. "It is not you, nor the men, nor the ship, nor even being so far from home. It is this duty, this assignment, this errand."

"Nevertheless, Captain, wanting out could pose a difficulty when we are more than a year from home."

Bliven fixed his gaze out the window. "Hm! Perhaps."

"What is it that you awoke to find so onerous?"

"You said it yourself, Mr. Miller, when we were in the Galápagos. Pirates—the oceans are lousy with them. I awakened and found myself thinking about something that Mr. Pitt said. You remember, he is the chief who fills the role of prime minister to the royal family in Hawaii. I gave him a tour of the ship."

"Yes, I remember him."

"I asked him at one point how they had been able to throw off the old pagan religion. And he said that it was mainly the women who had suffered under its superstitions and dogmas, and not just the poor common women, but the women of all classes. In their fear they said nothing, but their resentments grew, and perhaps they discussed it when they were alone among themselves. When there came an opportune time, when the old king died, the queens and the chiefesses rose up and struck. They just reached a point where they would not brook it anymore. And Mr. Pitt said something further. He said that when some of the priests made to fight to preserve the pagan idols, Kahumanu had no shortage of support when she determined to fight them.

"He said she tried negotiation but the priests wouldn't have it: they would rule or ruin. Even the sacred queen mother, who is almost a goddess, lent her influence, without effect. Each side assembled an army, and the great battle was fought near the western shore of the big island. Mr. Pitt commanded the queens' army, and Kahumanu herself commanded a fleet of war canoes off the shore, including her own, which was a double canoe mounted with a carronade. As the tide of battle turned in their favor, Mr. Pitt was able to drive the priests and their followers down to the beach, and there the queen was offshore, and she personally fired the piece, and every time she fired it, she cut down a swath of the old pagan priests. He said that the queen is not by nature a cruel woman, but when she got a bellyful of their arrogance and cruelty—when she realized that reason was lost on them, and that nothing short of death or total, abject defeat would make them cede their claim to rule the lives of everyone else with blood and terror—she accepted their terms. She merely accepted *their* terms. They demanded victory or death, and she gave them death. She cut them down by the score. She doubted not the justice of her doing so, nor does she yet."

Bliven paused and saw Miller studying him with piercing intensity. "And that, Mr. Miller, is how I awakened this morning changed, and feeling the same way—exactly the same way—about pirates."

"I see."

"The very idea that there is this class of men who actually believe that they have the right to take whatever they please from anyone who is too weak to resist them—such creatures do not deserve the courtesy of a fair fight. An entire ship full of such men is not worth the life of one of my officers or crew. They ought to be removed from the earth to make it safe for decent people, and given this, someone must do the winnowing. In the present time and in this place, that duty falls to me, and so I awakened this morning changed, and I feel changed immutably. I cannot explain it, any more than a caterpillar could explain how it awoke one morning and found itself turned into a moth. I felt . . . I felt I owed you this explanation before you should mark such a change in my temperament and wonder if I have gone mad."

Miller considered the whole exposition soberly. "Well, sir, surely no one could look upon your resolve to fulfill your duty to its outer limit, and do so while minimizing the risk to your ship and men, with any criticism. And yet—"

"What?"

"Did you not tell me at some time that your orders include the limitation to not engage pirates who work for the rajas allied with Great Britain?"

"They do. But, happily, I am informed that the Sultan of Johore just now employs no pirates, so any we find are fair game. Moreover, I sense that the British in their better senses are as revolted by them as we are; and third, this vessel has the right to defend itself against an attack from any quarter, regardless of their identity."

Miller nodded slowly. "As long as the other side fires first."

"I would say that is the safest course. We should never open a fight, but we must be prepared always to finish it."

"Do you imagine that we can clear the seas of pirates all by ourselves in our one ship?"

"No. Only the ones we come across. That is enough. But there is one thing more that I would tell you, not as a lieutenant under my command, but as my friend. It has also been working at my mind that not all pirates are seaborne. Pirates are but one species of the beasts of prey. The family includes also political tyrants, priests pagan or popish who employ fear or compulsion, men of business who profit by the ruin of others. I am no Jefferson, but I awoke this morning like him, as he famously wrote, having sworn eternal hostility to every form of tyranny. And yes, there is a specific event that may have triggered this miasma in my mind. I have learned by letter that my friend, the planter in South Carolina, is being ruined by having been led into financial risks that are proving disastrous, and if he is ruined, he who led him down that path is to take everything he has."

"And that is your friend who owns the large number of slaves?"

"Yes."

"Then forgive me, as your friend, but is slavery not the most terrible form of piracy? Is he not reaping as he has sown? Having devoured such small fish, is he not always in danger of being himself devoured by a larger fish?"

Bliven looked helplessly through the stern windows at what promised to be a hot day. "Miller, you have the damnedest penchant to cut straight to the heart of a dilemma."

"I thought that was part of my charm."

"He is my friend." Bliven barked out suddenly in laughter. "You know, when we were boys, we were midshipmen, and some bored and wicked lieutenants goaded us into dueling each other. Dale and Barron stopped us before we could kill each other."

"Dale? Richard Dale?"

"Yes."

"Heavens! I did not realize you served under Dale. What a great man to have known. I'm sorry, continue."

"They made us shake hands—or rather hold hands—and swear

before God that we would always be friends and defend each other's honor. That was about twenty years ago, and as time and events have separated us, we have held to that. When my wife met him she disliked him instantly for his owning slaves, and I defended him as coming from a different world. But as time has gone by, I cannot . . . I cannot defend it any longer."

"Then I may say, sir, that is to your credit. What is the adage? 'Hate the sin, love the sinner'?"

"But he would be quick to tell you, and indeed an old slave of his himself told me, suppose you freed them? Where would they go? There are no jobs, they could not buy land, no one would care for them. All we would create is a class of beggars."

"Is that not why we are creating that new country in Africa and we are to start sending them back to their own continent?"

"Ha! Liberia, yes, although I fear that experiment will fail from its own naïveté. They come from tribes as different as the English are from Mongols. We saw that from our own group that we smuggled into Boston a couple of years ago. So now we think to put them all onto a small patch of land and say, 'Here you are; good luck to you.'" He shook his head.

"Well." Miller stood. "I do not know the answers, but I applaud your wrestling with the questions. And as it comes to dealing with pirates, here or elsewhere, you have my full support."

"Thank you, but do not go yet. I want you to be present when I talk to the others."

Several moments more and Ross entered with Erb, Yeakel, and Fleming. "You wished to see us, Captain?"

"Yes, Mr. Yeakel. Gentlemen, our business in Singapore is concluded, except for taking aboard a Malay interpreter that Mr. Travers has been good enough to provide us. Mr. Erb, I wish you to procure a store of paints before we leave. We shall stand out of Singapore very smartly, saluting the fort and all that. But once we are out of sight, we shall hunt up some small estuary and put into it. There we shall do what we can to disguise ourselves as a large merchantman. Complete new paint down to the waterline, I think some dun sort of brownish green. When the gunports are closed, I want them to be invisible."

"I understand, Captain."

"All hands to wield paintbrushes so that we may be done speedily. Second, you must lay in enough civilian clothes for the men to wear whenever they are topside, not particularly new or nice."

"Yes, sir."

"Oh, and we shall need a name. Paint over *Rappahannock* and we shall call her . . . *Fortuna*. Also, Mr. Fleming, make some empty wooden frames on the weather deck, here and there, in no order. Then cover them with sails and anchor them down so it will look like we are carrying more cargo than we can stow in the hold."

"I understand, sir."

"Then, Mr. Yeakel, once we start up the Malacca Strait, I will set you a task. I will desire you to set your sails in a slovenly way. Spill a little wind. But set them only slovenly enough that you can trim them up for fighting at a moment's notice. Can you do this?"

"Certainly, sir." He grinned suddenly. "But it will require some skill, in the same way that a good singer must play a character who sings badly."

"Exactly. I did not know you to be a man of the theater, but the comparison is apt. We may be too large a vessel to trick anyone into thinking we are a commercial ship, but I am wagering that some pirate will be overcome by his greed. If he suspects we might be a merchantman, he will think us an uncommonly big one, and we must be carrying a great amount of cargo to steal. Let us hope that he is as unwise as he is greedy."

"What about our fighting tops, Captain?" asked Fleming. "Will they not give us away as a warship?"

"I have worried about that. Fortunately, they are smaller than the great broad fighting tops of a frigate, so with the sails set they may not be too prominent. I considered asking you to dismount them, but I do not want to diminish the ship's readiness for battle if a serious fight is pressed upon us. So then, paint the masts and fighting tops the same dun color as the hull; maybe they will blur together from a distance."

Fleming nodded. "Aye, sir."

"Now, gentlemen"—Bliven sat up straighter in his makeshift bed—"you know, for us to take a ship this size into such narrow waters, I feel a little like my grandfather's brother. He once crawled into a cave with a torch and a musket to kill the last wolf in Connecticut. I believe there is one further precaution we should take. We are entering these narrow waters with the intention of provoking an ambuscade. If we succeed, the attack will come swiftly and from close quarters. I wish to be able to repel it with decisive force, delivered quickly. Now, pirate ships here as elsewhere are lightly armed, and the weight of our broadside will be so excessive, I wish you to remove the twelve-pounder bow chasers to the stern. Cut new gunports for them there. Then I want you to hoist our forwardmost twenty-fours up to the bow as chasers. I believe that their additional few hundred yards of reach may serve us better there than in the broadside, which is adequate already. But you must inspect the deck and the knees beneath them: Reinforce the deck if necessary to support the weight of the guns."

There was a knock at the door and Jackson entered. "Excuse me, Captain, there is a small boat coming alongside. I believe it is the gentleman you are expecting."

"Thank you, Mr. Jackson. Take him down to the wardroom, if you please, give him coffee, and ask if he needs breakfast. I will come fetch him when I am dressed. Mr. Ross?"

"Sir?"

"Ready the other guest compartment for him, if you please."

"At once, Captain."

The following day they saluted the battery, Union Jack from the foremast and American flag from the spanker boom, and stood out regally, on a heading of west-southwest. Once alone, however, they made a swing to the south, slowed by constant soundings but still unobserved, into a small sound between Batam and Bulan Islands, far enough to be screened from the sea-lane.

Their transformation into a large and heavily laden merchantman required four days, even allowing for extra touches such as painting white squares and rectangles on the cream-colored sails, to appear from a distance as though they had been patched. They were just able to squeeze through the sound to its southeastern mouth, and made a wide starboard turn between Bulan and Tjombol, standing northwest into the Strait of Malacca. As they began their run, Bliven on the quarterdeck heard Yeakel ordering men to set the sails in ways that were not entirely proper, and smiled when he heard him bark at them for questioning why they were to do it wrongly.

They proceeded as slowly as a trolling fisherman, and were approached, still only distantly, by native proas, but otherwise excited no curiosity. In this attitude they sailed as far north as Penang, more than three hundred miles, before putting about and returning south under easy sail. Their disappointment was palpable, and Griggs, their interpreter, could offer no explanation or guess whether they had been discovered.

It was where the strait was constricted to less than six miles wide between Kukup and Karimunbesar Island that they began to be pushed southerly to the edge of the narrow channel.

"Damn this wind," said Bliven. "If we haul any closer we shall be blowing sideways!"

Suddenly they heard a deep, crunching groan as the bow lifted up and they felt their forward speed arrest and then grind to a halt. Without waiting on order Yeakel screamed to drop all canvas lest they be driven farther onto whatever it was.

"Captain," said Miller, "I believe we have hit something."

"Quartermaster, how is the tide?"

"At its ebb, sir."

"Well, that is one good thing. What is the sounding?"

"Six fathoms midships, sir, and aft."

"Then what have we hit? Mr. Miller, do you think we are aground?"

"I don't know, sir. It was not sudden, as if we hit a rock. It was more as if we drove onto a sandbar, but that could not happen within half the length of the ship."

"Captain?" It was the lieutenant of marines.

"Mr. Horner, what are you doing?"

Horner had pulled off his boots and stockings and was unbuttoning his coat. "I am a good swimmer, sir, I will go have a look. I have given command to my sergeant until I return." He pulled his shirt over his head, revealing a vast white chest, and before Bliven could respond, he jumped over the side vertically, feet first.

"I think you should grant him permission, sir," said Miller.

"Everywhere I look I seem to be confronted with initiative. Mr. Quarles!"

The midshipman ran up and saluted. "Sir?"

"Run below and bring us towels."

"Aye, sir!" He trotted toward the waist and disappeared down the ladder.

The officers gathered on the landward side of the ship, peering into the green water forward toward the bow, noting after a moment a string of bubbles breaking the surface. Presently Horner came up, heaving deep breaths, and before he could be hailed, he dove again.

When next they saw him he was coming nimble as a spider up the ladder. He took a towel from Quarles and rubbed himself vigorously. "You have hit wreckage, Captain."

"Wreckage? But we just came up this channel a week ago. How did we miss it then?"

Horner was quickly back into his shirt and pulling on his stockings and boots. "It is not an old wreck, sir. In fact, I would say it has been there less than a week."

"The wily bastards: they have sunk a hulk in the channel to hang us up. By God, that is why we have had no interest. We haven't fooled anybody. They have been watching the whole time and known exactly what we were about. Wily bastards! Mr. Miller?"

"Captain?"

"The next time you detect that I am underestimating an enemy's intelligence and abilities, you are to slap me on the back of my head. Do you understand?"

"I will be happy to, sir. But the question is, what now?"

"Deck! Deck ahoy!"

"What do you see?" called up Miller.

"A ship, sir, coming around the next island! Holy Christ, what is that?"

The officers crowded to the port rail on the channel side and raised their glasses. What became visible in almost aching slowness beyond a screen of mangroves was a gigantic barge, boldly painted in yellow and green and red.

It had not one but two outriggers, not for flotation or stability, as he had seen in Hawaii, but the outriggers themselves were large canoes attached to the main vessel with stout spars, and each containing twenty men pulling at sweeps, oaring the craft majestically from the cover of the island. It bore a single tripod mast bearing a huge crab-claw sail that was being raised even as it became visible. Both bow and stern swept up and terminated in peaks forty feet above the water, with a steering oar descending from the stern, and a single large gun projecting from the bow. In its waist stood a spacious open pavilion crowded with armed men who must have numbered a hundred, with a hundred more standing and gesturing on its roof.

"My God," whispered Griggs, "that is a karakoa. I have heard of them, seen drawings—never seen one. I did not know they still existed; the Spanish banned them centuries ago."

"The Spanish!" cried Bliven. "For God's sake, man, make sense!"

Griggs continued staring at it in disbelief. "It is a style of warship native to the Philippines. It is essentially the capital ship of the Boogis. They could overwhelm the Spanish galleons of the day, not with superior firepower, but by crashing into them and cutting down the crew in hand-to-hand fighting."

"Mr. Horner!"

"Sir!"

"Get your marines forward, with muskets and all the pistols there are, and send some men down to the gun room for more. Mr. Evarts!"

"Sir!"

"Get yourself down to the gun room, break out all the pistols and ammunition to the marines. Do you understand? Go!"

Miller came and stood by. "What are you thinking, Captain?"

"I am thinking I wish I had those paddle wheels from the *Constitution* right now."

"Yes, I quite agree."

Bliven's glance darted from starboard at the mangroves, to the channel that lay to port, up to his now furled sails, and forward to the gruesome-looking craft that was turning into the channel to bear down on them. "Mr. Miller, the next time you hear me disparage new inventions, you are also to slap me on the back of my head."

"Yes, sir."

"Hard. That is an order."

"I understand, sir."

Bliven cupped his hands and shouted forward. "Mr. Rippel, point your chasers, maximum elevation. Be ready to fire!"

"Captain, may I suggest something?" It was Yeakel, come back to the quarterdeck.

"I wish to God somebody would!"

"Sir, when we struck this wreckage, we were hauling as close as the ship would bear. If now we were to reverse the yards, as though we were tacking—wear ship, essentially—the wind should swing our stern around, and that might pull the bow free."

"Yes, and it might pull the bow off!"

"Yes, sir, there is that risk."

"Captain?"

"Mr. Griggs!"

"I need to tell you, sir, a karakoa is a big ship but it has a very shallow draught. I repeat: their purpose is not to make a pass and engage with guns. They will come right over the wreckage and spill their men onto your deck. You must pull off this wreck and get your heavy guns on them."

"Very well, then: Wear ship, Mr. Yeakel, wear ship!" It was essential to get a salvo off before the ship could move from where the bow chasers were pointed. "Mr. Rippel!"

"I have them, sir!"

"Fire, then!"

*Rappahannock* shuddered behind the twin booms of the two twenty-fours, and watched a hole pop open in the karakoa's single sail, followed by the ball's splash beyond; the second ball, they witnessed the splash even farther beyond—a good ranging salvo, but there was no time to follow it up before the ship would begin to shift. "Mr. Rippel!"

"Sir!"

"Roll your guns back! Get the weight off the bow!"

Through their glasses the officers witnessed the muzzle flash of the karakoa's single forward gun, and the sound reached them almost the same instant they heard and felt a sickening concussive crunch on their bow and a chorus of cries and shouting. "Miller! Get forward and find out what has happened!"

"Aye, sir!"

Bliven looked up to see the spread of men aloft, the yards turning even as the canvas of the courses and topsails fell and almost instantly filled with wind, and—the wind being against them—saw them billowing back against the masts.

Barely perceptible at first and then more by degrees, they felt the ship backing beneath them, and then with a deep rumble felt the bow slide off the hulk on which she had beached herself. "Starboard your helm!" roared Bliven. With the lieutenants at quarters, it was the quartermaster at the wheel.

*Rappahannock* began to cut a backward arc, increasingly changing her angle into the wind until it began to luff the sails. "Wear ship again, Mr. Yeakel; get some wind behind them where it belongs! Helm amidships! Mr. Jackson, ready on the starboard battery! Rolling broadside; fire as your guns bear!

"I understand, sir!"

"Hold your carronades until they are within range! How are they loaded?"

"With grape, Captain!"

"Good!"

The sloop crept to a halt and then slowly started forward. It was apparent as they moved away from the island that they would cross the course of the oncoming grotesque of a ship, now three hundred yards distant. It was the happiest turn of events that now they could deliver a raking broadside down its whole length.

"Captain!"

"Mr. Miller?"

"Their one shot has carried away our figurehead, and this deflected the ball. It came through the railing and knocked one of the chasers off its carriage."

"Was anyone hurt?"

"Two men hit with splinters. Lieutenant Rippel was hit with a chunk of railing and may have a broken shoulder. Dr. Berend has them in the cockpit now."

"And Mary Washington?"

"I fear she did not survive."

"Well, damn." Bliven knew without having to see that Jackson had run forward to point and fire the twenty-fours himself, and order them reloaded as fast as they fired. It was the Number Two starboard gun that boomed first, Number One having been moved to the fo'c'sle.

"It looks like we've got him," said Miller.

Eleven guns fired in succession, five to seven seconds apart; they had no time to loose the gun in the captain's compartment.

"Starboard your helm; come into the channel and make to pass him! Yeakel, reef our courses! Miller, take command of the carronades. Tell Jackson to open him up between wind and water as soon as we are abreast of him. You aim above the rowers in the outriggers; they are likely just slaves. Aim for the soldiers in that pavilion. You should have time to get off two salvos before they give up or sink."

"Yes, sir!"

Moving only under topsails, *Rappahannock* slowed, and once their length was even with the karakoa, the gun deck beneath them erupted with the unified broadside from the twenty-fours, the very muzzle blasts almost reaching the outriggers. Miller used that as his signal to discharge the grape-loaded carronades into the men who now sought cover, only to find none.

Before a second salvo could be prepared, the alien craft gave a great, almost animal-like groan, began to list, and then foundered to lie on its side in the shallow water, its port outriggers high in the air as though skewered on their yards, those men who had been rowing dropping off one by one. Blood and bodies rolled out of the pavilion, and from its roof the green water was streaked with red. Most of the men who could swim stroked for the shore and away from a British hangman. Only those nearest the sloop, or who were too injured to do more than float, permitted themselves to be rescued.

Bliven lowered two boats, with sailors to pull the injured from the water, and marines to cover them against any treachery. At the end he had thirty in his custody, whom he had confined in the cable tier, bound securely even as Dr. Berend saw to their wounds.

The lieutenants joined Bliven on the quarterdeck as the wrecked karakoa fell astern of them. He pointed to a green line on the horizon to the northwest. "Look there, gentlemen. I must admit my errors. I had thought that if pirates attacked us, it would be because we fooled them into accepting our disguise. Rather, they fought us because they thought to defeat us, and with the gall to do so in plain sight; Singapore is just right there. Who knew they would be so brazen?"

## { 12 }

## *Jade, and Slops*

SINGAPORE

20TH MAY, 1822

*My Ever Dear Love,*

*There is a British vessel, the trading schooner Eurydice, Capt. Blythe, leaving on the morrow for the Sandwich Islands, and he has kindly agreed to carry a letter addressed to you, and hand it to Mr. Jones our consular agent, who should if God is willing and all the connections be made, hand it to Rev. Bingham who will hand it to you.*

*I have now been in these environs long enough to have heard, a couple of times from different people, an old Malay adage: the first ship in the world was built to catch fish; the second ship was built to steal them. Piracy among the Malays has gone on for that long.*

*It is surprising to contemplate it, that piracy around the world should be so prevalent that it has grown into different shapes in different places. In our own part of the world, the buccaneers of the Caribbean were outlawed by all nations, even considered themselves to be a sort of nation, albeit a nation with no land to stand on—at least until the recent independence of the South American countries. They adopted pirates as ready-made navies, and those pirates are delighted to shield themselves under these new national flags. In North Africa, corsairs acted as an arm of the Mohammedan state.*

*Here in Malaya it takes on a subtly different complexion. Here there exists no unifying government. There are many competing little princes, each one in his silks and jeweled turban, each one ruling mightily over a realm the size of a few American counties, each one plotting and counter-plotting to pull down his neighbors before they can topple him. And into this free-for-all of native warfare come the pirates, selling their protection to the highest bidder, plundering the ships of his enemies, or of foreigners equally—until he should meet the pirates of his master's enemy, at which time the whole fracas moves from land onto the sea—which at least spares the hapless civilians who are slaughtered whenever some town is sacked. Human life here is held cheap, cheaper even than in Barbary.*

*What I hold to be of greatest interest here are two things. First, the pirates here are strictly correct to regard themselves as a separate nation. Indeed they are a distinct people called the Boogis. They are very numerous and are spread among several sovereign territories, but they are most emphatically a sea people, and even live in houses built upon pilings over shallow water. Their distinctive style of boat is called a proa, they can be both sailed and rowed, and they come in all sizes, from efficient little fishing outriggers to large war-galleys that* can, as I learned, challenge an American warship. Second, with all the Asiatic religions to choose from, these Boogis centuries ago converted to Mohammedanism. So I suppose I need not be surprised, considering the two wars that we fought with the Tripolitan states, that they consider piracy an honorable way of making a living, and believe that they have divine sanction to pillage the followers of other religions!

What is lost on them is any notion that piracy, itself, is wrong. After my one battle with them, we fished the captain and a few dozen of his crew from the water—although I confess I would happily have left them to the sharks, with which these waters are thickly teeming. When put to questions, captain and crew alike had no idea they had done anything wrong, they wanted only to know what potentate was so lucky as to have engaged me and my powerful ship! What is wanted is for some powerful Western country to conquer this lawless hell and impose order. From what I have learned here in Singapore, it begins to appear as though the British and the Dutch are going to divide that duty—British on the mainland and Dutch in the islands. The common people suffer so from the present petty tyrants, a colonial government could scarce leave them worse off.

The good news for you, my love, is that you needn't worry for my safety, for the pirates here are no better hands at fighting than the Algerines were twenty years ago. The proas in which they usually attack merchant vessels are large enough to carry perhaps twenty men while being rowed by a dozen others, and may carry one small gun, say a six-pounder or swivel piece. When they attack a merchant ship they come in a swarm, maybe six to ten proas at a time. As in the Mediterranean, they depend upon their reputation for cruelty to *convince merchant captains to surrender without a struggle and sue for mercy, which is customarily granted. But if there is resistance, or if the Boogis suspect that a captain is concealing valuable property from them—I do not wish to disturb you with a relation of what tortures they can resort to, and have done.*

*Their war proas are adequate for molesting the innocent, but as elsewhere in the world cannot stand up to a real warship for a moment. I commenced my run up the Malacca Strait, where they carry out most of their business, having disguised my vessel as a large merchantman. Perhaps it was foolish to even attempt to mask such a large warship as a trader, and we expended some pretty pennies in the effort, but apparently we deceived only ourselves—and some few other passing merchantmen in the Strait who hailed us to learn our cargo and where we were bound!*

*We were not unobserved, however, for upon our return the Boogis sank a hulk in the channel to foul us, and whilst we were engaged in getting free staged an ambuscade. They came round an island in a vessel of their same basic design, but much larger. They might have been upon us and worked some damage, but my bosun did some quick thinking and adjusted the sails to pull us free. Once we gained steerage their fate was sealed, and American powder and ball, and some good shooting, did its work. My casualties were three men wounded forward, when their one shot that they got off knocked a chaser off its carriage, and also lamentably carried away our figurehead. My men are recovering, but I fear that poor Mary Washington has been cast upon some lonely beach, or floats lost among the roots of a mangrove swamp.*

*In the morning we shall be bound for Canton to show the flag, confer with the American agent there, and report facts of salient interest to the government at home.*

*As for me, I cannot come back to you soon enough—and no doubt
to see little Benjamin twice the size I left him!*

> *I remain your very loving*
> *(and healthy and uninjured) husband,*
> *Bliven Putnam, Capt. USN*

> MRS. CLARITY PUTNAM,
> ABCFM MISSION
> C/O UNITED STATES CONSULAR AGT.
> HONORURU, KINGDOM OF HAWAII

When Bliven sent a note ashore to the resident commandant that he had pirates held prisoner aboard and asked how he should dispose of them, Travers came out himself in a large cutter with a guard of redcoated marines to take them off his hands. The two watched together from the quarterdeck as they were led barefoot up the ladder and relieved of their bonds long enough to climb down to the cutter.

"We heard quite a fearful rumpus across the strait yesterday," said Travers. "That must have been you."

"Yes. We were surprised they would attack us so close to Singapore. We were expecting it in some more remote place."

"Well, but being good pirates, they expected that you expected that."

Bliven signed the receipt that he was handing over the prisoners. "No doubt I should have expected that they expected that I expected—"

"And so on, yes." They laughed. "Where are you bound now, Captain Putnam?"

"Canton. Have you any advice?"

"Oh, God, fifty miles of mudflats. Best thing is to stop in Macau and take on a pilot. Plenty of them there, and they know the channels like the veins over their knuckles."

"I shall. Perchance do you know if Mr. Dunn is still the American agent there who I should call on?"

Travers's face turned sour. "Yes, to the latest that we know, he is still there. You shan't have trouble finding him, just look for a fat, pesky little old moralizing son of a bitch up to his knees in silk fans and jade goddesses, lamenting how the poor Chinese are induced to smoke opium. Once you are among the Thirteen Factories, you will find him quick enough, his is the place that looks like a curiosity shop."

"My thanks, Commandant." He did not ask into the fate of the pirates. He knew that, balanced around the world, there was an even chance they would hang, or be paroled back to continue their trade, whether on the promise to behave themselves or by the discreet passage of gold to their captors. In the morning they saluted the battery and stood out east.

ONE DIVIDEND THAT the Portuguese reaped from their glory days of exploration, even in their fallen state, was that they retained the commercial enclave of Macau on the west entrance of the Pearl River, that mighty third river of China after the Yangtze, and which actually carried more water, and silt, than the Yellow River, having laid down at its mouth a braid of channels through mudflats fifteen miles wide and more than thirty miles inland to Canton. Their first night under way, Bliven fished out his copy of Jedidiah Morse's *Compendious Geography* to see what he could learn about the place, and his amazement only began with the assertion that Canton held some one and one-half million inhabitants—he could scarce even imagine such a city—and every year exported some eighteen million pounds of tea.

Putting in to the harbor at Macau, Bliven selected from his choice of pilots a gray-haired man of indeterminate but certainly mixed race, by the name of Emanuel Sosa, on the evidence of his being the most experienced. With Bliven and his lieutenants on the quarterdeck, this English-speaking Chinese-Portugee directed Yeakel to shorten to fore and main topsails, and the fore and main topmast staysails. Yeakel complied, then caught Bliven's eye and shrugged his shoulders; but Sosa seemed to know exactly what he was about, for as *Rappahannock* creeped forward into life, they noticed that the darkest and greenest water always seemed to lie ahead of them. "Mr. Bosun, you fix sails to follow my turns, yes? Otherwise we hit bottom, maybe."

"Your pardon, Captain." Yeakel backed away. "It looks like I am going to be busy for a little bit."

The Pearl River estuary narrowed by degrees to a broad river that, as they ascended, divided and subdivided with stunning frequency, and at each confluence Sosa chose a channel and entered it, as unerring as he was laconic, with no chart of any kind for a guide. Human presence along the river, never entirely absent, thickened the farther they ascended, until houses became neighborhoods, and roads became thickly traveled streets, and at length they found themselves as much in the beating heart of a city as the Thames is the center of London. They beheld ships at anchor in a cacophony of trading schooners and brigs, and scattered liberally among them Chinese junks, which to Bliven seemed to distill some essence of what he had imagined China to be. So, too, did the uncountable sampans that shuttled about, pushed with steering oars—the transport of the common people who looked up at the big Western ships with a commercial eye, laden with trade goods, fresh vegetables, and girls.

Bliven approached him at the wheel. "Tell me, Mr. Sosa, have you recently piloted a large schooner, an American, the *Fair Trader*, Captain Saeger?"

"Not I, but my brother has." He cast his glance about. "Don't see him just now, but he may still be in here somewhere." From their northerly heading Sosa made a sudden ninety-degree turn to starboard, sending Yeakel into a flurry of turning the yards as almost at once they found themselves opposite a large square off the port side, with a row of buildings in European architecture lined up opposite the river.

"Let go your anchor!"

The heavy cable whirred through the hawsehole as their four-ton bow anchor crashed into the water, running out almost nothing as it settled into the shallow mud. Sosa left the wheel and joined the officers at the port rail. "Very well, gentlemen, let me tell you where you are. Starboard behind you is Honam Island; upstream beyond you lies Whampoa. Those need not concern you, for foreigners are most strictly limited to this square of Canton. It is called the Thirteen Factories, and there you see them."

His arms swept from left to right across the square, where three hundred yards away lay a row of stone storefronts with arched windows in a second story above them.

"Are they factories?" asked Miller. "They look more like mercantiles to me."

"They are mercantiles," Sosa agreed. "'Store' and 'factory' are very similar words in Chinese. Going farther in away from you on the left is New China Street, with the Danish trading house on the left and the Spanish on the right, and the French next to them. Then you see Old China Street. It is lined with local merchants, so when you let your men go ashore and they wish to purchase something to show they have been to China, that is where they will go. Now, listen to me good, both those streets, and Hog Street over on your right, pass through to Thirteen Factory Street. No one—and mark me, no one—may go beyond Thirteen Factory Street for any reason. Foreigners are not wanted in China, except in this one small place. Westerners are called *lo faan*; that means barbarians. I hope for your own sakes you will not test this boundary."

"I believe your meaning is clear, Mr. Sosa."

"Very well. Now, just east of Old China Street is the American factory, or shop, and next to it the Austrian, Dutch, and so on, the British on the far right; you see everyone's flags out front. The man you want to see about American matters is Mr. Dunn; inquire at the American factory. He lives upstairs. Is there anything else you need of me?"

"No, Mr. Sosa. You have been very helpful, and we thank you." Bliven extended his hand and he took it.

"Now, on the shore of this square you see two little customshouses. If you will lower a boat and take me to them, I can make my way from there."

"My bosun will see to it. Mr. Yeakel!"

"Sir?"

"Lower my gig, if you please."

Bliven accompanied Sosa to the customshouse and thanked him again before entering the square, heading straight but leisurely toward the American flag, and rather enjoying the penetrating stares of the Chinese who came to the Thirteen Factory Square to look at foreigners.

When he entered the American factory his attention was at once drawn to a plump man of forty with a sharp nose and small mouth and receding curly brown hair. He drew attention not for his appearance, nor even for his meticulous dress, but for the fact that he was conversing in rapid and apparently faultless Chinese with two wealthy-appearing locals. When he saw Bliven's uniform he excused himself, shaking not their hands but his own as he bowed himself away.

"Mr. Dunn, may I presume?"

"I am Nathan Dunn." He extended his hand and Bliven took it.

"Captain Bliven Putnam, United States sloop of war *Rappahannock*, just now come into harbor. May I speak with you for a few moments?"

"By all means. You must come up and have tea." He led him to the side of the mercantile, to a narrow stair that had not been visible behind a mahogany lattice screen. Bliven followed Dunn through a door and once in the apartment he stopped, stock-still in his tracks. "Good heavens! Is this the fourteenth century? Was that door a portal into the past? Where is Marco Polo? I have always wanted to meet him!"

With each sentence Dunn laughed harder, a shaking loaf of jolly amiability. "Oh, you are a breath of fresh air, Captain. We don't see many Americans here. Sometimes it is only Mr. Abeel, the missionary, and myself, and he is not always fun to be around." A servant entered from a rear room, and a few words in Chinese sent him away for tea.

"Well, that is a large part of why I have come, Mr. Dunn. Your country's policy is now to look outward upon the world more than in the past. I am here to show the flag and inquire whether you have any needs that you wish to draw the government's attention to. But first you must tell me about these . . . things! Never have I seen such an explosion of fine treasures. What did you do, loot the imperial palace? Do I need to sneak you out to safety before you are discovered?"

Dunn began again to laugh hard. "Stop, Captain! Mercy! Oh, my. Yes, I am a collector of fine Oriental crafts and art. But no, I have not raided the imperial palace. I am, however, supported in this endeavor by the emperor himself, who has permitted me to buy much of this."

"Yes, I heard something of your court connections from the British when I was just in Singapore. You do not seem to be their favorite person."

Dunn smiled, this time sardonically. "No, I should think not, and I can only imagine what they might have told you. You would like for me to explain my wealth and my connections straightaway, to ease your suspicions of my character? Very well, I shall save you the time. Let me ask you this, Captain, as you seem to have a better than average education. When you studied history, did you learn much about the colonial American economy, based upon that unholy triangle dependent on sugar and rum and slaves?"

Bliven smiled nervously. "Well, yes, but I am certain it was not put in such blunt terms as to injure my feelings of patriotism."

"No, it never is, but it will help you understand the China trade." Bliven found his change of mood astonishing, from the jovial to the precise and direct. "Here it is in a nutshell: There is enormous demand in the West for Chinese silk, tea, porcelain, furniture, and so on. In exchange, we sell our goods to them, but they are not interested in buying much of anything. This creates a great imbalance in payments. The British have discovered one product that the Chinese are very keen to acquire, and that is opium from British India; and once they become dependent upon it, they become desperate to acquire it. The British feel no qualms about balancing their payments by creating a whole class of wretched opium addicts. The emperor, however, despises what they are doing, and he has issued one decree upon another against the opium trade, and the British ignore them, of course. I, however, have found a way to balance our trade without opium, of which the emperor has taken favorable notice, and it puts English noses severely out of joint."

"May I ask how you worked such a financial miracle?"

Dunn wagged a finger in the air. "Ha-haa, you must not ask my trade secrets! But look around you. I was once a bankrupt in Pennsylvania, for which the Quakers threw me out of their Society. One creditor to whom I owed a great deal of money, instead of putting me in debtors' prison, set me up as a partner to manage his business. Now I have paid him off, and I have as much money as I will ever be able to spend, and I collect objects that demonstrate the Chinese way of life, as you see."

"Yes. I thought for a moment I had entered a museum."

"Well, in a way you have. When I take all this home, I intend to exhibit it. Just look: teak, jade, porcelain . . . Some of it is five hundred years old."

"Wait, though—I was just told that foreigners may not leave the Thirteen Factory Square. How have you managed to collect all this?"

"Because the emperor is so pleased with my stand against the opium trade, he has seen to it that I have the proper contacts, all over the country. It has driven the British nearly mad with jealousy, and I fear causes them to cling even harder to their infernal opium trade. And I may say that in this endeavor I have been most nobly supported by one of the leading hong merchants, a Mr. Ting Qua, whom I should like for you to meet. He can tell you more stories about the British than I can, and far more colorfully."

"Well, I am heartened to discover that an honest Quaker can prosper—"

"Former Quaker, we must say in all truth, but when they expelled me it was with the proviso that they would welcome me back when I was cleared of my debts."

"Why should they care? My word, that seems an odd stance for such an egalitarian religion. 'Simple Gifts' and all that."

Dunn's face hardened. "Yes, isn't it?"

Bliven sipped at his tea, and found it flavorful and robust without being bitter. "This is wonderful! Is this what you export?"

"No, the best tea never leaves the country. I am glad to serve it to you, you will never have better."

"I can believe it. Tell me, Mr. Dunn, do you have the acquaintance of an American trader, Jakob Saeger, of the schooner *Fair Trader*?"

"I have met him in the past. I have been here since 1818, and he was in the market several years before that, as I understand."

"I believe he may be in Canton now; that is where he said he was bound when he left Lahaina with a cargo. Our pilot said his brother brought him in a couple of days ago."

"Very possible. He would not stop here; he would go a little further upriver to sell to the craftsmen who buy the raw sandalwood."

"Is not all the commerce confined to this square?"

"Oh, he does not come ashore; they go out to him. Is your business with him urgent? If so, I can send a runner upriver and see if he is there."

"No, no, I thank you. He was once attacked by pirates of a kind I lately had to engage near Singapore. I just want to learn the details of his incident. Perhaps I shall send a boat out tomorrow and see if we can locate him. This was truly wonderful tea, by the way."

"Yes, well, we can't have you visit China and not experience fine tea."

Bliven stood, then reached to a table and picked up a slender jade goddess six inches tall. "My wife was raised to higher culture than I," he said. "If she saw this apartment, she would swear she had died and gone to heaven."

"Well! You will be in port for some days, I trust. If you think the art is enchanting, you must try the food. Will you come back and have dinner with me tomorrow evening? You can bring your officers. It will give me great pleasure."

"That is most heartily accepted. Thank you for your great kindness."

THAT NIGHT BLIVEN was sleeping so deeply, he did not hear Ross knocking on the door of the berth but felt him shaking him by the shoulder. He heard distantly, "Excuse me, Captain. I am sorry to wake you. Lookout reports that the city is on fire."

The shadows fell strangely in the compartment, lit by the dull glow of the battle lantern that Ross carried. "What? There is a fire in the city?"

"No, sir, the city is on fire."

"What! Oh, God!"

"Here are fresh clothes, sir."

In his mind's eye Bliven recalled his student days when he was consumed by history, of reading of the great fires—of the Alexandria Library burned by Caesar's fire ships, of Rome burning while Nero sang, of plague-ravaged London alight in 1666—when he would close his eyes and imagine the awful sights. He raced up the ladder to the spar deck, and there it was: tall yellow flames licking the sky against a duller orange glow, buildings silhouetted against them, the panic of helpless people screaming in the streets as they sought safety by the water, ready to jump in if they had to. He could tell from the smoke before it disappeared up into the inky night that the wind was from the east and coming toward the Thirteen Factory Square.

He sought out Lennox Jackson, who had the watch. "Did you see how it started?"

"No, sir. I first noticed it when I went forward on my rounds. It seemed farther away than now; it must be spreading very fast."

The square before the Thirteen Factories was filled with a swarm of people, horses, carts, wagons, rickshas—every mode of conveyance to rescue what of their inventory they could. It was impossible not to imagine the babble of languages audible there.

"Look there, sir." Jackson pointed. "Boats approaching off the port beam. Looks to be a string of them, sir, tied together."

Bliven's first instinct was to beat to quarters—an American ship in a foreign port, with the city in flames—but weighed this against being judged an ass for overreacting if the true story became known to be no threat. The dilemma was dispelled when a recently familiar voice issued from the first boat. "Ahoy, *Rappahannock*! Ahoy, can you hear me?"

Bliven strode quickly to the port rail. "Is that Mr. Dunn?"

"It is, sir, and thank God you are here! May I come aboard?"

"Certainly. Can you manage the ladder?"

"Yes, I think so."

It was almost time for change to the morning watch, and the commotion brought the bosun's mate and two seamen to the port boarding gate to help if they were needed.

Nathan Dunn was breathing hard by the time he gained the deck. "There is a fire," he gasped, "a terrible fire."

"Yes. Oh, Mr. Dunn, your things! Your wonderful things!"

"Ting Qua and his employees helped get my collection into the boats. He . . . he let his own business be consumed in the fire so that they could save it."

Ting Qua followed Dunn through the boarding gate. "Mr. Ting, are you all right?" He was the first Chinese that Bliven had ever addressed, and he was surprised by his gracile build and finely etched features. Plainly he was in shock at the night's events. "Yes, I think so."

The noise had awakened Evans Yeakel, who came topside to see if he was needed.

"Mr. Yeakel, would you awaken the cook and ask him to make some tea to warm these gentlemen?"

"I'll tend to it myself, Captain. It is only two hours until he must get up, and once awake he won't be able to go back to sleep." Yeakel clattered back down the ladder.

Bliven helped Ting to the hatch cover and sat him down. "Mr. Ting, we will have tea for you and your men shortly."

"That is most kind, Captain." It was alarming how frail he looked.

"Apparently, it is you who have been most kind. Is it true that your business is gone?"

"Yes, but my merchandise is easily replaced. Mr. Dunn's collection is a matter of personal interest to our emperor. The history and culture of my people is in these five boats. That had to take precedence."

Nathan Dunn had joined them. "Which does not diminish his heroism in the least. I don't know what to do. There is furniture and jade and porcelain, and I have not a yard of packing material to protect any of it. Captain Putnam, may I appeal to you to bring this material aboard your ship until I can figure out what must be done?"

"Of course, of course." Suddenly it occurred to him, not just an adequate solution, but one in which he would take some pleasure. "Gentlemen, excuse me, I think I can help." He raced back down to his cabin and met his steward. "Mr. Ross, please awaken Mr. Erb and tell him that I require his slops most urgently: shirts, trousers, stockings, everything that is made out of cloth that can be used as a wrapping. I think the whole ship is awake by now; find a couple of men, bring it up on deck by the armloads. Do you understand?"

"Aye, Captain, right away."

"Listen, now. You come back here after you awaken Mr. Erb. We have taken on board the American merchant Mr. Dunn and his factor, Mr. Ting Qua. They have saved from the fire a large collection of Chinese art and furniture. As it is wrapped, I put you in charge of storing it in the guest berths here. Stow things as tightly and efficiently as you can, but take care, for some of it is very ancient and fragile."

"You may leave it with me, Captain."

"Tell Mr. Erb that he may have his slops back as soon as we have worked out a more permanent arrangement."

Bliven rejoined Ting and Dunn at the spar deck's waist, to see that the fire had broken through the last line of buildings on the square, and the flames now illuminated the harbor without obstruction as it crawled along the line of factories. "Mr. Dunn, I fear we do not have any proper wrappings, either, but I am having shirts and stockings brought up that will meet the emergency. I will store your artifacts in the guest berths in my cabin."

"I don't know what to say, Captain Putnam. I am so grateful."

"Not at all." Somewhere in the back of his mind it occurred to him that he was being called upon to save the essence of a great civilization from being destroyed, and that it was he who should be grateful, but that was a thought better expressed later. "Do you feel able to superintend my men wrapping your objects and getting them stored?"

"Oh, Captain, just knowing that they will be safe gives me such energy as you cannot imagine. Yes, we will be fine."

Yeakel appeared bearing a wooden tray laden with steaming tin cups. "Swallow some tea first, gentlemen. Here you are."

As shirts and trousers began to pile up on the deck, Bliven smiled at the presence among them of linen napkins and tablecloths from the wardroom and the captain's table. Erb might have been having a little revenge, but it was well done.

"Captain, look!"

"Mr. Jackson, what is it?" called Bliven.

"Ship standing out of the harbor, Captain! I believe it is the one you have been seeking, sir!"

"What, at this hour?" Bliven ran around the hatch to the starboard rail, in time to be certain that the *Fair Trader* was putting to sea.

Dunn joined him, drawing long at his cup of tea. "Mr. Putnam, you sense there is a story there in his leaving, and I believe I can satisfy your curiosity as soon as we have completed the present task."

Miller and Rippel came up the ladder together, sleepy, and took cups of tea from the tray. Miller surveyed all—the fire, Mr. Dunn on the deck, a string of boats tied up, Chinese in long lines handing up treasures of art and stacking them on the deck. "Jesus," he said. "Can we be useful, Captain?"

"Bless you for coming up! Mr. Dunn will direct you."

"Yes, Lieutenant. You see this great pile of stockings here? And you see these small figurines there and all about, and these chests? If you gentlemen will wrap them in the stockings and pack them in the chests, and then stuff some more stockings around them so they do not shake about, that will get them out of danger and you can carry them down to the captain's cabin."

Down below, Alan Ross directed the incoming tide of riches as best he could. Cabinets and tables of teak and ebony he placed tops down onto the blankets in the berths so they should not be scratched; the chairs he set upright with chests on their cushions and larger curios protected within their legs. It took three hours, the end of which saw Bliven, Dunn, and the lieutenants in the sea cabin, less Rippel, who had gone on watch, having swapped tea for brandy.

Dunn was shifting uncomfortably. "Captain Putnam, I fear that after such desperate work, the human anatomy asserts itself. Tea in, tea out. Have you . . . ?"

Bliven indicated the door. "My privy is at your disposal." When Dunn returned, he sat at the table, disheveled, sooty, forlorn.

"Mr. Ross?"

"Captain?"

"Can you bring a basin of hot water and a towel for Mr. Dunn? He can wash up in my berth. And pull out one of my fresh shirts for him to change into."

"Right away, sir."

"Mr. Dunn, have you a place to stay?"

Only at that moment did Dunn allow himself the shock and exhaustion. "No, I—" He shook his head vacantly. "I don't know."

"Let us hang you a hammock," said Miller. "You need sleep before you think more."

"Oh, no." Dunn managed a smile. "I don't know how to sleep in a hammock. I should spin around and fall out like a ham."

"No," said Bliven. "Take him forward. Ask Dr. Berend to bed him down in the sick bay. It's a quiet corner; it has the softest beds and the cleanest sheets. We can talk when you wake up."

"You are a saint," sighed Dunn.

"On that other point you raised, if you can. What did you wish to tell me, about Captain Saeger and the *Fair Trader*?"

"Ah. Your pilot had it correctly. He came into port yesterday morning from the Sandwich Islands, as he told everyone, with a prime load of sandalwood, sixty-five piculs of it. He got top dollar for it, too, I can tell you."

"Forgive me, Mr. Dunn," said Miller. "That is a unit of measure with which I am unfamiliar."

"Oh, I am sorry. Indeed, it is a measure unique to the Asiatic sphere. It varies from place to place, but is generally defined as how much an average man can carry on a shoulder pole. For commercial purposes it has been standardized at one and one-third hundred-weight."

"So . . . ," figured Miller, "sixty-five times a hundred, plus a third—call it twenty-two hundred—would be about eighty-seven hundred pounds, so a little over four and a quarter tons."

"More or less," Dunn agreed. "Well, the buyers hadn't even seen a cargo of Hawaiian sandalwood in five or six months, so they had taken to buying it from India, which is a decidedly inferior tree. Well, sir, within a few hours they were coming back out to his ship, scream-ing and cussing and fit to be tied. It seems that the bundles were san-dalwood only on the outside; the interiors of the bundles were some useless wood of the same color. The merchants were in a state, threat-ened to have the law on him. They lightened him of every dollar they had paid him."

"Oh, Lord! Do you think he meant to swindle them?"

"I do not, sir. They said that his shock and nonplus seemed com-pletely genuine. I do not believe he knew what had been sold him."

"Were you a witness to this?"

"No, this is what I was told just tonight, after the fire began. The commotion about the warehouses was tantamount to a riot. Saeger insisted upon coming ashore and inspecting the wood himself. He took a scraping of every log and smelled it, vowing the most terrible vengeance on those who had done this to him. By the time they had separated the dross from the genuine commodity, it did not amount to more than ten piculs of sandalwood. This they were willing to pay him for, and did so."

"My God," whispered Bliven. "Well, if they did pay him for what good sandalwood he delivered, did that not satisfy them and end the trouble?"

Dunn shook his head. "It should have, but later in the day, representatives of the major trading companies went to see the governor, and he revoked Saeger's license to sell in Canton. Effectively, he has been banned."

"But why? If he was himself the victim of a swindle, and restitution was made, I do not understand why he should be outlawed from the city."

"Because, Captain, the major trading concerns, such as Marshall and Wildes, are his competitors. It was an opportunity for them to land a lethal blow and drive him from the business, and believe me, they wield considerable influence in a city that is China's only contact with Western commerce."

"My God." Bliven shook his head. "I cannot imagine anything more calculated to enrage him."

"What they paid him for the ten piculs was barely enough to provision his ship. And so tonight there was the fire. I doubt that anyone can prove how it started, but I note that it began among the craftsmen's shops and spread to the foreign quarter. I will learn after I rest how extensive the damage was. But I did hear one further thing that I should relay to you. Saeger was heard to say that when he returned to the Sandwich Islands, he would have his vengeance upon the savages who cheated him."

"Oh, no." Bliven shook his head. "Gentlemen, we must get back there. We must get back there with all speed. Mr. Miller, will you show Mr. Dunn to the sick bay?"

"Certainly, Captain. Mr. Dunn, it is down one deck and forward."

"Thank you. I can assure you, I am past being shy about wanting a place to lie down."

"Go get some sleep, then."

Dunn paused. "It is ironical, when you come to think on Captain Saeger. Here was this deeply mean and dishonest man who was finally undone and ruined by being cheated by someone else. Ha! And people think God has no sense of humor. Well, good night, gentlemen. I thank you once more for your kindness."

Miller returned and he and Bliven sat alone in silence for some moments. "That makes him look guilty as hell, does it not?" asked Miller. "Absconding in the middle of the night . . ."

"Yes." Bliven nodded. "He could have been slinking away in the dead of night from sheer humiliation, but if Dunn heard correctly, Saeger is damned by the words from his own mouth. I have a mighty fear that he is going to do something dreadful when he gets back among the Hawaiians. In the morning we must dispose of Mr. Dunn with all kindness and get under way."

## { 13 }

## *Queen to Her People*

All slept until daylight, when Ross brought coffee into the sea cabin, where Bliven was already awake. "Are the others up?"

"Yes, sir, they are having breakfast in the wardroom."

"Set me a place, if you please. I will be down directly."

All the officers pushed back their chairs and stood as soon as they heard his steps on the ladder. Ross held a chair back for him at a plate of eggs, pork, toast, and jam.

"We are sorry to have begun without you, Captain," said Miller. "We did not know you would join us until we had already started."

Bliven tucked his napkin into his cravat. "Well, in that case, gentlemen, you should have refreshed your plates. You could have had larger breakfasts. How are you this morning, Mr. Dunn?"

"Rested, Captain, thank you, for all you gentlemen have done."

"Not at all. Where is Mr. Ting?"

"We put him ashore at his own request. He was anxious to begin putting our affairs back together."

"I took him over myself, sir," said Miller. "While there, I took the liberty of engaging a pilot to take us back down. Mr. Sosa had not departed yet, so I hired him, since we already have confidence in him. I know you want to get under way at the earliest possible moment. He tells me that the tide will turn about noon, and we can depart then. Also, I made an inventory of the stores." He handed Bliven a folded paper. "We should have just enough food and water to get back to the Sandwich Islands without topping off again. I hope I have not taken too much upon myself without orders."

Bliven opened the paper and glanced it over. "Yes, well, that is part of your charm, Lieutenant." He beamed a sudden great smile to make it clear he was joking. "No, you have acted very properly. Now tell me, Mr. Dunn, I am curious but I have not understood. Exactly what is your relationship with Mr. Ting?"

"Ah." Dunn wiped his lips with his napkin. "That is readily explained. Although you saw from the Thirteen Factories—that is, as they used to be, until yesterday—we are allowed to sell our foreign goods, but it is not as direct as it seems. No white people are permitted to do business directly, so each of the factories has a resident hong, a Chinese middleman who the government appoints as our factor, or agent, to actually handle the transactions for us, for which they receive a cut of the profit."

Bliven thought for a moment. "That hardly seems like a necessary step in the commerce."

"Not strictly speaking, but it is a way for the government to impose an extra level of oversight and get some revenue without having to call it a tax. Besides, the hongs such as Mr. Ting more than pay their way, for China is a very closed society, and his presence makes people more comfortable doing business with us when they would otherwise avoid us."

"I see. Well, Mr. Dunn, have you thought about what you are going to do now? Oh!" He leaned over. "I see you are drinking coffee this morning, not tea?"

Dunn felt relief in being able to laugh. "Indeed, I have had no coffee the past year or more. It is a rare luxury, although perhaps not worth getting burnt out for." The others laughed with him, in appreciation of his courage. "Captain, no prudent man would flee a conflagration without rounding up his ready cash, so I am not without resources. If you would be so kind as to put me and my collection ashore when you deposit your pilot in Macau, I can rent storage and a temporary lodging there until we can learn what is to become of the foreign quarter here. Mr. Ting even now should be on a horse and halfway there to make the arrangements."

"So," said Miller to impart encouragement, "like a dropped cat, you will land on your feet."

"Of course." Dunn patted his ample stomach. "Even a very large cat can do that."

Back in Macau, Bliven watched as the guest berths disgorged their wealth, interrupting his study of the charts, which was a dismal task, for every way he studied them, every course he considered, the result was the same. Miller joined him after the cargo was off-loaded and Dunn had made his farewell.

"Michael, sit by me. Look at this; it is hopeless. From here to Hawaii, as the crow flies, is almost six thousand miles, and the trade winds hard against us the whole way. Saeger's schooner can attack the wind much closer than we can. There is no possible way to overtake him."

"Yes, but look, there are many places for him to put in between here and there. The Philippines, for instance. I have heard stories of sandalwood there. He might stop to investigate."

"How would he pay for it? No, my guess is he is headed straight back to Maui to get even with some people who think they have gotten the better of him. Look: I have considered every possible route, from north of the Bonin Islands to the New Guinea coast, and every way we try, winds and currents will be full against us. We will simply have to beat our way back. I was reading in Porter's Pacific book: there were days at a stretch when he just had to be content to be pushed off course, sometimes by a hundred miles, in order to make a few miles' progress in the direction he wanted. This is going to be a hard, hard haul. By the time we add our distance tacking, we must cover at least fifteen thousand miles."

"Well, now that we've been to China, have we not heard their saying? 'A journey of a thousand miles begins with the first step.'"

"Ha!" Count on Miller to find the hope in anything.

"Or in our case, a journey of fifteen thousand miles begins with the first order. Captain?"

"Indeed so. Take us out, Mr. Miller."

And so it was. They stood out east-southeast from Macau, six hundred miles to the channel between Luzon and the Batanes Islands, then eleven hundred miles east by north to avoid the mid-ocean hazard of the Parece Vela reef, then eight hundred miles due east to the Farallón de Pájaros, another thousand miles east by south to Wake Island, and then two thousand miles along the twenty-second parallel to the Sandwich Islands—five thousand, five hundred miles that would be tripled, at least, by the relentless tacking.

Those were the straight lines that they fought to keep to, and they did fight for every league, every mile, every chain length, boxing their course as they tacked, sometimes hauling close for a hundred miles while being taken thirty miles off their course, waiting for enough of a change in the wind to take them back closer to true.

After two and a half months, even the equably tempered Yeakel's nerves were raw, the ever-optimistic Miller had withdrawn mostly into silence, and in Berend's daily sick call he noted the usual complement of bellyaches and boils to lance, and several daily shrieking sessions with mercurous chloride squirted into diseased penises, screams that he judged were increased as much now by despondency as genuine malady. When they finally raised Diamond Hill, Bliven no sooner congratulated himself on his successful navigation than they were met by the clap of a gun from its summit.

All turned and saw the telltale jet of smoke wafting from its broad top. "It looks like they have set up a signal station," said Miller.

They coasted into Honoruru harbor and found they were the only ship there, which was unusual but not without precedent. Bliven and Miller were lowered in the gig and pulled up to the pier, and upon gaining dry ground saw no sign of life about the commercial warehouses. He looked east, and in the distance saw around the mission compound a gathering of people both white and native standing in the yard before the grass church.

"Well, Mr. Miller, we had best see what is going on."

As they approached they saw the Loomises and the Holmans standing together, the Binghams a little apart. The Chamberlains stood in a clot, Jerusha clinging to her husband as tightly as her children clung to her. Muriel Albright stood beside them, tall with the aid now of a cane, with three native warriors in close attendance.

Hiram Bingham stepped out to meet him. "Captain Putnam." They shook hands. "Your arrival is well timed. We are glad to see you."

"What has happened? Where is my wife?"

"Captain, calm yourself, and prepare yourself. They are safe, but the queen has taken them into arrest. The remainder of us are interned here, as you may guess by the line of *kapu* sticks surrounding the church and our houses. As soon as your ship was seen, she called the court to-gether. She requires your presence as soon as you touch ground, so we must go at once. Oh—Mr. Jones and the other agents are already with her. Here, he gave me a packet of mail to give you at once."

"Thank you." Bliven tucked the letters into a pocket without look-ing at them. The missionaries were herded toward the royal *pili* with the guard of warriors behind and flanking.

"You are certain she is safe?"

Bingham patted him on the arm. "I assure you, she and the baby are unharmed."

All ducked through the entrance of the *pili*, which was crowded thick with a confluence of natives and Europeans. The queen was dressed as Bliven had never seen her, not in a Boston frock but wrapped multiple times in a *pa'u* of stenciled tapa, her chest bare beneath a clasped *kihei*. Her hair was held up with silver combs, and around her neck was a weighty *lei niho palaoa* of twisted human hair six inches around, bound at her throat with the ivory tongue that spoke the law.

His eyes had not yet adjusted to the dimness when he heard the queen's booming voice. "Captain Putnam, come forward!"

Putnam marched in, saluting as he stood straight as a ramrod. "Your Majesty, I have been absent for several months. All was well when I left. Now my wife is not with her friends, and I find all in com-motion. What has happened? Where is my wife?"

Kahumanu pointed a finger at him. "It is well for you to express concern for her. Since this terrible thing has occurred, feeling against white people, including your missionaries, has run highly against them. My people are in a rage."

Retainers stood beside her, armed with war clubs and those tower-ing spears, and they wore crested war helmets that reminded him of the ancient Greeks. Behind her loomed her *kahili* bearers, their thick chests and tautly muscled arms bare, each with his loins wrapped in a tapa *malo*. Each bore a feather standard at least ten feet tall. Facing him a little to one side of her, Karaimoku stood stoic and grim, in the same native war garb, his massive plait of hair making him look like one of the disused war gods that stood forlorn in their temples but now come to life.

Bliven felt his heart pounding within his chest. "What terrible thing?"

"Captain Putnam," she growled, "are you not aware of what has befallen my people?"

"No, ma'am, I am in shock. The town seems almost deserted. What is the meaning of all this?"

"Hm! Karaimoku will enlighten you."

Bliven spoke first. "Mr. Pitt, you are dressed much differently than when I last saw you."

"Much has happened. Captain Putnam, there is a trading ship from your country, a schooner called the *Fair Trader*, Captain Saeger. You know him, as we believe."

"I have not met him, but I have been following in his wake. Some few years ago now he was attacked by Malay pirates. My government sent me there to establish our presence in those sea-lanes and engage any pirates that I found there. I went to Singapore and learned what I could of the local situation. They knew of Saeger and of his having been attacked. In the Strait of Malacca I engaged and sank a large pirate vessel. I then went to Canton to learn what I could of American affairs. Captain Saeger had left Lahaina for Canton shortly before I left here for Singapore. I found his ship anchored in Canton, having sold a cargo of sandalwood. I desired to obtain his statement of the attack made upon him, but before I could do so, fire broke out on the waterfront, and during all the commotion he was observed putting out to sea."

Karaimoku seemed even more like a walking idol as he moved

closer, and Bliven realized anew how much larger he was than himself. "Captain, did you mark whether his vessel was armed?"

"Yes, I am certain that it was. After being attacked in Malaya, he obtained some surplus carronades in Valparaiso, from the former British officers now in the service of Chile. As I have come to learn, that is not an uncommon practice among traders who must travel waters infested with pirates."

"Captain Putnam," continued Karaimoku, "a few days ago this same Captain Jakob Saeger put in to the town of Hana, on the windward shore of Maui, for the purpose of victualing and buying sandalwood. During these transactions, he got it into his head that he was being cheated. Rather than stop the proceedings and set things right, he bid the people then in canoes to come back out to him at an evening hour, and he would trade much more with them. When they did as they were asked, he turned the guns of his ship upon them, and opened fire."

"Oh, for the love of God!"

"He had loaded the carronades with grape. Before they could escape, more than one hundred were killed."

"Oh, my God. I am heartsick at such news."

"Captain Putnam!" Kahumanu pointed at him so suddenly that he almost expected her to shout an accusation. "The man who has done this crime is of your country. He sails in a fast ship, with guns against which we are powerless. In these islands you represent the power and justice of America. You have as fast a ship, and larger guns. Will you take my commission to find this man and bring him to us?"

"Ma'am, I am sensible of your feelings, and I am certain that your feelings are just. However, the law of my country is that if I apprehend him, I must bring him back to America to stand trial and receive punishment."

"Not so!" she roared deeply. "The crime is in my country. In your country, what crime is it to break the law in my country? What punishment shall he face? Do you imagine we do not know how lightly you regard us?"

"Captain Putnam," said Karaimoku more calmly, "my advisors tell me there is a word in your justice called 'jurisdiction.' It has to do with where a crime is committed, and whether you have the right to arrest him under your own law."

Bliven nodded slowly. "If he were to stand trial in my own country, I cannot deny that this might become an issue raised in his defense, and he might possibly escape punishment because of it."

Kahumanu looked at him dubiously. "You admit this?"

"I do, ma'am."

"I credit your honesty."

"And yet, Your Majesty, I beg you to understand that I have no authority to fire on a ship that flies my own flag."

"Indeed? We shall see about that. Mrs. Putnam, come forward!"

Bliven had not seen her before now—she had been concealed behind a file of warriors—but they parted, and Clarity made the few steps to stand before her and curtsied.

"Mrs. Putnam, my people are in a tumult. I am concerned how to guard your safety and that of your friends. Boki, come forward!"

Boki left Liliha in the assemblage and stood before her.

"Therefore, Mrs. Putnam, I remand you to the protection of the High Chief Boki. He will remove you and your child to his *ahupuaa* at Pupukea to await the outcome of this troubled time."

"What!" cried Bliven. He took a step forward, his right hand instinctively seeking out the hilt of his sword, but at the same instant a line of warriors formed a wall of shark-toothed war clubs between him and the queen.

"Now, Captain Putnam, let us see whether you can find the authority to deliver up this man to our justice!"

From the crowd issued a loud, approving murmur. Kahumanu held out her hands. "Mrs. Putnam, come to me."

Clarity mounted the dais and took her hands, the first time she had feared to do so.

So that no others could hear, the queen whispered, "Missy, this must be. My safety as well as yours depends upon it. I have laid a *kapu* of death upon any who would harm you. I will send a wet nurse with you for your child. Ask no questions now. Stand with Boki."

Clarity backed away and curtsied again. Four of the warriors who had leveled their spears at Bliven raised them and flanked her as she moved to where Boki stood.

Bliven clenched his fists. "Am I not to be allowed to even speak to my wife?"

"No!" thundered the queen. "You may greet her when you have done as I command. Karaimoku, you shall sail with him to Maui and discover the details of all that has happened. If you find this man, you will seize him and bring him here, and if not, you will make inquiries to determine where he has gone, and if he is within reach, you will pursue him. Captain Putnam, I do not forget that you have just arrived after a long voyage. Mr. Jones, come forward!" The raffish young American agent stepped out nervously and stood by Putnam. "Mr. Jones, as we have seen, the American and European ships that were here have put to sea in some haste. Therefore you will cancel what requests they have given you and provision Captain Putnam's ship, even so soon as tonight."

"Yes, ma'am."

"Karaimoku, if the missionaries on Maui have not been harmed, I make you responsible to gather them up and bring them here. They shall live with Mr. Bingham and the others in their houses here."

It was quickly apparent to Bliven that if their safety were the only issue, Clarity and Ben would have been better off being interned there with Bingham and the others, but this was no time to gainsay the vengeful giantess before him. His eyes met Clarity's, which were wide, but more assimilating than apprehensive. He thanked God, because if she had shown any fear, he could not answer for what he might have done.

Kahumanu swept her hand out violently. She shouted, *"E hele pela!"* with such force that her jowls shook; Hopu was within the *pili* and got Bliven's attention, then made a shooing motion with the backs of his hands.

"Forgive me, ma'am, I must have one word more," said Bliven.

The queen glared at him. "Speak."

"Ma'am, I may know the cause of this, for I have just come from Canton."

"Continue."

"When Captain Saeger reached that place with the bundles of sandalwood, it was discovered that the people who sold it to him had mixed in cheap, useless wood with it. When Saeger sold the wood to the craftsmen in Canton, the trick was discovered, he was accused of cheating them, and he was compelled to return their money. Of sixty-five piculs that he left your country with, only ten piculs were found to be true sandalwood. Even though he made good on this debt, men from the major trading companies went to the governor of Canton, who revoked Captain Saeger's license to trade there. They did this not because of the adulterated sandalwood, but to remove him from competition with them."

"Why do you tell me this?"

"Ma'am, at the time I left Canton, the waterfront was still burning. It is not proven, but it is believed that Captain Saeger set the fire to get even with the trading companies for what they had done to him. In Canton he was heard to say that he would avenge himself on those of your country who cheated him. Thus, I fear that he came here and committed this terrible murder at Hana."

"Do you say this to defend him?"

"No, ma'am. I say this to warn you to protect the trading district here in Honoruru. If he set fire to Canton, which is one of the world's great cities, why would he hesitate to burn down the commercial center here?"

"Karaimoku?"

"My queen, I will set guards in the city to prevent any setting of fires."

Kahumanu thought a moment more. "No, you will set guards to protect the places where people live. As to the trading companies and their warehouses, they have brought this upon themselves. Warn them, but let them hire their own guards."

BLIVEN WAS AWAKE early, attempting to draught a report of the disastrous situation on the islands, how and whether to include the possibility that he might have to fire on an American ship, or deliver up an American citizen to some sanguine native justice—notwithstanding that it was to save the lives of the missionaries. Even balancing the one worthless life against the twenty worthy ones he would save, the whole incident would easily spell the end of his naval career. There would be no shortage of superiors, and the superior acting, who would say that he should have turned his guns upon the town and the queen to compel the return of the missionaries, even if it caused the deaths of some or many. To write for instructions was useless, for no reply would come within a year.

Stymied, he set that aside and turned to the parcel of letters that Bingham had given him in Honoruru.

GALVESTON
PROVINCE OF TEXAS
EMPIRE OF MEXICO
25TH MAY, 1822

*Captain Putnam, my Friend,*

*You are no doubt in wonder at the heading of my letter, and entertaining your first thought that I am on board a ship, and have resumed my former life as a trader. It would be a likely guess, but a wrong one.*

*I confess I am in confusion, how to relate to you the calamities that have befallen me since our last letters. I shall tell you the worst of it first, that you may share my despair. My dearly loved wife and sharer of my life, Rebecca, is no more. As affairs on our plantation became ever more hopeless, she labored heroically, ever with optimism and determination, to turn things around. It wore her down, and when the yellow jack spread through the country last August it took her as one of its first victims.*

*And now for the rest. To add disaster to calamity, the damn'd banker who so confidently persuaded me to mortgage my holdings in order to buy more land, who so solemnly avowed that the only way to gain wealth was to fund it with debt (I have written you of him before), showed up at my door with a writ of foreclosure. In my most utter and profound shock I made protest that his promise had been, to renew the note as long as I met the interest, and paid something on the principal. His excuse was that those who had lent him the money to lend, had placed him in straits, and though he regretted it, he must pass on these strictures. I persuaded him to serve me the writ in thirty days, that I would endeavor to raise the money (for I knew he would rather have the money than my land) and then I made inquiry of a lawyer in Charleston. He said that though I had justice on my side, justice and the law are clean different things, that equity must ever kneel before the terms of a contract, and that I must prepare myself to lose all.*

*All was not lost, however, for I saw a hand bill soliciting colonists to remove to the Spanish province of Texas. The government there is seeking to build up the country, and is giving—I say, giving—land to Americans who will settle there and make the wilderness productive. Such is the excitement to remove to Texas that I could not even say, whether the news spreads faster by fliers and news papers, or by word of mouth.*

*Since my purpose in Charleston was to raise money, I had with me the jewelry of my late mother and my dear wife. It was not a great fortune, but considerable gold, with some small diamonds, rubies, &c., given across generations. These I sold, and it was enough to buy a sad small schooner then in harbor, which my servant and I, with our horses, sailed to Savannah. I left him with the ship, and rode home, to begin dissolving my household.*

*Oh, Bliven, you cannot imagine the grief. I had the space of two wagons, in which to decide what to take, and what must be left behind for the vultures. First was to empty the corn crib, smoke house, and pantry, so there would be food. Then sufficient clothes, bedding, and sundries, implements and seed to make a new planting. Most painful was to choose which of my people to bring with me, and who must be left behind, either to be sold or to stay working the place for new owners. In the end, I brought my two best field hands. Dicey is also with me to cook and keep house, although in honesty, since*

Rebecca's death her tenderness and sympathies to me have made her not just dear, but indispensable. I resolved to leave behind all my parents' fine furnishings, the bulk of the equipment, and some two dozen slaves, enough to repay most of the debt, and awaited my fate.

When after thirty days the banker arrived with his writ to have either the full amount of the note, or take possession of my land, I made him a fair exchange: I gave him his life, and signed to him the deed to my lands, and he gave me the money he had on his person, which happily amounted to some few hundreds of dollars. The law would find me guilty of a robbery, but I say, I am not the only victim of his dealings. If the man were found murdered in a ditch there would be twenty under suspicion.

I bound him securely, and left instructions for my people to "find" him in a day or so. I allowed myself to be seen traveling down the road to Charleston, but then took the cut-off to the Savannah Road, stopping to rest only as the horses needed rest, and reached there safely. We loaded all and everyone onto my little ship, hoisted sails and stood out for whatever new life is in store for us.

As I have heard it is the custom, throughout the South as it proceeds to ruin, I painted the letters GTT on my front door. This is more or less universally understood to mean, Gone to Texas, a vast new land of unbounded opportunity. It is beyond the reach of American law, or debtors prisons, but it is attained only at the cost of forsaking one's American citizenship and swearing allegiance to a different nation. This were an unthinkable cost, in the pleasant fiction of the patriotism in which we were raised. I greatly fear, however, that the America they told us of is not, in fact, the one that exists. I am assured that I am not alone in this sentiment. Indeed, I do not feel that I stand out in my present company, for nearly all of us now in Texas were ruined in some way or other back home. We are *people of good character who arrived at the end of one road, and now are compelled to take another.*

*This Texas colony is the venture of a young New Orleans man named Austin. His father began the project, and won the approval of the government, but then died just as he began recruiting settlers to remove there. The government renewed the agreement with his son, and the first of we, his Argonauts, are now in Galveston and preparing to remove to the mouth of the Brazos River, to await his pleasure. There has been some uproar, for in his absence there was a revolution in Mexico, which has thrown off the Spanish crown, and he has gone there to make sure that his contract is still good. It seems reasonable to assume that it is, but Mr. Austin is an observer of jots and tittles, and from all accounts is a man in whom confidence may be safely placed.*

*How the post will operate after we reach the interior is a mystery, but I am sure it will organize in some way. I will write to you again when I have a permanent address to tell how you may reach me. As you and I both served with some credit in the Navy of the U.S., you can imagine what a pain it gives me to subscribe myself*

> *Still yr friend,*
> *Samuel Bandy*
> *Citizen of Mexico*

BLIVEN PUTNAM, CAPT. USN
C/O AMERICAN CONSUL
HONORURU, SANDWICH ISLANDS

Bliven laid the letter on the table, leaned forward, and rested his head in his hands, whispering, "Oh, my Sam. Perhaps we are both coming to ruin."

Karaimoku emerged from his guest berth in Western dress—black suit, white shirt and cravat, and shoes—which drew Bliven's most surprised notice. "Good morning, Mr. Pitt."

"Good morning, Captain Putnam."

"Would you like some coffee, or do you prefer tea?"

"You have coffee?"

"Most surely."

"I will taste it. I have seldom had coffee."

"If you do not care for it, you may have tea instead." Bliven rose and crossed to the sideboard, and poured a cup of coffee, quietly calculating the geometry of not overfilling it, for the ship was heeling to starboard, hauling close while beating against the relentless trade wind, working their way to the leeward side of Maui. Liquids, he had long known, kept their own level regardless of whether the cup was level.

Karaimoku accepted it with thanks and then added, "Mr. Marín has told us much about coffee. He says that he thinks it will grow well here, and maybe become a valuable crop one day. He has not yet been able to obtain seeds or young plants to try. Where does this come from?"

"Martinique, which is a French island in the Caribbean. I have a friend who trades for it, and he gives some to my family every year for Christmas."

"Yes, we have heard that your people exchange gifts every year upon the birthday of baby Jesus." Karaimoku drew a chair back from the table and sat down, sipping the coffee and making an approving face. "Well, Captain," he said at last, "this is a fine kettle of fish."

Bliven allowed himself a tiny smile at another British expression that the islanders had acquired.

"I am your hostage," said Karaimoku. "Your wife is my brother's hostage, the missionaries are the queen's hostages. We are hostages all around."

"That is surely one way to see things."

"I like your coffee. It is stronger than tea, and has a more bitter flavor, but not so strong or bitter as our *awa*. How else can you see things?"

"That everyone may be telling the truth. That the queen did send my wife away with Boki to keep her safe from revenge, and that she has sequestered the missionaries to the chiefs to protect them. That I really do need you to help sort out things on Maui and protect the missionaries there. I do not regard you as a hostage in any way, Mr. Pitt, and I was truthful in saying that I will hunt this outlaw down."

Karaimoku nodded slowly. "But you have said you may not fire upon a ship of your own country. And, further, that you would be expected to bring Captain Saeger back to America to stand trial, that you could lose your rank if you turn him over to us."

"Yes."

"So what are you going to do, Captain Putnam? What are your intentions?"

Bliven screwed up his face for lack of answer. "Perhaps, we should have a kettle of fish for our dinner."

"Ha! That would be proper."

"I am worried about my wife from one aspect: I am far from certain that Boki can be trusted with her. Stealing other men's wives seems to be a custom among your people, even stealing one from your own brother."

Karaimoku sighed and let his head fall to the side. "Ah, yes. I was younger then, and not sure of my position. I was jealous of everyone, I think. When Kameeiamoku stole my wife, I thought I would burn alive, I was so angry."

"So you settled for burning Honoruru."

"Yes. To me then, being a high chief was about power over people.

The great king had not yet conquered the whole country; it was useful for people to fear us. Today, to be a chief is responsibility. It is not easy to balance power and"—he searched for the word—"obligation. The English struggle with it, the French even more. So will you, when your day must come."

Bliven measured the substantial justice in those remarks. "Would you like some more coffee?"

"Yes, thank you." The chief stood up. "I'll get it." Once he was on his feet, the ship gave a lurching heave to starboard and Karaimoku steadied himself against the table. "Sometimes, the passage between our islands is like this." Bliven found himself captivated by the thick black matte of hair that fell to the middle of his back. He was just at the point of finding it savage, but then recalled seeing portraits of European gentlemen from a hundred years previous whose voluminous primped wigs were not dissimilar.

"Yes, so I have heard about the force of your trade winds. I do not know that I would even attempt it in one of your canoes."

"Our canoes have their merits, Captain. See, your sails are wrong for this duty. You have big square sails that nearly lay you over when the wind comes across. In the rough seas we have outriggers to stop us turning over, and our sails are shaped like the crab's claw and can catch the wind in any direction."

"Yes. Around the world I have seen many different ways of sailing."

Karaimoku returned with the pot and filled Bliven's cup as well, nearly spilling some coffee when he accidentally stuck the table with his foot, which made him frown. "One question, Captain, if I may?"

Bliven looked up expectantly.

"How in hell do you walk around with these damned leather boxes on your feet?"

Bliven threw his head back and laughed. "Well, where I come from it is often very cold. I suppose that once we covered our feet to keep them warm, they did not become as tough and hardy as *your* feet."

"Hm!"

"Although I have seen some of your lava flows. Not even you would attempt to walk across them in your bare feet."

Karaimoku resumed his seat. "No, but we have sandals woven from grass that serve very well for that case."

"Shall we go up on deck?" They walked down the gun deck, their uprightness forming an acute angle with the deck, and then up the ladder and aft, where Rippel was at the wheel. They exchanged greetings and both Bliven and Karaimoku laid a hand on the binnacle, not because they needed it every second, but for sudden gripping when they were slammed with a swell.

"Tell me, Mr. Pitt, how long did it take Ta-meha-meha to conquer all the islands?"

"From the beginning?" He shrugged. "Thirty years, maybe. And still, some go a little of their own way. Tauai, which lies far to the northwest and where the missionaries' friend Tamoree is prince, is not completely subject to us to this day. And here and there are pockets and valleys where people do as they please."

"Indeed?"

"Oh, yes. Look at my brother's valley of Pupukea on the north shore of Oahu. It is still quite wild up there; even the old religion is still practiced. Years ago, Captain Vancouver of the English sent a watering party ashore, and the *kahunas* captured and sacrificed them for daring to steal water from a sacred stream. Our own chiefs learned to either respect them or leave them alone."

Bliven gasped. "And this is where he took my wife?"

"Do not be alarmed. When news was received of the killing at Hana, the queen was in a great rage against the white people. This pleased my brother greatly, and he encouraged her to be more cautious in her welcoming them and giving them so much influence over the country people. For now, at least, she and Boki are allies, and working together to restore order. I think that your wife is, to be sure, his hostage, but she will be well protected."

## { 14 }

## *Pupukea*

After the fraught encounter within the audience hall, Clarity left, under guard but not bound, with Boki and Liliha. With so many servants in their wake to pack and follow, there was little delay in mounting to ride. Clarity would have preferred horseback, but carrying the baby induced her to accept the offer of a closed sedan chair borne by six of their *kanaka*s, as Liliha arranged herself in another.

They traveled west for a very few miles before turning up a path to follow a stream that poured out of a valley that ascended up and up. Even through her distraction Clarity noticed the land becoming greener, more lush. They passed the household of Kaukaulele, the chief to whom the valley belonged. He maintained a house near the city from which to oversee his share of business, but preferred to live in the verdant cool of the valley, away from the stink and noise of a town, and Honoruru was quickly growing into a sizable town. Their ascent was gradual but became steeper as they approached a jagged lava wall that reared up in front of them, broken by a single gap for which the path seemed bound.

When they reached its summit, Boki turned his horse back and dismounted. "We can rest here," he told Clarity, and to her surprise offered his hand to help her out of the sedan chair. She walked a short distance, with Ben in her arms, to a grassy parapet, and what she saw took her breath away. The gigantic furrowed wall of a mountain stretched to the west, falling two thousand feet from the clouds down and down to a coastal jungle between the cliff and the ocean that lay in the distance, partly in sun and partly between the moving shadows of the clouds. Never had she imagined standing at such a height over a prospect, and sat down from dizziness. Even as a hostage she was glad to have seen it.

Boki joined her, her first perspective of looking up at him, and she realized that although he was tall and strong, he was not corpulent in the way of the other nobles, and his face lacked the low brow ridge and thick lips of his class. Clearly there was another influence in his ancestry. "Are you all right?" he asked.

"Yes, thank you. What place is this?"

"This is the *pali* of the Nuuanu Valley."

"Are we going down there?"

"Yes."

"Is the path safe?"

"Yes. People use it every day."

"Will you object if I walk until we reach the bottom? I am afraid sitting in the chair will make me dizzy."

He smiled for just a second. "You would not be the first. Yes, you may walk." She had not expected civility, but then remembered what Marín had said, that he was not as forbidding as his reputation, and that his opposition to Kahumanu and her society-altering program led her faction to paint him in perhaps too-dark colors.

The path down was steep, with switchbacks, but she let herself be diverted by the cliff wall that was covered in vines and flowers of species she had not yet seen, and the flashing colors of birds taking flight before them. Once at the foot of the cliff, they followed a well-worn path, perhaps the beginning of a road westward; when it began to rain, Liliha offered a large *kihei* for Clarity to wrap herself in, but she seated herself again in the covered sedan. One sight did begin to unnerve her. She was uncertain at first whether she saw the white of a bone lying within the dense green undergrowth, but as they continued it became undeniable, for she made out leg bones and the occasional rib cage.

Boki was riding immediately before her. "Chief Boki, may I ask why there are so many bones down here? Was this a place of sacrifice?"

"No, not really," he answered. "When the old king conquered this island many years ago, the Oahu king opposed him. There was a great battle on top of the *pali*. When Ta-meha-meha was victorious, the opposing soldiers were cast over."

*Well, that is lovely,* she thought. *Just when I thought this place was less brutal than I had believed . . .*

After several miles the track turned west at what she surmised was the north end of the island, then up and away from the coast, past a small lava-rock temple, of which there were several score dotting the island.

Boki dismounted and again helped Clarity out of her sedan chair, and she beheld something else that she would have listed as the least expected: an English cottage of red brick that could only have been imported, and glass windows with white-painted wooden sashes. It might have been lifted from central London but for its diminutive size and the fact that, once within, she found the floor not of wood but of packed earth. Still, it was furnished with the finest appointments.

"This is where you will stay," said Liliha. "You will find everything you need. The queen has commanded that we provide you a servant, one who has a new child and can nurse yours as well, if you wish. She is one of our *kanakas*, and we will send for her. Her name is Hewela. She does not speak English, but you know enough of our language to make your needs known."

AFTER TWO AND a half days' hard sail into oblique winds, *Rappahannock* entered Lahaina Roads and its relative calm in the lee of Maui's mountains. Yeakel swung the large cutter out on its davits, laden with Lieutenant Horner and fifteen heavily armed marines, waiting upon the captain and Karaimoku before lowering.

"Mr. Ross!" Bliven blurted suddenly.

"Sir?"

"Run to Mr. Erb. Here, take one of my shoes. Tell him I require a pair of marine boots of the approximate size, right away. I'm damned if I walk into possible trouble wearing these damned slippers."

Bliven waited impatiently until Ross returned and helped him into the boots with their high, scalloped tops.

When Karaimoku emerged from his berth, he was transformed, wearing a native *malo*, his shoulders draped with a striking cape of feathers of brilliant scarlet and yellow blazes sewn into a fine mesh, and he carried one of those ancient-looking crested helmets.

"Heavens," said Bliven.

"I am known here," he answered. "You will be safe as long as I am with you. You will not know what I am asking and saying, but I will ask for the missionaries to be brought down straightaway, and we will bring them back with us. I will learn all I can from the people."

They seated themselves in the cutter, and Lieutenant Horner and a dozen marines stepped in after them. Yeakel supervised their lowering. As the cutter touched the water ten sailors pulled at their sweeps. "I am sorry for the people of Hana," said Karaimoku. "They have known much suffering over the years. In the old days, every contender for king wanted to own it. The great Ta-meha-meha fought for it; so did his father and his uncle in their time." Karaimoku pointed to the hill that loomed south of them. "Kahumanu herself was born there, on a hill outside the town."

As they approached the beach, Karaimoku donned his crested *mahiole*, and the sight of a high chief in ceremonial war garb went far to quell the unrest of the throng that gathered. "Mr. Horner," said Bliven, "you come ashore with us and bring four marines; leave the others in the boat unless they are needed."

As soon as he said it, he realized this was the very thing that Captain Cook had done on the day he was killed, and for the same reason of not wanting to create too great a threat to the natives.

When Karaimoku began speaking, runners ascended the hill to where the missionaries were gathered at the edge of their compound, and in few moments they began walking down hurriedly, each carrying a portmanteau: Asa and Lucy Thurston, and Samuel and Mercy Whitney. Bliven looked them over quickly. "Is this all of you? Are you unharmed?"

"We are quite uninjured," said Thurston. "In fact our church and house have been guarded by our native Christians since the massacre at Hana."

"I am glad to hear it. Mr. Horner, have your men take their baggage and help them into the boat. Mr. Pitt, have you learned what you require?"

"More than enough."

"Well, then, promise them that I will do everything I possibly can to see that justice is done for them."

"I have done so already, and now we must hurry."

Two of the marines pushed them off the sand and then pulled themselves into the cutter, and the sailors went to their oars, port side pulling back, starboard pushing forward to turn them toward the ship.

"To whom do we owe the honor of our rescue?" asked Thurston.

Until that moment Bliven had scarcely noticed that after his nearly two years in and out and into Honoruru, the church in Lahaina did not know him. "Bliven Putnam," he said, "captain commanding United States sloop of war *Rappahannock*."

"Aha!" erupted Lucy Thurston. "You must be Clarity's mysterious husband! Now we understand."

"Shall you set off now in pursuit of Captain Saeger?" asked Thurston.

Bliven stared at him, astonished. "How did you know it was he?"

"So we deduced. He docked his schooner here in Lahaina for two days' drinking and making rude gestures up toward the church. He was disjointed that the local chief has joined our church and no longer permits the women of his district to consort with sailors. Made him quite enraged. He said he was going to the windward side to trade for sandalwood, and then he was going to Kona and to find a more agreeable port. We heard about the killing only a day later, so we believed it could not have been any other."

"My God. What do you think, Mr. Pitt? Do you think he might still be in Kona?"

"Maybe. We will not know unless we hurry."

Regaining Honoruru required only overnight with the trade winds behind them, where the entire missionary company was re-united, and Bliven and Karaimoku were given instant audience with the queen. He noticed at once that she still eschewed Western dress, and wore the thick *lei niho palaoa* of her royal rank about her neck.

"Karaimoku," she intoned, "what is the way of it?"

"My queen, what he suspected before has been proven true. When our people at Hana bundled the sandalwood, they placed it only on the outside. The inner logs were worthless."

Kahumanu's face twitched with rage.

"Ma'am," said Bliven, "this fact strengthens my suspicion that he set the great fire in Canton, and when he put to sea once more, he was next seen in Maui. The rest you know."

Kahumanu assimilated this as still and grim as a statue. Indeed, she sat motionless for so long that she might have been taken for struck dumb, but every soul at court knew she was calculating. The *kanakas*, the common people who loaded the wood, would not have dared such a thing on their own. She turned to Karaimoku. "From whose *ahupuaas* was this sandalwood taken? Which of our chiefs have done this thing?"

Karaimoku's sadness was immeasurable. "Kaiwikapu," he said at last. "And Na-ao-kaalelewa." The queen was from Hana; he knew that she knew these chiefs.

Suddenly she rose and, reaching to the side, took from her closest retainer a fearsome twelve-foot lance. It was then that Bliven noticed she had not been sitting on her Louis XIV gilt chair but upon a strong, shaped bench of yellow and brown koa wood. Using the spear as a staff, she advanced to the edge of the dais and stood immovable for two full minutes, glaring at those inside the royal *pili*.

She looked sharply down to her right, at the man with the writing desk. "Mr. Jenkins, have you set this all down in true account?" Bliven was surprised to see that she had acquired an amanuensis.

"I have, ma'am."

"Hear me, then, my chiefs and ministers. Through all our history, chiefs have governed the people on their lands, with no interference from the king, subject only to their portion of taxes, and providing soldiers in a war. See, all of you, where this has brought us. A hundred dead, our reputation ruined, we are made the victims of an evil man, those who have brought the word of God have been placed in danger. I say as I hold the spear of the Conqueror, those days are at an end. Hear my judgment! The lands of these two chiefs are forfeited."

A gasp rose from the court, followed by a receding murmur.

"If any deny my right to do this, speak now." The silence fell like a pall. "I give these lands to the Chief Naihetutui, and they shall be used to support the families afflicted by this terrible act. Now, Captain Putnam, do you know where this wicked man has gone?"

"We believe to the Kona coast, ma'am."

"Is it your intention to pursue him?"

"As soon as Your Majesty dismisses us."

"Go, then! Go, and let justice be done!"

Bliven and Karaimoku walked quickly back down to the pier, picking up at the waterfront the pilot that was now required.

"I thought for a moment she was going to sentence those two chiefs to death," Bliven remarked.

"It would have been better for them if she had," answered the high chief. "For a chief to lose his rank, to lose his land, to net fish and pull up *kalo* like the country people, is worse than death. I expect they will be dead within a year by their own hands, rather than suffer this. You have heard the queen's justice. You are an American, what did you think about it?"

"Well, I noted that she aimed her justice not for the government but to provide for the victims of the crime. I think in all honesty that it was well done, and fair."

Karaimoku clambered down into the gig behind him. "So did I."

As soon as they were back aboard, Miller asked if he might speak to the two of them, and they repaired to the sea cabin. "There are elements of this whole story that are not making sense to me," he began.

"Go on, Mr. Miller."

"First, Saeger left Canton the night before we did. With his ship, he should have beaten us here by three weeks. How is it this massacre took place only the day before we arrived? No one seems to have seen him before then."

"Good point."

"Second, the people he fired on were in canoes. They would have begun fleeing or diving into the water at first firing. How did he manage to kill a hundred people with only four guns, even loaded with grape?"

Karaimoku sat up, suddenly agitated. "Four guns? The people at Lahaina told me he had ten guns!"

Bliven and Miller stared at each other. "Lieutenant Miller, I suspect that you were correct in your suspicion weeks ago that he put in to the Philippines and acquired greater armament."

"Has he gone mad?"

"As a dog goes mad, I fear," Bliven answered.

"Captain Putnam," said Karaimoku, "I think you are in a pickle." Even in the tension, Bliven had to smile at a new Briticism from this native chief. "You have told the queen that you cannot deliver him up to a foreign country, and she has taken your wife hostage to the north shore of Oahu to make you do it. You have said that you cannot fire on a ship under your own flag. What are your intentions?"

Bliven stood suddenly, pacing a circle around the mahogany table, punctuating the air with his fist. "Mr. Miller"—he stopped just as suddenly—"make all preparations for getting under way, but do not hoist the anchor except on my order."

"Aye, Captain." He saluted and left.

"Mr. Pitt, come topside with me. You must help me think."

He was quickly up the ladder and aft to the quarterdeck, pacing back and forth. "What you say is true, but—my God, wait a minute. Wait a minute! I may not fire upon him. *You*, however, Mr. Pitt, are bound by no such restriction."

"What? *I* fire upon him? How? What with? What are you working at, Captain?"

"Yes, let us work at it." He pointed at him several times. "Mr. Pitt, you are a military commander, you have led armies, and I believe that the principles of military engagement are probably similar both on land and on the sea." He began walking forward and Karaimoku followed him.

"Yes."

"Let us say, you are at the head of your army and you look over your enemy's forces. Where would you attack him?"

"Where he is weakest."

"Exactly. Now, what do you think is Captain Saeger's worst point?"

"That he killed a hundred of our people."

"Yes, but there he acted out of vengeance. What is his greatest weakness, what can he always be counted to act upon?"

"His greed?"

"And what is he greedy for?"

"Money."

"Yes, but how is he accustomed to getting money here, in your country?"

"With our sandalwood." They approached the bow and Karaimoku interrupted himself. "You have placed larger guns in the front of your ship."

"Yes. This way when I come toward somebody, they know I mean to do business. Now, you told me something before that has been buzzing around in my mind like a bee. You said that on your brother's land, where they have taken my wife, there are valleys that are sacred to the priests of the old religion. Would they not still contain sandalwood?"

"Most surely."

"Of all your leading chiefs, who has the worst opinion of the white people."

"My brother."

"And who owes Saeger more money than anyone?"

"My brother."

"And who has the sandalwood that could cause him to come ashore?"

Karaimoku nodded emphatically. "My brother."

"So, if Saeger comes ashore to collect the sandalwood for the debt that your brother owes him, and he is captured by Boki's warriors—or your warriors—it would not have been by my hand, would it?"

Karaimoku stood stock-still. "Captain Putnam, I see that what you could not come to directly, you came back to by skittering around sideways. Here and now I give you a Hawaiian name: *Paiea*."

"What does it mean?"

"The crab."

"Ha! I shall wear it proudly. But come, how do we get Saeger ashore at Pupukea?"

"I do not know."

Bliven headed aft again, seeing the loose gear being stowed, and the master at arms beginning to take a roll of the crew. "Suppose, just suppose, that Saeger were handed a letter from your brother. In it he apologizes for his lateness in paying the debt and says that the queen and other chiefs, including yourself, have impressed upon him the importance of maintaining good credit with the foreign powers. With the end of the old religion, the forests that were once forbidden are no longer, and he is harvesting the sandalwood, if Saeger would care to come to Pupukea and get it. If you were Saeger, would you go?"

"I would consider whether it was a trap—and then I would go."

"Can your brother read and write?"

"Only to sign his name, I think. Maybe better by now."

"Well, then . . . well, then . . . How about this? You will write the letter on your brother's behalf. I will take it to Kona and hope that I get there in time. You will go to Pupukea as fast as you can, tell your brother everything, and be prepared to capture Saeger when he comes ashore. Do you think your brother will agree?"

"To capture and maybe kill this man? Yes, he will agree."

"Let us go below." In the sea cabin Bliven provided fresh paper and his desk set to Karaimoku, who began writing in a labored and elementary hand. "Now, if you say—"

Karaimoku's free hand flashed up. "Do not tell me. I know what is wanted."

"Yes, of course. If I may suggest, do not claim that Boki will pay his whole debt, or Saeger might suspect a trick. If you say you have enough sandalwood to pay seventy or eighty percent of your debt, and say you hope that will satisfy him for the present, it will sound more plausible, don't you think?"

Karaimoku looked up, his eyes wide. "Captain Putnam, you make an admirable sneak. And we must get him ashore," he added suddenly. "I will tell him that the wood comes from the sacred forest, so it is being kept in the temple and he must come get it."

"Oh, yes, that will do, that will do."

When it was finished he signed it "Karaimoku, High Chief and First Minister," and said, "Well. The bait is on the hook, and I must leave now with all speed. I will gather my warriors and go to my brother, who will gather his warriors, and we will prepare the priests in the temple there. The queen need not know any of this. We are doing her bidding, but she becomes alarmed when any soldiers gather that are not hers."

"I understand. You tell your queen only what she needs to know, and I will tell my government only what they need to know."

"We are plotters, you and I."

In the back of his mind he remembered saying this to someone else.

"I must go," said Karaimoku. "If you reach Kona and you are too late, send word quickly so we can disperse before arousing suspicion."

"I will. Mr. Ross!"

He came out of his berth. "Sir?"

"See Mr. Pitt up on deck and have him taken ashore in my gig."

"Yes, sir."

It would be a hard sail down to Kona, obliquely against the trade winds, perhaps two days. If Saeger got there and no word of his doings had reached there, he should be in no hurry to abandon its plentiful rum and willing women.

Those two days were exhausting before the winds eased in the lee of Hawaii Island's enormous mountains, and they eased around a point not named on the chart and into Kailua Kona's south-facing bay. It contained four ships, one of them a large topsail schooner, their hopes rising by degrees until they saw FAIR TRADER painted on its stern.

It was near nightfall, the bars would be filling, and the *Rappahannock*'s officers fanned out along the waterfront, knowing only that Saeger was inordinately tall, white-haired, and overbearing. It was Jackson who found him, in a place called Ka-eo's. Without being noticed, he tracked down the others; the lieutenants loitered in a nearby establishment as Bliven approached the open door, the smell of beer and piss, the growing noise. Of all things, he found himself thinking about Lady Macbeth: *Screw your courage to the sticking-place.*

He entered, and immediately saw a man who could only be Saeger at the far end of the bar. Bliven's uniform created a zone of quiet around him as he passed through and boldly up to the tall old man. "Excuse me, sir, are you Captain Saeger of the *Fair Trader*?"

He drew himself up to his full height. "I am. What can I do for you?" His suspicious nature seemed to hang in a protective cloud around him.

Bliven held out his hand. "Captain Putnam, United States sloop of war *Rappahannock*, just in harbor from Honoruru. I have a letter for you."

"Oh, well, that is good of you." When Bliven took it out of his pocket, Saeger said, "What, is it not sealed?"

"No, sir, it is rather an open letter. Let me buy you a drink and I will explain."

"Very well, if you wish." His voice was deep and sonorous, not what one would associate with a butcher.

"Rum or whiskey?"

"Rum, sir."

"Excuse me, please! A bottle of rum and two glasses."

They appeared almost instantaneously. "Two dollars, Captain."

He placed the coins on the counter. "May we sit at that table?" The feet of the chairs squealed on the wooden floor, one of the few he had seen.

"Now, what is this about?"

Bliven worked the cork out of the bottle and filled their glasses. "Captain, you have not been in Honoruru of late, as I understand."

"I have not."

"Are you aware that High Chief Karaimoku is now prime minister of the country?"

"No, I am not."

"You are aware, though, that he is the brother of High Chief Boki, who owes a great deal of money to Western captains, including your-self. Under pressure from European and American representatives, the government has begun a policy to redeem these debts, whatever it should take, as an issue of establishing the credit of their country. It seems, there are forests on Boki's estate that have never been har-vested for sandalwood." He handed over the letter. "He is offering to make good on part of his debt to you."

Saeger examined it as if it were a scientific specimen. "Here, now," he growled, his voice very broad as though he had let himself into the circle of a joke. "What do you take me for? Boki can't write, and this looks like he just came out of primary school."

"Quite right," said Bliven evenly. "He has learned to sign his name, but he cannot compose a letter such as this."

Saeger puffed out his cheeks. "Pff!"

"But his brother can." He turned the letter over to reveal the signa-ture. "The Americans and Europeans in Honoruru have united in telling them that no one will do business with them if they do not pay their debts, or at least as much of a debt as will be acceptable to him that holds it, such as you."

Bliven could tell Saeger was considering this, like the first nibble at a fishing line.

"Now, there may come a day when they regret it, but for now the chiefs are as addicted to gilt mirrors and mahogany furniture as their king is to liquor."

"That is true," grumbled Saeger. "They have no more self-control than children."

"Yes. Now, when Karaimoku gave me this letter, he vouchsafed that there are a couple of valleys on his brother's land that he knew still had sandalwood. In the old days those valleys were sacred to the priests, and no one has ever cut there. Those mountains are something on the order of three thousand feet high and catch the most rain, and so have the thickest forest. If Boki has wood now with which to make progress on what he owes you, that is likely where it comes from."

"It would stand to reason, yes."

"Well, I don't know the man myself, but I do have some acquaintance with Karaimoku, and he seems to place some faith in his word. To be sure, the queen remonstrated with him and the other debtor chiefs very severely on the damage they were doing to themselves and the country by ignoring their debts."

"M-hm."

Bliven laughed suddenly. "Of course, that number would include the king first of all, but I don't know what she can do about him."

"Truly said." Saeger drained his rum. "Well, if he makes a contract whilst he is drunk, that is no defense to let him escape its terms."

*No,* thought Bliven, *no indeed.* He held the bottle over Saeger's empty glass. "One more?"

"Thank you. You sailed all the way down here to tell me this?"

"No, no, it is a side errand, really. My ship is visiting all the ports, showing the flag, you see, meeting the local officials. The United States is broadening its horizons, as it were. Karaimoku asked me if I would carry this with me in case I encountered you."

"I see." Saeger began reading the letter in detail. "The forests used to belong to the temple. That makes sense; that is where they killed Captain Vancouver's men back in 'ninety-three for just putting in to water."

"One other thing, Captain Saeger. I have heard that some of the other big creditors, like Marshall and Wildes, have gotten wind that Boki intends to pay you what he can. I should warn you, they may reach him first with a better offer. If I were you, I should make haste."

Saeger considered it further and began to nod his head. "Indeed, I shall do so."

"You do know where Boki's lands are, at Pupukea?"

"Oh, yes, I know it well." Saeger stood, tall but crooked, and Bliven rose after him. Saeger extended his hand. "Good night, Captain Putnam. I am in your debt. May I keep this letter in case he tries to deny it all?"

Bliven took his hand. *You have no idea.* "Of course. My errand is complete. Good night, sir. Fair sailing to you."

HE WAS AWAKE and drinking coffee as through his stern windows he saw the *Fair Trader* stand out to sea from Kailua Kona's tiny little bend of a bay. He went up on deck; it was chilly because the sun was not yet above the hulking mass of Hualalai. It gave him a thrill to stand in the shadow of a volcano that had erupted, they told him, twice within his lifetime, and whose jolting earthquakes still struck and no one could say when next. West, across the bay, were the leaning remains of a huge grass *pili* behind a wall of lava rock, where the great King Ta-meha-meha had lived. How much he had missed, Bliven thought, by being born just an eyelash too late.

He tried to divine how long of a head start to give Saeger and his crew of the misbegotten. If he were able to arrest any of them, he thought, he must gratify his curiosity in learning how they had come to such a pass in life as to work for such a man as could snuff out a hundred innocent people. Were they equally distempered by nature, or had they like so many others followed their road as best they could, and eventually found themselves at a divergence with no good possi-bilities? Two days, he thought. Karaimoku must have reached Boki by now to prepare to trap Saeger within the walls of their Pupukea tem-ple and have their warriors ready for a fight if one were needed.

He went back down to his cabin, suddenly surprised at himself that in all this chasing about the Sandwich Islands he had never yet unshelved Jedidiah Morse's *Compendious Geography*. What must he have to say about this place? He found it on page 619, almost an after-thought: The people are darker than they are on Tahiti, but many with pleasant features; Captain Cook was killed here; the trade winds blow from the east; and the mountains catch the moisture, causing each island to have a wet side and a dry side. "Pfft!" With this much information, he thought, any old tar in Boston should write a geogra-phy, and he replaced it on the shelf.

He spread his chart of the Sandwich Islands on the table. Saeger had stood out to the northwest, surely the fastest and most sensible course; after he cleared the big island he would race along the outlet of the Alenuihaha Channel, then the winds would slack off in the lee of Maui, Lanai, and Molokai, and then with only a slight alteration to northwest by north they would cross the Kaiwi Channel and bear up the east coast of Oahu. It could not take more than three days to round the northern extremity of Oahu at Kahuku Point and drop anchor at Pupukea . . . and eternity.

No, he would not wait two days: they would embark the following afternoon. He did not wish to let events there go stale before he arrived.

Bliven plotted the same course he anticipated for Saeger. Once they were well under way, the lieutenants gathered in the sea cabin at his call, as did the lieutenant of marines—the bosun, for if they had to fight, it would be in the open, and his ship handling would be crucial.

"Gentlemen," he said, "in the future we may look back on these days and think them improbable, but the fact is that up to now our plan is working. When I spoke to Saeger, he betrayed no hint of disbelief or suspicion that I was playing him false. He took Karaimoku's letter with him and embarked the next day on this course we are trailing. And now, unlike the dog who chased a boar and got cut up, we must think in advance about what to do if we catch him."

He spread the chart of Oahu on the table.

"First thing, Captain, if I may?" Yeakel said. "Before we ever get into it with anyone, I would recommend that we shorten sail just as we round Kahuku Point. The last thing we want to do is give ourselves away and then overshoot the mark. It would take forever to claw our way back, and we might not be able to at all because the wind will have us running full and by."

There was a murmur of nodding approval. "Mr. Yeakel, keep up that thinking and you will make captain one day. Well done."

"Captain?"

"Mr. Miller."

"Let me speak cautiously here as we explore. By the time we get there, if all goes well, Saeger will have gone ashore, but we don't know with how many men. For that matter, if indeed he mounts ten guns, we don't know how many men are on his ship: he may have taken on Filipino sailors as well as guns."

"Or Boogis pirates, for all we know," said Bliven.

"Oh, yes!" whispered Miller. "That is true. Well, that emphasizes the point I would make: that even though this is an American vessel, our guns should be rolled out and ready for instant action before we ever see him."

"Yes, I quite agree," said Bliven. "Gentlemen?"

"Agreed."

Bliven ventured, "Do you suggest that we at least speak him, and give him a chance to surrender? Or allow to surrender whoever is on the vessel?"

"I suppose we should have to," said Miller, "even if just once."

Jackson shook his head. "If he has gone piratical, he knows that there is only one end for him if he does surrender. If I were him, I would see no choice but to fight it out."

"Against us?" Bliven's tone of voice suggested the madness of taking on a vastly superior vessel in a gun duel. "If he is not aboard, I believe we may count on it that they will hesitate in indecision. That will be a critical moment, for either they will, in the absence of the one who bullies them, abandon him and surrender or panic and open fire, in which case we will, as we have said, return fire in an instant. And then, once we have disabled their vessel, we will go ashore in force, say, fifty of our men with the fifty marines. Does anyone have another idea?"

Miller tapped the point on the chart showing the shallow scallop of Pupukea's inlet. "I believe that anything more detailed must wait until we see the lie of the land."

As they bore up the east coast of Oahu, all of them stood transfixed by the landscape, a thick, flat coastal jungle that ended abruptly at a vaulting wall of a mountain, two thousand feet high or more, corrugated by erosion from the veils of waterfalls that dissipated into mist before disappearing into the forest. When they passed the jutting promontory marked on the chart as Makahoa Point, they knew they were three miles from the northern tip of the island.

"Very well, Mr. Yeakel, reef your courses. Master-at-Arms, beat to quarters. Mr. Miller, see that the twenty-four-pounders are loaded with ball, the carronades with grape." The hollow thumping tattoo of the drum at the head of the ladder penetrated below, bringing men boiling up from below. There was the heavy creaking of the twenty-fours being rolled in, each one weighing forty-three hundred pounds and sitting on half-ton carriages. Belowdecks the boys scuttled into the powder magazine where only they could go, and Dr. Berend gathered up the more gruesome articles of his trade—more dire than his vials of mercurous chloride: his kit of tourniquets, knives, and bone saw—and repaired to his cockpit, donning the leather apron that he had not, thus far on this cruise, had to streak with blood.

"I am going below. I shall return directly," Bliven said. When he appeared again, he had changed his officer's shoes for marine boots, had his Yemeni jambia thrust through his belt, and carried his speaking trumpet in his hand.

By the time they reached land's end and saw open water open out to port, all was quiet again. "Very well, Mr. Yeakel, drop your t'gallant yards, shorten to stays'ls and main tops'l."

They turned west for three miles, and then from the moment they came southwest they saw their quarry at anchor, far ahead of them at Pupukea inlet.

"What is your sounding?"

"Eighty fathoms, Captain."

"Come two points to port. Bring us in a little closer."

With all in readiness, the silence on board was crushing, the wind in the rigging and the hiss of the water they cut through slower than before.

"He does not appear to be expecting company." They neared the shore obliquely until they could hear the breakers dull in the distance. "Sounding?"

"Twenty-five fathoms, Captain."

"Drop your sails; ready to let go the anchors. We will need both of them or we will drift over the cable and swing around. I don't want to do that unless it is useful." He found himself thinking again of Macdonough on Lake Champlain. "Bring us in about fifty yards off his beam."

"No sign of life," said Miller. "I rather wish we saw somebody."

"Sounding?"

"Fifteen fathoms, sir."

"Sails down. Let go your anchors!"

When the noise ceased, Bliven crossed to the port rail and put the speaking trumpet to his lips. "Ahoy, *Fair Trader*! Ahoy!"

After a moment's silence Rippel said quietly, "Nobody home?"

"Ahoy, *Fair Trader*! This is United States sloop of war *Rappahannock*. Where is your captain?"

Only a ghost ship could have appeared more lifeless.

"Ahoy, *Fair Trader*! I ask you again: Where is your captain? I require an answer!"

At last a voice came back, thin and surely without a trumpet. "Our captain is ashore!"

"Did you mark that accent?" asked Miller. "I don't know what it was, but it was nothing even remotely European."

"*Fair Trader*, who is your senior officer aboard?" Bliven turned to Miller. "I am getting annoyed. Preble would never have stood for this."

Still no more answer came.

"*Fair Trader*, I ask you for the last time, who is your senior officer?"

Both ships rocked in the swell for two minutes as the officers studied the lines of the sleek schooner. And then, in an instant, gunports snapped open where none had been visible before, and they found themselves staring at seven muzzles, a confusion of carronades and six- and twelve-pounders.

As loudly as his lungs would generate Bliven screamed, "Down!" even as he flung himself from the rail onto the deck. The schooner's side erupted in flame, so close that they felt the heat of the muzzle blasts and the impacts of balls striking the hull and railing, and the whistling chatter of grape from the carronades. From somewhere forward he heard screams and realized they had suffered casualties.

From prone on the deck Bliven cried, "Fire, all guns! Fire!" The *Rappahannock* seemed to slide sideways in the water from the recoil. As soon as he gave the order he reproached himself: he should have waited to ascertain their position in the swell, for as they rolled they might have shot into the water or over their rigging.

Peering through the smoke as it cleared, however, they beheld the entire side of the schooner appeared to have caved in five feet above the waterline, revealing compartments, bedding, open hold, and two guns knocked off their carriages.

"Reload! Get the wounded below!"

"Captain, look! They have a boat down."

They stood again and were able to see no one reloading the schooner's guns. "No, they already had a boat down. Now they are pulling for shore. Their guns were all previously loaded, and they don't have enough on board to reload them."

"Or know how," said Miller. "Look, they are Boogis, after all."

Horner called from the waist, "Shall we get a boat down and get after them, Captain?"

"No, hold where you are!" More quietly he added, "Gentlemen, the gunfire will have alerted the warriors of Boki and Karaimoku. These fellows won't get far. Mr. Jackson, get forward and then go below. Report to me damage and casualties."

"Aye, sir."

"Mr. Rippel, take a couple of men, go forward, and observe her from a different perspective, see if you detect any movement."

"Aye, Captain."

"Mr. Miller, get the master-at-arms to arm fifty men. I shall take them ashore with Mr. Horner's marines. You will be in command here. In a few moments, send Jackson ashore with twenty more. Mr. Yeakel, get both cutters ready to put into the water!"

"Yes, sir."

"Now, Mr. Horner, let us look to the shore. You see the beach where our friends just landed. Hm! look at them scampering up the trail, showing us where it is! They won't get far, I'll wager. Now, to the left of it you see a hill perhaps a hundred feet high, and on top of it and back from the edge you see walls maybe ten feet tall of lava rock. Looks like a fortification. Do you see it?"

"Yes, sir."

"That is our objective: that is where the chiefs were going to attempt to lure Saeger and whoever was with him. Once we locate the entrance, we will rush it. Now, whoever is inside, no matter how hostile, will be armed vastly inferior to us. Do not start shooting just because you see black people. Hold your fire until we discover whose they are."

"I understand sir."

"All right, get your marines into your boat."

\* \* \*

DAVID HORNER WAS first through the gate of the temple, leading his company of marines with bayonets fixed, the men behind him shouting to spike their ferocity; but once they were within the courtyard, they fell silent. Bliven and his company of seamen charged in behind them but were struck equally dumb even as they obeyed a command to broaden into a firing line. They beheld opposing them about twenty priests of the temple, or of this and other temples, for as Bliven realized in a flash the import of what Karaimoku had told him: that Boki, although he did not fight the new religion, nevertheless sheltered dissident *kahunas* in his own district. Boki may very well have been intending to ride a religious restoration to depose their giggling drunk of a king and his stepmother, whom Boki disdained, and himself take power. Kahumanu herself must have known how tenuous her own grip on power was; thus she had to be seen to turn against the missionaries in the wake of the Hana massacre. And what faced him now was not a clot of recalcitrant priests but the dragon seeds of Boki's new revolution.

Almost as one the *kahunas* produced and brandished an armory of native weapons that Bliven had seen pictured in the books about Captain Cook: the heavy war clubs studded with sharks' teeth; the wicked *pahoa* daggers, each with not one but two blades of razor-sharp volcanic glass, with the handle in the middle so that they could stab while thrusting both left and right. In their own era, in the savage days of early man, such weapons would have instilled terror, but against modern muskets they inspired pity.

"Sacrilege!" bellowed one of the priests, astonishing Bliven that he would have known that English word. That *kahuna* came to the fore of the group, genticulating hysterically. "You enter our *heiau*! You defile our temple! For this you will die!"

"Lieutenant," called Bliven, "do not fire unless you must!"

"No, sir, I understand! Marines, *en garde*, but hold your fire!" The company took a step forward, lowering their muskets.

Bliven advanced three steps toward the priests and began to understand from their bleary eyes and swaying that their determination if not their courage might have a chemical source. "Lay down your weapons," he said. "We have no quarrel with you. I give you my word, you will not be harmed." It was apparent that neither Boki's nor Karaimoku's warriors were anywhere around.

The pregnant silence continued for over a minute, until one of the younger and meatier of the priests suddenly descended into a kind of lewd half-squat. His eyes bulging, he uttered the most guttural bawl with his tongue stuck out halfway down his chin, at which the others followed suit.

"Stop this!" shouted Bliven.

Their shouting and brandishing of weapons went on until without any visible signal they surged forward, their war clubs high and daggers clenched.

"Marine company," cried Horner, "prepare to fire! Fire!"

The lava rock of the enclosing walls echoed the explosions of the muskets, and the charging priests were stopped for an instant. More than half fell, but then the others came on.

"Reload!"

"Ship's company," roared Bliven, "prepare to fire! Fire!"

There was another resounding volley, and pistols withdrawn from belts dropped those who were still standing. All waited with bayonets *en garde* to fight whoever should emerge from the cloud of smoke, but none came.

"Reload!"

Nimbly, the firing line of sailors disengaged their ramrods and stood their rifled muskets on their butts—powder, wadding, ram; ball, wadding, ram—

The smoke slowly lifted and revealed the completeness of what they had done.

"Why did they come on so?" Horner shook his head. "I did not wish to fire upon them—not at all." His distress appeared almost desperate.

"This was your first real action?"

"Yes, sir."

"Set your mind at ease, Lieutenant. You acted honorably."

Horner still looked, stricken, at the bodies before them.

"They were the last of their kind, David. They were the end of an era in human history. Perhaps they felt that such a momentous turning point should not be marked by a tame surrender. Maybe they wanted no part of a future without terror and human sacrifice. That was the world in which they became very powerful."

"Still, I feel quite terrible, sir."

"Good, for if you exulted, I would have to report you as unfit for advancement. But come. Come with me." They walked over to the nearest of the fallen *kahunas*. Bliven stooped and removed an obsidian-bladed *pahoa* from his hand. "Do you see this big dagger that I carry in my belt?"

"Yes, sir. I have wondered about it, but never asked."

"I took it from an Arab pirate in the Barbary War. It has brought me luck. And here is yours." He handed the *pahoa* over to Horner.

"Thank you, sir."

They surveyed the priests sprawled bloody on the ground, when a couple of them twitched and moaned. "Send someone back to the ship to fetch Dr. Berend. He will see if he can do something for any of them."

"Yes, sir." Horner turned and relayed the order to his corporal, who exited the temple at a trot and started down the path to the beach.

"And then I suppose you should form up a burial detail after Berend gets here and looks them over. Until then, we don't know that there aren't any more of them. Get some skirmishers into the surrounding forest. We don't want to be surprised."

The smoke had drifted away, and they looked across the courtyard toward the grass *pili* that must have been its sanctuary. "Jesus," said Horner, "look what they have done." Lennox Jackson joined them.

Lined up outside the grass-walled sanctuary, opposite a grinning wooden idol, eight tree-trunk stakes, each with a man's corpse tied to it, had been driven into holes cut in the rock. A tall figure was identifiable as Jakob Saeger, from his height, from the wisps of white hair and crooked teeth. His weight was supported not by his legs but by the native cords that bound him to the pole, for his legs had been broken, one knocked out to a sickening angle at the knee, the other smashed at the shinbone. The garrote that strangled out his life still bit into this throat, turning his pasty white face as purple as a plum, but he had not watched his own sacrifice, for two blood-crusted holes in his face showed where his eyes had been spooned out.

"My God, sir," breathed Jackson, "is this what the rest of the world is like?"

"A good deal of it, I fear."

"What they call a religion is a horror, sir," said Horner.

"Well, we were hanging witches in Salem barely a hundred years ago, so let us try to not feel too superior. Get your skirmishers to report, Mr. Horner. Well, with Saeger and his men dead, that would explain why the warriors have dispersed; that was Karaimoku's intention. I suspect that their hostage is at Boki's house and that trail would be an easy ambush."

Jackson suddenly crouched and extracted his pistol. "Sir, I saw movement within that grass house."

"Form up your company behind us."

With his heart in his throat Bliven entered the *pili*, with his men close behind, but it was as he first descried. They found only one person within, unarmed: the Chiefess Liliha, seated on a storage chest. She sat erect, bare chested, unbowed, and unmoved by the slaughter that had taken place a few feet away.

"Where is my wife?" he demanded.

Liliha made no answer but gazed at him, her expression seeming more than anything bemused.

He advanced on her, preceded by the point of his saber, which he placed just beneath her left nipple, where it made an indentation. "Chiefess, there might be a day when I could be induced to spare your life. But the day that my wife is held prisoner is not that day."

Liliha withdrew from the point of his sword, not in pain or panic, and breaking neither her gaze at him nor her quizzical smirk. "She is in my house. She and your son are unharmed. You may fetch them whenever your wish."

"Captain Putnam!" David Horner's voice came from the courtyard.

"In here!"

Horner ducked through the door to enter. "Sir, skirmishers report that the trails leading away from here are empty. The forest is too thick for anyone to come through there, except they be monkeys coming through the treetops."

"Very well. I shall take six of your marines with me to fetch the hostage. You will stay here. The chiefess is not to leave for any reason. And, Mr. Horner, do you know the myth of Circe?"

"Who, sir? I do not believe so, not at all."

"No, you wouldn't. In ancient Greece, the story of Circe was about an inveterate seductress who, after she had her way with men, turned them into pigs. Beware this chiefess. Do not allow her to leave, and do not allow her any liberties whatever. Do you understand?"

"Yes, sir."

Bliven selected his six marines and they ascended the trail to the house at a fast walk, running on its level and downhill portions. The sight of a Georgian cottage jarred him, as peaceful as it was incongruous, but he led the detail through the front door without knocking. Clarity was standing in the hall before the front door, and to the side Bliven could see the chair from where she had seen them coming.

With a huge sigh of relief he rushed forward and held her. "My love, are you all right?"

"Yes."

"Where is the baby?"

"In the bedroom, sleeping."

"You were well cared for, then?"

She gestured around the house. "As you see."

He held her again, longer, and looked around the parlor. "Of all the ways in which I might have imagined they live, Georgian Regency would not have come first to mind."

"Perhaps it did not fit in with the image they wished to project of being the defenders of the old ways."

Bliven nodded in agreement. "That would be hard to square with a love of luxury, would it not? Can you gather your things?"

"Already done, ever since I heard the gunfire. Cannons at first, then muskets. Are you all right, dearest?"

"Perfectly. If you can show these gentlemen what they are to bring, we must go."

When they regained the rock wall of the temple, Bliven stopped Clarity gently with a hand on her shoulder. "Perhaps you should wait out here. It is quite ghastly inside."

"No, do not shield me, I came here to see everything." They entered and saw Berend within, kneeling from one Hawaiian to the next, and Mutterbach with him. "How do you find it, Doctor? Can any of them be saved?"

Berend stood and shook his head. "No. Some of them may have been breathing at the time you sent for me, but they are dead as door-nails now."

"Captain Putnam?" David Horner hailed him from the door of the *pili*.

Bliven excused himself from Clarity, Berend, and Mutterbach. "Lieutenant Horner, have you had any trouble?"

"No, sir. But the burial detail begs leave to say the ground here is almost solid rock. It is not possible to bury the dead here."

"I see." Bliven looked over the *pili*. "The grass of these walls, and the timber frame, should be adequate for a funeral pyre. Commence to take it apart, then make a layer of grass and wood, then a layer of bodies, more grass and wood, more bodies, and so on. Do you understand?"

"Yes, sir."

"Is Liliha still within?" he asked as Clarity came over and joined him.

Horner stood aside so they could enter. "Yes, sir."

Bliven found her unmoved from when he had departed. "Chiefess, where is your husband?"

Liliha continued looking at him with the same limpid passivity.

"Madam, I ask again: Where is your husband? I require an answer."

"Captain," she said at last, "have you ever been to London?"

"What!"

"My husband and I are going to London. Our new king and queen are going there to pay their respects to the new British king and queen. As we are in the front rank of Their Majesties' retainers, it was natural that we should be invited to accompany them."

Clarity leaned toward him and whispered, "I will explain presently, but this question is best not pursued."

Bliven stood back from between Liliha and the door of the *pili* and sheathed his saber. "Very well, Chiefess, you are free to go. Tell your husband that I am glad we were not enemies in this. We wanted the same thing: justice for the innocent people who were killed at Hana, and that has been achieved."

"Good-bye, Captain." Liliha moved toward the door of the *pili*, brushing the back of her hand against the front of Horner's trousers. "Good-bye, Lieutenant. I hope we meet again one day."

As she exited, Bliven shot a look at Horner, who shook his head. "Circe, sir."

Bliven allowed himself a smile. "Were you tempted?"

"I should say, sir. Yes, I was."

"M-hm. And do you remember what Dr. Berend told the crew, about a moment of Venus followed by a lifetime of Mercury?"

"Vividly, sir."

"Good. One thing further, Mr. Horner." He gestured to the wooden idol that stood grinning at the corpses of Saeger and his men. "Have some of your men uproot this thing and bring it along."

"Very good, Captain."

When they were outside the temple compound, he touched Clarity's shoulder to stop her. "What did you mean back there when you said I should not question Liliha more closely?"

"Ah. Dearest, Hawaiian modes of expression are very subtle and very oblique. Her telling you about London was a way to say that if you abused her further, it would go down very hard with their good friend the king, and would damage the whole effort to Christianize these people."

They started down the path to the beach, their arms around each other. "Well, I confess," he said, "that particular interpretation did escape me. Did I miss much else while I was gone all those months?"

"Oh, Lord, I should think this was enough! But, yes, actually, there was a rebellion on Tauai not long after you left. They always have had an independent streak, as you may have heard. The queen sent Karaimoku and several canoes of warriors. They captured old King Tamoree and his family and brought them back to Honoruru as her 'guests.' Can you imagine? She said they were her *guests*!"

"My, how did that come out?"

"I thought she might have them killed, but she said she just wanted them to honor the existing alliance. So, to cement the alliance, she married the old king, and then married his son for good measure."

"You are not in earnest!"

"I am surely in earnest. I asked her about it, and she said European kings marry for alliance all the time, and she wanted this alliance to be good both for now and the future, so she married two generations."

"Oh, my God! Was that the son who is your friend Prince George?"

"No, no, this one was younger and much better looking. When I questioned her—very deferentially, of course—she pointed to Old Tamoree, and she said, 'Well, if I have to marry that old thing, I want some fun out of it, too.'"

"Ha! Oh, Lord—and what did Reverend Bingham have to say about this?"

"Not a word. As long as she comes to church and at least hears out his sermons, he knows better than to criticize her."

On the beach he lifted her and Ben up into the gig, not minding the little water that seeped over the soles of his boots. They were pulled out to the sloop, past the blasted remains of the schooner.

"Bosun's chair here!" Bliven called up.

Yeakel had seen them coming with Clarity and the baby and was almost finished rigging one.

"Oh, pooh. I could manage the ladder very well if I weren't carrying our precious one."

On deck Bliven helped her straight across to the ladder, then aft to the sea cabin, where he showed her his berth and the close stool, then held her tightly, running his fingers through her hair. "My love, do you think you have seen enough now to write your next novel?"

"Quite enough. My only complaint is there is not much left for me to make up from my imagination. If I merely report all this in its bare facts, it would be difficult enough for anyone to believe it."

He kissed her. "I leave that to you. I must go topside and confer with my officers. I shall return directly."

He found Miller on the quarterdeck, watching with wide eyes as the idol was hoisted over the rail, spinning slowly so that its mother-of-pearl eyes got a full view of the whole of the weather deck, its grimace of sharks' teeth holding in thrall those of the crew who beheld it. "Captain, that is rather a larger trophy than your Arab dagger. How do you propose to display it?"

"I noticed when we were in the temple that he is approximately the same size as Mary Washington, whom we lost in Malaya. My present intention is to have Fleming splice him onto her stump as a new figurehead. He will want to trim him down, of course: there are parts of his anatomy that we do not need to display to the world."

"Brilliant, sir, I approve. That did sound like quite the sanguine affair onshore. Dr. Berend tells me there were no survivors."

"No, there were not."

Miller looked ineffably sad.

"Michael, it had nothing to do with what I said in Singapore about wanting to exterminate the human predators of the world. Mr. Pitt was right: Boki's land was a refuge for priests who wanted to bring back the old religion. One that spoke English shouted that we had defiled their temple, and they attacked us in a most determined rush. One could not call it a fight—clubs and daggers against muskets. Very sad, in its way."

"And so they died, along with their way of life."

"The irony, Mr. Miller, is that one day historians who don't know crap will write that they were picturesque little natives living colorful little lives and we should have left them alone to sit for portraits and be interviewed by members of the Royal Society."

"That is rather a bold prediction, sir."

"Not so very much. Read Herodotus; read Livy. Historians have always romanticized distant savages, whether distant in geography or in time. But we accomplished the queen's business. Saeger and his crew are punished for their crime."

"Punished most horribly, from what Dr. Berend told us."

"Yes, they were very brutally killed. While I think of it, I want you to send a salvage party over to the schooner. Take off everything that can be used, make up parcels of their personal effects, to the extent that they can be identified. We will set her afire before we leave this place." With a toss of his head he gestured up to the temple, where its ten-foot wall of lava blocks was backlit by the pyre within it. "I have half a mind to demolish that thing with target practice. This part of the island has been a stronghold of the queen's opposition, and as their sanctum, she would probably thank us for knocking it down.

But I don't see much point in destroying one when there are a hundred still standing."

Miller nodded. "I quite agree, sir. I think we have made enough noise for one day."

Bliven went below, where he found Clarity in the privacy of his berth, feeding Ben from a packet of finely cut-up fruit and fish.

"Well," she sighed. "What now?"

"Now? We go to Honoruru, report to the queen, and then we go home."

"Home." She closed her eyes. "But wait, we can't do that. Captains are no longer allowed to sail with their wives, as I heard." He read in her eyes that she was already in a mood to tease.

He sat beside her and wrapped his arms around her and their son. "That is true. However, I am empowered to rescue and repatriate refugees whose lives are in danger." He lifted her chin and kissed her long. "If you are a poor, helpless waif, God help the rest of us."

The next day they were back in Honoruru, standing together before the queen. This time she was clad in bright blue English silk.

"Captain Putnam, our prime minister has given us a full account of what you have done. We hold that our justice has been fulfilled. I shall soon write a letter through Mr. Jenkins, our secretary, to your government expressing our thanks for your gallant and honorable conduct."

"I thank Your Majesty."

"And now, Missy La Laelae, come embrace me one last time."

Clarity approached, stopping to curtsy, as Kahumanu extended her meaty knee for her to sit on, as had once been their habit. "Missy, there is something that I desire you to know," she said quietly. "I did not wish to send you to the north shore with Boki. After the great killing at Hana, I had to speak as one voice with my chiefs against you all. If I had not done so, they could have deposed me. That would have meant the end of your god in my country, and with the chiefs in power, they could bring back *kapu*. These things I could not allow. I acted against my feelings for you, but I acted as queen to my people. Can you understand this?"

Clarity bowed her head for a moment. "Yes, ma'am. I cannot say you were wrong. You are still in power, justice has been done, the guilty men have been punished, and the missionaries are going to stay. So it seems you acted wisely."

"And now one last time, tell me some good thing of our Lord Jesus Christ."

She considered it briefly. "One thing that encourages me, when I am weary, when I see how much evil there is in the world that must be overcome and I am out of strength, when it seems like doing good things no longer has any point, I remember this. After our Lord was crucified and rose from the dead, He appeared to His apostles, the men who had followed Him. They were very sad, but He told them not to be discouraged, and that He would be with them in spirit, always, even to the end of time." She could tell from the tears that rose in Kahumanu's eyes that she had struck home.

The queen reached up, pulled a silver comb from her hair, and placed it in Clarity's. "Take this to remember me, and I wish you to remember me in your prayers."

Clarity was unprepared for her own rush of emotion. "Every day, my queen."

Kahumanu kissed her on the forehead and Clarity kissed her huge hand. A little nod and push at the back dismissed her and she slid off the queen's knee and backed away into a final curtsy. "*Ka mea Kamahao.*"

"*Mahalo*," she whispered lowly. "*Aloha oe.* Captain Putnam!"

"Ma'am?"

"The purser from your ship was heard inquiring of the American agent as to the proper price of pork and fish and other victuals. This was, however, after we had already provisioned your ship of our own generosity." She pointed a finger at him. "Do not let him cheat you."

"No, ma'am. I thank you."

As they departed the royal *pili*, Muriel Albright approached them, favoring one leg now with the use of a beautiful new cane of *koa* wood. "I wanted to see you before you left."

Clarity flew to her as Karaimoku placed a big hand on Bliven's shoulder. "Captain Putnam, we have had adventures together."

It still embarrassed him how tall the chief was next to him. "Yes. I am sorry that men had to die, but I hope that we have made the future of your country more secure."

"Your people say greeting and farewell by shaking hands. You and I now are going to do it our way."

"And what is that?"

Karaimoku placed his hands on Bliven's shoulders. "Do not be afraid, I shan't kiss you. I am going to place my forehead against yours, and we shall share breath for a moment."

By the time he pulled away they were both smiling. "And now we shake hands?"

"Yes."

Clarity shook her head slowly. "Mrs. Albright, will you not come home with us?"

"No, child. This is where God has led me. I am content to live out my days in this work."

They held hands. "I shall never forget you. It is hard, to feel that a good-bye is final."

"No, my dear, only if you believe that it is final. Perhaps I shall not see you again in this life, but in the next, you and I will surely resume our mockery of pompous reverends."

Clarity laughed helplessly, impatient that she could not see clearly through her tears. "Good-bye, dear Mrs. Albright."

Bingham drew Bliven aside. "Captain, I have a great favor to ask. After much discussion and prayer, one of our families, the Chamberlains, have concluded that their calling here was, perhaps, not well-thought-out. Two of their children are sickly. May we prevail upon you to take them home?"

"Reverend, unless I miss my guess, they are packed already."

"There you have us, sir. They can leave upon the instant."

"Get them down to the pier posthaste."

"Oh, God bless you!" He turned and walked toward their house as fast as his dignity would allow.

UNITED STATES SLOOP of war *Rappahannock*, twenty-six guns, Captain Putnam, discharged her pilot and stood out of Honoruru harbor on a fine afternoon, making her course west by south, running full and by with the strength of the trade winds coming straight over the taffrail.

Bliven sought out the ship's carpenter. "Ah, Fleming. The berth in my compartment—I wish you to widen it by a foot and a half."

"Very good, sir."

"And ask the sailmaker to stuff and sew up a new mattress to that dimension."

"Aye, sir."

"Can you do this by tonight?"

"With the freedom of your cabin and to make some noise, yes, sir."

"Go to it, then. Mr. Ross, I am afraid I'm going to have to exile you back down to a wardroom berth."

"Yes, sir. I have moved my things already."

"Have you? Well. And for the duration, you may knock and enter the great cabin, but enter the compartments only when bidden."

"Sir, I would have thought that went without saying."

"Do you think you can manage to serve a captain's table this evening?"

"Happily, sir! The queen loaded us to the gunwales with fresh food of every description. The sooner we eat some of it, the sooner we will have room on the decks to walk a straight line."

"Ha! Well, then, let us extend the invitation to the midshipmen and the warrant officers. Same menu, but they must dine in the wardroom, for I have my wife, the Chamberlains, and their children. They and the officers will crowd my own table. You will be serving us, of course, but take care you reserve a full plate for yourself. That will be a large number for dinner; dragoon a couple of the more presentable-looking seamen to help you."

After dinner, Clarity sat with Ben asleep in her lap, in a chair that she had turned to face away from the table, watching the night horizon where Diamond Hill had receded from their view, as Bliven came over and put his hands on her shoulders.

"Home now, my dearest?" she asked.

He sat beside her and wrapped an arm around her. "Home now."

"Oh, Lord, I suppose that means back around Cape Horn."

"In strictest confidence, my love: never again in this life if I can help it."

"Oh, that is good hearing. But what, then?"

"Once we reach a more southerly latitude, we are going to let the earth spin beneath us, and go home via the Cape of Good Hope."

"Africa?"

"My love, you will be the only lady in Litchfield to have circumnavigated the globe."

"Well! I don't . . . You take my breath away."

"And then, knowing the close interest you have in slavery and in bringing it to an end, I thought we might put in at Dakar. Perhaps when you see the beginning of those awful trips that the slave ships make, it will stoke that abolitionist fire under you a little bit."

It did not bear saying, but she knew that his own feelings about that sad subject must have modified more toward her own, or he would not have offered her a look at the slave markets and holding pens of West Africa. Ben awoke and wriggled. "I believe it is time for Baby and me to retire."

"Do you want anything?"

She shook her head.

He kissed her. "I am going to have a look topside. I won't be long."

As he went up the ladder and aft to the quarterdeck, it was surprising how the air had chilled.

"Good evening, Captain."

"Mr. Rippel, good evening. Are you ready to go home?"

"Ready, Captain? You have no idea."

Bliven ambled over to the port rail, grasped the mizzen ratlines, and let himself relax, filling his lungs with clean sea air and enjoying the relief of a long and difficult mission well acquitted.

"Good evening, Captain."

"Mr. Horner, good evening. What brings you up?"

"I don't know, sir. Couldn't sleep."

Bliven gave him a searching look. "Pupukea was your first real action, you said."

"Yes, sir."

"You keep seeing it?"

"Yes, sir."

"I understand. I was the very same at your age."

"Truly?"

"What you must do is ask yourself whether you acted wrongly in any part of it. You followed orders; you fired only when you were attacked. To have not done so would have cost our lives instead of theirs. If you hate the violence and the bloodshed, good for you. That is what will make you a good soldier."

"I understand. Thank you." He stood quietly for several minutes. "Captain, may I ask you something?"

"Of course, Mr. Horner."

"It is not of any great moment, really, but I have been curious."

"Speak up, lad, what is it?"

"Well, sir, in your wife's book—is it . . . true . . . about the guns and the ramrods at the Battle of Derna?"

Bliven let out his breath slowly as he pursed his lips and sucked at them as he gave his lieutenant of marines a look both askance and withering. "Mr. Rippel?"

"Sir?"

"You have the deck. I am going below. Good night, Mr. Horner."

"Good night, Captain."

HONORURU
20TH AUGUST, 1822

*My dear Commodore,*

*In my last report, from Canton, I advised that Capt. Jakob Saeger, schooner Free Trader, whose attack by Malay pirates now some years ago was an impetus for sending my vessel to the Pacific, was thought to be in harbor at the time I arrived there.*

*Once in Canton, agreeable to instructions, I made the acquaintance of the American agent, Mr. Dunn, who was happy to learn of his country's increasing interest in foreign contact and commerce. Before I could make contact with Capt. Saeger, a general fire destroyed much of the business community. After this I learned from Mr. Dunn that Capt. Saeger was indeed in port, and caused a great commotion when it was discovered that the sandalwood which he sold was deceptively mixed with a useless wood, for which he was compelled to return their money, and was banned from further commerce.*

*The authorities in Canton, after investigation, concluded that the fire which destroyed the foreign quarter of the city was of unknown origin, but spread with such devastating effect owing to the overcrowded and unsanitary conditions. My own suspicion, though it is founded principally in my own instincts, is supported by relevant circumstantial evidence such as the location of the fire's first detection, and that it was deliberately set by Capt. Saeger, his motive being to destroy the stocks of sandalwood belonging to his competitors.*

*Mr. Dunn was unharmed in the conflagration, although the American mercantile was destroyed. Further, the collection that he has assembled of Chinese art and ancient artefacts, was rescued onto boats and rowed into the harbor by the swift action of his Chinese factor, Mr. Ting Qua, who allowed his own commercial merchandise to go up in flames rather than witness the destruction of his cultural heritage. This gallantry, while it has no bearing on my mission and will not appear in my official report, I found to be highly commendable.*

*I learned from Mr. Dunn that Capt. Saeger was heard to say, that he would avenge himself upon the Hawaiians who had sold him the false sandalwood. I therefore returned to the Sandwich Islands as fast as possible, although this required a hard sail of ten weeks into unfavoring winds. By the time I arrived, I learned that Capt. Saeger had most treacherously called a gathering of native canoes to come trade at his ship, but instead turned his guns upon them—he had acquired four small carronades from the British at Valparaiso, on the claim of needing to protect himself from the Malacca pirates—and with a broadside of grape shot killed more than a hundred native Hawaiians at Hana, on the island of Maui, who had sold him the adulterated sandalwood.*

*With the country in an uproar, and with my vessel the only one capable of finding and arresting Capt. Saeger, I accepted the Queen's request to locate him. Also at her direction, the American missionaries who have been dispersed through the islands, were sequestered in the households of powerful chiefs for their protection. The head of the missionaries, Mr. Bingham, and a couple of others, have assured me that they have not felt in personal danger, that the Queen and most of her court have converted to the Christian faith, and that the Americans here feel no need nor desire to be evacuated and withdrawn—with a few exceptions as I shall detail presently.*

*Learning of the events in Hana, I set off in pursuit of Capt. Saeger to force an end to his depredations, which in addition to being criminal were harming the reputation of the United States. Off the district of Pupukea on the north shore of Oahu, I learned that Capt. Saeger and some of his crew had gone ashore with the prospect of a profitable bargain in obtaining pure sandalwood. There they were captured and meted out mortal justice by the high chief of this district. His own conversion to piracy was attested by his remaining crew opening fire on my vessel, inflicting three fatalities and* wounding five among my men. Once I returned fire, the result was his vessel was burnt to the waterline, with his men escaping to the shore in small boats. The deaths of Capt. Saeger and those with him, I can confirm by having gone ashore and found and buried their bodies.

Back at Honoruru I made report of these facts to the Queen, who expressed her satisfaction, not with the deaths of Saeger et al., but that justice had been done—a conclusion with which I can not but concur. She also expresses her continuing good will toward our country, and her gratitude for the religious instruction and practical help—doctor, teachers, etc., brought by Mr. Bingham and the other missionaries of the Congregationalist Church.

A few of them imparted to Mr. Bingham that they no longer felt safe there, and desire to return home, viz. Daniel and Jerusha Chamberlain and five children. Despite my disinclination to take on civilians, two of their children are in delicate health, and I am well founded in my opinion that my ship's surgeon Dr. Craighead Berend will offer the best medical care they could obtain in this part of the world. As I am now bound for Boston by the straightest route possible, I am bringing the Chamberlain family with me. And as my intention is that no ship now here will reach there before us, I will deliver this letter by hand at that time.

> Yours, sir, with great respect,
> Bliven Putnam, Capt. USN
> Commanding Sloop
> Rappahannock

ISAAC HULL, COMMODORE
CHARLESTOWN NAVY YARD

\* \* \*

IT WAS LATE when Bliven blew out the lamp in his study and clicked open the door to his compartment. Even with the widened berth, he was almost atop Clarity when he crept beneath the covers, and she awakened. "Did you finish your letter to Hull?"

"Yes." He kissed her.

"Were you able to finesse your . . . well, liberties, with the facts?"

"I had to borrow some of your creative imagination, I'm afraid."

"Well." She buried her face in his nightshirt. "What they don't know won't hurt 'em."

# GAZETTEER

The Hawaiian language was not standardized for purposes of writing for nearly a decade after the arrival of the first missionaries. When the language was simplified, for instance, *R* became *L*; *T* became *K*, and so on. Personal and place names were known differently before then, at the time of our story. To keep within its time frame we have chosen to use the terminology as it was used in 1820. Also, while Hawaiian names are now properly rendered with the appropriate spelling and diacritics, the first Americans in Hawai'i, in the absence of a written language, spoke and wrote in phonetic approximations. Again in faith to the story's times, we use the names as known in the time. We have made one exception to this. So many people are now accustomed to the name Hawaii that to call it by the name it was usually called in 1820, Owhyhee, would do more to confuse people than illuminate the language.

# GAZETTEER

| NAME IN 1820 | NAME AFTER STANDARDIZATION |
| --- | --- |
| Karaimoku | Kalanimoku, chief aide to Kamehameha I, who transferred his loyalty to Ka'ahumanu when she became *kuhina nui* |
| Honoruru | Honolulu, chief settlement on Oahu |
| Kahumanu | Ka'ahumanu, widow of Kamehameha I, who shared power with his dissolute son Kamehameha II as *kuhina nui* |
| Kairua | Kailua, royal capital of the Kona district on the west shore of the Big Island (a second Kailua lies on the north shore of Oahu.) |
| Kamamalu | Half sister, wife, and queen of Kamehameha II |
| Kepurani | Keopuolani, queen and near goddess, mother of Kamehameha II |
| *kuhina nui* | Principal advisor to the king, a combination of prime minister and coruler |
| Henry Obookiah | Opukaha'ia, Hawaiian refugee to America from the Kamehameha conquest, who was the first to conceive the missionary effort |
| Prince George Tamoree | Kaumuali'i, son of the king of Kaua'i, sent to America to learn Western ways |
| Reho-Reho | Liholiho, given name of Kamehameha II (ruled 1819–25, sharing power with Ka'ahumanu) |
| Ta-meha-meha | Kamehameha, dynastic name of the first five kings of Hawai'i; also Kamehameha I, who was the first high chief to conquer the islands into a unified country (ruled 1810–19) |
| Tauai | Kaua'i, northernmost of the principal Hawaiian Islands |

Other Hawaiian names, such as Hopu and Boki, did not change.

# FURTHER READING

American Board of Commissioners for Foreign Missions. *A Narrative of Five Youths from the Sandwich Islands, Now Receiving an Education in This Country.* New York: J. Seymour, 1816.

Bingham, Hiram. *A Residence of Twenty-One Years in the Sandwich Islands, etc.* 3rd rev. ed. Canandaigua, NY: H. D. Goodwin, 1855.

Dwight, Edwin Wells. *Memoirs of Henry Obookiah.* Philadelphia: American Sunday School Union, 1830.

Haley, James L. *Captive Paradise: A History of Hawaii.* New York: St. Martin's Press, 2014.

Holman, Lucia Ruggles. *The Journal of Lucia Ruggles Holman.* Honolulu: Bernice P. Bishop Museum, 1931.

I'i, John Papa (Mary Kawena Pukui, trans.; Dorothy B. Barrère, ed.). *Fragments of Hawaiian History, as Recorded by John Papa I'i.* Honolulu: Bishop Museum Press, 1959.

Jarves, James Jackson. *History of the Hawaiian Islands, Embracing Their Antiquities, Mythology, Legends, Discovery, etc.* Honolulu: Charles Edwin Hitchcock, 1847.

Judd, Laura Fish. *Honolulu: Sketches of Life in the Hawaiian Islands.* Reprint ed. Honolulu: *Honolulu Star-Bulletin*, 1928.

Kuykendall, Ralph S. *The Hawaiian Kingdom.* 3 vols. Honolulu: University of Hawaii Press, 1938–1967.

Ledyard, John. *A Journal of Captain Cook's Last Voyage to the Pacific Ocean, etc.* Hartford: Nathaniel Patten, 1783.

Malo, David (Dr. Nathaniel B. Emerson, trans). *Hawaiian Antiquities (Moolelo Hawaii).* Reprint ed. Honolulu: Bernice P. Bishop Museum, 1991.

Matson, Cathy, ed. *The Economy of Early America: Historical Perspectives & New Directions.* University Park: University of Pennsylvania Press, 2006.

Porter, Capt. David. *Journal of a Cruise Made to the Pacific Ocean in the United States Frigate Essex, in the Years 1812, 1813, and 1814, etc.* 2 vols. 2nd ed. New York: Wiley & Halsted, 1822.

Rothbard, Murray N. *The Panic of 1819: Reactions and Policies.* New York: Columbia University Press, 1962.

Stewart, Charles. *Journal of a Residence in the Sandwich Islands by C. S. Stewart, During the Years 1823, 1824, and 1825.* 3rd ed. facsimile. Honolulu: University of Hawaii Press for Friends of the Library of Hawaii, 1970.

# ACKNOWLEDGMENTS

———••◦•••———

For matters concerning the history of the American Board of Commissioners for Foreign Missions, I thank my friend Mike Smola, curator of the Mission Houses Museum in Honolulu, with continuing thanks to my St. Martin's Press editor, Charles Spicer, for the chance to research Hawaii history.

For indispensable help in getting through writing another novel, I thank my friends and readers Greg Walden, Greg Ciotti, Evan Yeakel, Steve Clodfelter, Bill Young, and my oldest friend and most faithful reader, Craig Eiland of Tulsa, Oklahoma, who missed by three weeks seeing the final product.

Upon the book's editor, Gabriella Mongelli, enough praise cannot be heaped. I knew from her edit of the first five chapters, when she made strategic suggestions and relied on me to provide tactical solutions, that working with her would be a joy—as much as with my previous Putnam editors, Nita Taublib, Christine Pepe, and Alexis Sattler, each of whom left her

## ACKNOWLEDGMENTS

impress on these books. Highest thanks is reserved for Ivan Held, the god-father of the series. I revere you all . . .

. . . almost as much as I revere my agent, Jim Hornfischer, who brought the original idea to me and brokered a chain of books that has been the light of my career.